WHAT ECHOES RENDER

TAMSEN SCHULTZ

*everafter*ROMANCE

EverAfter Romance
A Division of Diversion Publishing Corp.
443 Park Avenue South, Suite 1008
New York, New York 10016
www.EverAfterRomance.com

Cover Design by Sian Foulkes
Edited by Julie Molinari

This is a work of fiction. Names, characters, places and incidents either are the
product of the author's imagination or are used fictitiously. Any resemblance to
actual persons, living or dead, events or locales is entirely coincidental.

For more information, email info@everafterromance.com

First EverAfter Romance edition March 2017.
Print ISBN: 978-1-63576-037-8

To Nav, even though you don't like Ardbeg as much as I do

And to Rai and Liam, for making me laugh just a
little more often than you make me want to cry

CHAPTER 1

ALERTED BY THE CLICK OF her heels on the industrial floor, several heads raised from behind nurses' stations as Jesse Baker walked down the hall of Riverside Hospital's intensive care unit. Housing the sickest of the sick, this floor was, naturally, one of the quietest in the hospital. But even so, as Jesse made her way from the sixth floor elevators toward the east wing, the silence seemed to have seeped into everything around her, dampening movements and slowing time; the people, the lights, the machines, all seemed to be moving in their own worlds.

But then again, it had been a somewhat surreal day altogether.

Rounding the corner to her destination, Jesse came upon a man standing with his back to her. Wearing cargo pants, work boots, and a navy blue t-shirt emblazoned with the firefighters' emblem and "AFD," he stood with his hands in his pockets, as still, as contained, as everything else around him. From the back, he looked youngish. And fit, judging by his shape. He wasn't what Jesse had been expecting. But her surprise was only of the curious kind that happens when one isn't actually aware of one's expectations until presented with something that doesn't meet them.

His head turned at the sound of her approach and she caught a glimpse of his profile. His brown hair, streaked with gold, touched the top of his ears. His nose was straight and his skin the color of a man who spent time outdoors. When he turned toward her, she noted the emblem over his pectoral, a miniature of that on the back of his shirt.

"You must be the investigator from the state," Jesse said, striding toward him with her hand outstretched, her voice sure.

She didn't miss the way his eyes took her in—taking stock, not judging—as his hand closed around hers. His fingers and palm were rough, the hand of a man who did more than just type on a keyboard.

"I'm Jesse Baker," she said. "The Hospital Administrator."

"David Hathaway, Arson Investigator."

"And Albany Firefighter, if your shirt is anything to go by?" she asked. The official who had called to alert her about the visit had only mentioned the investigator's arson credentials.

He nodded. "The state called, I assume?" he asked.

She confirmed with a nod then glanced around the hallway, wondering if maybe they should go somewhere else to talk. She'd never been in this kind of situation before. But he resolved her indecision by taking control of the conversation.

"You run the show then, Ms. Baker?" he asked with a vague gesture of his hand meant to encompass the facility.

She inclined her head, going along.

"Such as it is. And please, call me Jesse," she added.

"It's a nice place," he responded, his eyes sweeping the area. He looked about her age, mid-to-late thirties. And though his attempts to put her at ease weren't subtle, she appreciated them nonetheless.

"Have you been here long?" he asked, returning his gaze to her.

Despite everything, she let herself smile a bit at that. She looked young, always had. She wasn't young, in any sense of the word, but people always thought she was a good ten years younger than she was. Including, apparently, David Hathaway.

"I've been the administrator for six years, but I've been at Riverside Hospital for over twelve," she answered.

His brows shot up in surprise and then he seemed to catch himself.

"Then I can't imagine much surprises you these days," he said, his voice indicating that his mind had returned to the reason for his visit.

Again, she dipped her head.

"Generally, that's true. But this, well, this situation *is* new to me, Mr. Hathaway."

"Please, call me David."

She nodded then looked down the empty hallway again. What she'd gleaned from the first responders, and the news, was that the house that had gone up in flames earlier in the day. It was so rural that, while the neighbors eventually saw the smoke, no one had heard anything. And based on what the state official had told her, the cause of the fire which had brought Aaron Greene to her hospital was still, officially, undetermined. But he had also told her, confidentially, that there had been an explosion. What kind, she assumed, was the investigator's—David's—job to figure out, but the man from the state had intimated that it might not have been accidental and may not have been meant for the house. Which left her thinking what he'd no doubt intended her to think: Aaron had been involved, somehow, with a bomb.

The thought made her sick, and knowing what it might do to the community, if in fact Aaron had been planning to detonate a bomb somewhere in the area, she had every intention of keeping it quiet until the state made an official ruling. So, even though she and David weren't talking about anything confidential—yet—she didn't particularly want prying eyes and ears nearby. Especially since it was still possible that the explosion wasn't anything intentional.

"I've never met an arson investigator investigating this kind of thing," she continued as she stepped to the side of the hall, toward an empty room. He followed and seemed to sense her desire to keep things quiet as he moved close enough for her to lower her voice as she spoke. "And while we have our fair share of kids doing stupid things, I can safely say, Aaron Greene and his father are our first…" She let her voice trail off, not wanting to say "bomb victims."

A frown touched his lips and she knew that he heard the concern in her voice. Concern about the explosive that had ripped through the Greenes' rural farmhouse, to be sure, but also concern for those involved and what it all might mean. But he didn't know the community the way she did, didn't know how its people would react or respond, and wisely, she thought, he held his tongue, handing her a folded piece of paper instead.

"The warrant for Aaron's medical records?" she asked.

He nodded and she gave it a cursory glance before refolding it.

"How is he?" David asked.

"He's in serious condition," she answered. "It was a toss-up as to whether we should transport him to Albany or not. But he seemed to stabilize here so we've kept him. They have a better burn unit there, but he'll get more individualized care here since we're a bit smaller."

"And he's part of the community," David suggested but didn't seem to be judging.

"There is that part of it, yes," Jesse answered then gestured for him to follow her. "Aaron and my son Matt are in the same class," she explained as they began to walk toward Aaron's room. "As is Danielle Martinez, the daughter of the doctor who worked on him." They turned the corner and headed toward the end of another hall. "But believe me," she added, "if we thought he'd have had a better chance up there, we would have sent him."

And they would have, but it had been a judgment call, like so many decisions in hospitals were. And thankfully, it looked like it was a decision that was going to work out okay. Aaron *was* in serious condition, but he was stable.

David didn't seem to feel the need to comment, so, with the exception of the click of Jesse's heels, they made their way down the hall to Aaron's room in silence. She stopped in front of the large glass window that separated the hallway from the room where Aaron lay. For a moment, they observed the young man—his body, bandaged and unmoving, hooked to machines that monitored the life still fighting for a chance within him.

The smell of burnt clothes and flesh had been awful when he'd first come in over seven hours earlier. Even now, there were still hints of it lingering in the hall, although it had mostly been suppressed by the antiseptics used to clean every surface in the ICU and by the glass wall dividing the patient from the hall. There was also the plastic containment unit Dr. Martinez had ordered constructed around Aaron as an additional layer of protection.

"Did they know him?" David asked, presumably referring to her son, Matt, and Dr. Martinez's daughter, Danielle.

"Not well." She shook her head. "But while Riverside is a small town, Windsor, where we're from, where Aaron is from, is even smaller. And it's an even smaller high school."

"Everyone-knows-everyone kind of place?" he asked.

She nodded. They stood, not speaking for a moment, and she wondered just what an arson investigator would be thinking about what he was seeing in front of him.

"So, what do you think?" he asked, surprising her.

"About?" she responded, not entirely sure what he was asking her.

"About Aaron," he clarified, keeping his voice low. "Do you think he was the kind of kid to build an explosive device?" he asked, confirming her assumptions about just what he was investigating.

She glanced at David, caught a little off guard by the question, before letting her gaze fall back on the boy. He was eighteen, so not legally a child anymore. But lying there alone, he looked small and helpless.

"I think that, whether he constructed a bomb that killed his father or he was the victim of it, it's going to be a tragic story," she said, her voice soft.

She could feel David's gaze on her as she stared at Aaron for a moment longer. As a mother, her heart broke for the young man. She knew enough about his life to know it hadn't been easy for him these past few years. Not that she thought that would be an acceptable excuse if he did end up being responsible for building a bomb that ruined his home and killed his father, but she believed what she'd just said. Whichever way things turned out, it was going to be a tragedy.

Not wanting to sink too far into maudlin thoughts, Jesse straightened and turned away from the glass window to face the investigator. "I'll take you to my office and we can pull the files. I'll also call Dr. Martinez so that she can come up and answer any of your questions," she said. "Once you have what you need from us up here, we can head down to the morgue where Dr. DeMarco is finishing up the autopsy of Brent Greene, Aaron's father."

David recognized her comment for what it was, more of a plan than a request, and he gestured with his hand for her to precede him. She led him back down to the elevators and to her office located on the first floor. When they arrived outside her office, Kayla, her assistant, looked up from her desk.

"Here is the official warrant for the records for Aaron Greene," Jesse said, handing the paper to Kayla, who took it from her without a word. She had no doubt Kayla would know exactly what to do with the document. Kayla was one of the brightest, most detail-oriented people Jesse knew, despite the fact that, unlike herself, her assistant actually *was* young, very young.

Leaving Kayla to her task, they entered Jesse's office where she offered David a seat. He declined, opting instead to take a slow tour around the room, checking out her pictures and books while she sat down at her desk to make a quick call to Abigail Martinez and bring up the electronic medical records. Hitting the print button she sat back and waited for the documents to spit themselves out.

"Is that your boy Matt?" David asked, pointing to a picture. It was one of her favorites of her oldest son. Matt was sweaty and his hair was sticking out all over the place, but the grin he wore, along with the medal from the track championships, reminded her of the little boy he'd once been.

"Yes, it was at the all-state track meet last year," she answered. "He came home with several medals," she added, not bothering to hide the hint of parental pride. Her printer stopped and she walked to a file cabinet to retrieve a folder from the bottom drawer for David to take the papers in. Straightening away from the cabinet, she turned to find him watching her. She held his gaze for a split second, then he looked away.

"You must be very proud," he said, turning back to the picture. For just a beat, Jesse felt a touch off balance. That he was an attractive man hadn't escaped her notice, but she was so used to being heads-down working during her time at the hospital that recognizing a person as anything other than a colleague was a skill she had long ago lost. Or maybe not. Because that look had felt like more than just a collegial exchange.

Deciding she'd imagined it, she turned back to the printer to pick up the documents as she answered. "I'm proud of both my boys. They're good kids."

She handed him the file and he looked about to ask another question when a knock sounded at the door.

"Are you ready for me?" Abigail Martinez asked as she popped her head through the doorway. At more than a decade older than Jesse, Abigail's short, dark hair was streaked with gray and her face held hints of her age. But her deep brown eyes danced with almost childlike humor just as often as they reflected the strain of her job.

Jesse offered her friend a smile and welcomed her in, thankful for the break in the conversation that was turning a bit too much toward her family. It's not that she had anything to hide, but no matter how good-looking David Hathaway was, he was still a virtual stranger.

After making the introductions, they agreed that Abigail would bring David back to Jesse's office when the two had finished going over Aaron's injuries and medical condition. After that, Jesse would take him down to the morgue where the autopsy on Brent Greene would be finishing up. In the meantime, she had paperwork to finish, reports to review, and a newsletter to write. Good times.

Jesse watched the two leave as an errant thought filtered into her head. David Hathaway might be an interesting distraction, but, like most parents, she already had more on her plate than she could handle. Really.

• • •

David walked through the hospital with Dr. Martinez as his mind stayed in the office with Jesse Baker. He had watched her lean over to pull a folder out of a cabinet drawer and for a moment his mind had gone blank. She had more than caught his attention as she'd come striding toward him in the hallway earlier—with her long blonde hair pulled back into a ponytail, she wore a fitted V-necked sweater the same color as her brown eyes and a not-quite demure skirt that hit just below her knees, but hugged every curve. A pair of four-inch heels that he was sure were an attempt to disguise her petite stature were the coup de grâce. He'd thought her too young to run Riverside Hospital and had initially thought maybe the administrator had sent an assistant to handle the inquiry into Aaron Greene. And to say he was surprised when she said she'd been there for twelve years was an understatement. He vaguely remembered thinking it put her closer to his own age if she had started right out of graduate school.

But then when she'd bent over in her office, pure male instinct had taken over and the only thought that had flitted through, and stuck, in David's mind was that he saw no panty lines under that nicely formed skirt—that and the short list of reasons why he saw no panty lines. All very nice thoughts, in his opinion.

Then she'd straightened and looked at him. The shape of her standing before him, slightly turned at the hip and glancing over her shoulder, had reminded him of the bombshells from the fifties. She wasn't tall, maybe five foot four in her heels, but she looked like someone had taken Marilyn Monroe, blonde hair and all, and just shrunk her down without changing any of the proportions.

David had never been very attracted to skinny women and, for good or for bad, Jesse Baker had reminded him of that with every move she made, from her confident walk, to the way she slid into her chair, to the way she held his gaze for just a moment after she'd straightened away from the file cabinet.

But then she'd handed him the file. And he had reminded himself that he wasn't there to flirt, a skill that was so rusty he was pretty sure he'd lost the ability altogether anyway. No, he was there to figure out if eighteen-year-old Aaron Greene had built a bomb that had gone off earlier in the day, destroying the peaceful spring morning as well as Aaron's home, his body, and his father's life.

David gave an internal sigh as he followed Dr. Martinez and begrudgingly admitted to himself that it was probably a good thing she had arrived when she did. He had no business digging into Jesse's life, asking about her sons. His own life was finally, after years and years of effort, becoming less complicated. He didn't need to fuck that up by flirting with a woman he'd just met. A woman he knew nothing about and who was, most likely, married. So, dutifully, he wrenched his brain away from the tempting curves of the hospital administrator and focused on the horror that Dr. Martinez was about to lay before him.

Forty-five minutes later, he had the gist of what he needed to know. Aaron had suffered third-degree burns on 10 percent of his body and had another 20 percent affected by first- and second-degree burns. The bulk of the serious injuries were centered around his right palm, left forearm, and down the left side of his torso. The majority of the second-degree burns impacted the left side of his body—his leg, shoulder, and that side of his face. He was in shock, unconscious, and would likely remain so for at least another day or two. If he didn't come to in that timeframe, Dr. Martinez indicated that his chances of survival would drop significantly.

She and her team were competent, more so than he'd expected walking into the hospital of a relatively small town. But while Windsor, where the explosion had happened, with its mix of wealthy weekenders and hard-working, blue-collar full-time residents was a town with a low crime rate, Riverside was a different story. David knew it was gentrifying, but he also knew from his chief that, for decades, Riverside had seen more than its share of crime, violence, drugs, and poverty. And the hospital, by necessity, had responded accordingly.

After going over everything and peppering Dr. Martinez with a number of questions, David followed her back to Jesse's office where they found her sitting behind her computer screen, leaning back in her chair, chewing on her lip. She looked up at them from under her eyelashes with a decidedly irritated expression.

Dr. Martinez laughed, the first laughter he'd heard from anyone since he'd walked into the hospital. "Let me guess, the monthly newsletter?" she asked.

Jesse let out a huff. "I hate this thing," she responded. She stared at her computer for a moment more before sitting forward and shutting it off.

"I foolishly started it three years ago and now everyone expects it," she explained, looking at David as she stood and began gathering her things.

Beside him, Dr. Martinez chuckled. "It's true, everyone does expect it. But only because you have a way with words."

"Ha, anyone who manages a facility filled with two hundred doctors better have a way with words," Jesse countered. "Anyway, I'll figure it out later." She closed her laptop and slid it into her bag. "Will I see you at the meet later?" she asked Dr. Martinez, pulling the bag's strap over her shoulder. "Matt and Danielle are both on the track team. We only have a couple of meets left before they both graduate," she added as an aside to David. A hint of parental sadness tinged her voice. He knew the feeling.

The two women made plans to meet at the high school and when it was clear they were finished, he thanked the doctor. She'd agreed to keep him updated and it was all he could ask for at the moment.

"Ready?" Jesse asked, once Dr. Martinez had left. He nodded and followed her out.

"You seem to have a good staff here," he said, making small talk as they left her office.

"I know, not what you'd expect from a small-town hospital, but you're right, we do," she answered. "Don't get me wrong," she added as she hit the down button outside the elevator. "We're not nearly as equipped as Albany or even Pittsfield, Massachusetts, but we're pretty good for our size and location. You must not be from around here?"

They stepped into the elevator and he was surprised to catch a delicate whiff of her perfume. It was hard to smell much of anything not industrial or biological in a hospital, but he definitely caught her scent. With a shake of his head, he answered.

"No, I moved here about ten months ago from Northern California."

"What brought you here? I love it, but it's not a well-known area."

David shrugged. "I like it, too. Colder than where I'm from, but I wanted to be on the East Coast and Albany offered me the chance to be both a firefighter and an arson investigator. I've done both, but in the past several years, I've mostly done the investigation part. I like it, but I missed being part of a team." That was part of the story—all true, just not all of the story.

"And how does that work?" she asked. The elevator dinged and the doors slid open, revealing a basement hallway. Stepping out, she directed him to the right as she clarified, "Being a firefighter and an investigator, I mean."

"In big cities they're usually different roles," he said, following her through the dim corridor. "But in areas like this, with lots of rural municipalities, towns and counties that don't have the need or funds to keep someone like me on staff full time rely on the state. So I'm employed by the State of New York as a part-time investigator and the rest of the time I work for the Albany FD."

He finished explaining just as Jesse stopped at a pair of closed doors. As she looked up at him, he noted that she had the longest eyelashes ringing her eyes, which he now realized were more hazel than brown.

"Sounds like a reasonable compromise," she said, her hand on the swinging door.

He shrugged.

She studied him for a moment, then took a deep breath. "You ready?"

After his sharp nod, they pushed into the morgue, a serviceable room containing a single table, a desk, and a woman washing up at the sink. On the table lay a form under a white sheet. The woman turned and looked at them over her shoulder as the door clicked shut behind them.

"Jesse," she smiled. "I'm glad you came down, I wasn't sure if you were going to." She finished rinsing her hands and grabbed a couple of paper towels before turning all the way around.

Presumably this was the medical examiner. She was another attractive woman, but in a very different way than Jesse. Even in her scrubs, it was easy to see she had an athletic build, though she looked like she'd either put on weight recently or was in the early stages of pregnancy. She was a lot taller than Jesse and had dark hair and Mediterranean skin. In looks, about the only thing the two women had in common was the way they wore their hair. As his eyes met the woman's, he recognized a look of idle curiosity in her expression.

"I wanted to make sure we were still on for tonight?" Jesse asked.

The other woman's eyes swung back to her friend.

"And by the way, this is David Hathaway, the arson investigator," Jesse said. "David, this is Dr. Vivienne DeMarco. She is, among many things, our medical examiner. She's also a professor at the university in Boston and an FBI consultant."

The introduction was meant to impress him and it did. He wondered how such a small town had landed such a person.

"She's also pregnant and shouldn't be working so hard."

David turned at the new voice and saw a man in a sheriff's uniform stride into the room with a resigned expression on his face. The officer walked up to Dr. DeMarco and gave her a swift kiss.

"You shouldn't be standing so much." The man's voice was soft with affection.

"I'm pregnant, Ian, not ill. Now, don't be rude," Dr. DeMarco responded as she gestured toward David with her head. The sheriff ignored her statement for a moment and stared at her with a look of repressed exasperation. When she arched a brow at him, he rolled his eyes and turned toward David.

"Sheriff Ian MacAllister. Also Vivienne's husband. But call me Ian, please," he said, holding out his hand.

"David Hathaway," he responded, taking the proffered hand. The assessment the sheriff subjected him to was swift, but David didn't doubt it was complete. Something in the man's bearing screamed competence. Probably military-trained competence.

"It's nice to meet you. Can't say I'm a fan of the circumstances, but what can we do?" Ian said with a shrug.

David couldn't agree more and said so.

"So, is there a reason you called me here?" Ian asked his wife, who elbowed him in response.

"Yes, now don't be pushy," she answered. "Let me just finish up with Jesse and I'll be right with you both."

The two women walked toward the door. It was obvious they were good friends and they seemed to be making plans to meet later that night for dinner. It was amazing to him that they could be talking about such a thing considering where they were. Oh, he was used to it. Sort of. He'd been around enough burned bodies that the smell didn't completely turn his stomach anymore. And, well, Dr. DeMarco—he understood that, given her job, she probably had a cast-iron stomach.

But it said a lot about Jesse that she hadn't flinched a bit when they'd walked into the room. He didn't get the sense that she spent a lot of time in the morgue or saw all that much violent death, but she just seemed strong. Able to take what life put in front of her. Today it happened to be a body burned to nearly nothing. He had to admire her for that.

"So what's the public story?" Ian asked, pulling David's attention back to the situation at hand.

"About?" David countered, feeling a little slow.

Ian lifted a shoulder. "I haven't heard much of the news today, but if they suspected a bomb was the origin of the fire, it'd be all over the media. We wouldn't be hearing about anything else. So even if that's what you are investigating, the public story must be something else."

David studied the sheriff, taking in the man's matter-of-fact assumption that what was being made public might not be the real, or entire story. It made David wonder about Ian's background. Not that it mattered one way or another.

"Officially undetermined, but we're mentioning a possible gas explosion," was all he said, figuring that as law enforcement, Ian should probably know the company line, so to speak.

Ian raised his shoulders in an "it'll do" gesture and they fell back into silence. David didn't miss the fact that he wasn't the only one whose eyes seemed to gravitate to the two women.

"They might be talking about you," Ian said, out of the blue.

David turned at Ian's voice. "I beg your pardon?"

"My wife is steadfastly trying not to look in my direction. That usually means she's up to something," he said. "And my guess is, given the way Jesse is shaking her head and rolling her eyes, Vivienne is probably trying to suss out whether or not she's interested in you."

David wasn't quite sure what to say to that. At least Ian had answered the question of whether or not Jesse was married. But still, even knowing small towns had lots of small-town gossip, being sucked into it after knowing a man for less than five minutes left David with very little to say. And he must have looked it because Ian let out a big laugh.

"Don't worry. If there's a single guy within a forty-mile radius, my wife is trying to set Jesse up with him. I try not to get involved. But there it is."

"There what is?" Dr. DeMarco asked, returning to their side of the room. David watched as Jesse gave him one last look before pushing the morgue door open and leaving him alone with the couple.

"You, trying to set Jesse up," Ian responded as he crossed his arms over his chest, all but daring his wife to argue. She opened her mouth, then shut it, then opened it again before pursing her lips and glaring at her husband—like a puppy caught in the act.

"I have no idea what you're talking about," she finally retorted. "Now, if you'd both like to turn your attention to Brent Greene, I will present you with my findings."

"Please," Ian said, making a grand gesture toward the table. David encountered a lot of people in his line of work. Some earned his respect, some he enjoyed working with. But it seemed that everyone he'd met in just the last few hours during his visit to Riverside were people he might actually like. Not just as colleagues, but possibly as friends.

They were genuine in the way they worked together and treated each other as professionals. But they also seemed to somehow cross over and have real relationships outside of work—meeting for dinner, cheering their kids on together—or, in the case of Dr. DeMarco and Ian, working and living together. Maybe there was something to be said for small towns.

"Now, Mr. Hathaway—" Dr. DeMarco began.

"David," he interrupted.

She acknowledged his interjection with a nod then continued. "You might be wondering why I called Ian here. Aside from being my husband, of course." She cast a smile at Ian over her shoulder and her husband's lips lifted in return.

"I assumed it was because arson, of any sort, is a criminal investigation and him being the sheriff and all," David responded, his curiosity piqued. If Dr. DeMarco had found something to indicate it was more than arson, this could get interesting.

"It is, of course. But let me direct your attention here." She led both men over to a large computer screen and pulled up a couple of x-ray images. Both showed a skull. "Now, Mr. Greene's ultimate cause of death is smoke inhalation," she said.

"He wasn't killed by the fire? Or the explosion?" David clarified.

"No," she shook her head. "He was dead before the fire got to him and the injuries that I did find that resulted from the explosion wouldn't have killed him."

"But you did find evidence of an explosion?" David asked.

Dr. Demarco nodded. "Most definitely. But I found those injuries mostly on the lower part of his body and not severe enough to be the cause of death. So, as I was saying," she continued, "the smoke is what ultimately caused his death, but I want to draw your attention here." She pointed to the forehead area of the x-ray. David stepped closer and peered at the area. At his side, he felt Ian do the same.

"Is that a series of fractures I see?" David asked, frowning.

"It is," she answered.

"He was hit on the head before he died from the smoke?" Ian clarified.

"He was. And whatever it was he was hit on the head with, or by, was powerful. This bone here," she circled the area of the forehead, "is a very strong bone. As you can see from the x-rays, there are several small radiating fractures. It would take a hard instrument and a strong person to do that."

"And not something that would happen if he fell and hit his head?" David asked.

"Definitely not. Not enough force," she answered.

"Can you tell if it happened before or after the injuries he got from the explosion?" David asked.

Dr. DeMarco shook her head. "Not by the injuries themselves. The best I can tell from the remains is that they happened either close together or at the same time."

"But?" Ian pressed, obviously hearing something in his wife's voice.

She cast him a glance, then spoke. "But if we look at the placement of the injuries, not the injuries themselves, I would posit that he was hit on the head, fell down, and *then* the explosion went off, sending debris and such into his legs, particularly the lower portions which were probably closest to the origin."

Ian bobbed his head. "Okay, so a forceful hit to the head knocked him out."

"So, what would do that?" David asked.

"And who?" Ian added.

"As to who, that's your job, babe," she said with a grin. Out of the corner of his eye, David saw Ian roll his eyes at his wife's dry tone.

"As to what," she continued, "I'd say something thick and hard."

"Like a baseball bat?" David offered.

She shook her head. "Not round, something flat. Like a two-by-four or the like."

"Like something that would have burned up in the fire." The sheriff's voice wasn't thrilled and David could sympathize.

"You think a third person might have been involved? Someone who whacked the dad?" David asked.

"That's not my territory," she answered.

"It *is* her territory, Hathaway. Maybe not officially, but by experience. And don't let her fool you into thinking otherwise," Ian interjected, clarifying for David. For a moment the sheriff's eyes narrowed on his wife, as if trying to figure her out, then he shrugged.

"For some reason, she's trying to stay out of it, though. Not sure why, since she never has before, but I'll figure that out later. Officially, an assault like this would be my case," he said, studying the image. "Unless of course the state or the feds take over, depending on what you find, Hathaway," he added, taking a step away from the computer screen.

"But if someone were to ask me," Dr. DeMarco continued, ignoring her previous statement with a sly smile directed at her husband, who shot David a look as if to say "I told you so." "I'd say you should look into the possibility of a third person, but my guess is you'll find that Aaron did it," she pronounced as she placed her hands on the small of her back and stretched, displaying her growing belly.

"You need to sit down, Vivienne," Ian said, noticing his wife's movements with concern.

"I'm fine," she waved him off.

"Why?" David asked, cutting off the protest that was no doubt forming on Ian's lips.

"Maybe to stop his father," she offered, her head tilted as she studied the images.

"Stop his father from setting off the bomb or stop his father from stopping *him* from setting off the bomb?" he pressed.

She took a moment to answer. "You'll have to figure that out," she finally said. But it was clear from the way her gaze slid to the side that the good doctor definitely had her opinions.

David frowned and mentally went through what Dr. Martinez had told him about Aaron's condition. "Aaron's injuries might be consistent with an attempt to defuse a bomb," he posited, thinking out loud more than anything. He hadn't really formed any opinions yet, didn't have enough information. But he wanted to throw it out there and see what this couple did with that option.

"Or they might be consistent with someone who was attempting to build one and accidentally set it off," Ian suggested, though his tone was more pragmatic than persuasive or argumentative.

"Would this injury have killed him, Dr. DeMarco, if the smoke hadn't?" David asked, pointing to the x-ray images.

"Call me Vivi, please, and yes, it probably would have if he didn't seek treatment for it. The force of the blow was strong enough that the impact of the fractures would have caused damage and bleeding of the brain. Left untreated, his brain would likely have swollen, eventually killing him."

"So if it was Aaron who hit his father and then set off the bomb, he's probably responsible for his father's death either way," David said.

"But if he hit his father and tried to defuse the bomb, he was likely acting in some form of self-defense," Ian countered.

David had to admit that, even though he would track the evidence where it took him, the idea of Aaron Greene being involved in this debacle as a hero rather than a killer appealed to him. He knew it was possible for a kid to be cold-blooded, to build bombs and set fires that killed people. But he preferred to give the young man the benefit of the doubt. And though everyone he'd met so far at Riverside had maintained professional detachment and no one had raved about Aaron being innocent, it was clear from how they talked about him, how they talked about the situation, that everyone was having a hard time buying he was the bad guy in all this.

CHAPTER 2

Perched on the bleachers with the other parents, Jesse watched Matt and Danielle stretch and warm up on the inner ring of the track. Matt must have said something funny because Danielle threw her head back and laughed. Jesse smiled. Looking at the two of them, it was hard for her to believe that at their age she had already met and become engaged to Mark, Matt's father.

And within a year of that, she'd had Matt. It hadn't been easy being married so young, and with a baby to boot, but Mark had been quite a bit older and, at least for the first several years of their marriage, loving and supportive of her.

Resting her elbows on her knees, she gazed at the two kids warming up as she reflected on her own journey from teenager to adult. Mark had been adamant that she continue college as she'd planned. And despite having Matt, and a little more than two years later, James, she'd finished in four years and then gone on to graduate school.

She'd started working at Riverside shortly after that, and when the boys were seven and five, they'd bought a house in Windsor. With two young kids, a marriage, and a full-time job, most of those first ten years or so seemed a blur.

Then, suddenly, the boys were riding their bikes into town, going to school dances, and in just a few short months, Matt would be off to college. When she was living it, her own path hadn't seemed so strange, but watching her son now, she wished him, and Danielle, many more carefree years as young adults.

"Thinking this will all be over soon?" Abigail sat down next to her, offering to share a blanket she'd brought. It was a warm spring night, but Abigail was constantly cold.

Jesse smiled. "Actually, I was thinking that I hope they don't lose their carefree ways for many years to come," she said, feeling Abigail's eyes on her.

"You did start young," Abigail conceded.

Jesse gave an unladylike snort. "You can say that again. And while I don't regret it—how could I?" she said with a nod to Matt. "I wouldn't wish it on them. I'm going to miss him, but I'm glad he's going off to college this fall. I just hope he takes advantage of it all."

Abigail gave her a little bump of support. "You're a great mom. He's a good kid. He'll do great. And speaking of great kids," Abigail's voice trailed off as James, Jesse's younger son, came jogging up.

"Mom," he said, stopping in front of the two women.

"Hi, honey. How was your physics test today?" she asked.

Like a typical fifteen-year-old, James rolled his eyes. "Easy, cakewalk," he answered.

The scary thing was, it probably was a cakewalk for him. Her younger son was a bit of a science and math savant. Something he probably inherited from his dad.

"Coach wants us to warm up with the varsity team," he continued. "But then Cameron and I want to head into town and grab something to eat. Can you pick me up there after the meet?" As a freshman, his main track season had ended a few weeks earlier, but like his brother, James was a runner at heart, and with a few off-season meets still left in the school year, the chance to run and socialize wasn't one James would pass up. It also didn't hurt that his current love interest had joined the team.

"Sure, bring your phone though, so I can reach you if I need to. Do you need any money?" Jesse asked.

"Nah, I got it. You're the best," he answered, then jogged off.

Jesse watched him join a group of kids. Both her boys looked a lot like their dad, she mused. Olive skin, dark-brown hair, and lanky forms. But they both had her eyes. And not that it mattered, but she secretly liked that fact. They were good-looking boys, but most importantly, to her especially, they were generally good kids.

"Like I was saying, you know you're doing something right when your fifteen-year-old tells you you're the best," Abigail pointed out.

Jesse laughed. "It's not like we don't have our days, but you're right, I think we're all lucky to have each other. Oh, look." She spotted Vivi walking toward them and waved her over.

"Well, well, well, if it isn't the little vixen," Vivi said, smiling coyly as she sat down beside them.

"I have no idea what you're talking about," Jesse answered. But of course she did, and both Vivi and Abigail snickered.

"What are you doing here? I thought we were going to meet later. Isn't Ian all up in arms about you having been on your feet all day today?" Jesse asked, trying to change the subject.

"That sounds like a nice change—I've been sitting on my ass all day." All three women looked up at the sound of a fourth voice to find their friend Matty Brooks walking toward them. She eyed the empty bleacher seat beside Vivi, looked to be debating whether or not to stand, then sat.

"Plugging away on your next book?" Jesse asked.

Matty was a renowned author of political thrillers. Having spent most of her life inside the DC beltway, she was a fairly recent transplant to Windsor, as was Vivi. But still, Jesse and Abigail, who'd lived there their whole lives, had become fast friends with both women. It didn't hurt that she and, though to a lesser extent given the age difference, Abigail had grown up with Vivi and Matty's husbands.

Matty let out a dramatic sigh. "My deadline is in a month. I know I shouldn't be freaking out about it yet, but I've reached the point where I can't stand my characters anymore," she answered.

"But that's a good thing, right?" Abigail asked. "Doesn't that usually happen when you're almost done?"

"A coping mechanism because you're about to have to let them go?" Vivi added with a grin.

"Don't shrink me, doctor lady," Matty shot back with her own smile. Not only was Vivi a medical doctor, she also had a PhD in psychology.

"When *is* your next book out?" Jesse asked.

"End of June. We'll have to have a launch party," Matty added in a tone that suggested the party might be the only thing that could incentivize her to finish.

"It will be a month of parties, with all the graduations, too," Jesse mused. It was still a little hard to believe that her baby was graduating from high school in less than a month. Her baby whose six-foot-three frame was about to start his first race of the meet. By unspoken agreement, all four women fell silent as they watched Matt lap the track four times and easily finish in the first position. Jesse glanced at the time clock. He'd be happy he won but not with his time.

"So, what are you both doing here?" Jesse asked, returning her attention to Vivi and Matty.

"Ian is helping Meghan serve ice cream out front," Vivi answered. Meghan Conners owned a local ice cream shop. A young, single mom who'd not only had a really rough childhood, but she'd also been tortured and nearly killed by a crazy man around the time Vivi had come to town the year before. Meghan had proven to be a fighter, for both herself and her young son, and had recovered from the ordeal; however, Vivi and Ian tended to take special care of her. She was working hard to grow her ice cream business and it wasn't a surprise Ian was there to help.

"I wanted to help, too, but Ian insisted I sit down. The overbearing beast," Vivi added with a grin.

"Oh, you love it when he's overbearing," Matty shot back. Vivi's grin turned into a smile.

"And what about you, Matty?" Abigail asked.

"Kristen Harwick joined the JV team this year," Matty explained. "Of course her father, the bastard, hasn't been to a single one of her meets, so Dash and I are here," Matty said, referring to her husband.

"Kristen's dad is a very busy man," Abigail offered.

"Kristen's father is an ass. But at least she has us. Dash is just getting us some food."

Before Dash had married Matty and moved into her house, Kristen had been his neighbor. Matty had met the young girl last fall when she'd gone with Dash, a veterinarian, to care for Kristen's horse, Bogey—the only living thing that had truly seemed to care for Kristen at the time. Having known what it was like to have an absentee father, Matty and the girl had become quick friends. Matty, a city girl at heart, had even allowed Kristen to teach her how to ride.

Jesse turned her gaze away from her son and glanced at her friends, all of them happily married, and for more than two decades in Abigail's case since she'd married Joe Martinez right out of college. For a moment, she wished Carly and Kit were there, her two good friends who were single, like her. She and Mark had had a good run, but the fact was, she was alone now. And while she liked it most of the time, liked it enough not to want to change it, sometimes the affection and familiarity she heard in her friends' voices when they talked about their husbands caused a little pang in her heart.

"So, tell me about the hottie," Vivi said, returning to the topic Jesse had hoped they would drop. Especially now that she was sitting amongst the married set.

"The state sent an arson investigator down to look into what happened this morning at the Greenes' place," Vivi filled Matty in. "And he's definitely some serious eye candy."

"*And* he was making serious eyes at Jesse today," Abigail added.

Jesse rolled her eyes. "We were talking, of course he was looking at me."

"Oh, I didn't realize your ass could talk 'cause that's where I saw him looking," Vivi interjected, making her other two friends hoot. Jesse tried to keep a straight face but failed in the face of so much laughter.

"Oh look, Danielle's race is starting." Her attempt to redirect her friends wasn't fooling anyone. But this was exactly why she didn't date. She loved her friends, but dating someone, or even showing an interest in someone, would lead to questions about dates, and then questions about more dates, and then questions about where it was all leading, and all the things she just wasn't interested in talking about. Not that having a hot night with David Hathaway wasn't appealing—who was she kidding, of course it was appealing—but it wasn't worth the complications if people found out. Maybe, when she was older and the kids were out of the house and she was beyond the age where everyone still considered marriage as par for the course, she might start dating. But at the age of thirty-six, with a group of married friends, mostly *newly* married friends, and some even expecting children, that age was a long way off.

Mercifully, her friends let her off the hook after that. They spent the rest of the meet cheering the kids on while chatting off and on about nothing of substance. And beyond general sounds of sympathy, no one seemed inclined to talk about the fire that had claimed a life and left a young man in the hospital. But then again, no one other than Vivi, Abigail, Ian, and Jesse knew it was more than a fire. It would come out eventually. David's investigation would become public. But for now, she was thankful people were still sympathizing with Aaron rather than speculating about his character.

The meet came to a close and Matt stopped by to let her know he was going into town with his teammates for pizza. After making arrangements for Matt to pick up James, Jesse spent a few more minutes saying good-bye to her friends then made her way out to her car to head home, having opted to skip dinner with Vivi and Ian. It had been a long day, starting with work at seven a.m. Now, twelve hours later, she was ready to head home, pour a glass of wine, and sit on her porch.

Or not.

"Crud," she grumbled as she reached her car. It was sitting so lopsided in the parking lot there was no missing the two flat tires. At a loss for a moment, she just stared. The tires were fairly new; the whole car was only two years old. That she would have two flat tires didn't seem logical and her mind was having a hard time accepting it.

A car door slammed shut somewhere in the parking lot behind her and the wind picked up, bringing with it the smell of freshly cut grass, the sound of kids laughing, and the pinch of reality biting her on the butt. Mumbling a curse, she slipped her keys back into her purse and grabbed her phone.

"There a problem?" came Ian's voice as he and Vivi pulled up beside her.

"You could say that," Jesse said, motioning to her tires even as she kept the phone to her ear. "I'm trying to get a hold of Richie to have him give me a tow. Or bring some tires out to replace these."

Ian parked, and he and Vivi both slid out of their car and approached Jesse. Richie, the town's auto mechanic, wasn't answering his phone at the moment, so she hung up and stood with her friends, gazing at her car. Beside her, Ian contemplated her little Subaru for a moment before going down on his haunches beside her rear tire. He stayed there for a minute or two before moving to examine the front tire.

Standing back up, he frowned. "Someone slashed them."

"What?" she stuttered. It wasn't unheard of to have petty vandalism in Windsor. It had just never happened to her.

Vivi went through the same motions her husband just had. "I can see it. Here," she said, pointing to a small slice in the rear tire. "And here," she said pointing to an identical one in the front tire.

Jesse hadn't seen the cuts when she'd first noticed the tires. She'd been so surprised to see them flat in the first place that she hadn't looked further. But now that it had been pointed out to her, it was obvious it hadn't been an accident or something she'd driven over that had caused the problem.

"Anyone been bothering you lately?" Ian asked, reaching for his phone. He didn't say a thing but she had known Ian long enough to know he was calling some of his fellow law enforcement.

Jesse shook her head. "This is city jurisdiction, not county," she pointed out, knowing full well that Ian, the county sheriff, would ignore her. But still she tried and added, "You don't have to call anything in. I'm sure it was just kids messing around."

Ian responded with a flat look. "All the more reason to see if we can figure out who might have done this. If it's kids, we might have a chance of stopping them from choosing a life of crime," he said.

She rolled her eyes at his over dramatization of the situation. His lips twitched as he started speaking into his phone.

"Your husband is overreacting just a tad, don't you think?" Jesse asked, turning to Vivi.

Vivi shrugged. "Probably. It's what he does when he thinks someone he cares about might be in harm's way. But it can't hurt to get a police report. It will help with getting insurance to cover the cost of new tires," her friend answered practically.

It was a good reason to at least have a report taken—one she hadn't thought of. Whether she would actually report it to her insurance or not remained to be seen. It would probably be easier just to pay for the things herself than to go through all the paperwork it would take to get reimbursed.

"Vivienne, why don't you take Jesse home? Carly and Marcus are going to come along. I can take it from here and they can give me a ride home," Ian said, still holding the phone to his ear.

Vivi looked to her for input. For a moment, Jesse thought about staying. It would hardly be a hardship to answer a few questions and then arrange for her car to be towed. But then again, Ian liked to take care of people. It was part of who he was. And at the moment, having someone take care of her, just a little bit, didn't sound so bad.

"Thank you, Ian. I'd appreciate that, if it won't be too much trouble?"

He shook his head in response and began filling Carly and Marcus, two of Windsor's police officers, in on the plan. She grabbed her computer from the trunk of her car then climbed into Ian's truck with Vivi behind the wheel. Ian came to the window and after Jesse agreed to touch base with him later to get the details about where to pick up her car in the morning, she and Vivi drove out of the parking lot and headed north through town. She was thinking of the glass of wine on her porch again when Vivi spoke with a grin.

"So, tell me about this arson investigator."

Jesse groaned.

CHAPTER 3

"DAVID, THIS IS JESSE BAKER at Riverside Hospital. You asked me to call you when Aaron Greene was awake." Jesse tapped her pencil on her desk as she spoke.

"How long ago?" he asked.

He had a nice voice, she realized as she listened to it on the other end of the line. Not too eager, but not cautious either. It had the practical and confident quality of a man who knew his job well.

"About twenty minutes. Dr. Martinez has been in with him, but I wanted to let you know," she answered.

"Has anyone else been in there?"

She paused before answering. She didn't think she'd done anything wrong but wasn't sure.

"I have."

He didn't speak for a moment, but she could hear the sound of him closing a car door.

"I'm on my way, and please don't let anyone else other than the doctor in with him," he said.

"Fair enough, if you agree to meet with me before you go in," Jesse said. She knew she had no right to make such a request, but an urge to protect Aaron had made her say it anyway.

David said nothing for a moment; over the phone she heard the rumble of a car engine starting in the background.

"I'll call you when I get there," was all he offered.

Jesse sighed, hung up the phone, and glanced at the clock. It would take him about forty-five minutes to reach Riverside from Albany. For a fleeting moment, she wondered if he would look the same as he had two days earlier. She kind of liked his work look; it was sturdy and rugged and spoke of a man who worked hard physically. Mark had always worn suits. And while he'd worn them well, they sometimes seemed more like part of an image he'd wanted to portray than a part of the man himself.

With a shake of her head and an intentional reprimand to bring her mind back to task, she pulled up her latest draft of the newsletter. With any luck, she would be able to finalize it before David showed up.

Forty minutes later, Jesse sat back and stretched her arms over her head. She'd just hit the send button and was newsletter-free for another month. As if on cue, her phone rang. She smiled when she saw David's name on the caller ID.

Their conversation lasted less than a minute, then Jesse slipped her phone into her pocket, locked her computer, and made her way to the lobby to meet him.

• • •

David was standing in the lobby perusing staff pictures when he heard the click of Jesse's heels. He turned to watch her walk toward him. It was hard not to appreciate the view. Today she wore a green dress that made her eyes look brighter and fit her petite curves perfectly. The slit up the side was probably tasteful, but coupled with her high heels, well, it made his mind wonder things it shouldn't.

She was talking on the phone as she approached him, and holding up a finger to ask for a moment, she gave him an apologetic look as she finished her conversation. He nodded and shifted his gaze back to the inanimate pictures on the wall.

"No, that's great, Julie. Thanks, I'm really looking forward to picking it up. What time are you open on Saturday? Ten? Great. I'll be in early so I can get it out in Saturday's mail. No, no worries, it wasn't your fault it was delayed. Right, thanks again, and I'll see you Saturday."

She hung up and gave him a chagrined look. "Sorry. I ordered a quilt for my parents' fortieth wedding anniversary from the local shop in Windsor. Julie, the owner, has lots of friends in Amish country who make things for her. It's going to be gorgeous, I know, but it came in a little later than expected so I'll need to be sure to pick it up and mail it on Saturday. Their anniversary is next week," she explained. He almost smiled at the subtle look of confusion that crossed her face when she finished speaking—as if she didn't understand why she'd told him everything she had.

"Will it make it to your folks on time?" he asked, taking a step back as a woman pushed a food cart past them, followed by another woman carrying a little girl. He'd been in his fair share of hospitals over the years but he still found it surprising how similar most of them were. The staff and volunteers all wore the same type of uniforms and the visitors tended to have one of two expressions on their faces—happiness or fear. Sometimes it was subtle, but in his experience, it was always one of those two.

When the hallway door closed behind the passersby, he turned his attention back to Jesse. The quilt had nothing to do with why he was there at Riverside, but he didn't bother to stop himself from making small talk. He also didn't bother to wonder why he was taking the time to make small talk in the first place.

She nodded. "Yes. They live in Washington State, so as long as there aren't any problems and I can actually get it out in Saturday's post, it should be fine. Of course, I can always send it overnight, and I will if it comes to that, but I'd rather not spend an arm and a leg if I don't have to," she added.

"Amen to that," he muttered in agreement. He knew he should ask to see Aaron right away, but standing there, looking at Jesse, he realized that despite looking as good as she did, she looked more tired than she had a few days ago. He frowned.

"How have you been?" he asked.

The personal nature of his question caught them both a little off guard, but she recovered quickly and smiled at him.

"Fine," she answered. "Except for having my tires slashed at my sons' track meet Monday night, everything is fine. I would say

35

it's just one of those weeks, but every week seems to be one of those weeks, if you know what I mean?" she added with a smile.

He did, and he liked to see her smile. But he didn't like what he'd just heard. "You had your tires slashed?"

She nodded and lifted a shoulder in a what-can-you-do gesture. "Some kids, I imagine. It happened at the school," she added.

David frowned. That kind of vandalism wasn't something he expected to hear about in Windsor. Cow tipping, maybe. Kids trespassing to party, definitely. But destruction of property with a knife? He was about to ask her if she'd reported it, then he cut himself off. She didn't seem too concerned about the situation and he knew she was a friend of the sheriff's, so if she *had* been concerned, she no doubt would have gone to Ian.

"I'm sorry to hear that," he said. Then turning the conversation back to work, he asked why she had wanted to see him before he headed up to the ICU.

Her smile faltered and she gestured for him to follow her. She started speaking as they walked toward the elevators, her voice low enough for only him to hear.

"I know you have your job to do and I don't begrudge you doing it. If Aaron was responsible for that fire, he needs to be held responsible. But he hasn't had it easy these past few years," she started. When they stepped into an empty elevator, her voice went back up to its normal level and she continued. "I asked Matt about him," she said. "And no, before you ask, I didn't say anything about the investigation. We just talked in general terms."

Jesse had been working in a hospital for a long time, and she struck David as a woman who knew a thing or two about the importance of privacy. He hadn't been about to accuse her of breaching any laws regarding an ongoing investigation. But he *was* curious about what Matt had said.

"What did your son say?"

"Well, you probably know all this already, but Aaron's mother died a few years ago. They were really close. She was a sweet woman. His dad wasn't bad, just never really around, probably more mentally absent than physically absent, though he was a truck driver for a year or so when Aaron was little. Anyway, his mom supported them, and his dad could never really get it together. He never held a job for any length of time, never really seemed to do much of anything to help out," Jesse answered.

"But," he prompted as they stepped out of the elevator and into the ICU.

"But after his mom died, his dad seemed to kind of lose it a little bit. We'd see him in town, picking fights, that sort of thing. Matt told me that a time or two he saw Aaron come to school with bruises on him."

David could tell from the way her voice went hard that had she known of this before, she would have been sure to have done something about it. Unfortunately, he knew from experience that sometimes there just wasn't anything anyone could do. That didn't mean he or anyone else had an excuse for not trying, but it did mean that it was impossible to save everyone.

"His dad was beating him?" he asked, just to clarify. If this was true, it was new information in the investigation. And it could go both ways as to whether or not it would help Aaron. It certainly gave the boy motive to hurt his father, but if his father was going off the deep end, maybe Aaron just got caught in the middle.

Jesse glanced at him and shrugged. "I couldn't say for certain," she answered as they made their way down the hall. "Matt did ask Aaron if he needed any help with anything and Aaron said no, but that *is* what Matt thinks. Matt's feeling really guilty about it now. About not doing something more to help his classmate," she said, almost on a sigh.

"It's hard to help people who don't want to be helped," he offered as they came to a stop outside Aaron's room.

She turned to face him as she responded, "And it's hard for a seventeen-year-old boy to understand that, let alone accept it."

Having been one himself once, albeit twenty years ago, David understood what she was saying.

"So, you wanted to tell me what?" he asked, his eyes locked on hers.

"I didn't really have anything specific to tell you. Like I said, you have to do your job. And while I know a lot about what I do, I know nothing about what it takes to do what you do."

"But?" he pressed.

She turned to face the massive window that looked into Aaron's room. "But I'd ask that, if you can, maybe take it easy on him a little bit," she answered quietly.

He watched her profile as she gazed into the room He didn't doubt she was every bit the professional he recognized her to be, but standing there, looking at Aaron, he knew she was looking at the boy as a mother, as a protector.

"You don't want me to use my thumb screws?"

Startled by his comment, she turned her big hazel eyes on him. And then smiled at his expression.

"Am I being too protective?"

He shook his head. "Everybody needs someone to look out for them. Maybe he's involved, maybe he isn't. But judging by the way you and your colleagues are tiptoeing around him and my inves- tigation, I expect he's the kind of kid who's going to tell me the truth. And telling me the truth will make everything a lot easier."

She studied him for a long moment, before nodding. "Thank you."

"No need to thank me. I'm just doing my job." And he was, just maybe a little more pleasantly than he usually did. "Do you want me to stop by when I've finished?"

Again, she looked surprised, and pleased, by his offer. "Yes, thank you, again. I'd appreciate that. And in the meantime, I'll let you get to it."

He watched her walk away, admiring the sight, before turning back to Aaron Greene. Over the last two days, he'd developed his own theories on what had happened. Now it was time to see if he was anywhere near the mark.

"Aaron?"

The boy's head turned a fraction as David entered the room. He approached the bedside so Aaron could see him more clearly without having to move.

"You're the investigator." Aaron's voice was scratchy and muffled by the bandages around his neck and lower jaw, but otherwise coherent. "Mrs. Baker told me you'd be by," he added.

"She called me after you woke up. I was hoping we could talk." David looked into Aaron's eyes and saw moisture gathering.

"Yeah, I think we should talk."

● ● ●

David slid the door closed behind him. On the other side, Aaron was taking a much-needed rest. The boy had told him everything he needed to know—David didn't think it was everything Aaron needed to, or should, say about the past few years since his mother had died, but it was what David needed to close the investigation.

He headed down the hall and rather than taking the elevator he opted to jog down the stairs to Jesse's office. She'd be glad to hear what he had to say and he was feeling good about being able to deliver news that would make her happy. Well, maybe happy was too strong a word given the circumstances, but information that would give her some peace.

But then again, closing the investigation meant he'd no longer have a reason to visit Riverside. He'd no longer have a reason to run into Jesse.

He didn't live all that far from Windsor, just a few towns up I-90 toward Albany, but it was a world away from the close-knit hamlets that made up the Windsor townships. Aside from Windsor proper, there was Windsor Center, North Windsor, East Windsor, and Old Windsor—not that he'd looked into it. The area looked the same as where he lived, but somehow, maybe because of the close proximity of so many small towns, it actually felt like a community, rather than a haphazard collection of houses and a post office like in his township.

As he hit the landing of her floor, he mulled over the idea of asking her out. He was pretty sure she was single, given that the sheriff had hinted about his wife, Vivi, scheming to set David and Jesse up. But that could mean a lot of things in this day and age— maybe she was newly separated from a husband, or maybe there was never a husband at all. He didn't really know her story, and not knowing her situation, or her expectations, made him somewhat hesitant to pursue her. Because the truth was, after the way he'd spent the last twenty years of his life, he wasn't altogether sure he wanted to start dating anyway. And something about putting the two unknowns together just didn't seem like a great idea. Not intellectually, anyway.

Pushing aside all thoughts and questions of dating, and focusing on the task at hand, David walked into the administrative offices just as a man in scrubs walked out. Kayla, on the phone, waved him toward Jesse's open door. Knocking on the doorframe he poked his head in and found her standing by the window talking on her cell. She glanced over and motioned him in with a wayward smile.

"Just a quarter cup, James. No. Yes, it goes in the spot to the left. No, not hot water unless you want your shirts to fit me. Yes, that's right. Good. Okay, I'll be home in an hour or so. Yes, love you, too."

She ended the conversation, gave the phone an exasperated look, then shook her head with a smile.

"Sorry," she said, turning toward him. "First quilts, now this. I do actually work on occasion."

"Everything okay?"

"Everything is fine. Except for my younger son's socks and white shirts. He washed them with his new red sweatshirt. Everything is pink and of course he doesn't have anything clean to wear tomorrow so he has to fix it tonight," she explained with good-natured patience.

"At least he does his own laundry," David offered.

Her eyes went up to the ceiling. "There is that, I suppose.

Please, take a seat." She gestured to the empty chair in front of her desk but didn't move to sit herself.

"If you don't mind, I'd rather stand," he responded. "I was just getting out of an insurance fraud deposition when you called earlier. I've been sitting all day."

She smiled and perched at the end of her desk. "I was wondering about the suit," she said with a nod to his formal attire.

He caught and held her gaze for a moment. She'd been thinking about him. Again the thought of asking her out crossed his mind. Then one of the pictures on her shelf caught his eye. Two smiling young boys and a man standing on a mountain trail surrounded by maple trees in their full autumn glory. Leaves of vibrant reds, oranges, and yellows framed the three figures and littered the trail floor. Judging by what he remembered of the photo he'd noticed during his first visit, one of the boys was obviously Matt, Jesse's oldest son. And given how much the younger boy looked like the older one, he assumed it was her younger son. He couldn't say for certain who the man was, but based on the body language in the picture, with an arm slung around each boy's shoulders, David would wager it was their father. And wondering why Jesse would have a picture of the boys' father up in her office when she was single served to remind him of just how many unknowns there were between the two of them.

"You'll be happy to know I'll be closing the investigation and filing my official report tonight or tomorrow morning," he said, bringing his eyes back to the woman in front of him.

A single brow went up. "Am I allowed to ask how your conversation went?"

"You are, but it's just between us for now. Until I file the papers, that is," he added. When she nodded, he continued. "Aaron didn't talk too much about what his dad was like before the last few weeks, but I got the sense that what your son noticed was spot on. And in the last few weeks it had just gotten worse and more erratic.

"Aaron said he would come home to find his dad online looking up explosives. But as soon as he realized Aaron was in the room, he'd close everything down and go out drinking. Eventually, he'd come home drunk and raving about how the restaurant where his wife worked was responsible for her death. In his mind, they worked her to death. Made her heart go out. At least that's what Aaron got out of his father's ramblings and accusations."

"Too blinded by guilt to acknowledge his role in how much she worked? That she might not have worked so much or might have taken care of herself more if he'd bothered to help pay the bills?" Jesse posited.

David lifted a shoulder. "Yes, that was Aaron's take. Anyway, last Wednesday morning he woke up and came into the kitchen to find his dad actually assembling what Aaron assumed was a bomb, given what he'd seen his dad looking at online."

"And they fought?" The inevitability in her voice echoed his.

He nodded. "A big fight, according to Aaron. A fight that explains his broken arm," he added, then paused to reflect on the horror the young boy had been living with and in. David let out a deep breath and continued, "Finally, in desperation, Aaron grabbed a two-by-four his dad had brought into the house as part of the station he'd set up to assemble the bomb. Aaron nailed his dad in the head and dragged his unconscious body away from the explosives. Or whatever it was his dad was building."

"And he went back for the bomb? Why would he do that?" Jesse asked. Her hand had unconsciously come up to her throat, an empathetic reflection of the vulnerability Aaron must have felt.

David paced to the other side of her office, feeling her eyes on him the whole time. "He said he wasn't sure what it was or, more likely, didn't want to believe what he suspected. He said his dad wasn't too literate or savvy, and even if it was a bomb, Aaron thought he might be able to dismantle it himself."

"And protect his father," she said on a sigh. "If no one knew, no one would be able to do anything."

He nodded. "I don't think Aaron grew up being abused. I think the abuse started when Aaron was old enough to see the pain his father was going through." His eyes had landed on some award that Jesse had won, but he wasn't really looking at it. It was just somewhere to fix his gaze.

"And old enough to make excuses for him," she added.

David nodded even as his attention was drawn to a picture of Jesse and her two sons, smiling, on a beach somewhere. It was a far cry from what they were talking about now. "He was making excuses for his dad, for sure," he responded. "But not the same kind that someone who'd been through systematic abuse would make. I think he honestly thought that if he could just help his dad through this rough patch, he'd go back to being the dad he was before."

"Such as he was."

"Such as he was," David agreed. "But while he may not have won any father-of-the-year awards, he didn't beat his kid," he pointed out. For what it was worth.

"So what happened?" she asked.

"It was a bomb, a crude one, and Aaron tried to defuse it. Tried to take it apart. But his father was better at building bombs than Aaron thought and he had somehow managed to set up a functioning trigger. Aaron figured out he wasn't going to have much luck and was backing away when it went off. The explosion blew him clear of the room."

"And, next thing he knew, he ended up here." The tone of her voice told him that she was well aware that what Aaron was going through wasn't the *end* of anything. The boy would have a long road in front of him, both emotionally and physically.

"And he ended up here," David repeated. He picked up another picture, this one of the two boys when they were much younger, he'd guess about four and six. It looked to be taken in an evergreen forest somewhere.

"Orcas Island in Washington State. My parents live on Whidbey Island; we went to visit and took a side trip to the San Juan Islands." For a moment, he had no idea what Jesse was talking about, then he realized he was still holding the picture. He set it down carefully and shoved his hands in his pockets.

"So, will there be any charges brought against him?" She stood and walked back behind her desk.

"No, he was trying to do the right thing. Trying to protect himself and other people from the imminent danger created by his dad. There won't be any charges filed at all. In fact, we should probably be thanking him. If he hadn't taken action, who knows how many people would have been hurt if his dad had succeeded in detonating it at the restaurant?"

Jesse let out a deep breath and slid into her seat. "Thank you for telling me."

"You knew all along he wasn't involved, didn't you?"

She tilted her head. "I'm way past the age of thinking I know anything for certain about most people, especially teenagers. That said, I would have been surprised if he'd turned out to be nefarious. But of course, isn't that what the neighbors always say? 'He was such a nice boy.'"

He smiled at her mimicry. "So, how did your son's meet go the other day?"

"He did well, the team did well. Matt won a couple of races, but of course he's not happy with his times," she answered without missing a beat.

"A little competitive?" David asked as a smile tugged at his lips. Given how young Matt's mother was and how far she'd come in her professional life, it wouldn't surprise him in the least if the apple didn't fall far from the tree.

"Mostly with himself so I guess I shouldn't complain. And even if I did, that would be a little bit of the pot calling the kettle black," she added with a self-deprecating eye roll.

He could feel her watching him as he wandered around her office, examining more of her photos. She had a lot, not an unusual amount, but enough to see that she was a devoted mother. And judging by the smiles on the boys' faces, a good mother, too.

"And your younger son? Is he a runner, too?" He knew he was just shamelessly fishing for information now. Maybe he wasn't as on the fence about asking her out as he'd thought.

"He is. He's athletic like his brother, but mostly I think he joined because there are a couple of really cute girls on the team." David glanced over his shoulder just in time to see her smile a private, motherly smile. "Both the boys do well in sports and school," she added. "But James is the real science wonk. He'd rather be in the lab most of the time."

"Any kind of science in particular?"

"No, anything science or math," she answered. After a pause, she gave a small laugh and added, "I've seen enough budgets in my life to be proficient, but what he does, what he can understand, is way beyond me. He'll be going to a special program this summer in Boston for high school science students. And of course, Matt starts college there this fall," she added.

"It's a big step, sending a chick out of the nest," he commented. He should know, he'd just done it several months ago, but he didn't bring that up. Instead he walked back to the front of her desk.

"It is, but it's a good thing. I'm excited for him," she said.

"And his father?" He almost grimaced at his own recognizable intention because there it was, the obvious casting of the line.

"My husband died about two years ago. A fire actually, in his office at the university in Albany. He was an economics professor. Probably where James got his affinity for numbers." Her hands were folded on her desk and her voice hadn't broken in the slightest. And yet, staring at her face, he felt off balance at that piece of information. Sure he'd been fishing, he just hadn't expected to pull up the fact that she was a recent widow. And now he wasn't quite sure what to do with it.

On one hand, he had confirmation that she was single. On the other, if he asked her out now it would seem opportunistic. He rocked back on his heels in silence for a beat, then cleared his throat. She gave him a small smile that hinted she sensed his discomfort.

"Well, thank you for stopping by, David," she said, rising from her seat and holding her hand out. On reflex he reached out and shook it as she continued. "I appreciate you telling me about your investigation and we'll be sure to treat Aaron well."

She was dismissing him, letting him escape from his own lame inability to process the fact that she was a widow. And not just a widow, but one whose husband had died in a fire. What were the odds?

"Anytime," he responded. "If you have any questions or if Aaron needs someone to talk to, please give me a call."

Jesse nodded and before he knew it he was heading out to the parking garage. It hadn't been his most suave moment and more than once on the walk between her office and his truck he considered going back to ask her out. But on the way, his phone rang, duty called, and the moment passed.

CHAPTER 4

Jesse curled a foot under her and gave a little push off the floor with her toe to send her rocking chair into a gentle, soothing motion. Tucking her other foot against the rung of the chair, she sipped her coffee and looked at the view out across her lawn and down to the swimming pond. It was a cool morning, but she liked these moments of quiet before the day really started.

She watched a pair of Canada geese fly by and smiled at their distinctive, obnoxious honking. A frog croaked and a hawk soared and circled overhead. She loved her big wrap-around porch; it had been the reason they'd bought this house. Ten years ago, she and Mark had come to this piece of property and seen not much else other than potential. An old, dilapidated farmhouse, a pond that was overgrown, and fields that hadn't been sown in years. The original part of the house had been built in the late 1800s, making it about a hundred years younger than most of the other farmhouses in the area. Its age, and hence its architectural style, also made it less appealing to the weekenders who seemed to only want houses in the Greek revival style indicative of the time when the area was full of revolutionaries and the country was first being formed. Jesse loved both styles of houses but because there wasn't a demand for homes in this particular style—not to mention in the condition it had been in when they came upon it—she and Mark had been able to buy it for a song. And over the years they'd refurbished, rehabilitated, and cleaned things up.

And still, all these years later, her favorite simple pleasure was sitting on her wrap-around porch watching the world go by at a snail's pace.

Pushing off with her toe again, she heard the porch door open. "Mom?"

Her older son came out with his own cup of coffee. His hair was sticking up with a severe case of morning bedhead and he was dressed in his pajama bottoms and no top, the chill of the morning seeming to have no effect on him.

"Hi, honey. You're up early."

He took a seat and a sip. "It's almost nine, not that early."

"For a Saturday?" She arched a teasing brow at him.

"Okay," he smiled back. "It's a little early. But I promised Allie I'd come down and help decorate for prom tonight."

"Are you all ready? You have everything you need?" she asked. Looking at Matt, it was hard to believe he was getting ready to attend his last high school formal. It felt like only days ago that he'd been struggling with the question of whether or not to ask a girl to his *first* formal.

Matt nodded in response to her question. "Thanks for arranging the car tonight. Allie and I aren't going to do anything crazy, you know," he said, referring to his date.

She smiled at that. Matt was not a crazy kid, probably more responsible than he should be, and she had little doubt this stemmed from the death of his father.

"I know, but I just thought it might be nice to be driven around a bit, and you're welcome. Are you still doubling with Danielle and Todd?"

Matt shook his head. "No, Allie wanted to go with Brittney and Jay, so we'll be picking them up on the way."

"That's too bad." Matt and Danielle had been close friends, practically since birth. "But I suppose you'll see them there," she commented.

He grinned. "We have less than a hundred and fifty kids going, I think it's a pretty good bet we'll see each other."

They sat in silence for several minutes. Jesse sensed her son had more to say to her but something was holding him back. After years of being his mom, she knew the best thing to do was to wait and let him come to her.

Finally, he spoke. "Mom, Danielle and I would like to go see Aaron. We called down to the hospital yesterday and they said visiting hours were today from two to four. Do you think we should?"

Jesse considered this. Matt and Aaron weren't the best of friends, not really friends at all but more like friendly acquaintances. And Aaron, a young man, might not want to be seen in the state he was in. She knew what Aaron had sacrificed and why, and she had told Matt some of it, the parts she thought David wouldn't mind her sharing. But she didn't know if Aaron saw it the same way—saw his own sacrifice. She didn't know if Aaron would want to be reminded that he wasn't going to prom; that he wasn't active and doing all the things the other young men in his class were doing. The male ego was a fragile thing.

On the other hand, she'd been his only visitor. David and Abigail had seen him, of course, but she'd been the only one who'd stopped by to visit without having a professional reason.

"Why don't I ask him on Monday and let you know?" she offered.

"We'd kind of like to go today, if we can. It's been long enough that he's been alone."

Her son's insight caught her off guard and really, what could she say to that? Still, she wanted to ask Aaron first.

"Dr. Martinez is running rounds this morning. Why don't I call her? She can ask him and then let Danielle know?"

Matt let out a sigh of relief. "Thanks, Mom. I can't imagine what his life has been like these past few years."

"No child should."

"And it's not over for him, is it?"

"Unfortunately, not by a long shot. He has a long recovery ahead of him."

Together, they pondered this for a moment, before Matt stood.

"Thanks for checking in with Dr. Martinez for us. I'll let you know if we end up going down."

"Please do, and keep me updated on what's going on today. I have some errands to run." She glanced at her watch. "One of which I'm running late for already, but other than that, I'll be around here."

He nodded and headed back into the house as she rose from her seat. She wasn't quite ready to start the day, but she'd promised Julie she'd be at the quilt shop at ten and if she was going to call Abigail before that, as well as shower and get dressed, she needed to get a move on.

• • •

Jesse looked at the clock on her dash as she pulled into a spot across the street from Julie's Spin-A-Yarn shop. She wasn't too late, just about fifteen minutes. She spotted Julie out front chatting with Jason, the owner of the local health food store, and waved. Main Street was still quiet this time of day, except for those partaking of breakfast at Frank's Fed Up and Fulfilled Café, and both proprietors looked up and waved back as she got out of her car.

She smiled and was just sliding her keys into her purse when a deep sound reverberated around her. In a flash, Jesse felt like she was being swallowed, like a weight was pressing against her entire body, stealing the air from her lungs, making it impossible to scream. A cacophony of sounds assaulted her ears, then suddenly everything seemed to slow down. Somehow, the noises that had seemed so angry before became dampened and muffled. With no time to comprehend or react to what was happening, she watched as the windows of Spin-A-Yarn erupted outward, exploding onto the street toward her.

CHAPTER 5

ON INSTINCT, JESSE SPUN AWAY and hit the ground as shards of glass scattered around her. She didn't know how long she stayed there, but slowly it registered that everything was silent. From her position, lying on the street, she stared at the ground in confusion for several seconds before reality hit her with the subtlety of a two-by-four. There had been an explosion of some sort. A real explosion.

Her head came up cautiously and she tested her body. Moving easily and not sensing any serious injuries, she gazed at the debris around her; then, suddenly panic stricken, she turned to look for Julie and Jason. She saw them both, holding onto each other, crouched against the front wall of the health food store but still on their feet.

She made to get up and move toward them just as a giant orange and blue flame leapt through the shattered front window of what had once been Julie's shop. Jesse shrank back against her car even as the flame was seemingly sucked back into the building. For a moment, she saw no signs of the fire, then it became more visible and she could see flames licking the walls of Spin-A-Yarn. Sitting up, she shook the glass from her purse, grabbed her phone with a shaking hand, and hit the emergency button as she stood up. After giving the dispatcher the details, she took a few tentative steps toward the shop and craned her head to get a better view. She didn't want to get too close, but she needed to see if anyone was inside. She wasn't an EMT, but she was trained in first aid and knew enough that she might be able to help someone if they needed it before real help arrived.

But Julie was already running across the street to stop her from moving any further.

"Jesse! Stay where you are, we called 9-1-1." Julie seemed to be shouting, but Jesse could just barely make out her friend's voice.

"So did I," Jesse answered, pausing not far from her car. "Is there anyone in there, Julie? We need to be able to tell them if someone is in there," she said, pointing, needlessly, toward the building, now clearly in flames.

"No," Julie shook her head, also still in a daze. "There's no one in there. It was just me, and I stepped out just a few moments ago."

Jesse brought her attention back around. "Are you okay? You were standing right there. Are you hurt?" she asked, her eyes scanning her friend as she spoke.

Again, Julie shook her head. "Stunned, startled, and I'm shaking like a leaf in a windstorm, but I'm not cut or bruised or bleeding."

Examining Julie one more time just to be on the safe side, Jesse then cast her gaze up and down the street. People were coming out of their shops, some looking stunned, others scared, but all were curious. Thankfully, it appeared that no one was hurt.

"But you, Jesse. You've got glass all over you," Julie said.

Jesse turned her eyes back to her friend and saw genuine concern etch itself onto Julie's face. She must have looked worse than Julie was saying. But she felt fine, and as if on automatic pilot, she started to list the things she thought they should be doing.

"We need to get people out of the stores on either side of yours," she said, taking another tentative step away from the safety of her car.

Julie looked about to protest, but then gave a curt nod. "Jason was just starting to do that when I came to check on you. He was planning to head to the shops north of his store. Let's go together and make sure everyone is out of the stores down the south side."

With arms linked together, for emotional as much as physical support, they made their way along Main Street evacuating people from the shops. The police, who were housed not two blocks away at the end of Main Street, were on the scene by the time the two women had cleared the last shop. The fire trucks were now in place, and the EMTs had arrived and insisted that Jesse let them clean and bandage the cuts she'd sustained. Feeling babied more than she thought necessary, she let them do their jobs and was soon sporting several small bandages across her arms and hands.

Sitting in the back of an ambulance, Jesse watched as a fire-fighter called out from the burning shop and two more ran a second hose inside. It was a mostly volunteer department, but they seemed to be efficient. And with the police keeping everything under control and the fire department doing their thing, she let herself breathe for a moment. That's when she really started shaking.

Without a word, the EMT, a young man who looked too young to be so efficient, finished the last of her cuts and wrapped a blanket around her. It wasn't cold out, but the way the blanket enveloped her made Jesse feel a bit more secure.

"I hate feeling this way, all shaky and discombobulated," she clarified, probably unnecessarily, to the man who had most likely seen more than his fair share of people in shock.

"But I have to admit, I'm glad I'm not alone in this," she added as Julie came and sat beside her. Both women spent a few moments just watching the events unfold before them. By chance, Jesse happened to look over at her car. Absently, she noted that though she'd just gotten it back with two new tires, she'd probably need a new paint job now. It wasn't bad, but a few bits of glass had made it across the street and dinged one side of her car.

Even staring at everything in front of her—the glass in the street, the firemen, the police, the bystanders milling about—it was hard to believe what had just happened. Try as she might, she couldn't remember the last time there had been a fire on Main Street. A couple of times a year there might be a fire at a resi-dence. But mostly, the fire department was used for cleanup during weather emergencies or after auto accidents.

"You know, for what happened, for how it felt when it happened, the damage out here isn't all that bad," Julie commented.

Jesse took a good look around her, a real look, not one tainted by adrenaline or fear, and saw that Julie was right. The windows had been blown out, but most of what was left of the glass and wooden panes was lying in the street—none of the surrounding buildings seemed to have been damaged.

"It sure felt like something, though, didn't it?" Jesse said. It was more of a comment than a question, but Julie nodded, still looking quite dazed.

"Do you think my quilt will survive?" Jesse was just relieved that all the people nearby had survived, but still the thought had crossed her mind. And then the inanity of the question hit and she started to laugh. After a second, Julie joined her.

"Jesse!" A voice called to her from down the street. She looked up to see Frank, of Frank's Café coming toward them. She groaned. Frank wasn't the most hospitable guy on a good day. And today was most definitely not a good day.

"Jesse! Julie, you too! Come down to the Café. I'll get you some coffee, or a mocha, and you can sit down while they finish up out here."

Jesse eyed him with suspicion. If it weren't for his magic egg and bagel sandwiches and heavenly mochas—mochas she was sure came straight from the Mayan gods—everyone in town would stay well clear of the man. But here he was, offering her a free one. She glanced at Julie, who looked just as confused as Jesse felt. She couldn't figure out what was more bizarre, the fire or the fact that Frank was being nice. But at the moment she didn't have the energy to debate the issue so she shrugged off the blanket, slid from where she was perched on the back of the ambulance, and headed down the block.

Within minutes, she and Julie were seated at a table for two—not a table for four because Frank didn't let two people sit at a table for four, not even in times such as this—sipping their mochas and watching everyone working to put the fire out and control the curious gawkers. She knew that she was more or less stuck in town for the time being—she'd need to answer some witness questions, and even if she didn't, her car was boxed in by a couple of fire trucks. But even so, when her sons both called and wanted to come down, she strictly forbade it—she was fine, no one else was hurt, and the police needed to keep the streets clear. Instead, she asked James to keep studying for his upcoming biology final and told Matt to get ready for his prom. She promised them both that she'd be home in time to take some pictures of Matt in his tux before he left that evening.

Ian and Vivi stopped by to check on her and Julie, as did Carly Drummond, a friend of Jesse's and one of Windsor's four police officers. But only Vivi pulled up a third chair and stayed to chat with them. Jesse liked to think Vivi was just being a good friend, but she guessed it was probably a little bit of the shrink in her that kept the doctor there, too. Vivi wasn't exactly subtle about assessing both her and Julie for shock. Still, it was kind of nice that Vivi cared enough to check in on them—not that she would expect anything less.

By the time she finished her second mocha, the clock tower had struck one, the last of the big fire trucks had driven away, and Julie had left to begin the long process of figuring out how to rebuild her shop. Main Street was cleared for driving and the only remaining evidence of the fire was the foam and water residue on the street, the empty windows of Spin-A-Yarn, two police cars, and an SUV with the Windsor Fire Department logo on it.

The fire would be investigated, a tidbit of information that, when Jesse heard it, made her think of David. She wondered if she'd see him in town. She'd already given her statement to Carly and the acting Deputy Chief of Police, Marcus Brown, and wasn't sure she'd have anything more to add if questioned further, but the thought of seeing David again was, well, intriguing.

As if she had tempted fate, she paused at the driver's side door of her car and watched as a truck pulled up behind her. Even with the glare of the windshield, she could tell it was David behind the wheel.

"Jesse?" He was frowning as he climbed out of his truck and strode toward her, his voice laced with concern.

"Hi, David. We really should try meeting under more pleasant circumstances one of these days." Of course, she'd tried to go for flippant, but the second the words were out she realized how they might sound, like she was suggesting they should actually plan to meet somewhere else. She opened her mouth to explain but he waved it off.

"You were here?" he asked as his brows dipped low.

She nodded.

"How are you? You weren't hurt, were you?" He was taking a closer look at her, no doubt checking for injuries.

"No, I'm fine. A few cuts from the window glass, a little shaken, and now a little tired, but not all that hurt. I was just getting out of my car when it happened. Thankfully, no one else was hurt. Why are you here? Are you investigating this?"

He nodded, still looking her over, his eyes lingering on the bandages like he didn't believe she was actually okay. For some reason, his reaction made her smile.

"David." His eyes travelled up and met hers. "I'm fine, really."

He searched her face for a moment, then nodded and let out a breath. "I'm glad to hear that."

He lifted his hand as if he was going to touch her, then let it drop. He was wearing the same thing he'd worn the first time she'd met him: a navy shirt, cargo work pants, and boots. There were a lot of men in Windsor who never saw a suit when working, but none seemed to wear their workman garb as well as he did.

"So, did Vic call you?" she asked.

He frowned and shook his head. "I don't know who Vic is, but MacAllister called me. Or rather he had someone named Marcus Brown call me."

She smiled. "Marcus is the Deputy Chief of Police. He took over the position when Ian left to become sheriff. Vic is the Chief of Police. He's a real… well, let's just say he isn't the easiest person to deal with. A word of unsolicited advice: work with Marcus and Carly—she's Marcus's partner, for the most part. Professionally, not personally. They're very good at what they do and good people, too." She realized she'd been rambling and abruptly cut herself off.

He gave a half smile. "Thanks. Marcus mentioned there were three witnesses. I assume you're one of them?"

She nodded. "And Julie Fitzpatrick, who owns the store, and also Jason Henry, who owns the health food store next door. I was here, by my car, and they were outside in front of Jason's shop when it happened. There were a couple of other people around, too, but they were mostly inside their own shops or inside Frank's." She gestured toward the café.

David turned and assessed the scene, looking up and down the small Main Street. People were still gawking, but some of the shops had reopened. An acrid, bitter smell permeated the street, and Jesse figured it was a mix of the ashes, the burned wood and fabric, and whatever retardant the fire department had used.

"I'm going to need to interview you and the other witnesses before I leave today, but I need to talk to the fire captain and I want to see if I can get inside first."

Jesse opened her mouth to say she'd already given a statement to Carly and as it was, she didn't have much to say. But she stopped herself. Having him in front of her, knowing he was going to handle the investigation, made her feel something, something good and safe, and on a day like today, she wouldn't mind taking advantage of that just a little bit.

She nodded. "I've been here all day, though, so if you wouldn't mind, I'd like to go home, shower, and maybe rest a little bit. You have my cell number. Why don't you call when you're ready to talk to me and I'll drive back down into town?"

He eyed her for a beat. "Or I could finish up here and drive to you?"

The thought of him in her house was awkward. She hadn't really dated anyone since Mark had died, and she wasn't sure what the boys would think having a man in their home—a man that was, she assumed, judging by his lack of ring, single and not someone they'd known forever. But then again, he wasn't there for a date. She might find him attractive, and she was pretty certain it was reciprocated, but he also had a job to do. And the idea of talking about the fire over a cup of tea in her own home held a lot more appeal than doing so at the police station or back at Frank's.

"That would be great, thank you." She reached into her purse and pulled out a business card. After scribbling her address on the back, she handed it over.

"Well," she said, pulling out her keys. "I guess I'll talk to you later?"

He looked at her again and then his hand came up and wrapped around hers. The sudden strength and calm of his touch stilled everything inside her. She hadn't even realized she'd been shaking.

She looked down at his large hand covering her much smaller one. His skin was darker than her fair, English coloring. The hair on his forearm was the same gold, flecked brown as that on his head. With her eyes, she followed his arm up to his shoulder then moved her gaze up to his face. The look of concern there was unmistakable.

"You're much taller now that I'm not wearing heels." It was an inane comment but the day seemed to be filled with them. A refuge from the ugliness, she supposed.

He smiled down at her. "I'm barely five ten."

"Eight inches taller than me. But then again, most people are taller than I am, so I shouldn't be surprised."

"I put you at five one."

"Five two, thank you very much."

"Barely," he prodded with another smile.

"Okay, fine," she rolled her eyes. "I'm *almost* five two."

He chuckled and, for a moment, they simply looked at each other.

"Hathaway." Ian's voice interrupted them. David dropped her hand as the man approached.

"MacAllister."

"Ian," she said in greeting when he stopped in front of them.

"How are you, Jesse? Are you headed home?" Ian was a worrier, but Jesse knew why so she simply nodded and answered.

"I am headed home and I'm fine. Did you send Vivi home?" she asked.

"She went home to walk Rooster. Our dog," Ian added as an aside to David.

"You know she probably saw through that request, don't you?" Jesse teased. Rooster practically lived outside; he didn't need to be walked. Ian just didn't want his wife near the scene any longer.

"No 'probably' about it, but she loves me so she humors me," Ian responded with a self-deprecating shrug.

Jesse laughed at that. There had been a time, when Ian had just come back from serving as an Army Ranger, that his friends and family had worried about him and his ability to readjust to civilian life after almost fifteen years in the service. Having to recover from both an IED attack that had left him hospitalized for months and bouts with PTSD didn't help. But then Vivi had come along—a woman who knew how ugly the world could be but was strong enough to spend every day trying to make it better. And now here they were, starting their own family. Ian worried incessantly, but that was part of his makeup. Fortunately, Vivi seemed to take it all in stride and, as he'd suggested, even humored him every now and then.

"Has Jesse been filling you in on the players?" Ian asked, turning to David, who nodded.

"Yeah, if the building's been cleared, I want to get inside and get an idea of what happened. But I need to talk to the fire captain first."

"Robbie's the fire captain," Ian said with a nod toward a man sitting in the Windsor Fire Department SUV. By the way he was hunched over, the captain looked to be filling out paperwork.

"You'll have to work with Marcus on the rest. I'm pretty sure the building is clear, but he'll have to give you the go ahead," Ian added.

David raised his eyebrows in question.

Ian wagged his head. "I used to be on the police force but was elected sheriff last summer. We're in town, so we're in Windsor police jurisdiction. Anything outside of the town limits is my territory, but inside is all Vic's."

"You don't strike me as territorial, MacAllister," he commented.

Ian shrugged. "I'm not. I don't care who the hell solves crimes or gets the bad guy or the credit for getting the bad guy, but Vic sure as hell does. So feel free to get in touch with me if you have any questions, but for the most part," he paused and raised a hand, gesturing someone over, "you'll be working with Marcus."

Marcus came jogging up and Ian made the introductions. After Marcus asked how she was feeling and she'd replied, Jesse used the moment to make her escape. They needed to get down to business and she, well, she really needed a hot bath.

• • •

David watched Jesse pull away in her car. Twice in one week her car had taken a beating. But it wasn't the car that occupied his mind. Not that he would admit it, but his heart had just about stopped when he'd pulled up and seen her on the street. She'd just been standing there, staring at the gaping holes of what had been her friend's shop. That she was there at all, let alone that she was one of the witnesses, didn't sit well with him.

He turned back to the deputy and Ian, the latter giving him the kind of look a guy gives another guy when he knows more than he's going to say.

"Is the building clear, Deputy Chief Brown?" David asked with nod to the shop.

"Call me Marcus," the young deputy chief responded. "And, yes, as far we know. I don't know how structurally sound it is, but the fire was out pretty quickly and the crews scoured for any hot spots, but you should talk to Robbie."

As he spoke, the man himself climbed out of his SUV and came toward them. He was a big, barrel-chested man, with gray hair that brushed his shoulders and a walk that told David he couldn't wait to leave.

David understood the captain's desire. Robbie was probably tired, maybe even a little shaken, but as the investigator, David needed to talk to him about what his men had seen when they'd first come on the scene and entered the building. Also, as the fire captain, Robbie had jurisdiction, and in order to leave, he had to officially hand the investigation over to David.

Surprised was probably too strong a word, but David was definitely pleased when the captain was able to deliver a clear and succinct account of the fire. His men had arrived within ten minutes and had been inside within fifteen. He reported that the fire had seemed to burn hottest in the middle of the room, though the flames looked to have moved through the area by catching the displays on fire. They had seen no signs of forced entry and had searched the building for people and found it empty.

When Robbie finished his report, he shook hands with David and handed him his card. A few seconds later, David watched the Windsor Fire Department SUV make a U-turn and head south out of town, then he turned his attention to the building.

"You're not going in alone." Ian's voice was flat and certain. David had been considering it. Neither of the two men in front of him had fire experience, though he'd bet they'd both seen their fair share of hairy situations. But still, going in alone wasn't a good idea. It never was. So he'd have to make do.

"Given MacAllister doesn't have any jurisdiction in town, are you up for joining me, Marcus?"

The deputy chief shrugged, "Yeah, I guess I am."

"Do you have any equipment?"

"Hard hat, boots, and a flashlight," Marcus answered.

"Here," David said, reaching over to pull an extra coat from the back of his truck. It was heavy and made of material that would do its best to protect the wearer from all sorts of fun things like fire, shards of debris, and, of course, water. Marcus slipped the coat on as David grabbed his kit and donned his own gear.

"You going to hang around?" David asked Ian.

"Like a good citizen, nothing more," Ian grinned. It was hard not to like the guy.

"Here, then, like a good citizen, keep an ear on that, will you?" He tossed the sheriff a two-way radio; he and Marcus would each carry a similar device. David didn't anticipate any problems, but it was good to have someone on the outside to call for help if they needed it. Not to mention that arsonists, if there was in fact an arsonist, were sometimes known to return to the scene; if that happened, it would be good to have someone who could radio in a warning.

The three men crossed the street. A couple of people stopped to stare, but no one approached them. When they reached the bottom of the three steps that led into the building, another police officer moved out from the shadows just inside the store. She had curly blonde hair and hazel eyes that were more brown than Jesse's, which tended more toward green. He figured this was the Carly whom Jesse had mentioned, and Marcus's introductions confirmed it.

"Ready?" David turned to Marcus, who gave him a nod. Checking his hard hat, David stepped into the store. The smell of the fire assaulted his senses. He wasn't sure whether it was good or bad that he never got used to the acrid odor that permeated his nostrils and made them sting. Knowing that overwhelming his senses was the only way to shut them down, David took a few deep breaths and then stepped further inside.

Flicking on his flashlight, he did a cursory perusal from where he stood. Without electricity, the room was darker than one would expect in the middle of the day and his light illuminated only a small fraction of the space. Still, he moved its beam over the walls and floor, noting that most of the damage was toward the rear of the building.

Water had probably ruined the quilts and yarns displayed in the front section, but, as compared to the back, there was very little fire damage by the front door where he stood. Tracing his light further back into the shop, he noted a particular section of blackened wood, a half-circle mark that was charred more deeply than the wood around it. And it was in the middle of the mark that he assumed the checkout counter had previously sat. As it was, there was little left other than a stand of random pieces of lumber and metal sticking out at odd angles. He couldn't see behind it from his current position, but he'd wager that the half circle he saw now was probably a full circle with the former counter sitting in the middle.

"Was there damage upstairs?" David asked, shining his light upward. Based on what he saw, he suspected the fire hadn't reached the second floor and Marcus quickly confirmed his impressions. "And is there a basement in this building?"

"Yeah, the door is over there," Marcus answered, shining his light toward the rear right corner of the shop. "Some of the basements along this side of the street connect to one another. There are doors that are, or should be, locked between them, but at one point, the same person owned this land and he liked being able to move back and forth between the theater-cum-brothel and some of his other, more respectful, shops."

"Not a bad setup, if you're so inclined," David answered glibly, his mind already on the possibilities. Given what he was seeing he was already coming to some opinions, but he didn't want to risk missing anything so it was a trip to the basement for him.

"I'm going to head down into the basement, but I'm going to do it slowly. I have to walk around what looks like the origin of the fire and I don't know about the flooring. So watch where I walk and if I make it, take the same path. If I don't, don't follow me."

Marcus chuckled a bit behind him. "Live dangerously much?"

"Nah, this is child's play. Now, if we were on the roof, that would be a different story."

"If you say so," came the disbelieving reply.

David inched his way toward the basement door, skirting the edge of the room as much as possible. But with racks and debris strewn about, it wasn't easy. It was so silent that each time the floor creaked it sounded loud as a bullet, giving his heart a good start.

About halfway to the door, his foot went through the floor. He could hear Marcus let out a curse, but David stayed focused on slowly pulling his foot out so as not to disturb any of the floorboards around him. When his foot was free, he let out a breath and found a new, hopefully sounder, location for his next step. When the spot held, he continued on back until he reached the door.

Standing next to the doorway, he took a deep breath and released the tension in his body. Yes, doing this on the roof would have been worse, but contrary to what he'd said, it wasn't exactly child's play. He called Marcus over. After coaching him for several steps, David decided that his voice was distracting Marcus more than helping him and the Deputy Chief was probably better off without a firefighter watching his every step.

So he turned his attention, and flashlight, to the remains of the checkout counter. Sure enough, around the back of the rubble was another half-circle of deeply charred flooring. It was more confirmation of what he'd suspected when he'd seen the front—whatever started the fire had likely been centered in, or under the counter. He had his opinions on that, too. But he wanted to see the basement before talking it through with Marcus.

Seeing Marcus just a few steps away, David tried the basement door and, finding it unlocked, pushed it open. Taking a good look at the stairs, which were stone and seemed to have been left untouched by anything other than maybe a little water that had seeped under the door, he headed down, ordering his temporary teammate to follow him at a reasonable distance.

Once David hit the landing, he directed his flashlight around the room. It smelled less of the fire down there, though the odor still lingered, and more like how a dank, musty, subterranean basement should smell. From above, water dripped through the floorboards and hit the storage boxes and shelves with individual plopping sounds. But much like the front of the store that mostly showed only water damage, there was very little indication of a fire down in this part of the building.

"It looks relatively unscathed down here," Marcus said as he came down into the basement. David mumbled an agreement but the two continued to direct their flashlights around the room just in case.

"Let's take a look at the doors," David suggested. "Is this one of the basements that's connected to the others?"

"Yeah, this shop, the health food shop, and shoe store all connect."

"Who would know that?" David asked as they made their way through the room. The floor was concrete and, with the exception of an odd box scattered here and there, the room was mostly well kempt.

"Anyone who has ever owned or rented one of the buildings on this side of the street. Plus any of the family or friends the owners or renters might have told. Probably the delivery people and the historical society, too."

David chuckled. "So you're saying just about everyone."

"Maybe not *everyone*, but close." They heard a creaking noise above them and both shined their flashlights upward. "Could that come down on us?" Marcus asked, referring to the flooring above them.

"Possibly, let's just stick to the sides. There wasn't as much damage to that part of the shop. Hopefully, the floors will be sounder there," he said.

"Hopefully?"

"We always live with a little bit of hope in this line of business," he responded as they reached the door that he assumed led to the next shop's basement. It looked closed and locked. "Doesn't look like it's been opened or tampered with." He ran his light up and down the doorframe.

"Carly and I will check the other side, too, just in case," Marcus commented.

David nodded his agreement with that decision and then swung his light back the way they'd come, toward the rear of the building. "What are the doors like upstairs?"

"There's the front door and a rear access. According to Julie, the front door needs to be locked and unlocked with the key. There's a deadbolt on it also. The backdoor needs a key to get in, but locks itself when it closes."

"There." David's light landed on a small casement window not far from where the stairs ended. It was ground level and about two feet high and three feet wide. And it was broken.

"Shit." Marcus's tone was an excellent reflection of David's own sentiments.

"We don't know if this means anything yet." David said. "Could be that window was broken days or weeks ago or was broken in the fire."

But either way, they'd need to look into it. Making their way back toward the stairwell, they stopped about two feet away from the damaged rear window. Glass littered the floor. David realized he hadn't noticed it on his first perusal of the room because the window was broken clean out with no shards or pieces remaining in the frame. The drop into the basement from outside was less than six feet, and while it would have been difficult for someone his size to fit through the window, it would have been possible.

To the left of the window he noted another door—a big, heavy metal door. Through the window he could see a set of stairs leading from the basement to the alley behind the shop and he figured it was a delivery door.

"I think if someone went through the window, that door won't tell us much," David pondered out loud.

"But we'll check anyway. I'll send Carly back to the alley to collect evidence and look for footprints. It's mostly pavement back there, but there are some gravel areas," Marcus said.

"And what about those buildings?" David asked with a nod

out the window toward several houses that looked to have once been homes but were now businesses. Between the back of the quilt shop and those businesses lay the alley, the railroad tracks, and a road, but each house looked across at the backs of all the buildings on Main Street.

"None will have CCTV, if that's what you're thinking. Depending on when this window was broken, someone might have seen something. But I doubt it. Someone would have reported it if they had. If it happened last night, there were some track repairs going on just north of town and some of the rail cars were parked here for most of the night," Marcus answered.

David grunted at their bad luck, but took it in stride. Having seen what he needed to in the basement, he made his way back up to the main floor of the shop with Marcus following behind him. He could see Ian on the front steps chatting with Carly. They both looked up and raised a hand in acknowledgement.

Knowing this was when things were about to get interesting, that this was when his investigation *really* kicked-off, David took a deep breath and got started. But it didn't take long to find what he was looking for.

"Marcus."

"Yeah?"

When he was sure he had the other man's attention, David motioned with his head toward the beam of his flashlight. Highlighted in its circle of light was a medium-sized metal canister. It was lying on its side, ripped in half, blackened, and twisted, about six feet from where the checkout counter had once stood.

"You've got a firebug," David announced.

CHAPTER 6

"Is that what I think it is?" Marcus asked.

"If you think it's a dirty bomb and the remains of a well-designed, if somewhat crude, timing device, then, yeah, it is what you think it is."

"Shit," Marcus said on an exhale.

"A man of few words."

"Aren't dirty bombs nuclear bombs?" Marcus asked after a moment. David almost smiled at the anxiety he could hear Marcus trying to hide.

David shook his head. "In common lexicon, yes, but in my line of business, we refer to homemade bombs as dirty bombs. They tend to be less precise, though often no less dangerous, than explosives made by professionals." David studied the remains for a moment longer before adding, "And based on what I see from here, it looks like you have a creative arsonist on your hands."

Standing beside him, Marcus took a deep breath of reconciliation. "Okay, so how do we go about this?" he asked. "I've never investigated an arson before. We had a serial killer here last year who was after Vivi, and we captured one of the heads of an organized crime syndicate last fall, but I've never worked an arson case before."

David was staring at the deputy chief. "A serial killer and an organized crime syndicate? In *Windsor*?"

"I'd like to point out that both perpetrators were out-of-towners, not locals," Marcus rejoined.

He let out a small bark of laughter at both Marcus's fact *and* his indignation. "Of course they were," he replied. Then, turning his attention back to what looked like the area of origin, David brought the conversation to the task at hand.

"An arson investigation is like any other, only we'll have the lab run some additional tests on the residual contents of the device we collect and maybe see if we can find out if similar devices have been used in other fires. Other than that, and being extra careful that the floor doesn't collapse under us while we collect evidence, it's the same process."

"Motive, means, and opportunity," Marcus muttered as he nodded in agreement.

After another assessment of the scene, both men agreed they'd need Carly's help if they had any intention of getting out of there before dark. So, after they gave her a quick update on the situation, the three of them got to work photographing, documenting, and collecting samples, pieces of the debris, and anything else that caught their attention. David, being the most experienced, gathered the pieces of the device that had caused the explosion. And while he didn't say anything to either of the police officers, he was wagering they'd find that the canister held a natural gas of some sort—something easy to get a hold of, yet effective, maybe propane.

The clock was striking five as David sealed up the last of the evidence boxes and handed them off to Carly to take to the state lab in Albany. He would check in with the lab tomorrow, but for now, he needed to get a few witness statements. Marcus had arranged for Julie and Jason to be at the police station for him to talk to. Based on what he'd heard from the two Windsor officers as they collected evidence, Carly had already taken official statements from all three witnesses. Judging by how meticulous she had been about documenting the scene and evidence, he suspected Carly's reports would contain everything he needed to know. Still, he'd have a quick talk with Jason and Julie while the officer made copies of those reports for him.

So that just left Jesse. As he walked the two blocks to the police station, he pulled out his phone, dialed her number, and agreed to meet her at her place in a little over an hour. He wasn't sure about the professionalism of his decision to go to her home, but after his day, and hers, he wanted to make sure she was okay and safe. And it would be easier to do that if she could stay in her own space.

And though a little less than an hour later he still believed his decision to go to her place was the right one, as he pulled up her driveway he considered the fact that he could have timed it better.

The house itself sat on a hill and was wrapped by a porch on three sides. The front faced the tree-lined main road, and the driveway, which stretched out before him, came up alongside the east side of the house. As he followed the gravel drive, on his left he passed a swimming pond then a sweeping lawn that went all the way up to the house. On his right sat what looked like a small outbuilding or maybe a barn.

It was beautiful, and the word "cozy" crossed David's mind, but there was no mistaking the fact that he was fifteen minutes early and had obviously arrived right in the middle of an important family moment. He was reluctant to interrupt, but he knew it was too late to turn around and come back on time, so he pulled up and parked next a gorgeous vintage Bentley.

Standing near the porch, Jesse, having changed from the jeans and t-shirt she'd worn earlier in the day into a pair of leggings and long sweater, was taking pictures of a young man dressed in a tuxedo.

She called David over, even as she continued snapping pictures.

"Matt's headed off to his last high school formal and I'm tormenting him with pictures. Matt, this is David Hathaway, the arson investigator I mentioned," she said, making the introductions.

Matt stepped forward and shook his hand. "Matt Baker, tormented son."

David's lips twitched at the good-natured, put-upon look on the boy's face. He was tall, several inches taller than David, and looked very little like his mother other than having the same hazel eyes.

"Mom!"

David spun as another boy burst from the house behind them and then skidded to a stop. The boy's eyes went to Jesse, then to him.

"And this is James," she said to David. "James, this is David Hathaway," she added in answer to James's unasked question.

Jesse must have mentioned him to the boys because recognition dawned in James's expression and he stepped forward to shake hands. The boys looked so similar that if it hadn't been for the obvious age difference and the few inches of height Matt had on James, they could have been twins.

With a more pressing matter at hand than a visiting arson investigator, at least as far as the younger teenager was concerned, James turned back to his mother. "Mom, Chelsea and some of the others are meeting at the video store, then going to her house for pizza and movies. Can you give me a ride into town? She can bring me back."

Jesse arched a brow at her younger son and smiled. "I'm kind of in the middle of an investigation, or at least in giving my witness statement," she said with a nod in his direction. "David was nice enough to drive out here, I'm not going to head into town until we're done," she added.

David watched the boy's expression dim and figured there must be something about this girl, Chelsea, that lit the fire in James's eyes. But he was pleased to see James didn't argue with his mom.

"We can drop him," Matt offered, gesturing to the car and the driver patiently waiting several feet away. "The video store is on the way to Allie's. We can just drop him and go on from there."

"Mom?" James all but pleaded. It was an interesting look into Baker family dynamics. They'd suffered a major loss in the death of Jesse's husband, the boys' father, but he would wager that theirs was a family that had pulled together rather than fallen apart.

"If Matt doesn't mind, it's fine with me," she conceded.

"Thanks, Mom," James called as he dashed back inside, not

bothering to wait for his brother's response. "I just need to grab my shoes and a sweatshirt," he added, his voice trailing off.

Jesse and Matt shared a conspiratorial smile.

"It's Chelsea, Mom. I'm telling you, she's the one," Matt said.

Jesse shook her head. "I still don't believe it. I think it's Heather; find out if Heather is going to be there."

"Mom and I have a bet about which girl James is interested in," Matt explained to David. "Mom's going to lose. I have the inside info, since I go to school with him."

"I have the inside info because I see his phone bill and know what number he calls most often," Jesse retorted.

"Ready?" James asked as he came jogging back outside, putting an end to the familial betting ring.

Matt nodded and they climbed into the back of the Bentley. David stood with Jesse as she watched her sons disappear down her drive, a wistful expression on her face.

"Hard to believe they're so big?" he asked.

She lifted a shoulder. "I just remember thinking that this day would never come, and then, suddenly, it's here. I know it's a cliché, but there really is a reason it's such an overused one, because it's just so true."

He stood silently at her side, giving her the time to have her moment. He wondered if she missed her husband, if she wished he were there beside her right now, rather than him.

He cleared his throat. "Shall we?"

She turned and blinked at him. "Yes, of course," she said with a shake of her head. "Come inside, I'll get us something to drink."

He followed her through some French doors that were clearly the home's main entrance, even though they were located at the back of the house by the parking area. The doors led to a small mudroom that then opened directly onto a sizeable kitchen with a large butcher-block island in the middle and a breakfast bar to the right. Beyond the bar was a small sitting area and back toward the rear of the house, to the right of where they'd just come in, there was a small alcove with two well-worn chairs and a potbellied stove nestled in the corner. From where he stood, he could see the start of a hallway that ran from the sitting area toward the front of the house; he didn't know where it led but assumed he'd find some of the bedrooms and eventually the front door if he followed it.

Taking a few steps further into the kitchen, to his left David saw what looked like the main room of the house. It was a big space—not by modern standards, but by the standards of the time the house was built—that was centered around an enormous, stone fireplace. To the right of the fireplace, toward the front of the house, a sofa, two chairs, and some built-in, cushioned benches were arranged to create a seating area. To the left of the fireplace, close to the kitchen, sat a long farm table that looked like it had seen many years of family dinners. The house was, David realized, a true family farmhouse. With the mostly open flow and size of the rooms, it would be easy to heat with the fireplace and pot-bellied stove. And while it was probably designed years ago for the practical living of a family that was likely surviving off the land and watching every penny, now it seemed homey, welcoming, and warm.

"Nice place," he commented, resting a hip against the island.

She smiled. "Thanks, I've been here just over ten years. We've done a lot of remodeling since then, like changing the old canning cellar downstairs into a guest room and TV room. And with the master on this floor, and the boys' bedrooms upstairs, it's not a huge house, but I've always loved it," she said. Her affection for her home was clear and genuine.

"Now, can I get you something to drink? Coffee? Tea?" she asked, moving into the kitchen.

"I'll have whatever you're having," he answered.

She gave a small laugh. "I was going to have a big glass of wine. You're welcome to join me, if you can?" He nodded "yes" and moved to look at a picture attached to the refrigerator with a little flower magnet.

"I also have beer, if you prefer. It's in the fridge," she added, gesturing toward the appliance as she poured a glass of red wine.

"Do you mind?" he asked. He liked wine, but he preferred beer.

She shook her head. "Not at all. Help yourself." He opened the refrigerator door as she recorked the wine. When they both had drinks in hand, they made their way to the little alcove.

"Did you talk to Julie? I'm not sure how much any of us will have to offer since we didn't really see anything." Jesse sank into a big chair and curled her legs up under her as she spoke.

He took a seat in a chair opposite her.

"I wish it were a simple investigation," he started, "but it looks like the fire was set intentionally."

He took a sip of beer and watched her big eyes go round in surprise. Leaning forward to rest his elbows on his knees, he waited for his information to really sink in.

"I don't—I mean," she stuttered. Then, seeming to get herself under control, she started again. "I don't know what I should say first: Twice in one week, what are the odds? Or, who would do such a thing?"

"I know," he said. "Unless the target of an attack like what we saw today is involved in a bad situation, the seemingly randomness of it all is always hard to believe. It's no surprise that what happened today came as a shock to everyone involved since, from what I gather, Julie is about as clean as they come."

Jesse gave a rueful laugh. "Unless you count a few speeding tickets from the speed trap just outside of town, I'd say so. What did she say?"

"She was about as speechless as you. She wasn't able to come up with anyone who might do something like this, but she's thinking about it."

Jesse was shaking her head. "I just don't know what to say. Could it have been some kids?"

He thought about the device he'd found. It wasn't sophisticated, but it was more complex than anything kids looking to create mischief would build. And though he didn't discount the abilities of a troubled kid, he thought if that had been the case, a quilt store wouldn't be the top choice for making a statement. He shook his head.

She took a dazed sip of wine and stared into her glass for a moment. "And to think we were supposed to be in there. Julie always opens at ten and, well, you overheard my conversation the other day, I was supposed to meet her there at ten to pick up my quilt. I guess she and I can both be glad I was running a little late."

The thought of Jesse being in the shop when the bomb went off chilled his blood and he found himself forcing his fingers to loosen their grip on his beer bottle.

"So why don't you tell me what happened," he prompted.

She gave him a confused look, like she didn't know what she could possibly have to add. But then she took a breath and told him what she'd seen, what she'd felt, and what she'd heard. As she recounted the details, what few she had, his eyes traveled over her. He could see a few of the bandages on her hands and one fairly large one on her neck; he wondered how many nicks and scratches she'd gotten, just how deep they ran, and how many more there might be that he couldn't see. The image of her lying in the street, blood streaming down her neck, caused his heart rate to kick up and he felt the edge of panic creeping into his chest. Willing his mind to focus on what she was saying, he took a sip of his beer and listened.

When she was finished, when she got to the part where the police and fire department showed up, he told her she could stop. He didn't need to hear the rest. They sat in silence for several moments before she spoke again.

"That probably wasn't all that helpful, but if there's anything more I can do, please tell me. Julie is a friend and I would hate to see her, or anyone else for that matter, get hurt."

"Can you think of anyone who might have wanted to do this to her shop?"

Jesse seemed to give the question some serious consideration before she shook her head. "Not that I know of. She's lived here a long time, is part of the community. Her son is close to my age. I think he's living in the city now—New York, that is. He's a lawyer. Maybe he has a dissatisfied client?" She paused to give that idea some thought, then shook her head and added, "Other than that, I can't think of anyone."

The idea of someone going after the mother for the sins of her son wasn't all that far-fetched, but it didn't really seem to fit the facts of this situation. If a person were going to go to the trouble of hurting or scaring someone's parent, they would usually be more precise in the method. But still, it was worth looking into.

"Thanks," he said. "If you think of anything else, just let me know. For now, the evidence is up at the lab in Albany. We'll just have to see what it tells us." He sat back and took another sip of his beer.

She gave him a faint smile. "Like CSI?"

He laughed. "Not quite, but the same idea. It's actually pretty cool, the things they can do there."

"James would love to hear this. All the science, and the practical application of it, is right up his alley. Maybe I should get Vivi to take him up there one day," she mused to herself.

"Vivi? As in the medical examiner and sheriff's wife?" David wasn't sure what Vivi would have to do with anything and the confusion must have come through in his voice.

Jesse gave him an indulgent smile. "Vivi is our county medical examiner, and I as I mentioned when we first met, she's also a professor at one of the universities in Boston. Sameer Buckley, the head of the Albany lab, was one of her first students. And just so you know, in addition to her medical degree, she has a PhD in Forensic Psychology. I know I also said she is a consultant with the FBI, but she's actually one of the foremost investigators of cold cases in the country. Oh, and she also used to work for the Boston PD."

He blinked. "Oh, wow." He knew his voice sounded impressed. Hell, he *was* impressed. "So I guess she could get James a tour anytime."

Jesse's smile was genuine. "She could. I just had never thought about it until now. He's been to the hospital, of course, but he'd probably find the lab interesting, too."

"They seem like good kids."

Taking a longer swig of the local ale, he crossed his ankle over his knee. He was starting to relax for the first time all day. As if to help him along, a big, fluffy orange cat sauntered out of nowhere and stared at him with yellow, assessing eyes. After a moment, it jumped up onto his lap and made itself comfortable.

"That's Mike. I hope you don't have any allergies?" Jesse said.

"Nope, I even kind of like cats. Imperious little bastards that they are," he answered.

She laughed and he realized how much he liked the sound.

"So, senior prom tonight?" he asked as he stroked Mike, who'd started to purr loud enough for someone in the next county to hear.

"It's hard to believe, but yeah. He'll be off at college next year, then James will be gone three years after that. I've never been alone, and while I couldn't be more excited for them, I have to admit it's going to be weird without them around all the time."

"Yeah, it is weird."

Her eyes shot to his and he realized what he'd said. He didn't usually talk about his personal life, especially not in the middle of an investigation. But this time, well, he found himself doing just that.

"I have a daughter," he said. "She's finishing her first year of college this year."

Jesse studied his face for a long moment. "So we're both members of the young parent club? You can't be much older than me, if you're older at all."

"I'm thirty-seven. Miranda was born when I was eighteen."

"I was nineteen when Matt was born," Jesse supplied.

"But it sounds like you had a good husband? A good partner?"

She wagged her head. "I did. What about you?"

"Her mother was never involved—first by choice, then by court order. Miranda and I are very close, and while I wouldn't take it back and don't regret having her, being a single parent is tough and I wouldn't wish it on anyone. And being one at such a young age is something that I find almost incomprehensible, even though I lived it."

"What happened?"

Her voice had softened and for the first time in a very long time, David felt like talking about those first few years—years when emotions ripped through him like typhoons, changing direction and intensity with what felt like a sadistic kind of whimsy. Maybe it was because he sensed Jesse would understand—at least some of it—or maybe it was because he just missed having people around on a daily basis who really knew him. As he sat there in her cozy house, he realized that since moving to Albany nine months earlier and leaving his entire family and all his friends behind, not to mention the home Miranda had grown up in, he'd been feeling somewhat unsettled. Somewhat uncertain about what to do or who to be. And so he talked.

"Valerie was two years older. I was seventeen when we met. I'm sure you have no problems imagining what an ego rush it was to have an older girlfriend." He paused, thinking back on the time. "God, I really thought I was something, you know. Anyway, it's amazing, and lucky, that the *only* lasting thing that came out of that relationship was Miranda. Most of the time we used protection, condoms, but every now and then I let her convince me we could do without. She was way more experienced than I was, and looking back on it, I should have seen it for what it was. At the time, I was so wrapped up in how 'cool' the whole thing was. I didn't have a clue, or probably even the ability to have a clue, as to how messed up she was. Her home life was crap—one parent neglected her, the other was a drunk. Her mom had lots of boyfriends, despite being married, and I'm pretty sure she let them get a little too close to her daughter a time or two. But not being such a bright teenager, I only saw what I wanted to see."

He stopped to take a sip of beer, hardly believing he was telling Jesse all this. But, not willing to stop, he went on.

"We'd been together about seven months when she told me

she was pregnant. She wanted to have an abortion, of course. A baby would seriously mess up her social life. I don't know what I was thinking. I'm not very religious, kind of an Easter/Christmas churchgoer, if you know what I mean. But still, I couldn't see doing that. Maybe it was ego. Hell, I'm sure it was. But there was no way I was going to let her abort my child if I had anything to do with it."

"What about your parents?" Jesse asked, tucking her feet further under her. Her voice held curiosity but no judgment.

"They didn't know any of this was going on until I came home and told them Valerie was six-months pregnant. I'd pleaded and persuaded and somehow gotten her to agree to have the baby. And my parents, well, they were shocked. Not exactly how they'd hoped things would work out for their only child. But they were, they *are*, amazing.

"Anyway, two days after giving birth to Miranda, Valerie walked out of the hospital. I didn't see her again for seven months."

He took a deep breath and realized that Jesse's house smelled of ginger cookies. He smiled; ginger cookies were some of Miranda's favorites. He made them with her every Christmas.

"When she came back, did she come for Miranda?" she asked quietly.

"At first, I thought so. And I kind of panicked. I wasn't sure what I would do if she wanted the baby because I was already wrapped around Miranda's tiny little finger and it was a toss-up who adored her more, me or my parents. But after a few long nights of waiting on pins and needles for Valerie to give me some indication of what she wanted, of why she was back, my parents suggested I give Valerie an ultimatum: that she was either in all the way or out all the way."

"And did you?"

He nodded. "Turns out, it wasn't much of an ultimatum. Valerie wasn't really interested in Miranda, she just wanted to pick up where we left off, physically that is."

"But your ego wasn't so flattered the second time around, was it?"

He laughed. "You've raised two kids, you know what those first few years are like. It was a miracle if I could even find the energy to shower after being up all hours of the day and night. So between that and my changed priorities, no, Valerie's offer really didn't hold any appeal. And when it became clear to her that Miranda *was* my priority, Valerie bailed again." He paused for a moment and let the years wash over him. "You know, it's funny, most young guys would kill to be used for sex." He hadn't really given it much thought over all the years, but looking back on it now, he could almost understand why Valerie had been so shocked when he'd turned her down.

"But not you," Jesse said.

He shook his head. "Not me, not then. Probably not now either, but back then it actually pissed me off. I couldn't believe what she was asking."

"I'm not sure whether to feel sorry for her or think it was probably a good thing that she left."

David stroked the cat, lost in thought again for a moment. "Both, I think. Again, hindsight is twenty-twenty, but I think maybe she kept coming back to me because I came from a strong family. Family that stood by each other, fought for each other, that kind of thing. I think she probably wanted the same thing."

"But didn't know how to ask for it."

He nodded again. "But it was also a good thing because by then she was starting to develop a drug habit and the thought of having her around Miranda wasn't something I was willing to allow."

Jesse got up and poured herself another glass of wine, then silently gestured toward the fridge in question. He gave his own silent assent and she grabbed another beer out for him, popped the top, and brought it over.

"So, what happened?" she asked, curling back up in her chair and pulling a lavender blanket over her feet. This time of year, the weather was warm during the day, but the evenings were still chilly. He glanced at the potbellied stove and the firewood in the copper bucket beside it and thought about offering to make a fire. But then Mike stood, circled, and plopped back down.

"She didn't show up again until Miranda was seven," he continued, answering Jesse's question. "By then, Miranda and I had moved out of my parents' house and were living in our own place. Valerie just showed up on the doorstep one day. Of course, Miranda had no idea who she was, so when Valerie started calling herself 'Mommy,' Miranda burst into tears. In all fairness, Valerie kind of scared me, too. The years hadn't been kind to her and it was definitely showing. Needless to say, I wasn't having any of it. So I hired a lawyer the next day and proceeded through a nine-month period of hell that ended with Valerie terminating her parental rights."

"That must have been brutal."

"It was, more so for me. I think I kept most of it out of Miranda's life, but even so, I'm sure she picked up on a lot more than I give her credit for. But it worked, and after that we never saw her again."

"Do you know where she is now?" Jesse asked.

"She died a few years after that. She OD'd in some seedy hotel in San Francisco. Miranda knows the whole story now, though," he added.

They were quiet for a few minutes as he lost himself in memories of those years. He was pretty sure Jesse was giving him space to rebalance after relaying his story.

Then she spoke. "How did you do it?" she asked. "I mean raising a daughter on your own when you were a kid yourself? I had a husband who was a good man, a good father. I also had my parents until about seven years ago when they moved out west, and Mark's parents for a few years when the boys were really young. And *even then* it was hard. I can't imagine having done it on my own when they were little."

He gave a half smile. "I'm pretty sure that raising kids is hard no matter how old you are when you do it. But yeah, it was hard. But I wasn't completely on my own. Like I said, my parents were amazing. We made an agreement that they would help with child-care costs as long as I kept a full load at the community college and kept my grades up. They also let us both live with them until I was well on my feet. I managed to buy a small place by the time Miranda was six. It was near my parents' place; I didn't want to move too far away from them given how devoted they were to her. And it worked out. I studied chemistry in college and during my last year met a guy whose brother was a firefighter in Truckee, the small town near Tahoe in California where I grew up. The hours seemed good and I liked the camaraderie of it. It was a more adult version of what I'd missed by not going away to a four-year school."

"And the arson investigation?"

"I kind of fell into it. Given my background in chemistry, they asked me to attend a couple of courses on accelerants and other flammable materials. One thing led to another…" His voice trailed off.

"And here you are. But how did you get here? I mean to this area?"

He let out a self-deprecating laugh. "Like you, I was excited for Miranda to go off to college, do all the things I didn't get to do. She's a great kid and I know she'll do well…"

"But you still want to keep an eye on her."

"Guilty," he said, not bothering to hide the accompanying smile. "She's in a seven-year undergrad and medical degree program in Providence. Albany had an opening in their fire department; I figured maybe it was time for me to break out of my shell, too."

"And do you see her often?"

He shook his head and looked down at the bottle in his hand as a wave of emotion washed over him. "Not as often as I would like, but then again, if she lived at home, I probably wouldn't see her as much as I would like either. But she's off starting her new life and doing really well. She loves the program, the people, her professors. We talk a lot, almost every day, but I only get to see her about once every five or six weeks."

"You must be very proud."

He looked up at her words, an echo of his own from only days earlier.

"Yeah, I am," he said. She smiled at him and their eyes held. Then Mike's claws dug into his thigh and he drew back, breaking the moment. With a glance at the clock, and the empty second beer in his hand, he frowned.

"It's almost eight. I've kept you way too long."

She waved him off but rose from her seat. "I'm glad you stayed. I mean, it was good to talk with you, and to be honest, from a purely selfish standpoint, it was nice to have something to think about other than myself."

Following her into the kitchen, he placed the second empty bottle on the counter by the first one.

"How are you feeling? I see your bandages are still in place." He wanted to examine each and every one of them, peel them off and make sure the EMTs had done a good job.

"They're fine." She rubbed a hand over the back of her neck in a self-conscious gesture. "I won't be surprised if I'm a little sore tomorrow, though. I fell to the ground pretty hard. But other than that, I'll be fine."

"Do you have any plans for tomorrow, or will you be able to take it easy?"

"Easy, definitely. I'm having lunch with my friend Kit, but nothing else. Not even laundry."

"Sounds like the perfect lazy Sunday," he said. *Well, an almost perfect lazy Sunday*, he thought to himself as an image of Jesse lounging around in bed popped into his head.

"Hopefully. You?" she asked, oblivious to where his head was.

He cleared his throat. "I'll be working up in Albany with Dr. Buckley, seeing what we can come up with on this fire."

Her mouth tightened at his words and he wished he hadn't

reminded her of what had happened, wished he'd been a little more conscientious.

"I'm not sure if you can, but *if* you can, will you keep me updated?" she asked, walking him to the door.

As he stepped outside, he pulled his keys from his pocket. "To the extent that I can, yeah, I'll keep you updated. I have your number."

"And you know where I live." She wrapped her arms around her middle. Whether she did this because she was cold or as a defensive gesture to keep the events of the day at bay, he didn't know.

"And I know where you live."

A soft breeze lifted a few pieces of her hair and blew them across her face. He almost reached out to brush them back. To touch her. To maybe ask her out on a real date where they could talk about movies and food and the weather. Not teenage parenting and arson. But her own fingers came up and tucked the wayward strands behind her ear.

"Thank you for coming out. I appreciate how much you went out of your way for me."

He wasn't sure if that was another dismissal or not. He studied her eyes but they gave nothing away. So, rather than put her in an awkward spot, he stepped back, while at the same time deciding, then and there, that he wasn't about to let this thing go—whatever it was between them. Maybe what he felt when he was with her was the start of something. Or maybe it wasn't. But right now the moment just didn't feel right to try and find out. And if there was one thing his job had taught him, it was the importance of intuition.

So he drove away with the image of her standing in the doorway watching him leave burned into his mind.

CHAPTER 7

As Jesse entered The Tavern, she waved to Rob, the bartender and owner. Seeing Kit at a booth in the back, she made her way across the room. Her friend stood to greet her with a kiss on the cheek as she arrived at the table. Jesse took off her coat and slid into her seat.

Kit, wearing a smile, already had a glass of white wine in front of her. "What are you smiling about?" Jesse asked, motioning to Rob to bring her a glass of whatever wine Kit was drinking.

Jesse had met her friend a few years back when Kit, an author, had contacted her and asked if she would provide information about hospital processes and procedures for one of her novels. Jesse had been glad to be her go-to gal on the subject; Kit's world was so different than her own day-to-day life, it had been fun. Over the months they'd been in contact, their relationship had grown from that of professional acquaintances to friends and now, years later, she considered Kit one of her closest. Last year, she had introduced Kit to both Vivi and Matty, and Vivi now acted as a consultant to Kit, as well. And since neither Matty nor Kit were inherently jealous people, the two of them had also grown close, bonding over the industry.

Between Abigail, Kit, Vivi, and Matty, Jesse knew she'd hit the jackpot of girlfriends.

"My brother is coming to town. I was just thinking you might make a good match for him," Kit said with a waggle of her eyebrows, answering Jesse's question.

Jesse stared at her for a moment, then burst out laughing.

She'd never met or even seen pictures of Kit's brother, but if he looked anything like a male version of Kit, there was no way she would be a good match for him. Kit was stunningly beautiful, with long auburn hair and eyes of a striking gold color. But more importantly, she was tall. Probably close to five foot eleven. She would wager that Kit's brother was well over six feet. Everything else aside, the mechanics of it would be awkward. Not to mention the fact that, in all the years she had known her, Kit had very rarely mentioned her brother. This alone raised some red flags.

Oh, yeah, and she was also kind of pining for a certain arson investigator.

"That is *so* not going to happen," Jesse said with a roll of her eyes before turning and thanking Rob who'd just delivered her drink.

Kit, shrugging, seemed to have expected the response. "Worth a try, at least. I wouldn't mind if he had a reason to come around a little more. Then again, we tend to do better when we don't see that much of each other. So, what have you been up to?" Kit asked, propping her elbows on the table and leaning forward.

For a moment, Jesse thought Kit might be kidding. But then she realized she hadn't talked to her friend much over the past several days. So, taking a deep breath, she filled Kit in on everything from Aaron Greene to her car to the explosion in Spin-A-Yarn. At some point, Rob came along and took their lunch orders, and by the time she'd finished recounting her last several days, their food had arrived.

"Holy shit, Jesse. You were really there?" Kit asked, speaking of the explosion. "I read about it, of course, but not much was reported beyond 'No one was hurt.' I also saw the damage when I went to Frank's this morning. Everyone there was speculating, but I hadn't heard you were there when it happened."

Jesse took a long sip of her wine. "Let's just say, I think it took a few years off my life." She paused for a moment then added, "I don't know how people like Ian can do it—live every day knowing that at any moment a bomb might go off beneath them. And for years, too." The kind of anxiety he must have lived with every day as a Ranger wasn't something that just went away and it was no wonder he had a tendency to worry.

"No kidding," Kit agreed. "But, I'm just glad you're okay. And Julie, too."

"Me, too. I'm also really glad the kids weren't with me," she added. As a parent, she naturally wouldn't have wanted her kids anywhere near what had happened. But it was more than that, and both she and Kit knew it. Mark had been gone for two years, having died in a fire, a fire that had destroyed his office in less than ten minutes due to a gas leak and ancient insulation. She had no idea how her boys would react to seeing such a similar situation play out in front of them. It was a reminder she didn't think they'd ever need, especially not so soon after their father's death.

For a moment, she and Kit ate in silence, then Kit spoke.

"So, do they know what happened?"

The six-million-dollar question, Jesse thought. She shrugged, "I don't know, but David is investigating it." She was just taking a bite of her sandwich when she realized her mistake.

"David? And who might *David* be?" Kit asked. As if to emphasize the real intent of her question, she put her fork down, steepled her fingers, and cocked her head as she waited for an answer.

Jesse tried her best to seem matter of fact, but unfortunately, she was talking to a writer and there was very little that escaped Kit's notice.

"He's an arson investigator. He also investigated the fire at the Greene place, which is how I met him. He came in to the hospital to interview Aaron. Then Ian called him in yesterday when the thing happened at Spin-A-Yarn."

Kit seemed to be thinking on this. "Is he the extremely good-looking, tall guy I saw with Vivi at the hospital?"

Jesse frowned. "Yes, but he's not that tall. I didn't know you were at the hospital last week."

"I wasn't." Kit grinned. "Come on, Jesse. You know you'd never tell me anything about him if I just flat out asked."

Jesse shot Kit a repressive look, hoping to end the topic. It didn't work.

"Come on, tell Mama everything," Kit chided. Jesse regarded her friend for a long moment. It actually wasn't a bad idea, talking to Kit about David. She was one of her few single friends, and she wasn't looking to settle down anytime soon, so Kit probably wouldn't try to push her into anything. But still, what did she really have to say about him anyway? That she *thought* there was a mutual interest but wasn't sure. Or that he hadn't asked her out and she didn't know if she'd go on a date anyway? It all seemed too angst-ridden—too schoolgirl-like—to give any voice to.

"Just say it," Kit interjected as if reading her thoughts. Jesse eyed her friend's eager but set expression and realized that Kit wasn't going to drop the subject so she might as well put it all out there and get it over with. She took a big sip of wine.

"Okay, here is the story. He's attractive. Very attractive," Jesse started.

"Hallelujah," Kit interjected.

"Are you going to let me talk?"

Kit made a motion of zipping her lips shut.

"So, the thing is, I'm pretty sure he's interested in me," she continued, not feeling entirely comfortable saying what she was saying.

Kit snorted. "Of course he is, every man alive that's interested in women is interested in you. Sorry," she added, slapping her hand over her mouth in response to Jesse's raised eyebrows.

"But here's the deal." She paused, took a deep breath, then released it, along with everything on her mind about David. "I don't want to deal with all the shit I dealt with when I was married. Don't get me wrong, I loved Mark and the life we built together, and I wouldn't change it for anything. But I don't want to do it again. I just don't have it in me to go through everything a relationship takes, *again*."

Kit dipped a few French fries in ketchup and popped them into her mouth. She appeared thoughtful as she chewed.

"So, who says you have to?" she asked after a moment.

Jesse let out a rueful laugh. "Do you know how many of my friends are newly married or have been happily married for a long time?" It was phrased as a question but they both knew she was making a point. "I would probably still be married if Mark hadn't died." Maybe, she amended to herself, if they'd been able to come through his infidelities intact. No one other than Jesse knew about those, though, and she preferred to keep it that way, if only for the sake of the kids. "If any of our friends see me out on a date, or even hear I'm dating someone, they'll be all over it. Even if I tell them to drop it. Believe me, none of them will be able to contain themselves."

Kit bobbed her head. "I know Matty and Vivi, and you're right, they won't be able to contain themselves," she conceded. "So have a secret relationship with him. Or one of those friends-with-benefits things that seems to be so popular these days," Kit suggested.

"Nice idea." And it was, only it wasn't. "But the thing is, he has a daughter. I know that sounds totally unrelated, but he was eighteen when she was born and now he's on his own for the first time. On the one hand, it seems like it might be a perfect solution, right? Like he might want to sow his wild oats, or however that saying goes. But on the other, he told me the other day how the mother of his daughter came back a few months after abandoning him with their baby and basically wanted just that—wanted to use him for sex. And to say he wasn't into the idea would be an understatement," she said, remembering how adamant David had been when recounting that part of his story.

Kit inclined her head but didn't look convinced. "He had a kid *as a kid* and I assume the mother left him to do all the work, so of course he wasn't into it when she came back. Who would be? But now he's an adult with no responsibilities other than his job and being a good parent to an adult child. My guess is it might be different at this stage in his life," Kit suggested.

She gave this some thought. What Kit said was true; it might be different. He was in a very different stage in his life, no doubt about that, but Jesse wasn't sure. She wasn't sure what *she* would think if someone came to her and said, "I want a relationship that actually isn't a relationship."

"Maybe. But he's a good guy and he deserves someone who can give him what he wants. Someone who can give him simple things, like dinners out in public," she said with a shake of her head.

"But do you know what he wants?" Kit asked with a pointed look.

Jesse blinked. "Meaning?"

"Do you know what he wants? I mean, have you asked him?"

Jesse drew back at the thought of asking such a personal and intimate question of someone she barely knew. "Of course not."

"Then maybe he wants the same thing you do. But, all that aside," Kit said, cutting off her objection, "I think that begs the bigger question, what do *you* want?"

"What do you mean?" Jesse frowned.

"I mean, if you could create your fairytale relationship for this stage in your life, what would it look like?" Kit clarified.

Jesse stared at her friend, at her unblinking golden eyes, and realized Kit was asking a serious question. "I don't—I don't actually know what I want. I know what I *don't* want," she answered.

"But you haven't given yourself the opportunity to think about what you *do* want, right?"

Hesitantly, Jesse nodded in response to her friend's question.

"Maybe you should start thinking about that," Kit suggested. "And then maybe, once you sort it out, you can run it by David. He's a man who seems like he's seen and done a lot in life already. My guess is he won't be at all shy about telling you what he wants."

Jesse thought about David and recognized the truth in what Kit was saying. But because it was hard to really imagine, or acknowledge, what she actually wanted, it was nearly impossible to guess whether or not he would want the same.

With a sigh, she looked up, caught Rob's attention, and ordered another glass of wine.

At her desk several days later, Jesse couldn't get her conversation with Kit out of her mind. She wasn't a prude or particularly old-fashioned, but she had never really thought about her options beyond dating someone seriously or having a one-night stand. If she wanted to avoid the questions and pressures of her friends, dating someone was out of the question; living in a small town put everything more or less out in the open. As for a one-night stand, she could travel somewhere else, but that really held no appeal for her. A night of mind-blowing sex held great appeal, of course, but she was old enough to know that, while one-night stands in novels were always mind-blowing, in the real world, the odds were against it.

She sighed and picked up the paperwork on her desk, forcing herself to focus on the task at hand. All she had to do was finish Aaron's charity case application and she would be more or less done for the day. While an aunt, a sister of Aaron's mother, had shown up out of the woodwork and was set on helping Aaron as much as she could, hospital stays were expensive. Jesse had spoken to both the aunt and Aaron several times and then sorted out what expenses the aunt could cover and which would need to be put into the application to apply for funds from the hospital. It wasn't usually her job to do those applications, but there was no way around the fact that she'd taken a special interest in Aaron.

Thinking of Aaron made her think of Julie and as she signed the documents in all the right places, she wondered how that investigation was going. Jesse hadn't been downtown all week so she hadn't seen if rebuilding had started yet, but had heard from Vivi that new windows were in and the interior cleanup had started.

As if on cue, there was a knock at her door and David popped his head in.

"Hi, I was in Windsor so thought I'd come down to visit with Aaron and update you on the Spin-A-Yarn investigation," he said, still standing in the doorway.

For a long moment, she just stared at him. His friendly expression turned into a questioning one when she didn't respond—she just hadn't expected to see him and was caught by surprise.

"Uh, do you want me to come back?" he asked.

She shook her head and spoke, finally. "Sorry, I was in the middle of paperwork, plus it's Friday. My mind hadn't made the leap from this," she held up the files, "to arson."

He grinned and stepped into her office, closing the door behind him.

"How are you?" he asked.

She signed the last of the papers, tucked them all neatly into the file that would be sent to the board for review, then looked up at him. "I'm good. This week has been a lot quieter than last week was, that's for sure. And you? Is there something going on with Aaron's case?"

"Glad to hear your week is going well. And no," he shook his head and took a seat across from her. "Everything's fine. I just came by to make sure Aaron didn't feel too alone, I didn't know he had family in."

That was, well, that was sweet. She cleared her throat.

"Yes, his aunt came in on Monday. I was just thinking about her. I hadn't known Aaron's mom had a sister, so I was a bit suspicious, I admit. But Aaron recognized her. He said she'd always sent him cards and packages on his birthdays, but apparently his mother and her sister were more or less estranged after his mom married his dad."

"I'm glad he has someone. It's going to be a long road."

She smiled. "I was thinking the same thing. Have you met her?"

He shook his head. "No, I stopped by the nurses' desk and they told me he'd been moved out of the intensive care unit and that his aunt had come. I figured I'd drop by to see you first, then go see him."

"Jesse?" The door opened and her assistant's head appeared.

"It's eleven thirty. If you're going to be at Carl's by noon, you should think about leaving."

"Or I should already be out the door?" she rejoined with a smile. Her assistant was unflaggingly professional and Jesse was sure that, one day soon, she'd lose Kayla to someplace far more glamorous than Riverside.

"I'll get the packages ready," Kayla said, then closed the door again, leaving the two of them.

"You're on your way out?" David asked.

She inclined her head. "Yes, I'm taking the afternoon off, but before I do that, I need to stop by and visit an old friend. My predecessor had major heart surgery down in the city last week and is back home now," she spoke as she gathered her jacket, computer bag, and purse. David stood with her.

"Here you go." Kayla reentered the room with a huge bouquet of flowers and a box Jesse had previously filled with homemade food items that Carl and his wife Angie could just put in the freezer, then reheat as needed. The box also held cards and small gifts from just about everyone who worked at the hospital during Carl's tenure—a testament to his leadership.

"Are you going to need a hand with these?" Kayla asked, eyeing Jesse whose hands were already quite full.

"I can give you a hand," David offered.

Jesse saw just a tiny movement in Kayla's eyebrow, but her assistant handed the items over to David without a word.

"Thanks, David, I appreciate it. I just need help out to my car and then I've got it," she said.

"So, do you have plans after visiting Aaron?" she asked as they left her office and made their way through the halls to the front of the hospital. Not surprisingly, her heart managed to find its way into her throat. Unintentionally, she let out a laugh, mostly at herself. She couldn't even ask him if he wanted to grab lunch with her without getting nervous—there was no way she'd ever be able to ask for more, as Kit had suggested.

"You okay?" he asked.

"Everything is fine. I just sometimes think I look like I'm moving into or out of this place when I walk around with so much stuff," she lied, lifting the bags in her hands.

"Jesse." A voice called out from behind them. A voice she knew too well.

As she came to a stop and turned around, David paused beside her. "Dr. Bennet, what can I do for you?" she asked.

Ken Bennet's eyes went from her to David then back again. "You left your phone in my office," he said, holding out the device. "And we didn't get a chance to schedule a follow-up to our conversation," he added, his gaze flicking to David again.

That, of course, had been intentional on her part. Dr. Bennet was a great surgeon but a terrible head of his department. She had enough past history with him to know that the "conversation" he wanted to have would be nothing more than an hour of her listening to him complain about his budget. Or complain about the nurses. Or complain about the hospital's equipment. Jesse often mused that Dr. Bennet was the perfect example of someone who was incredibly attractive on the outside and incredibly unattractive on the inside.

"Thank you." She took her phone from him. "Kayla can schedule something. Call her and she'll take care of it," Jesse said, knowing full well that Kayla would be careful not to find an open spot for Dr. Bennet for several weeks. Not that her calendar was actually that booked up.

Dr. Bennet looked about to protest, but she cut him off. "I'm running late for my visit with Carl, Ken. Call Kayla, please."

The surgeon's mouth pursed but then he gave a terse nod and turned to walk away, in the process almost running into a woman pushing one of the food carts. Jesse braced herself for the explosion she expected to come from Dr. Bennet's lips, likely blaming the woman for being in his way—he wasn't known to be forgiving, or even very rational—but to her surprise, all that came were some irritated mumbles as he stalked off.

Jesse turned to give the woman with the cart an encouraging

smile but saw that she'd just ducked her head and carried on, leaving Jesse and David standing in the middle of the hall.

David shrugged in response to her what-can-you-do shrug then gestured for her to continue on down the hallway.

"You asked if I have plans after visiting with Aaron," he said as they entered the lobby area of the hospital. "I have to be back at the firehouse tonight, but I have a couple of hours."

They scooted past a young woman carrying a toddler toward the intake desk and an old man with a walker being helped by a nurse. As they stepped outside and headed toward the parking area, Jesse took a deep breath and inhaled the crisp spring air.

"Carl lives just on the other side of the Rip Van Winkle Bridge," she said. "I'm not going to stay longer than half an hour. Do you want to grab some Mexican food around one-ish?" she asked as they approached her car. There, she'd done it. But just what had she done?

They reached her car and she saw him frown as he studied its chipped paint.

"That sounds good," he replied, almost as an afterthought. "Are you going to get this repainted?" he asked.

She opened the trunk and dumped her computer bag in, then she took the goods from David and set them gently beside her bag.

"I think I'll have to or it will just get so much worse this winter," she answered, trying to sound as casual as David. "I know it's a long way off since we're just heading into summer, but I may as well. Um, do you know the restaurant I'm talking about? It's the only Mexican one in town. It's on Phillips Street between Fourth and Fifth Avenues." In for a penny, in for a pound.

His eyes left her car and looked straight into hers. He nodded. "I've never been there, but I know where Phillips Street is. It should be easy enough to find."

"Great." She opened her driver's side door and threw her purse across into the passenger seat. "I'll see you at one?" When he didn't immediately answer, she turned and looked up at him. He was watching her.

"See you at one," he repeated, his eyes not leaving hers. She managed a nod then climbed into her car, shutting her door behind her. He stepped back as she started the engine. Watching him in her rearview mirror as she drove off, she knew he didn't leave the parking lot until after she'd pulled out. He was a gentleman in so many ways. But with the way he looked at her sometimes, she knew he could also be anything but.

• • •

David was still on her mind as she pulled onto Route 23A and headed back toward Riverside. She'd had a nice visit with Carl and his wife, Angie. She was happy to hear, and see, that her predecessor and former boss was doing much better than she'd expected. His spirits, always high, were what she'd expected, but it was nice to see that he was healing physically, too. And as for Angie, she seemed to be taking everything in stride, trying not to hover, but also trying her best to keep her overactive husband mostly inactive.

Jesse switched on the radio as she noticed a bank of dark clouds moving in from the south. She wasn't exactly surprised to see a storm coming; she'd thought it had smelled a bit like rain earlier. But still, the day had started out clear and sunny and she hadn't brought an umbrella. As the first drops began to fall and the weather station sited a series of moderate to severe thunderstorms moving in her direction, she flipped on her wipers.

Within minutes, the sound of the rain on her car was deafening. She no longer needed the weather report to tell her what was happening, so she turned the radio off and focused on driving. Her whole life she'd experienced these kinds of intense storms—storms that lasted anywhere from five to forty minutes. They'd blow in with startling intensity and blow on up, usually northward toward Albany or the northwest corner of Massachusetts. Sometimes there wouldn't be any damage, but sometimes they'd leave downed power lines or toppled trees. Judging by the looks of it, and sounds of it, she wouldn't be at all surprised if this one left some wreckage behind.

She gripped the steering wheel and cursed the fact that she was behind a semitruck; not only did it block her view of the road ahead, it also kicked so much water up onto her windshield that it was almost impossible to see more than a few feet in front of her.

Glancing at the clock on her dashboard, she realized David was going to be at the restaurant waiting for her in twenty minutes. She might make it on time but was more likely going to be five or ten minutes late. Still, he didn't seem the type to mind too much, and as her car slowly paced the miles toward the bridge, she found herself looking forward to having a margarita to kick off her weekend almost as much as she was looking forward to seeing David.

She glanced in her rearview mirror and could see more clearly looking backward than forward. Behind her was a large blue ancient-looking SUV, possibly an old Suburban. It looked steady as a rock and she gave a fleeting thought to the wisdom of buying a small Subaru. But she loved her little car and it got her everywhere she needed to go, so she took her eyes from the behemoth behind her, refocused them on the semitruck ahead, and thought about David.

She'd been surprised when he'd stopped in to see her—that he'd even come by the hospital at all. Her impromptu invite to a late lunch hadn't been well thought out and seemed to go against everything she'd been trying to tell herself, everything she'd told Kit. A restaurant not three miles from the hospital was pretty conspicuous. But then again, nothing had happened between them, so at this point, a lunch could easily pass as quasi-professional or friendly.

The road rose up as it approached the bridge and she fell back from the semitruck a bit hoping to gain some visibility. Behind her, the driver of the SUV must have been thinking the same thing because it dropped back as well. Following the Suburban was a string of cars, but because of the weather, no one seemed anxious to speed up or pass.

From her position well behind it, she watched the semi get blown around by the winds that blew at much higher speeds over the bridge. She felt her own car being buffeted by the same weather, but not having a trailer attached, it managed much better than the truck, although they both made it across the bridge without incident.

Letting out a small breath she hadn't realized she was holding, she watched as the semitruck pulled into a small diner with a big parking lot just over the bridge. She couldn't say she blamed the driver for needing a break. Those truck drivers had way more experience than she ever would, but still, she wouldn't want to handle such a big rig in the kind of wind this spring storm was bringing. Especially when the storm was likely to blow over in only a few more minutes.

Jesse had been focusing so much on the truck in front of her that she was startled when she glanced in the rearview mirror and saw the blue Suburban riding her tail. Apparently, the driver was no longer bothered by the weather and felt a sudden need to hurry.

Not at all interested in having a car that close to her bumper on a wet road, Jesse's eyes scanned the side of the road for a place where she could pull over and let the SUV pass. She didn't have that far to go before she'd need to turn north off of Route 23 to head into Riverside, but given her druthers, she'd rather not continue with such an aggressive driver behind her. Unfortunately, after the diner where the semi had pulled off, there didn't seem to be any other spots to pull over. The shoulder was fairly narrow on her side and beyond the shoulder there was just a ditch and then a field, which left her with almost no room to maneuver. She let out a small huff of frustration and then forced herself to let it go. Her turn was less than a mile away; the driver behind her would just have to deal with it.

Or so she'd thought.

Out of the corner of her eye, she caught a flash of blue over to her left. Her head whipped around to the driver's side window, and to her horror, she saw the front end of the massive automobile coming up next to her. On instinct, she slowed down to allow the SUV to pass. The road had only two lanes and was an easy one to speed on. But it was also a gently winding road with a double yellow line. Not that the driver of the SUV seemed to care much about either the speed limit or the no-passing zone as it came alongside Jesse.

Slowing down more and inching her way to the side of the road a bit, she thought about stopping altogether, then dismissed the idea. There were too many cars behind her. She also thought about speeding up and forcing the SUV to come back in behind her rather than continuing alongside her as it was doing now. But driving aggressively wasn't all that appealing to her at the moment, so she opted to slow down just a little bit more, hoping that the driver, whom Jesse could barely see, would finally pass her and continue on his or her way.

But the Suburban's pace slowed to match hers. The driver didn't seem interested in passing or falling back and the vehicle just maintained its position right beside her. It was the first sign that something wasn't quite right and, for the first time since she'd noticed the SUV, Jesse began to get nervous. It was one thing to deal with a driver who felt the need to speed or drive somewhat recklessly. It was another thing entirely to feel like someone might actually be trying to scare or harm her.

Looking in her mirror again, she saw a couple of cars still behind her and hoped their drivers were noticing what was going on. Maybe someone would call the police—at the very least, maybe someone would get the SUV's license plate. With one hand on the steering wheel, she fumbled in her purse and pulled out her phone. Hitting the button to bring it to life, she keyed in her password and started to dial 9-1-1. Maybe she was overreacting, but something just didn't feel right.

And then she saw another semi-truck. Only this one was headed right toward them.

CHAPTER 8

LIKE A DEER IN HEADLIGHTS, Jesse froze for a split second. The SUV was still beside her, and heading in their direction, in the same lane as the SUV, was the semi-truck. She dropped her phone and gripped the steering wheel with both hands. She had enough presence of mind not to slam on her brakes, but she did take her foot off the gas.

In retrospect, she wasn't sure if that been a good idea or not. Because when the SUV sped up and swerved back into her lane, its back end rammed the front left side of her car and she didn't have the power or control to get out of the spin caused by the impact.

Her fingers strained against the leather of her steering wheel as she battled for control of her vehicle. She hadn't been going very fast, not in the rain, but on the wet road, her driving skills were being ruthlessly challenged. In a blur, she saw flashes of blue and heard the horn of the semi and sound of rubber skidding across pavement. The next thing she knew, the car slammed into something solid and came to a sudden stop. Stunned by the impact, the only thing Jesse was able to immediately grasp was the feel of her seatbelt straining against her chest and the airbag cushioning her cheek.

She sat still—hands on the steering wheel, chest pressed against the canvas of the belt, eyes closed—for a long, long moment.

"Are you okay?"

"Is she hurt?"

"Did you see that crazy driver?"

The voices all came to her slowly, filtering through her rattled mind before settling in her brain and registering. Hesitantly, she lifted her head from the deflating airbag.

"Don't move. The police are on their way," someone said to her. She ignored whoever had issued the order and continued to raise her head. Confusion was swirling through mind and body as she struggled to take in the situation. After a few moments, she figured out that her car was face down in the ditch beside the road. The windshield and driver's side window were shattered and little shards of safety glass were everywhere. She had a blinding headache and her neck hurt, but other than that, she seemed to be able to feel and, after a quick test, move everything. She noticed her hands were still clutching the steering wheel and so with great effort, she uncurled and stretched her fingers in an attempt to loosen the joints.

"I'm okay." Her voice wasn't exactly steady, but it was strong enough for the person nearest her to hear.

"Still, I don't think you should move until the paramedics get here."

She turned and looked into the blue eyes of an elderly man, somewhere in his seventies, she'd guess. His face wore a look of concern. Behind the elderly man was a younger man, maybe late forties, and beside him was a young teenage girl. They were all watching her.

Jesse braced her feet against the floorboard and pressed herself back into the seat. "No, I'm okay. I'm just going to get myself out."

The older man mumbled some sort of protest but then insisted on helping her. He called the younger man forward and together they pried open the damaged driver's door. Once it was open, Jesse tried to unbuckle her seatbelt, but her weight pressing against it made it almost impossible to get the latch down. Or maybe it was her shaking hands.

Feeling more and more helpless with each passing moment, she found herself battling an unexpected rush of tears. Probably sensing her frustration and shock, the younger man leaned inside the car and held onto her, easing some of the tension off of the seatbelt as he reached around and unbuckled it. She was glad his body was braced somewhat against hers because, with the angle of the car, she would have pitched forward when the belt released if he hadn't been there.

"Do you think you can stand?" the man asked, still holding her steady in her seat.

She nodded and he called over his shoulder to someone. Jesse watched as the teenage girl scrambled forward to help them.

And with the assistance of her three Good Samaritans, a dazed Jesse climbed out of her car. Bit by bit, the events of the accident were coming back to her as was her strength. She wasn't about to hike out of the ditch yet, but she could stand.

"I don't suppose anyone saw what happened," she said, to no one in particular, as she noticed two more people standing up on the road staring down at her.

"That crazy driver in the blue SUV," someone started.

"It's as if he wanted to drive you off the road," another offered.

"Didn't get his license plate…"

"Didn't have one…"

She heard the words and phrases, but she soon realized that in her current state, she wasn't going to make any sense of what they meant. Thankfully, she heard sirens approaching and knew that, because they were in an unincorporated part of the county and thus sheriff territory, Ian's people would handle things for now. Having spent enough time in hospitals, she knew she wasn't at her best just then. When her mind was clearer, and her heart rate back to normal, she'd work through it herself.

Almost as if she was reliving the events of the Saturday before, the EMTs arrived, then the fire department. Eventually, Ian showed up. It seemed like a lot of hoopla to her; she just needed to get her car out of the ditch and to the mechanic. She knew Ian would be taking statements and getting all the information he needed from the people who'd stopped to help. Once she was feeling a little more under control, she'd learn what she wanted to know from him.

Sitting on the back of the ambulance having her eyes checked for the third time in forty minutes, Jesse heard her phone ring. Some nice person, probably one of the first firefighters on the scene, had brought her purse up. Ignoring the scowl of the EMT working on her, she answered.

"Hello?"

"Jesse?" David's voice came through the line. "Is everything okay? I'm at the restaurant and I'm pretty sure it's the right one."

She'd completely forgotten. "I'm so sorry, David. I should have called you earlier. I'm not going to make it today."

He paused before answering. "Okay," he drew out. "Are you all right?"

"I'm, well, I'll be fine. There was a little accident on my way back into Riverside," she explained.

"What kind of accident?" She didn't need to see his face to know he'd snapped to attention.

"A crazy driver tried to pass me on a two-lane road. A truck came along in the other direction, I ended up in a ditch and the crazy driver is long gone. But I'm—"

"Where are you?" he cut her off.

"What?"

"Where are you? On the road? Are you far?"

She frowned. "No, I'm less than a mile after you turn onto Route 23 toward the bridge. Maybe ten minutes from town."

"I'll be right there."

"You don't need to come..." She hadn't finished her sentence before she realized it would be fruitless. He'd hung up.

Even though she'd told him he didn't need to come, the idea of having him there appealed to her. And so she knew that exactly eight minutes had passed since David had hung up. She'd watched the clock.

"Jesse," he said, jogging up to her. "Are you okay?" He put his hands on her shoulders and searched her eyes. Probably looking for signs of a concussion, she told herself.

"I told you, I'm fine. If it weren't for Ian barking orders, these poor guys probably would have left me twenty minutes ago."

David either wasn't listening or didn't agree because he turned around and barked his own orders. "She's shaking, why doesn't she have a blanket? Someone get me a blanket."

"I'm fine. It was just still raining when the accident happened so I got a little wet. Now, I'm a little chilled," she said, knowing he wasn't really listening.

"You're a little stunned is what you are," he responded. "Not full blown shock, but close." A blanket appeared in his hands and he wrapped it around her. Then, tucking it around her body, he pulled her close to him and rubbed his hands gently up and down her arms. She hadn't realized how cold she'd actually been and she leaned into him, drawing warmth from his body.

"Hathaway, what are you doing here?" Her head came up slightly at Ian's voice. David lightly, but firmly, pressed it back against his chest.

"Jesse and I were supposed to meet for lunch. When she didn't show, I called. I just got here," he answered.

She was tempted to look up in the ensuing silence, but instead she closed her eyes.

"Are you a little better now?" It took her a moment to grasp that David was talking to her and though she was feeling tired, she was definitely feeling better—warmer, stronger, more normal. She nodded.

"I want to talk to Ian for minute, get an idea of what happened. Do you mind?" he asked, pulling back just enough to see her face.

She glanced at Ian, who was watching the byplay. It shouldn't have mattered, but she knew this little scene would be the first thing he'd tell Vivi about when he got home that evening.

"Of course, I'm fine." She managed to make her voice sound professional. David gave her a curious look but didn't say anything. A minute later, she watched his head disappear down the side of the embankment.

• • •

"You don't really need to see this," Ian said to David as they scrambled down toward the car.

"Yeah, I kind of do. I may be an arson specialist, but I *am* an investigator," he managed to say through the fear and anger that had been clawing at him since he'd learned about the accident. When they reached the bottom of the ditch, he paused and took in the scene. Jesse's car was nose down in the bottom of the ditch. He could see the deflated airbag and pieces of glass everywhere. The front left corner of the vehicle was crumpled and the front axle was also visibly broken.

"It's a miracle she wasn't injured more with all the broken windows," David said, attempting to ignore the churning in his gut.

Ian made some sort of murmur of agreement.

David turned to Ian, looking him squarely in the eyes.

"Tell me what happened." It was just shy of an order, but Ian, being gracious enough to overlook his tone, responded, recounting, presumably, what the witnesses had told him.

When Ian got to the part about the SUV bumping Jesse's car, David's eyes went back to the front panel of the vehicle. Wanting a closer view, he stepped toward it and went down on his haunches. He could see streaks of blue embedded in the black paint of her car.

He was studying the pattern when Ian spoke again. "Is there something going on between you and Jesse? Not that it's any of my business, but she is a good friend."

David didn't take his eyes off the car. He wasn't really sure how to answer that question. Yes, there was definitely something going on. But it wasn't anything he felt ready to talk about or could even explain without sounding like an idiot. Especially since, by the standards of the day, most people would say nothing was going on. They had never kissed, the only time he'd touched her beyond purely professional confines was just moments ago when he'd wrapped her up in the blanket and rubbed her arms. Hell, they hadn't even been out on a date.

Opting to ignore the question, he pointed to the blue paint and asked, "Are you going to get a sample of that?" Ian might take offence, but he figured the guy probably knew a thing or two about strategic silence.

"And do what? Spend time and resources looking for someone because they *might* have committed a crime? Maybe it was just an oblivious driver."

At Ian's almost flippant tone, David straightened and fixed him with a glare. "I hear your wife and Dr. Buckley at the lab in Albany are good friends. I'm sure he wouldn't mind doing it as a favor to her. Seeing as how you're all friends and everything."

Ian's lips lifted into a smile and David knew he'd been "had," if only subtly so. The sheriff knew exactly how David felt about Jesse.

"I've already got a sample and a complete set of pictures on the way up to the lab. Knowing Sam, he'll probably have something for us tomorrow or the day after," Ian answered with a knowing grin.

David gave a snort. "Anyone ever tell you you're kind of a bastard?"

Ian shrugged and his grin widened. "Devious maybe, but not usually a bastard."

"Yeah, that fits, too," he said. But Ian was good people. So far, David hadn't met anyone in Jesse's life that wasn't.

The thought of her brought his gaze back around to the car. He frowned.

"What are you thinking, Hathaway?" Ian asked.

Not taking his eyes from the car, David answered with his own questions. "Does Jesse have any enemies? People who don't like her? An ex-boyfriend, maybe? Or even any patients who've felt they didn't get the care they should have?"

When Ian didn't answer immediately, David turned his way. The sheriff stood steady, feet apart, arms crossed over his chest, and stared at him with his unusual, light green eyes.

"No," Ian drew out. "Not that I know of. She's a regular mom with two good kids. There are people she is close with and those she isn't, but as far as I know, no one really dislikes her or has a reason to consider her an enemy. I don't think she's dated anyone since Mark died, and as for the hospital, I wouldn't know. She's never mentioned anything and definitely never reported anything to me, but it's possible that even if she'd received a threat I wouldn't have heard about it. She's compassionate by nature so she'd be more likely to try to make things better for the person who'd sent the threat than turn it over to the authorities."

David grunted. "Yeah, that's what I thought." He turned his gaze to the clearing clouds and tried to calm the turmoil building inside him.

"What *else* are you thinking?" Ian demanded.

"I'm thinking we might need to have a little chat with her," he answered as he watched a hawk soar above them.

"About?"

David lowered his eyes to meet Ian's gaze. "About why she's been the victim of three violent attacks in less than two weeks."

Ian stared at him. Hard. But in his gut, David knew there was something wrong, something involving Jesse, so he met the man's scrutiny and didn't back down.

"Explain." It was the most authoritarian David had heard Ian's voice.

"Her tires last week, the explosion at Spin-A-Yarn, and this," he said, gesturing with his head to her totaled car.

"Her tires could have been some kid. Spin-A-Yarn isn't even her shop, how would someone know she'd be there? And as for this, it could have just been an accident." Ian shifted his arms and jammed his hands onto hips.

David took a deep breath. The air was still damp with the rain and he could smell the wet asphalt and fresh-cut grass in the field beside them.

"If it were kids, why two tires and not just one? Someone had to be pretty confident they could slice two tires without getting caught. A nervous kid doesn't really fit that bill, unless you have some regular delinquents in Windsor?" He didn't wait for Ian to answer before continuing. "As for the explosion. Jesse was supposed to be there. She'd made an appointment with Julie to meet her there at ten. Even *I* knew about it. She was making the appointment on the phone when she met me at the hospital last week. If she hadn't been running late, both she and Julie probably would have been standing right at the cash register when the device went off. And finally," he held up a hand when Ian opened his mouth. "This. You know as well as I do that this was no accident. That's why you sent evidence up to the lab."

Ian gave him another long, hard look. "She was supposed to be at Spin-A-Yarn?"

David nodded. "At ten, to pick up a quilt for her parents' anniversary. I heard her on the phone—who knows who else might have heard or who else she might have mentioned it to?"

He could tell Ian was thinking, putting the pieces together. The sheriff's eyes strayed to the field, but he was looking into the middle distance, his mind clearly focused on this new information.

Finally, Ian shoved a hand through his hair and dropped his head. "Shit."

"Yeah, my thoughts exactly."

Crossing his arms again, Ian remained silent for a while. Finally he spoke. "I think Vivienne should talk to her." That seemed like passing the buck to David and he said so.

"It isn't though," Ian insisted. "I know you know Vivienne is an ME—"

"And an FBI consultant," David interjected.

Ian nodded and continued. "She is, and while she prefers to work cold cases, she also does a lot of work with the behavioral science unit."

"Profilers?"

"Yeah. I know, not my favorite either, but Vivienne is good. Really good." From the tone of his voice, he couldn't tell whether Ian thought this was a good thing or not. "Anyway, if she talked to Jesse, Vivienne would probably see things—hear things—we wouldn't."

"But why not tell her now and then have your wife talk to her this afternoon?" He didn't want Jesse going about her daily life with no idea that maybe, just maybe, she needed to be more vigilant.

"Because I don't want to scare her." Ian held up a hand to ward off the protest on David's lips. "Look, I know you think something is probably going on here. And I have to admit, when you string it all together, I don't like the looks of it either. But we don't really have any proof that someone is targeting her, or even any reason why they might be. Are you free for an hour or so?" Ian ended his reasoning with the question.

David nodded.

"Good. Stick with her. Vivienne will be back from Boston in about an hour. I'm sure she'll be more than interested in heading straight over to talk with Jesse."

"And what about tonight or tomorrow?" David asked.

"Nothing has happened at her home. It's all been in other places. She has an alarm and her farm is in my jurisdiction so I can be sure to have someone nearby until we have a better sense of what's going on. Or even *if* something is going on," he added.

David thought about Ian's plan, and though he didn't like it, though he would have rather taken Jesse and tucked her away at his place, it made some sense. Not to mention the fact that, instinctively, he knew she wouldn't allow herself to be coddled anyway. He didn't think she'd take unnecessary risks, but she wasn't a shrinking violet. Still...

"She may be tiny, but she's tough, Hathaway."

He looked at Ian, whose expression bore something akin to sympathy. David nodded.

"Let's go, then," Ian said and together they headed back up the embankment.

Jesse was now perched on the fender of David's truck, the paramedics having left while he and Ian were talking.

"I'm not sure if I need to call a tow truck or what the standard operating procedure here is," she said to Ian as they approached.

Ian waved his hand. "I took care of it. Richie should be here soon. He's got the equipment to pull it out of the ditch and he's a good mechanic. He'll be able to work with your insurance to sort things out."

"Thanks." Her voice was soft but strong and she looked like she was coming back to herself more and more with each minute.

"You have the afternoon off, right?" David asked, remembering what she'd told him earlier.

She nodded. "Yes, I do. Thankfully. But the track team is headed up to Ithaca tonight for an off-season weekend track meet. They're taking the bus there, but I told the boys I'd come by the school to see them off before they leave at three thirty." She looked at her watch, then back at both David and Ian.

"I'll take you," David stated more than offered.

"Are you sure it's not a problem?"

He hated how tentative she sounded asking him for help. "No, it's not a problem."

She drew back a bit and he realized just how sharp his voice sounded. "I start a three-day shift tonight but I don't have to be in for four hours. I was going to take the back roads on my way north anyway, a stop at the school will be right on the way." His attempt to soften the edginess he felt seemed to work, and she offered him a smile.

"Thank you, I would appreciate it."

"No problem. I can take you home afterward, too."

She shook her head. "I can grab Matt's keys from him and drive his car while he's away. After that, I'll get Wanda out. It's been awhile since I've driven her, but she runs."

"Wanda?" David asked. Ian looked interested, too.

"My husband's '68 Shelby. It took him ten years to restore her. The boys and I decided not to sell her after he died, even though we hardly ever drive her."

For the first time in several hours, a smile played on David's lips. The image of her in that car was striking. She'd look like Cybill Shepherd from *American Graffiti*.

"Why don't you guys head out so you can catch the boys and have some time to reassure them that you're all right. I'll finish up here and Vivienne will probably stop by later this afternoon," Ian suggested.

David started ushering Jesse toward the passenger door of his truck but she paused in front of Ian. "Vivi doesn't need to come see me, Ian. I'm fine. She should stay home and rest."

"Probably, but it will be a lot harder for me if I don't tell her what happened and she finds out tomorrow. So if you could just humor me, I would appreciate it."

She laughed. "Whatever you say, Sheriff. And thanks for your help." She went up on tiptoe and gave him a kiss on the cheek.

"Anytime, you just need to take care of yourself. Drive safe and call me if you need anything. Otherwise, we'll be in touch when I have more information and I'll make sure Richie calls you about the car."

Jesse nodded and climbed into the truck. David shut the door behind her and motioned for Ian to walk with him as he rounded the vehicle.

"I'd start at the hospital, if I were you," David suggested. "It's the most likely place someone might have a bone to pick. Her assistant can help you, I'm sure."

Ian gave a small nod. "I'll do that, but not until after Vivienne talks to her. I'm not going to go behind her back or frightened her staff. Jesse is a reasonable woman and expects to be treated as one. Over the years, I've learned it's easier to accommodate that and deal with my own anxiety than try to keep anything from them, 'cause it always bites you on the ass in the long run."

He raised an eyebrow. "Voice of experience?"

"Maybe a time or two. But it didn't take long to learn that lesson." Ian grinned.

Nodding his agreement, David climbed into his truck. As he shut the door, fastened his seat belt, and turned his key in the ignition, he watched Ian raise a hand up in a subtle wave, then turn and walk toward his own truck. His gaze turned to Jesse, only to find her rubbing her neck and temples—any moment of light-heartedness he'd just been feeling vanished immediately. Without a word, he pulled out onto the road and headed toward Riverside. From there he'd take a local route north to Windsor.

"Are you okay?" she asked.

He blinked. "Am *I* okay? Of course, *I'm* okay. Are you?"

She sighed. "I'm fine. A little sore. I'll be even more sore tomorrow. A lot more sore than I was last weekend."

"You *have* managed to take a few beatings this week." He managed to sound reasonable, he was pretty sure.

"Yes, my life isn't usually so…"

He wasn't sure if he would be able to keep himself from exploding if she said "exciting." There was nothing "exciting" about what was happening to her.

"Intense," she finished. He forced his fingers to relax on the steering wheel. "Thank you, again, for taking me back to Windsor," she added, her voice quiet.

"It's not a problem." Okay, maybe he hadn't been so good that time around. He glanced over at her and she was watching him. With a *look*. He knew that look. He'd used it often on Miranda. When she was fourteen.

He took a deep breath and let it out slowly. "I'm sorry, I didn't mean to snap. It's just that the thought of someone almost running you off the road has set me a little on edge. I see the worst of the worst in my job—like you, I bet—and sometimes it's hard to keep my mind from going to all those places. All those 'what if' and 'could have' places."

He afforded another look at her as he pulled through the center of Riverside and started to head north. Her expression was almost unreadable, but he was pretty sure he detected a hint of understanding in her eyes. And then she turned and looked out the passenger window.

"Yeah, me too. I'm trying not to think about it, actually.

Trying really hard. So, if you don't mind, maybe we can talk about something else? Didn't you come by my office earlier to update me on the fire at Julie's?"

He wasn't sure this topic would make her feel any better, but at least it was a few days, rather than a few hours, in the past. "I did. I stopped by and met with Julie this morning before I came down to the hospital. The device was fairly crude, a simple canister of propane and a basic timing device. Thankfully, the checkout counter was sturdier than the bomb maker anticipated because the canister was a good size and the timing device, though not sophisticated, worked perfectly."

"Meaning?"

"Meaning the explosive did what it was supposed to do. Sometimes, when we see crude explosives like that, we hope it was a fluke or that we'll find some indication that the maker just got lucky. But whoever left it in Spin-A-Yarn was meticulous about their workmanship, even if it was an elementary device."

"I watch all those crime shows and I'm sure they are about as unrealistic as the hospital shows, but they always talk about bombers having signatures. Is that true?" she asked.

"To an extent, yes. If you have a serial arsonist or an explosives expert, you do tend to see patterns. But with the device we collected from the shop, we've determined that the design came off a website."

"Kind of like buying ready-to-wear rather than couture?"

He smiled. "If that means what I think it means, then yes. It will be harder to tell it apart from other devices that might have been based on the same instructions."

He slowed for a light that had only just turned green and when the car in front of him picked up speed, he accelerated too, being sure to keep a good distance between him and all the other drivers. Jesse didn't look too gun shy, but it would be hard not to be after having just been through what she'd been through.

"So, what about other evidence?" she asked.

He wagged his head. "Our preliminary tests came back inconclusive. We know we don't have any prints or shoe marks or anything like that on or around the building structure. Not even on the pieces of the broken window we collected. But we're still running some tests on the device itself. Given the state it was in, it's not as straight-forward as printing from a sheet of glass or a door knob."

"No, I don't suppose it is. So, what do you do now?"

"Now, we wait for the second round of tests to come back and then we'll probably do a third. No one was hurt, but you can be sure that everyone from the state commissioner on down wants to know exactly what happened so that we can rule out terrorism. A bomb going off in small-town America is the perfect way to conduct psychological warfare. Thankfully, the people of Windsor don't seem to be panicking."

He could feel her eyes snap to him in shock and he wished he hadn't added that last little bit. Just because he and his teammates had to think that way every time they discovered that an explosive was used in a fire didn't mean everyone else should.

"You don't really think it was an act of terrorism, do you?" she asked.

He gave a curt, adamant shake of his head. "I do not think it was an act of terrorism in the sense you're thinking. I do think that any time someone detonates or threatens to detonate an explosive device it is *a* form of terrorism. But not like 9/11 or the bombings in London or Madrid."

"So, what *do* you think?" She sounded like she wasn't sure whether to believe him or not.

"I think it was someone who very deliberately picked *that* shop and *that* time to set off a bomb. I think we'll find it has something to do with Julie or the people around her. It feels very targeted to me and not part of a larger political statement."

"So then, if they didn't succeed at whatever they were trying to do, do you think we'll see more?"

Now *that* was the million-dollar question. He wanted to say no, but given that someone had very nearly just run Jesse off the road, he couldn't make that statement.

"I sure as hell hope not."

CHAPTER 9

J̲ESSE CURLED UP IN HER favorite rocking chair and sipped a glass of wine. Matt and James were off to Ithaca and the night was, hopefully, going to be a quiet one. The boys had both wanted to stay home with her when she'd told them what had happened, and truth be told, she wouldn't have minded the company, but this was the last meet of the year. It wasn't meaningful from a rankings standpoint, and Matt already had his scholarship locked up, but it was a fun one and one the kids enjoyed every year, so she'd sent them on their way.

Looking at her watch, she decided that she didn't have the time for a quick walk before Vivi arrived. As Ian had predicted, Vivi had called her only minutes after she'd heard about the accident from Ian. At first, she'd tried to get Vivi to stay home, put her feet up, and relax—not only was her friend pregnant, but she'd just spent the last few days in Boston teaching. But now that Vivi was on her way, Jesse was kind of glad that she was coming. It was quiet at home, which was a good thing, but for the first time in a long time, it felt kind of lonely. Even the sound of her phone vibrating beside her, as soft as it was, startled her.

She picked it up, looked at the number, and smiled. A girlie feeling of happiness crept into her chest.

"Hello?"

"How are you?" David's voice sounded gruff, but not gruff in an unpleasant way.

"I'm fine. Sitting on my porch having a glass of wine while I wait for Vivi. Thinking maybe I should get a dog when Matt goes to college." She hadn't really been thinking about getting a dog, but maybe she should.

"Do you ever wear your hair down?"

That caught her off guard. "Huh?"

"Your hair, it's always up. Do you ever wear it down?"

She smiled to herself again. He'd been thinking about her—and not just about her as a victim of an accident or the explosion at Spin-A-Yarn, but her as a woman.

"Sometimes, for special occasions."

"Like what?"

"Weddings, charity events, things I have to dress up for."

"Hmmm," was his only response.

"I've thought about cutting it," she added.

"Don't," he cut her off.

"But I have that kind of hair that's not wavy enough to be cute or straight enough to be easily managed. And since time is such a hot commodity as a working parent, I just leave it long and pull it back."

"Huh."

"Is that why you called?" Her voice was teasing but she was secretly kind of pleased. It had been a long time since a man had been this forward in his interest. Usually, when men found out that she was a widow, they became overly respectful. And usually that was fine because she had no interest in them anyway; it actually made things easier. David had been overly respectful when she'd first told him about her husband that day in her office. But she was very glad to hear he was moving through it.

"Yeah, sort of," he answered. The hint of embarrassment she heard in his voice was kind of cute. "I just pulled up to the station. I'm on shift until Monday night, but I'll keep in touch," he said.

"Okay. You know where to find me."

"Stay safe, Jesse." The fierceness of his voice was offset by the tinge of tenderness she also heard.

"I'm always safe, David. It's the people around me that seem to be causing the chaos."

He made an indecipherable sound. In agreement, she assumed.

"You do the same, David." They disconnected and, for the first time, she thought—really though—about his job. She knew him as the investigator, but he was also a man that ran *into* fires, not away from them, for a living. The thought sat uneasily in her stomach. But if this thing between them went anywhere, it was something she would have to get used to. With another sip of wine, she opted to push that thought aside for the time being. Yes, she was worried about him. But at this point, there was no sense in worrying how she might handle the dangers of his job if they were ever in a relationship of any sort.

As if to make changing her mindset easier, she heard the wheels of Vivi's car on her gravel drive and soon saw the car itself pulling up to the house. Walking to the driveway, she arrived just in time to watch Vivi haul herself out of the car. Smiling, Jesse remembered how cumbersome she'd felt at that stage in her pregnancies.

Vivi caught her eye and laughed. "I know. It's like I'm suddenly pregnant. I don't think I showed much for the first several months and now I'm starting to feel a bit blimpish." She got herself upright and closed her car door. "How are you?"

"I'm fine," Jesse answered. "And you don't look blimpish by any stretch. But you do look considerably more pregnant than you did five weeks ago. Want to go inside and I can get you something to drink?"

Vivi shook her head. "If you're up for it, I'd rather take a short walk first. I've been sitting all day between department meetings and driving."

Not one to deny a pregnant lady, Jesse agreed. After taking her wine glass inside and slipping on a pair of shoes, she joined Vivi and the two headed for the trail that looped around the perimeter of her property. Years ago, when Matt had first gotten into running, Mark had created the tractor-width path as a place for him to train. Since they lived on a road that had no sidewalk or even much shoulder to speak of, it had been a great idea. Even now, the boys still used it to train and she used it when she wanted to go for a walk but not deal with the cars, few and far between though they were.

"So how are you really?" Vivi asked as they headed up the hill toward the back end of her land.

"I'm really okay. I still have a little bit of a headache, but I took a couple of ibuprofen and will take some more before bed. I'm sure I'll be sore tomorrow, but this walk will probably do me some good."

"You should book yourself a massage tomorrow."

"Already done," Jesse grinned at her friend. "And a pedicure."

"That's my girl," Vivi said with a laugh. "So, Ian told me what happened. Do you want to talk about it at all?"

Jesse thought about it for a minute. "There's not really much to talk about. I saw the SUV behind me, but didn't think anything of it until it was beside me. Then, everything happened so fast—I'm sure Ian got more information from the folks who stopped to help than he got from me."

"Did you see anything in the SUV? Did you get a glance at the driver?"

Even though Ian had asked her these same questions earlier, she knew she was in a better frame of mind now than she had been then, so she gave it some thought.

After a moment, she shook her head. "Honestly? I didn't see much. The windows seemed darker than mine, not tinted *really* dark, but maybe just a little bit. The driver was small and he was wearing a red baseball cap. When he was behind me, he was short enough that I couldn't really see him and when he was beside me, the truck was so much taller than my car, all I could see at that point was the top of the baseball cap."

"You keep saying 'he.' Do you think it was a man driving?"

Jesse wagged her head from side to side. "No, I'm not really sure. I just said that because most of the time around here it's men who seem to drive those big SUVs. And while I know plenty of women who drive them too, I'd say the majority are probably men.

But other than that, no, there's no reason why I called the driver a 'he.'"

They walked in silence for a few minutes. Beside her, Vivi took very deliberate steps, her head down in thought. In fact, she looked to be thinking quite a bit.

"Care to tell me what's on your mind, Doctor?"

Vivi glanced up, then looked chagrined. "Ian wants me to ask you about a few things."

Jesse frowned. "Okay. But I'm not sure what to think when Ian sends you on an errand. It's either some girlie questions that he's too uncomfortable to ask or something sensitive that he's worried about screwing up."

Vivi smiled at this assessment of her husband. "Definitely the latter."

She took a deep breath. "Okay, lay it on me."

"How have things been at work?"

That wasn't quite what she'd expected and Jesse looked at her friend in surprise.

"Fine. You know, the usual stuff—budget issues, godlike surgeons, and the nurses' union. But nothing out of the ordinary. Why do you ask?"

"Because Ian is concerned that there might be a pattern developing."

Jesse paused at the top of the hill under the guise of thinking about what Vivi was saying, but she also wanted to give her pregnant friend a little rest.

"Pattern?" she asked as she looked back down on her house. She loved this view of her property, her little farmhouse with the big chimney, the old barn, which had been Mark's former office, to the left. She could even see a hint of the pond.

"There have been three incidents in the last two weeks that have directly involved you. Your tires, Spin-A-Yarn, and what happened this afternoon. When I found out you were supposed to be at the quilt shop last weekend, I have to say, it made me a little concerned, too. You didn't mention to Ian that you'd had an appointment with Julie that morning. He's not very happy about that." When Vivi was done speaking, she cast Jesse a worried look then gestured her onward across the back part of the property.

"I didn't really think about it, and how did you find out anyway?" Jesse commented as they began to walk again.

"David might have mentioned something to Ian."

"Might have?"

Vivi inclined her head. "Did. He seemed very concerned. He was the one who brought it to Ian's attention in the first place. Since Ian didn't know about your appointment, he hadn't made any connections. But when David suggested he look into it? Well, let's just say Ian isn't all that happy about it."

"It wasn't something I intentionally kept secret. Obviously not, since David knew and anyone else I might have mentioned it to."

"We'll get to that part later. But back to my original question. Have you received any letters or phone calls at work from people unhappy with you or the hospital?"

Jesse had to laugh at that. "Yeah, all the time. I don't actually see most of them. They go to our internal patient care review team. They do read them all, and if a letter warrants, they'll look into the sender's complaint and we have a whole process in place for handling it. If the team finds a complaint that might pose a high risk to the hospital or other patients, they'll bring it to me and we'll do a full scale investigation."

"And have you seen any of those kind of letters in the past six months or so?"

"Maybe two or three. But they were specific to a physician or nurse. Nothing that blasted the hospital in general."

"Still, would it be possible to get a look at those letters?"

Jesse wanted to say "Yes, of course." But the reality was that some of those letters contained confidential information. They wouldn't be considered protected health information, which was protected by federal law, but she didn't want to run afoul of any other privacy laws that might be implicated by the letters.

"I don't have an objection, especially since you're doing it because you seem to think someone might be out to harm me, but I'll have to check with our lawyers. If we can legally give them to you, or Ian, really, we will. But if we need a warrant, I'm going to have to require one. I hate to be a stickler, but I don't want to put the hospital at risk of a lawsuit or anything like that."

Thankfully, being a professor and a consultant with the government, Vivi knew a thing or two about privacy and the law, so she nodded.

"Thanks, now let's also talk about who might have known your movements so Ian can also start with that line of inquiry. Who knew you would be at the track meet?"

"Only every parent of every other kid on the track team. We're all at the home meets almost all of the time. And then there are the kids, and anyone at work who knows the boys run. And those at work who do know the boys run often ask about upcoming meets, so anyone who might have overheard those conversations would know," she answered in a sardonic tone, knowing full well her response wouldn't help.

"That narrows it down."

Jesse could understand Vivi's sarcasm, but it made her smile. Life wasn't as clean as they liked to make it appear in the movies and there was no way she would be able to identify anyone who might have looked out of place eavesdropping on her conversations.

"So how about Spin-A-Yarn? Who knew you'd be there?" Vivi asked.

"I obviously don't know everyone who knew I'd be there, but the boys knew, Danielle Martinez knew, most of my friends at the hospital, including my assistant, Kayla. I was talking on the phone to Julie when I saw David, which is how he knew."

"So again, anyone might have overheard you?"

Jesse inclined her head.

"What about this afternoon? Who knew you'd be on that road?"

"Kayla, because she knows everything about my schedule.

Again, the boys knew because I was making some dinners to freeze and take down to Carl and Angie. I had to buy some extra containers and had a little chat with Josie at the Extra Mart. And again, a lot of folks at the hospital. As you know, Carl was my predecessor. He still has a lot of friends there so folks dropped off a number of cards and small gifts for me to take, knowing I was going over there. And then again, David knew because he helped me carry the stuff out to the car."

They'd come back down the hill and were now adjacent to the house on the opposite side from where they started. They could continue on and loop down the front part of the property line, but Jesse was starting to feel a little sore. And maybe a touch nervous.

"You up for a drink? I have some tonic water, decaf tea, and a bunch of other stuff," she asked with a gesture toward the house.

"I would love some tea. The days are generally warm now, but it's still a bit chilly in the evenings."

They made their way inside, and Vivi sat at the breakfast bar while Jesse put the kettle on and laid out some teas for her friend to choose from. When Jesse slid onto a stool beside her, Vivi looked up.

"So, maybe I should be a little more vigilant about using my alarm?" Jesse asked. "I was also just considering getting a dog. I was sitting outside and realized that in a few months Matt will be gone and James won't be far behind. A dog might be nice."

Vivi snorted. "You can have Rooster."

"You love Rooster."

"Yeah, we do. But I had to get up early to drive into Boston yesterday, and Ian was trying to sleep in because he'd been up on a night call. Rooster, who has been even weirder than usual since the pregnancy, regressed into his puppy days and started howling at me. I couldn't get him to shut up."

Rooster was by far the goofiest-looking dog Jesse had ever seen. His fur was gray and wooly, his eyes were the color of a wolf's, and his ears were these enormous things that stuck straight out to the sides. And more often than not, his tongue was sticking out.

"What did you do?"

"The only thing that would shut him up was to put him in bed with Ian."

Both women were laughing now.

"I bet Ian loved that."

"I didn't stick around to see the show. I skedaddled as fast as I could. Before either could protest anymore."

Jesse was laughing when she got up and poured Vivi's mug of hot water. Even though *she* wasn't looking for wedded bliss, she couldn't be happier for her two friends. As she came back to her seat, her phone vibrated on the counter. Looking at the number, she was grateful it wasn't David again. But the fact that Ian was calling her and not Vivi was curious. She hit speaker.

"Hi Ian."

"Is my wife there?"

Jesse glanced at Vivi.

"Yes, I'm here," Vivi answered

They could hear him let out a deep breath. "I've been calling you. Where is your phone?"

Vivi looked around like she might find it on the counter, then felt her pockets. "Oh, I must have left it in the car. Sorry."

"But you're fine?"

"We're both fine, thank you," Vivi answered smoothly. "We just went for a little walk and had a little chat about who might be doing some of these things that have happened."

"Any thoughts, Jesse?" Ian asked.

"No, Vivi can fill you in. But my life really isn't all that exciting. I have no idea who might be doing these things, or even if they are actually related. I have a hard time believing your suspicions, but I'm also not interested in being the proverbial virgin in a horror movie flick. I'm taking you all seriously, even if I'm not sure what to really think about it."

"Good," he grunted.

"Have you eaten dinner yet, Ian?" Vivi asked. When he said no, she turned to Jesse. "Do you have plans, Jesse?"

She shook her head.

"Ian, why don't you stop by Station Pizza and bring some food up here. We can hang out for a while, eat, catch up. It's been a while since we've had the chance," Vivi suggested.

Jesse wasn't fooled. She knew her friend was trying to make this easier by not leaving her alone to think about all the things that go bump in the night. She could have said no, but it was also true that she hadn't had a lot of time to catch up with her friends lately. The end of the school year was always crazy.

"Jesse?" Ian asked.

"If you don't mind sharing your wife after she's been gone for a few days, I would love it."

"It's a plan. I'll get the usual and be up in about an hour?"

They agreed and hung up.

"It's a plan?" Jesse repeated with a smile, making Vivi laugh.

"I know, Ian always has a plan."

CHAPTER 10

THE NEXT MORNING, JESSE TAPPED an old, familiar business card on the kitchen counter and stared at her phone. The thought that she was overreacting had crossed her mind about a thousand times. But so had the thought that if she didn't do this, she could end up regretting it later. With a sigh, she grabbed her phone and dialed the number on the card.

"Wilton Dillard."

"Wilton, it's Jesse Baker, Mark Baker's wife—widow," she corrected.

"Jesse! How are you? I haven't heard from you in, well, a while."

She smiled at that. Her lawyer was too professional to say, "since Mark died."

"Yes, it has been a while. That's why I wanted to call. I haven't updated my will or taken a look at the trust since Mark died. I was thinking that maybe we should meet to make sure everything is still in order."

She knew this was the right thing to do. Whether someone was actually after her or not, it was something she needed to do for her kids' sake, something she'd been meaning to do for a while but had just never gotten around to. Only, doing it now made her feel like she was tempting fate.

"Yes, yes, of course. When would you like to come in? I can meet you tomorrow?"

Leave it to Wilton to meet with her on a weekend. He was in his late sixties, still sharp, and had lost his wife almost ten years earlier. Jesse was pretty sure he went to his office every day just to give himself something to do. She was also pretty sure he didn't have enough business to keep him all that busy, with Windsor not being that big of a town. But she could picture him there at his desk—reading the paper, maybe flipping through law journals.

"This weekend isn't good. The boys get home tomorrow afternoon and I'll want to go through some of my paperwork first. How about Monday morning? Say nine thirty?"

"Nine thirty it is." He didn't even hesitate. "I have copies of the will documents here, but why don't you bring what you have as well as a list of your accounts, insurance, things like that, and we can make sure everything is taken care of?"

She agreed and ended the call, still wondering if she was overreacting. The good news was, no one would need to know and she could overreact in private.

Glancing at the clock, she decided to head to Stockbridge early and grab some tea before her massage. Not surprisingly, she was much more sore than she'd been the day before. Pretty much every muscle in her body ached, and her neck was so stiff it was giving her a headache. It wasn't anything she hadn't expected, but it still sucked.

She paused, picking up her purse as her phone rang. She looked at the number then answered.

"Hi, Matty."

"Dash ran into Vivi this morning and she told him what happened yesterday. Are you okay?" Matty's words came quickly, without so much as a hello.

"Sore, but okay. I'm on my way out to get a massage now," Jesse answered.

"Good, I hope you get two. Come to dinner tonight, it will just be us and it will get you out and moving. I know that probably doesn't sound all that appealing right now, but moving around will help."

"I know it will, but tonight doesn't work." She needed to get the paperwork in order for her visit to Wilton's office on Monday. And she wanted to do it before the boys got home.

"Then brunch tomorrow," Matty insisted. "Kit is coming over and might bring Caleb, her brother, if he bothers to show up—her words not mine. Although, to hear her talk of him, brunch might be too civilized."

The mention of Kit brought back the memory of their conversation last week. "Did you know she was thinking about setting me up with him?" Jesse laughed, still in disbelief. Matty hooted.

"That would be interesting. I'm picturing a male version of Kit, and if he's that, he's probably a good fifteen inches taller than you. Hmm, I'd almost like to see that. You know, if I were a voyeur, of course."

Jesse laughed even harder. "I know! That's what I said to her. We wouldn't fit. Honestly, I don't know what she was thinking."

"Given that she seems ambivalent about him herself, I'm not sure what she was thinking either. So, will you? Come to brunch?"

In a flash, Jesse ran through everything she needed to get done to prepare for the coming week—from pulling things together for Wilton to getting some work done Sunday to make up for the hours she would miss in the office Monday morning. It would be tight, but she thought she could do it all without too much headache.

"Yeah, I'll be there. What can I bring?"

"Nothing but yourself, you have enough going on right now. We'll take care of it all and if you do bring something, I'll retaliate and seat you beside Kit's brother. If he comes," Matty added.

It was hard to imagine that with her life, her friends, her kids, and her job, there would be someone out there that could hate her enough to want to hurt her. It really just didn't make sense.

But still, that didn't mean she was going to take Vivi and Ian's opinions lightly.

• • •

David pulled his phone from his locker and looked at the time. It was nine a.m. on a Sunday. He wondered if Jesse was up. She was a parent, so he'd guess that she'd lost the ability to sleep past eight or eight thirty once the first baby had come along. On a whim, he jogged down the stairs and stepped outside with his phone. He needed to shower and change—he smelled like smoke—but he found he wanted to talk to her first. He'd spoken to Ian late last night and had heard the tone of growing suspicion in the sheriff's voice. And now, well, he just wanted to know she was okay.

"Hello?" Her voice was heavy with sleep. He could hear sheets rustling, like she was rolling over in bed. His body reacted with a jolt at the thought of her in bed and it crossed his mind that maybe he shouldn't have called.

"So this is what you sound like when you're sleepy. I didn't wake you, did I?"

It took a second for her to respond, if she hadn't checked the number before she'd answered she was probably still sorting out who he was.

"Good morning, David." He could hear the smile in her voice. "Yes, this is what it sounds like when I'm sleepy, but no, you didn't wake me. I've been lying here for about thirty minutes just enjoying the coziness of it all."

Listening to her voice just then, he suddenly *really* understood the appeal of phone sex.

He cleared his throat. "How are you feeling?"

"Better than yesterday, that's for sure. I had a massage."

He'd just been imagining her in bed and now he had to picture her on a massage table? *Sheer torture*, he thought.

"And went for a nice walk." She continued. "I'm still sore, but definitely on the mend. How are you?"

"We just got in from a call. No one was hurt and everyone got out of the apartment building, so I'm doing fine. So, did, uh…" He didn't want to kill this easy sense of intimacy, but he needed to know she was being careful.

"Did Vivi and Ian talk to me? Yes, they did. Vivi came over

after I got home the other day and then Ian ended up coming over and joining us for dinner. We talked through a couple of scenarios, and while I'm not dumb enough to discount the intuition of three investigators, it all seems so unreal."

He could understand that. In fact it didn't make much sense to him either. She seemed to lead the life of a normal working mom. Not the kind of life that attracted violent people. But even so, his gut told him there was something to it.

"I'm sure it does. Did you guys talk about the possibility of it being someone associated with the hospital?" He heard her moving around more in the sheets and even the topic of conversation couldn't keep his mind from going where it wanted to.

"Yes, we did. I'm happy to have Ian look at the letters we've received, but I'll have to clear it through our lawyers on Monday first. He also wants to be able to talk to some of the nurses and doctors to see if there was anyone that was particularly unhappy or upset recently that might *not* have sent a letter, so we'll make sure to get everything in place for him to do that, too."

"Lawyers?" He knew all about legal procedure from his work, but having it applied in a way that slowed down an investigation meant to protect Jesse, well, it pissed him off.

"I know, can't live without 'em, can't kill 'em."

He chuckled. "So what are your plans for the rest of the day? When are the boys home?"

"They'll be home around one. I'm headed over to see my friends, Matty and Dash—they invited me to brunch at their place with our friend, Kit and maybe her brother, too. It's not clear whether he is going to be in town or not, but I hope so since we're all kind of dying to meet him. Kit holds things very close to the vest and seems to have a love/hate thing going on with him so it could be interesting."

Jealousy reared its ugly head for a moment and while he wanted to say, "have fun," he couldn't quite bring himself to.

"Well, at the very least, it might be interesting," he managed to say.

"If he shows up. We're not sure he will. But even if he doesn't, it will be good to see Matty, Dash, and Kit. And Matty is a phenomenal cook, so I'll be well fed, too."

"Sounds nice. I'm about to go in and rummage up some scrambled eggs and toast."

"Hmm, sounds good. I hope you at least get some coffee with that gruel?"

He chuckled. "Yes, lots of it." He paused and then in a rush went on. "Any chance you're free for dinner this week? I'm open after Monday night, but back on shift Friday night."

"Oh," she said.

He knew a "no" was coming, but at least he could hear what sounded like real regret in her voice.

"I wish I could. But this is the last week of school for the boys, and with Matt graduating next weekend, we have a ton of events and parties over the week."

"That's okay, believe me, that's something I understand." And he did. It had been an amazing time when Miranda had graduated the year before. Something he didn't want Jesse to miss a minute of.

"But the boys both go away the week after. James is headed into Boston for a math camp and Matt is headed down to, of all places, the Jersey Shore for an extended senior week. Maybe sometime that week?"

He smiled to himself. "Yeah, that would be great."

They said their good-byes and David slipped his phone back into his pocket. Turning to head back into the station he almost walked into Dominic, one of his teammates.

"Who was that?"

The question was nosy, but Dominic was a nosy guy. Not out of malice by any stretch, and he could keep a secret like no man's business, but being the youngest of seven, nosiness came with the territory for a guy like Dominic.

"Nothing," David answered, walking toward the station door.

"Really?" Dominic grinned. "'Cause it didn't sound like

nothing. It sounded like you were asking someone out? I'm like a brother to you, you know you wanna share the details."

"Yeah, we're one big happy family here. But everyone has their secrets, right, Dominic?" They actually kind of were like a family, one big obnoxious, teasing family.

A look of surprise flashed across Dominic's face, then he grinned to cover it up. "I don't know what you're talking about, Hathaway."

"Oh yeah? Does red hair, about yea tall," he held up a hand to the height of Dominic's shoulder, "ring a bell? Cute as a button."

"Sorry," he said, following David in. "Still don't know what you're talking about."

"I saw you two cuddled up at Maggie's last Thursday. She was wearing a wedding ring, and since you're not married, I'd say we all have our little secrets."

"Shit." Dominic actually went a little pale, making David feel a bit sorry for him.

"Look, Dominic, I'm not going to tell anyone, and while I don't condone it—at all—you're a grown man, it's your decision."

"Her husband is a bastard."

"They always are, Dominic." He had heard similar stories before, even been suckered by them a time or two.

"Meaning?" Dominic asked.

"Meaning nothing. You'll figure it all out yourself." And David walked away. Leaving Dominic standing there looking concerned, like maybe he was missing something he shouldn't be.

Maybe the woman's husband really was a bastard, but David would wager he was probably just neglectful and the wife was hoping to shake things up a bit. The fact that she hadn't bothered to take off her wedding band or diamond had tipped him off. And after all his years on the job, he could spot a firefighter groupie before she even *thought* of giving him a come-hither look. Who knew? Maybe Dominic's date was telling the truth; maybe she wasn't using him. But he wouldn't bet on it.

Still, the conversation brought home one of the things he

didn't like about his job. He didn't like everyone being up in his business all the time. It wasn't that he had anything to hide, but those first few years on the job when he'd been a single, twenty-two-year-old dad with a four-year-old daughter, he'd endured a lot of ribbing and teasing from his teammates in California. Good-natured ribbing, mostly. And his team had eventually become like family to Miranda, but it had been a lot for him to deal with at such a young age. There were times when he just wanted to leave his private life at home. Not have it dragged out into the open.

Over the years, when he'd dated on and off, the teasing never got to him too much because there was never anyone serious. Not that he was thinking that he and Jesse had something serious going on now, he just felt the need to keep it to himself. He didn't want his teammates asking about her or demanding details from him. He didn't want to do that this time, not with her.

So, stepping into a hot shower, he made a decision. He'd do everything in his power to keep whatever was developing between him and Jesse private. And if that meant not talking to her when he was on duty, then so be it. It felt a little draconian, but he knew in his gut that it would make things easier. Not that it was all about him, but he just didn't want to have to endure all the talk; he wanted to be able to enjoy getting to know her and not have to explain everything to everyone in the station. He just hoped that, when it came down to it, she would understand.

• • •

Jesse parked Matt's car on the other side of Matty and Dash's barn. She grabbed the bottle of champagne she'd purchased the day before and climbed out. Under normal circumstances, she wouldn't bother locking her car, but today she made a point of it. Turning toward the house, she saw a man stride out from behind the barn.

Stepping back on instinct, she held on to her keys. He froze, took in the situation, then held up his hands in an effort to show he wasn't a threat.

"You startled me," she said.

"You must be Jesse." He took a few steps toward her, moving slowly so as not to startle her any more. "I'm Caleb Forrester, Kit's brother."

He took another few steps closer and she knew he was telling the truth. He wasn't as tall as she'd thought he might be and his hair was blond, a strong contrast to Kit's auburn color, but he had the same startling gold eyes as his sister.

She smiled and held out her hand. "It's nice to finally meet you, Caleb." He moved all the way over to her now and took her hand in his. He had an intense look about him, in the set of his shoulders and the way he stood on his feet, that he looked to be trying hard to hide.

"Did it get too…" She debated what word to use so as not to offend him. But then, judging by his eyes, she bet little actually did offend him. "*Normal* in there for you?" She gestured toward the house. "You look like you're out here pacing." *Like a lion or tiger*, she thought. His eyes certainly matched the description.

A smile teased at his lips and he shoved his hands in the pockets of his jeans. "I'm not all that used to civil society."

Jesse smiled. "I'd say we're not all that civil, but it would be both a cliché and a lie. We can, though, on occasion, carry on an interesting conversation or two. And you should be glad that I'm the only one with kids. At least this way you won't have to hear about school politics."

"And are there a lot of school politics?" he asked as they made their way up the drive toward the house.

"We're a small town. If someone doesn't say 'bless you' when someone else sneezes, it becomes a political issue. But with Kit and Matty around, we usually end up talking books or writing."

"And are you a writer?"

"I would like to think I have a good story or two in me, but what I don't have is time, skill, or interest. I leave that to the pros and I'll stick with running my hospital."

"And the PTSA and the children's health cooperative for the county and the pancake breakfast for the volunteer fire department. Don't let her fool, you, Caleb," Matty spoke as she opened the door and took Jesse by the arm. "She's a woman of many talents and even more energy."

Jesse looked at her friend, who was steadfastly avoiding eye contact, then to Caleb, who was looking back at Jesse, studying her.

"I don't doubt it for a minute," Caleb said, meeting her gaze.

For a moment, her heart sank. She really didn't want this brunch to be about setting her up with Kit's come-and-go brother. But then she saw the glint in his eye, as if he were inviting her to have a little fun at everyone else's expense. He wanted her to know that he wasn't taking them seriously, so she shouldn't either. She gave a small dip of her head to show that she accepted his invitation and he smiled.

"Champagne anyone?" she asked, holding out the bottle.

"I thought Matty told you not to bring anything." Dash, Matty's husband, stepped forward and took the bottle from her hand. "But I have to say, this is better than what we have, so I'm glad you did."

Jesse was about to offer to open the champagne when a cacophony of toenails pounded across the floor and five dogs came bounding into the room. Matty had not only inherited her brother's house after his murder the year before, but also his canines. Along with all his other animals—cats, rabbits, chickens, cows. Luckily, Dash was a vet, and in his opinion, there was no such thing as too many animals.

"Didn't you lock them downstairs?" Dash asked as he popped the cork.

"I did, but Isis has opposable thumbs and knows how to open the door," Matty replied, referring to the beautiful ridgeback that was hanging back and keeping an eye on everything. Jesse smiled as Dash handed her a glass of champagne, moving about like there wasn't three hundred pounds of dog in his kitchen. Caleb had hunkered down and was giving Bob, the yellow Lab, some love.

"In case you were wondering, Caleb, Isis does not have opposable thumbs. The door jam bent out of shape when the dogs were roughhousing one day and it doesn't close very well," Dash supplied.

"I don't know, opposable thumbs sounds so much better," Caleb replied as he gave the Lab one more rub, then rose. When he declined the glass of champagne Dash was offering, Jesse wondered if it was because he didn't drink at all or just didn't drink champagne.

"I'm thinking about getting a dog," Jesse commented as Matty ushered the four-legged mob out the door. "What do you think, Dash?"

"A specific breed or just any dog?" Dash asked.

"Just a dog. Something big, though. Or something that will grow into something big. Do you ever come across puppies that folks are trying to give away?" she asked.

Dash motioned his guests toward the back porch where the table was set. It was another beautiful spring day and Jesse took a moment to appreciate the gentle warmth of the morning as everyone sat.

"I do." Dash replied. "Usually, farm dogs that get pregnant before their owners have a chance to get them fixed. I'm also on the board for the shelter so I see plenty of dogs there, too. Are you looking for companionship or protection or something in particular?"

"Just a dog," she said quickly. Too quickly, judging by the curious look Matty gave her as she set out a truly amazing spread of food before sitting down herself. Raised by her Puerto Rican mother and wealthy DC socialite grandmother, Matty cooked an extensive repertoire of dishes, all of which made Jesse's mouth water.

Jesse shrugged, hoping to seem casual, and then played the empty-nest card. "The boys will both be out of the house soon. I thought it might be nice to have some company, that's all. I'm not in any hurry, but if you wouldn't mind keeping your eyes open, Dash, I would appreciate it."

Dash agreed, as she knew he would. Unlike Ian, who had a fairly intense personality, Dash was about as laid-back as a person could get. That wasn't to say he was lazy, not by a long shot, but very little bothered him, and being raised in a close family with long ties to the valley, there was very little he wouldn't do to help out a friend or neighbor.

He was good for Matty, too. Jesse had seen some of the subtle changes in her friend since she'd arrived in town almost a year ago. She had liked Matty from the start—her strength, fire, and sense of humor were hard not to fall in love with. But coming from a rough background, Matty was a woman with a big heart and even bigger trust issues. With help from Dash, she was starting to give her warmth and affection more freely. Most of which was being given through food, Jesse judged now, looking at the gorgeous brunch laid out on the table before her.

"What time did you start cooking this morning?" Kit asked, obviously thinking along the same lines. Caleb hadn't said much of anything; sitting to her right, he was eyeing the table like he wasn't quite sure what to make of it all.

Matty waved a dismissive hand in the air. "I figure after the week Jesse has had, she deserves a huge, overindulgent meal. Start, please," she added, gesturing to the food.

"What kind of week have you had?" Kit asked as she helped herself to a couple of eggs layered over fried plantains.

Caleb's eyes fell to Jesse, silently asking the same question.

She shrugged and tried to wave this off as well. "I had a little car accident on Friday. I'd say it's not a big deal, and in the grand scheme of things, since no one was really hurt, it isn't a big deal. But it did shake me up a bit, that's all," she said, taking the platter of eggs and plantains from Kit.

"Why didn't you tell me? I would have come over and kept you company or brought you food or, even better, some whiskey," Kit said.

Jesse smiled at her friend's remark. "I know you would have, Kit, but it wasn't that big a deal. Seriously. I was, and still am, a little sore. My car is in the shop. But other than that, things are fine."

Kit stared at her for a long time. Jesse's eyes flitted to Caleb and for a moment she wondered if he knew more than what was being said or if the intense expression he wore was just normal for him. A little confused by his reaction, she looked away, but not before she saw a small frown form on his lips.

"Wow, add that to the bomb last week, and you *have* had a rough time," Kit finally spoke, taking a long sip of her champagne.

From the corner of her eye, Jesse saw Caleb put his coffee cup down. She wished Kit hadn't brought all this up. She knew it was a topic of conversation, how could it not be, but she wished they didn't have to talk about it now.

"It wasn't exactly a bomb, not in the traditional sense, anyway." She tried to downplay the situation as she cut into a succulent piece of ham.

Kit lifted a shoulder. "Yes, it was a bomb. It may not have been the kind of bomb used to take apart a bus, but it was an explosive device."

Jesse was just going to leave it at that, but Matty piped in. "So is David investigating that, too?"

"You know about David?" Kit asked. Jesse all but groaned.

"Yes, from Vivi and Abigail." Matty answered as she picked up a cheese-filled pastry, pulled a piece off, and popped it into her mouth. "He was investigating the fire that killed Aaron Greene's father. How do you know about him, Kit? Have you met him?" she asked after swallowing.

Kit shook her head and both women looked at Jesse. She looked at Dash and he came to her rescue.

"Do you understand a word of what they are talking about, Caleb?" Dash asked.

Caleb shook his head. "I got 'bomb' and 'explosive device,' but other than that, I'm lost." Unlike everyone else at the table, Caleb seemed to be more focused on his coffee than his food.

Jesse desperately wanted to end this conversation. Not only was it becoming all about her, but she really didn't want David brought into it. She sent Kit a warning glare, reminding her without words that she had no wish to discuss him with anyone. Kit had the grace to look just a tiny bit apologetic. And to make up for it, Kit gave Caleb a condensed version of the explosion, leaving any mention of its investigator out of it. Matty then jumped in and added what she knew about the accident.

When Kit and Matty had finished their accounts, Caleb turned to Jesse. "I thought you told me you were all civilized out here?"

"We are." She sat up straighter, but downed the last of her champagne, nonetheless. "Just a fluke thing, is all." She hoped.

"You have to admit," Dash spoke, cutting into the potatoes his wife had fire roasted with peppers and onions, "it's a crazy coincidence that those two things happened to you in less than a week."

She thought about mentioning her tires being slashed, but since the conversation had already gone on long enough to make her uncomfortable, she didn't. "Vivi and Ian think it's a bit unusual, too. They're looking into it."

"Vivi and Ian?" Caleb asked.

"Friends," she said. Then, when he frowned, she added, "They are both local law enforcement. Ian is the sheriff but was an Army Ranger for almost fifteen years. Vivi is an ME, but was a detective and also consults with the FBI as a profiler. Although her specialty is cold cases."

Caleb turned and looked at his sister with raised brows. "I had no idea there were so many interesting people around here." It was clear in his tone that his sister had failed to mention a few things about the people in her life. And he wasn't happy about it.

But Kit just met his gaze, cocked an eyebrow, and popped a small, fruit-filled pastry into her mouth. "Imagine what you might learn if you came to visit a bit more often," she eventually pointed out.

The two stared at each other for a long moment. There was an underlying tension in Kit that Jesse had never seen or experienced before. Caleb and his sister were obviously very different. And though Kit had said that Caleb did something with or for governments, she hadn't specified what that was, exactly—Jesse thought it was more likely that Kit didn't actually know. For a moment, she wondered if he was one of those mercenary or private security types she'd read about but had never been sure actually existed.

"What do you do, Caleb?" she asked in an attempt the break the tension between the siblings.

"I beg your pardon?" he said, turning back to her.

"For a living. Do you work?"

He took a sip of coffee. "I work for the government. What are Vivi and Ian looking into?"

Studying his eyes, Jesse got the sense that not only did Caleb want to avoid talking about what he did for a living, but that he knew she didn't want to talk about what was going on, or potentially going on, with her. It wasn't exactly tit for tat, but by turning the conversation back to her, he'd given a subtle warning to drop the conversation about him. Interesting.

She was about to say "nothing" when everyone else at the table prompted her to explain as well. Shooting an annoyed look at Caleb, she told them what little she knew—only that Vivi and Ian were going to look into complaints at the hospital and maybe talk to a few folks. When she'd finished recounting the facts, she made it clear that she knew nothing more and all but pleaded to change the topic of conversation.

As if to help her out, Bob suddenly came tearing by on the lawn dragging a stick three times his size with the rest of the dogs in hot pursuit behind him. It wasn't much of a conversation starter, but it did move their banter onto lighter things.

After the gluttonous meal, Matty and Dash banned everyone from the kitchen while they prepared another pot of coffee and started some cleanup. Kit's cell rang and she headed into the study to start what would likely be a lengthy conversation with her publisher. Jesse and Caleb found themselves alone at the table. Needing to move around after such a big meal, she stood and walked to the porch railing. In a few weeks, when the bugs started to get bad, Dash would put up screens to enclose the area, but for now it was open, and inhaling deeply, she took in the scents of spring—fresh grass and lilacs. Caleb came to stand beside her.

"You looked like you weren't quite sure what to do with all that food," she commented.

He shrugged. "I can't remember the last time I sat down to a home-cooked meal, let alone one that size." She turned and looked at him, again, wondering just what kind of life he led.

"Tell me about David," he said. It wasn't a request, but his command confused her for a moment. That he'd mentioned David at all was a surprise. As was the fact that he felt he could demand anything of her. She didn't feel put out or self-righteous about it; actually, she was more curious than anything else.

She turned back to the lawn as the dogs came racing back into view. "He's an arson investigator. I met him at the hospital two weeks ago when he came to interview a young man who'd been burned in a house fire here in town. I guess there aren't that many arson investigators in the area so when the explosive went off at the quilt shop, he was assigned to that as well."

"And was he around when you were run off the road?"

"He was there, yes. We were supposed to meet for lunch. He called when I didn't show up and came out to the scene. He was the one who suggested that Ian look into things, given there had been three incidents in less than two weeks."

"Three?"

Crap, she'd let that slip. Briefly she told him about the tires, and begrudgingly added that the vandalism had happened the same day she'd met David—she'd thought about holding that piece of information back but got the sense that Caleb could and would find out if he really wanted to. But she did make a point of asking him not to bring it up to the others. Ian and Vivi knew, since they'd been there when it happened, but no one else needed to know. Why make them worry about her any more than they already were?

"And are you seeing this guy?" Caleb asked baldly.

Her eyes flew to his for a moment, startled by such a personal question.

In a flash, her mind went to David, to his voice, to his phone call earlier that morning, to his concern over her.

Thankfully, Kit walked out just then, and Jesse was saved from answering the question. She didn't think Caleb was the type to banter David's name about, so, unlike with the others, she didn't find herself feeling the need to keep this thing with David, whatever it was, a secret from him. She just didn't know how to answer the question, exactly.

"Is Jesse telling you about how I thought about trying to set you two up?" Kit asked with a mischievous smile. It was obvious she was trying to prod her brother more than anything else.

Caleb's eyes sought Jesse's—this time he looked startled. She smiled. "I told her it would never work. Seeing as this is the first time in years you've set foot in Windsor and most of the time Kit doesn't even know where you are, things would just be more complicated than I'm interested in. Besides, I thought you would be taller and the mechanics of things would just, well, they'd be awkward. Matty agreed with me on that point, I'd like to add."

His lips quirked into a grin. "The mechanics?"

She gave a dramatic sigh. "I know, tall and handsome is the stereotype fantasy man, but being five foot two, for me, 'tall' is a relative term. Speaking from experience, a huge height difference does sometimes, well, like I said, it can sometimes make things awkward."

Kit laughed, and on Caleb's face Jesse saw the first real smile he'd allowed himself all morning. He was an attractive man; of that there was no doubt. But judging by the vibe she was getting from him, he was no more sexually attracted to her than she was to him.

"So, how tall is David?" he asked, crossing his arms.

"Caleb!" Kit chided. But when she didn't answer, Kit turned to her. "Well, how tall is he?"

Jesse rolled her eyes and shook her head. "You, my friend, will probably never know."

"You're not going to introduce him to your friends?" Caleb sounded genuinely curious now.

"It's a long story, Caleb," Kit said, taking her brother's arm and pulling him toward the house. "But suffice it to say, I'm encouraging her to go for the sex and not the happily-ever-after."

"Kit," she warned, following them into the house.

Without turning around, Kit waved a hand at her. "And I shall say no more on the subject."

As Dash and Matty entered the kitchen, Kit said, "I need to go. My publisher just called—we need to set an itinerary for my Europe tour so I have to review some dates in the next few hours."

Matty expressed her disappointment, but, being a writer herself, she was sympathetic. Jesse considered staying to chat with her friends for a while longer, but then remembered the work she still needed to get done before meeting with her lawyer the next morning. Plus, she had to pick up the boys in thirty minutes. Leaving now would give her just enough time to make a quick stop at the grocery store before swinging by the school.

"I'll walk you to your car," Caleb offered, surprising her. She glanced at Kit who was frowning at her brother. Matty and Dash looked curious. Rather than making a fuss and drawing more attention to his offer than was warranted, she agreed. After bidding her friends good-bye, the two headed down the driveway.

"What do you know about David?" he asked.

"I beg your pardon?"

"What do you know about the guy?"

She wasn't an idiot; she knew where this was going. And she also knew Caleb couldn't be further from the truth.

"Like I said, he's an arson investigator. He's also a firefighter who moved here a little less than a year ago when his only daughter, whom he raised on his own from the day she was born, started college in Rhode Island."

"And the first incident happened on the day you met him." They reached her car, and much to her dismay, he made an obvious scan of it, then took her keys. Unlocking the door, he ordered her to step back before he started the engine. When it turned over just fine, he pulled it forward enough to be able to see the ground that had been underneath it. Putting it in park, he got out.

"Looking for bombs?" Her voice was dry; she couldn't help it. He didn't seem to notice.

"Among other things." He was searching the ground now; for what, she didn't know. Brake fluid maybe? Would that leak onto the ground?

Finally, looking satisfied with whatever he'd found, or hadn't found, he turned to her. "You should have Ian look into David."

"No," her answer was emphatic.

"Why not?" His arms crossed over his chest.

"Look, I'm not some Pollyanna who only sees the good in people. I work in a hospital, in a *county-funded* hospital. I've seen what people can do to each other. And while in your world, whatever world that may be, everyone may have questionable intentions, in my world, *this* world, that isn't the case."

He studied her for a long moment and then cracked a grin. "Well, I guess you just put me in my place."

She rolled her eyes at him. "I'm pretty sure that David's only intentions regarding me aren't of the violent sort. And don't think for one second that I think I've put you in your place. I don't know who you are or what you do, but I have a sneaking suspicion you're going to check into him anyway."

He tilted his head in response and stepped aside so that she could get into her car. "You're one of Kit's friends. I don't see her all that often, but I do care about her. And the life she's made for herself. You're a part of that."

"Then, just for the record," Jesse said as she climbed into the driver's seat, "you're wrong about David."

"Duly noted." He shut the door and she backed up, then began to pull away.

She watched him in the rearview mirror as she headed down the drive. Whoever Caleb Forrester was, he was not a man to be messed with. And even though she didn't think he was even close to the truth when it came to David, he seemed like the kind of man who would be good to have on her side if she ever needed it. She just hoped she would never need it.

CHAPTER 11

JESSE SAT IN THE CHAIR across from Wilton and gave him a blank look. At least she thought it was a blank look, since that was how she felt.

"Trust? Mark and I never set up a trust for the kids." Wilton returned her look with one that would seem condescending coming from anyone other than the paternal man in front of her.

"I know you never set up that kind of trust. Or at least not with me. But Mark came by to talk to me about it a while back. It was a month or two before he died. He said he was thinking about setting something up for the kids. I gave him an envelope of material to go through at his leisure."

"But we don't have that much money, why would we need a trust?" She was still confused. Maybe not so much by the idea of setting up a trust for the kids, but by the fact that Mark had been considering it before he died but had never mentioned it to her. It was true, their marriage wasn't as rock solid as people thought it was, but it was unlike him to make a decision like this, about the boys' future, without her.

"There are many reasons to set up a trust, and they aren't just for the wealthy. You know they help avoid probate and can make the transfer of the estate much smoother, which is why you have the one trust you do. But since we're having this conversation, which I'm happy to have by the way, I assume he never mentioned anything to you?"

Jesse shook her head. No, Mark hadn't mentioned anything to her. But what that meant, she wasn't sure.

"Well, it's something to consider, especially now," Wilton said, leaning forward to sort through some papers.

"What do you mean, 'especially now?'" She hadn't expected to enjoy this morning meeting with her attorney, but she also hadn't expected to feel two steps behind from the moment she walked in.

"Well, Mark's insurance money, of course. And the settlement from the university for his case. You signed all the documents, all the court filings, Jesse. Don't you remember?" he asked, as he pulled a few sheets loose and handed them to her.

She shook her head to clear the cobwebs. Of course she remembered doing those things, and the evidence was right in front of her. But she had been in such a daze then, and, well, until Wilton had reminded her, she *had* sort of forgotten that the money existed. Her job paid her well, Matt was on scholarship, and the house was paid for. She and Mark had gotten into the habit of saving early—for both retirement and the boys' college—so those accounts were healthy, too. She hadn't needed the money, so when the settlements came in, she vaguely remembered asking Wilton to put it into a safe account somewhere.

"Where is the money and how much is there, exactly?" She felt ridiculous asking the question, but better to be asking it of Wilton than anyone else. He gave her a look that seemed to express both sympathy and disapproval at the same time.

"The insurance money is in a mutual fund and the settlement is being managed by a broker I recommended in the city."

"Is there anything left?" The economic downturn must have made a dent in it to some extent.

"Actually, yes. Both accounts are doing well. The insurance started at a million and has made about 10 percent. The settlement was slightly more than that and has made about 6 percent."

Jesse blinked. She and the boys had over two million dollars. It was a lot of money. Maybe not by the standards of the ultrarich. But for someone like her, someone who lived simply and didn't need much, it was a lot of money.

"Wow."

Wilton chuckled. "I'm not sure if this changes things for you, but maybe we should talk about those trusts and what might make sense for you and the boys?"

Jesse looked at her longtime lawyer and friend, still absorbing the news. Then, finally, she spoke, "Yes, yes I think we should talk."

• • •

Later that night Jesse curled up in bed with her computer and a glass of wine. The boys had made dinner and, miracle of miracles, cleaned up, too—even after finishing all their homework. It was the last week of school, and truth be told, they didn't have that much homework. But Matt had one more paper due tomorrow and James had two exams left. One was math and one was biology so she didn't feel the need to check up on him as much as she would have if one had been an English class.

She could hear them now upstairs, getting ready for bed. For a moment, she leaned back against her pillows and just listened. She could hear them walking around in their rooms and imagined them picking up their things, putting their backpacks together, and changing into their pajamas. Every now and then she could hear the murmur of their voices and occasionally one would laugh. Maybe they were talking to friends on their phones, or maybe, she liked to think, they were talking to each other.

It was hard to imagine that in three months Matt would be gone. And three years after that, James would follow. Time had gone by so fast, even the bad times, that it still caught her off guard sometimes.

Thinking of the passage of time brought her mind back to her morning meeting with Wilton. Throughout the day, whenever she'd had a spare moment—which, between working on the hospital budget and working with the lawyers on Ian's request, wasn't often—she'd thought about what Wilton had said. She still couldn't shake the fact that Mark had talked to him about trusts for the kids without mentioning it to her.

Maybe he just hadn't had the time to look into it before he'd died, or the time to tell her. There was probably a logical explanation, but still, something just didn't sit right.

She looked at her phone lying on her bedside table and considered calling someone. But what would she say? Mark's actions weren't totally out of character and everyone would tell her that. Everyone who'd known him anyway. She considered calling Vivi or Matty, neither of whom had known Mark, but dismissed the idea. She would probably sound like a crazy suspicious wife to the two newly married women. David popped into her mind. He would probably have a good perspective, but the thought of calling him to dish on her deceased husband felt, well, weird.

Finally, after mulling it over for what seemed like too long, she came up with an alternate plan. All of Mark's things, except his clothes, were still in his office in the barn. Several months after his death, she'd asked some friends to come over and help close it up. They'd boxed everything up and weather- and rodent-proofed it. Jesse had kept it locked away ever since. She hadn't had the energy to go through everything, or, honestly, the interest. If there was anything Mark had been keeping to himself, chances were she'd find it in his office.

But not wanting the kids to know she was going through their father's things, she decided she could spend the hour or so she had alone in the morning, after they left for school and before she left for work. And once they were off at their various activities next week, she'd have a lot more time. With the plan fixed in her mind, she pulled her computer over and opened up the latest budget.

As she perused the numbers, she tried pushing aside the disappointment creeping into her mind. Having dismissed the idea of calling David to ask his advice, she no longer had a reason to call him, fabricated or otherwise. But it would be nice to hear his voice. What they would talk about, who knew, but it would still be nice to talk.

Jesse's eyes travelled to her phone. She didn't know what time he got off work, where he was, or if he could even talk. Much less whether or not he'd want to. Still, her eyes lingered.

After a few more minutes, she decided not to be so girly about it and picked up her cell phone. As she hit the button to bring it to life, it vibrated in her hand.

"Is it too late for you?"

She smiled into the phone. "No, I was just picking up the phone to call you."

"You were?" The surprise in David's voice made her laugh.

"And that surprises you?"

"No, well, maybe. I just know you have a busy week this week. I remember what it was like. And then I was debating whether or not to hang up, thinking it might be too late given everything that's going on. How are you?" he asked.

"I'm good, much less sore. And you?"

"Good, the rest of the weekend was mostly uneventful. That's a good thing but the time passes slowly, that's for sure. How was brunch? Was the enigmatic brother there?" Jesse was pretty sure she heard more than just curiosity in his voice, but he was doing a good job trying to hide it.

"He was, yes. Caleb," she answered. "He's not quite what I'd expected. He's very intense, but he has a better sense of humor than Kit led us to believe. The topic of Ian's investigation came up. Caleb insisted on checking my car before I left. Seemed like a bit of overkill, but he's not the kind of guy to be swayed in his opinion."

"I guess we should be grateful for that." He didn't sound so sure. "How are things going with the boys this week?"

Jesse was glad for the change of subject, she was kind of done thinking about herself and the situation for a while. She still had her plan, but as for the rest, well, it was definitely more fun to talk about all the graduation and end-of-year activities going on. And so they did, for the next fifteen minutes or so. And when they hung up, it seemed natural, though unspoken, to assume they'd talk again soon.

"Mom?" James poked his head around the door. For a split

second, a feeling of being caught doing something she shouldn't have been doing paralyzed her. But then she realized James probably hadn't heard anything, and, even if he had, she hadn't been doing anything wrong. She hoped.

"Yeah?"

"I heard you talking, is everything okay?" His eyes darted to her clock. After Mark had died, phone calls at odd hours had taken on a whole new meaning.

"Everything is fine. It was just a friend calling to check in," she reassured him.

"How are you feeling?" James asked as he came in and stretched himself across the foot of her bed.

"Better. My neck is still a little sore, but I'm better every day. How are things going with you? Are you ready for your test tomorrow?"

He nodded. Her youngest had something on his mind but she knew better than to ask. Unlike when talking to Matt, with James she often just had to keep him talking and whatever was on his mind would eventually come out.

"Do you have everything for your week in Boston?" she asked.

Again he nodded.

"Tell me about the track meet. You gave me the stats, but did you have fun?" She knew they'd had a blast, but she was trying to get him to start talking. And it worked. For the next few minutes they talked about the meet—about who did what, where they ate their meals, who was dating whom, and who was taking advantage of the time away from parents. There had been chaperones, but not one per kid.

"Do you miss Dad?" James suddenly asked. The question didn't come entirely out of left field; she knew James had wanted to talk about something. But coming right at the end of a story about Callie Laidlaw tripping and taking a header just before the finish line, it caught Jesse off guard.

She blinked. "Yes."

"Were you guys happy? I mean, you seemed happy, but I'm a kid. Were you really happy?"

Jesse bit her lip. The question was so like James. Her younger son was someone who gave a lot of thought to a lot of things. He'd probably been mulling this question over for a while. Maybe not even consciously at first, but he'd grown up a lot in the past two years.

"We were happy. We married young and had our ups and downs, but every marriage does. We built a good life together," she answered.

He looked at her like he knew she wasn't telling him everything.

"Do *you* miss him?" she asked, turning the tables.

He nodded. "Yeah, I do. It's weird because it's not like we spent a ton of time together. I mean I love him and he was a good dad, but because we kind of liked the same things, you would have thought we would have spent more time together. So I miss him. But then sometimes I wonder what I'm missing. I don't know if that even makes sense."

She studied James, who was picking at a loose thread on her duvet. "It makes sense. Your dad was busy a lot. He took on a lot when we married—kids, my college and then grad school, the house. I think he just got in the habit of making sure everyone had what they needed to get through the day and then his job was mostly done. Because, for a long time, that was a feat in and of itself. But he is still your dad and there's a lot in your life that he's not going to be a part of now that he's gone. Even if he would have only been there in the shadows, so to speak, he was always going to be there. And that's gone now so, yes, what you said does make sense."

James's eyes darted to hers then back to the duvet. A few beats passed before he spoke again. "It's like I sometimes feel like I miss him more for what he could have been than for what he actually was, and it makes me feel kind of mean. Maybe a little ungrateful for all he *did* do for us."

"I can't tell you how you should or shouldn't feel, but I can tell you that he loved you boys very much, and maybe more importantly, he knew you loved him too."

James picked at the thread for several more minutes before speaking again. "He was a good man, wasn't he, Mom? I only know him as my dad, and now that he's gone, no one is ever going to tell us otherwise. But was he really, Mom? A good person?"

Jesse didn't want to think about how she should answer, so instead she asked, "Is someone telling you something else?"

James shook his head. "No, it's just that sometimes people aren't who you think they are. Most of the time, we get the chance to figure that out, but I can't do that with Dad."

She frowned. There was obviously more to this than what he was saying. "Do you have someone in mind when you say that?"

James dipped his head to the side. "Did you know that Chelsea's parents are separating?"

No, she didn't know that. She shook her head.

"Turns out that her mom has a big gambling problem," James said.

"I had no idea." And she hadn't, the news came as a complete surprise to her. Chelsea's mom was one of those PTSA power moms with close ties to the community. She was a good woman who'd done a lot of good things for both the school and the town.

"Yeah, turns out Chelsea didn't know either, until her parents told her last night that they're separating and her mom is going into a treatment center."

Jesse let out a deep breath, feeling for the girl. "I'm sorry to hear that. How is Chelsea?"

"She's pretty messed up. Trying to hold it together, but it's hard. It's just, well, it just made me wonder if there were things we didn't know about Dad."

There were, but she wasn't about to tell him. There was no need since it wasn't anything that would affect them, not the way Chelsea was being affected now.

"No," she shook her head. "Not things like that. He had his faults, we all do, and I don't want you to think he was perfect because he wasn't. But he was a good man."

James studied her face for a long moment before giving her a small smile. "Thanks, Mom. I know it was kind of crazy—"

"There's nothing crazy about wanting to know or talk about your dad," she cut him off. "That's the other thing I don't want to happen; I don't want us to avoid talking about him when maybe we might need to."

James hesitated for a moment, then asked, "Does it bother you?"

"To talk about him? No," she said, shaking her head. "I don't know that I'd want to talk about him all the time, because we do need to move forward, but I like talking about him with you boys, remembering the good times. And maybe some of the not-so-good times, too. Answering your questions. You each would have had a different relationship with him than I did, but since you won't be able to know him as adults, I want you guys to feel like you can ask me about him."

"And you'll be honest?" He was sort of teasing her, she knew. But she also knew it was a small test.

"To the extent that I can. My perception of your father is just that. Mine. I have my own filters. I see him and my relationship with him through those filters. I can tell you my perceptions. As to whether or not it's the truth," she shrugged.

After a beat, James gave her another small smile. "Thanks, Mom. I guess I should hit the hay now."

She nodded. "You do have a test tomorrow."

"Biology, Mom. Piece of cake," he said as he stood up.

"Good, then I'll expect an A."

He paused at the door and shot her a cocky look that reminded her of Mark from all those years ago. "At *least* an A, Mom."

Jesse laughed softly as her son made his way up the stairs to bed. He and Mark hadn't always had the easiest of relationships. Love between them wasn't the problem, but their personalities hadn't always meshed. She was glad James had come to her to talk about his dad and she hoped she'd said and done the right things. But then again, as a parent, it seemed like she was *always* hoping she'd said and done the right things—it was par for the course.

CHAPTER 12

"He's he-ere," Abigail said in a singsongy voice when Jesse answered her office phone.

"What?" Jesse asked. It was the Monday after graduation and between the graduation events and parties, sending the boys off to Boston and New Jersey, and trying to keep up with work, she could barely keep her head on straight. Let alone try to follow her friend's line of thought.

"David Hathaway. You know, the arson investigator," Abigail said.

Feeling stretched almost to her limit with everything going on, Jesse almost snapped that she knew very well who David Hathaway was. But then she remembered that, as far as most of her friends were concerned, she'd only seen him a few times and always on work-related business. They didn't know that she'd spoken with him every night this past week except the nights that he'd been at work.

Then Abigail's words sank in. He was here. At Riverside. She looked at her calendar and remembered that he was off shift as of last night. They'd talked as he'd driven home, but work hadn't come up. She wondered if she'd forgotten, if he'd said something about wanting to come by. But nothing came to mind. Which, to her, meant he was likely there to see Aaron, who was going home in two days.

"And?" Jesse prompted.

"And don't play sly with me. He couldn't take his eyes off you, Jesse. You might want to consider asking him out. Or something," Abigail added, leaving no doubt as to what "or something" could be.

She sighed. "This isn't a conversation I want to have right now, Abigail. Or ever, for that matter. I'm knee-deep in budgets, Ian is still looking for someone who might be intent on hurting me, and my firstborn just graduated from high school. I have a lot on my mind. I don't need to complicate things by dating anyone." Which was exactly why she was keeping her phone conversations with David to herself.

"Is it because of Mark?" Abigail asked, her voice softening.

"Because of, what? No." Jesse insisted, then took a deep breath and forced herself to calm down. She knew Abigail was only trying to be a good friend, encouraging her to explore options and all that, but this was exactly what she'd been trying to avoid. She just didn't have time for conversations like this. And all those that would follow if she started dating someone and her friends got wind of it.

She glanced up and her gaze caught on a picture of the boys. She also wasn't sure how she would cross that bridge when or if she came to it. She didn't think her boys would begrudge her dating someone, but she wasn't altogether certain they were ready for it right now.

"Look, Abigail. Thanks for being such a good friend, and no, it's not because of Mark that I'm not interested in dating," she began, in a much calmer voice. "I still miss him, yes, and the kids do, too. But I know he's not coming back and I have moved on. The fact of the matter is, I don't have the time or energy to date anyone. It's just too much work right now, Abigail. I know that sounds like a cop out, like I'm avoiding intimacy. But it's not that. I just know myself and know that I don't have what's needed to put into that kind of relationship right now."

Her friend was silent for a long moment, then Jesse heard Abigail take a deep breath and let it out. "We just want you to be happy, Jesse. All of us do. And we know you and Mark had a good relationship and nothing will replace that, but you might find the companionship comforting is all. But I hear you, and while I will promise to try my best not to get too excited when I see someone interested in you, I can't promise to keep my mouth shut all the time."

Jesse smiled, at a lot of things. She wasn't all that interested in *comfort* when it came to David. And she knew her friend well enough to know that she'd be lucky if Abigail limited herself to loaded and meaningful looks. But she'd take what she could get.

"Thank you, I appreciate that. And if or when I'm open to dating again, I'll let you know so that you can parade a stable full of eligible men in front of me." It was a peace offering that both women knew would never happen. Not only would she not be interested in a stable full of eligible men, but Abigail, as a married woman whose friends were mostly married, didn't actually know very many single men.

Abigail chuckled. "If I knew a stable full of such men, I think I might be more interested in parading them in front of *me*."

Jesse laughed and the two women hung up. But no sooner had she set the phone down than Vivi called to give her the same news. In the hospital for some routine work, Vivi had run across David talking to one of the charge nurses. More prepared this time around, she had almost the exact same conversation with Vivi as she'd just had with Abigail, only she suspected Vivi picked up that there was more to the story than Jesse was letting on. Thankfully, if that was the case, Vivi was also a good enough friend not to probe too much.

Knowing those calls were out of the way and no one else was likely to call for the same reason, she went back to her work. In addition to finishing the budget, she had to start on the next newsletter so she got busy brainstorming some article ideas.

An hour later, a knock sounded at her door. She didn't need x-ray vision to know who it was. She beckoned David in, and when he stepped through the door, she was struck, again, by how attractive he was. She hadn't seen him in over a week and hadn't realized just how good he would look to her after all that time. And judging by the way he was taking her in with his deep-brown eyes, she'd bet he felt the same way.

They stared at each other for several long moments until David cleared his throat and moved into the room. He checked to make sure the door had closed behind him before he sat down across from her. It wasn't exactly where she wanted him, but it was probably the best place for him.

"Did you stop by to see Aaron?" she asked.

He nodded. "It looks like he's doing well. He and his aunt seem to have bonded."

"He'll have some scarring, physical as well as emotional, no doubt. But you're right. I've spent some time with both of them and they appear to have formed a good relationship," she agreed.

They stared at each other again.

"I, ah, was wondering if you wanted to go to dinner this week. Now that the boys are gone and I have a couple of days off," he finally spoke.

Jesse felt her heart rate kick up at the thought. She wanted to say "yes," she really did. But her phone beeped and she glanced down at a new text message. From Abigail. "Is David in your office? Is he asking you out?"

Her conversation with Kit a few weeks ago floated through her mind. What did she really want? She'd given it *some* thought, but looking at David sitting so close, she suddenly knew exactly what she wanted. Of course, asking for it was a whole different story.

She rose from her seat and paced over to the window.

"That doesn't look good." His tone was dry, but not altogether put off by her lack of enthusiasm.

"It's not that. It's not what you think," she said, looking at her view of the parking lot.

"I'm equal parts curious about what you think I think and what it really is."

She turned and faced him. His expression was wary, but there was also a hint of something more. Something that made her think she should watch her step and try to be as brutally honest as she was capable of being. Because, the way he was eyeing her, he didn't look like he was at all above crossing the room and just taking what she was sure they both wanted if he sensed the opportunity. She took a step back.

"I'm not saying I'm not interested," she started.

"But?"

"But it's complicated." That sounded lame, even to her. She held up a hand to stop the comment that she saw forming on his lips. A comment that she had not doubt would not be all that sweet.

"My life is busy. Really busy. I know you know what I'm talking about. So it's not that I don't want to be with you…" Her voice trailed off.

"What is it you do want, Jesse?" He stood and walked toward her but stopped several feet away.

She shook her head and looked down at the floor.

"Tell me," he pressed.

She bit her lip and hazarded a look at him. Predatory did not begin to cover his expression.

"I'm not sure I can," she managed to say.

"Because you don't know or because you don't want to tell me?"

"Because it's so against my nature and I'm afraid I'll sound like a complete bitch, not to mention that there's a chance I might remind you of Miranda's mother."

That seemed to give him pause and he frowned. "You're not a thing like Miranda's mother and I doubt anything you could ever say would change that."

He seemed so sincere that it was now or never. So she dove in before she had the sense to stop herself. "What if I said I want a relationship, but not one anyone knows about?"

"Keep it a secret?"

"Sort of."

"Sort of?" He had the gall to quirk a little grin.

"Look, I told you it's crazy. I'm crazy to think it and it's not at all fair. It's just that a friend suggested I think about what I want, what I would really want from someone like you. Okay, what I would want from *you*," she corrected when he his brows shot up.

"And?" he prompted.

"And it's not very flattering to me."

"Try me." He took the last few steps toward her and stopped just inches away. She couldn't quite meet his eyes, but it wasn't any better looking at his chest. Not when she had an urge to place the palms of her hands against it and feel his heart beat under them. She looked down at the floor again, but his fingers came up to her chin to tilt her head up, forcing her to meet his gaze.

"Tell me what you want, Jesse."

"You, of course," she whispered. She saw the response in his eyes so she hurried on before he acted on it. "But I don't want candlelight dinners or dates. I don't want expectations and I don't want to have to juggle schedules. I don't want to argue about laundry or dishes and I don't want to spend my time talking to my friends about you and explaining why we are or aren't serious. I know you're just talking about a date, but with friends like mine, many of whom are newly married, a date takes on a whole new meaning. And with everything else that's going on in my life, I really don't want to spend my time explaining myself."

She was flushed by the time she'd finished. Never before had she had such an explicit conversation. She'd been so young when she'd met Mark and had wanted so many different things.

"You've told me a lot of things you don't want, Jesse. What *do* you want?"

She hesitated for a second and tried to look away, but his hand, still under her chin, wouldn't let her. He wouldn't let her run. So she didn't.

"I want companionship. I want sex—hopefully, good sex," she added with sheepish shrug. "I want monogamy and respect and privacy. I want all the good things of a healthy relationship without anything that makes it messy. I want something that's mine. Something that would be ours. Not something I have to share with or explain to anyone else. I don't know if it's even possible, but that's what I really want," she added quietly.

"You want your cake and you want to eat it too."

Her heart sank. He had every right to be offended. But she'd be lying if she said she wasn't disappointed.

"I told you it would make me sound like a bitch. But you're right, I want to have my cake and eat it, too," she conceded.

"And what do you think I want?" His finger brushed across her lower lip. She blinked. Maybe he wasn't as offended as she'd thought.

"I don't know. But I know you deserve more than I can probably give you. What do you want?"

His eyes dropped to her mouth. Like a damned cliché—she couldn't help it—she licked her lips. His thumb stilled, then fell away. Then he dipped his head down and pressed his lips against hers. The kiss was subtle as if he was testing her, testing *them*. Her heart leapt into her throat at the taste of him, at the feel of him against her. He drew back for a moment as if debating whether to pull back or push forward. And then he was back and it was no test.

With a certainty born of what, she didn't know, his lips moved over hers as he slid his hand to her neck and tilted her head up. He urged her mouth open and she complied, not once thinking about stopping him. And when his tongue slipped between her lips, something gave inside her and she became more than just a recipient. Opening her mouth to him, pressing against him, she became a participant, wanting to give more, wanting to take more—just simply wanting more.

How long they stood there like that, she had no idea, but soon, too soon, she became aware of David pulling back. Pulling away from her. When she opened her eyes, he was watching her. His lips were damp and he was flushed. He looked like she felt. For a moment, she wasn't sure what to say after a kiss like that. And then she knew. She knew what she needed to know.

"What *do* you want, David?" She repeated the question she'd asked before the kiss. This time with more confidence.

He brushed his thumb across her wet lips once more and looked at her.

"I don't know, Jesse." He shook his head. "No, scratch that. I know what I want right now, but that's not what you're asking, is it?" It was a rhetorical question; they both knew what they wanted at that moment. But her question was deeper. What did he want and could he live with what she wanted?

He shook his head. "I don't know, Jesse. I've never given it too much thought. I just thought maybe I'd meet someone and it would go from there."

"Then maybe you should think about it. I know where I need it to go, at least at this stage in my life. If that doesn't work for you, I'll understand. But you need to think about it before we just 'go from here,' because if it's not something you want, or can even live with, then as much as it pains me to say this, we'd both be better off leaving it alone."

"Right person wrong time?"

She inclined her head. "It's possible, but until you give it some thought, we won't know."

For a second, he looked as if he wanted to say something, but he pulled back. Stepping away, he gave a curt nod of acknowledgment. "I've never done this before, Jesse. Been so intentional about things."

"I know. If it makes you feel any better, I've never done *any* part of this before. Remember, I was eighteen when I got married—I didn't think about these things then and haven't ever had cause to since."

His eyes searched hers as he shoved his hands in his pockets. She hoped he understood what she was saying. This was hard for her too, and she needed him to respect that by giving it the same amount of thought she had—maybe not the same level of thought, but enough to know that whatever he decided wasn't a whim.

Again he nodded. "We'll be in touch?"

She lifted a shoulder. "I hope so."

"I'm back on shift in two days, so if I don't talk to you before then, I'll be working for a few days after that."

She hoped he would call her before then, but she nodded, knowing it was only fair to give him the time and space he needed. It wasn't as if she was asking him to marry her, but she was asking him to give up a lot of the "usual" aspects of a relationship without having any idea how important those aspects might be to him.

"Good-bye, Jesse." It didn't sound final, but still, she didn't like the sound of it, even as she replied with the same.

And she *really* didn't like the sound of the door closing behind him.

• • •

With a groan of appreciation, Jesse slipped off her shoes, changed into a clean pair of jeans, and padded into her empty kitchen. It was Friday. Finally. And what an exciting Friday night it was. Having just spent a good bit of time going through her deceased husband's things, maybe she'd even be so crazy as to warm up some leftovers. *At least I only have one cat*, she thought to herself. A cat who happened to be sitting on the middle of the kitchen island, daring her to tell him to get down when he knew full well he wasn't allowed up there in the first place.

She sighed, thought about dinner again, then opted to pull out a bottle of wine instead, ignoring Mike, who was watching her every move. She was pouring herself a glass when her phone rang. Like a schoolgirl, for a split second, her heart stuttered as she hoped it was David. She hadn't heard from him since that day in her office and didn't know if she ever would.

Glancing at the number she wasn't surprised that it wasn't his, but a little shard of disappointment lodged in her belly.

"Hi, Kit," she said.

"Hi, yourself. What are you up to tonight?"

Jesse gave a dramatic sigh. "I just put on my pity party dress and poured myself a glass of wine."

"Get out a second glass. I'm coming over."

"It's not that kind of party, Kit."

"It is now."

Jesse stared at her phone. Kit had hung up on her. And she knew her friend well enough to know that she'd be pulling up the drive in less than twenty minutes. And sure enough, she was.

Jesse greeted Kit at the door, handed her a glass of wine, and then set the alarm behind her. By unspoken agreement, they moved to the couch in the family room. Propped on opposite ends, they pulled their feet up and tucked a throw blanket over their legs.

"So, what's going on?" Kit asked after she'd settled herself in comfortably with a pillow on her lap.

Jesse gave a reluctant shrug. "I'm feeling sorry for myself. That's all."

"Because?"

"It's no big deal. I'll be fine. It will all be fine."

"Of course it will, but that doesn't mean you can't allow yourself a moment of self-indulgence. Come on, lay it on me," Kit insisted.

She considered brushing her off, but then realized she didn't really want to. It was kind of ridiculous and maybe she just needed to say it all in order to move through it.

"Okay," she started. "Here goes. My car is still broken, Ian is investigating eight people who filed complaints against the hospital who he thinks were angry enough to possibly take it out on me, I just spent two hours going through Mark's things, I'm pretty sure I scared David away earlier this week, and my kids are growing up and moving away. Oh, and I'm contemplating becoming a cat lady."

Kit chuckled. "I can kind of picture you as a cat lady."

Jesse glared at her. "Thanks."

"That's what friends are for. Now, let's talk. What's the story with Ian's investigation?"

Jesse took a big sip of wine and filled her friend in on what little she knew. Ian, like many rural county sheriffs, was short staffed, so even though he was doing the best he could, things were moving slowly. He and his team had identified twenty-three complaint letters they'd wanted to look into. Over the past two weeks, he'd winnowed it down to six that they thought were worth investigating more fully. Two other patients or family members had been identified through interviews.

"So you basically have to sit tight and hope they come up with something soon. And for someone who likes to be as in control as you do, that sucks," Kit summarized.

"That and the fact that I'm living with the possibility that someone might really want to do me harm and I still have no idea why."

Kit wagged her head. "Okay, fair enough. You're allowed a little self-pity for that. Now, what about Mark? Why were you going through his things?"

She told Kit about the conversation she'd had with her lawyer and how it just didn't sit right with her.

"I know you probably think I'm crazy, but I'm telling you, it wasn't like Mark to look into something like that without talking to me about it."

"Maybe he didn't get a chance. The fire was just a few months later," Kit pointed out.

"Mark couldn't buy peanut butter without asking me first. And yes, before you ask, it was annoying, but after so many years of marriage, you pick your battles." She sighed. "I know you're right, though. I probably won't find anything."

"But you're determined to try."

Jesse nodded.

"I could help," Kit offered.

"Thanks," Jesse said with a smile, "but since I don't know what I'm looking for, it would probably be better if I did it myself. You only knew him peripherally at best and only for a short time. I'm probably the only one who would notice something out of character for him amongst his things. But thank you."

Kit seemed to consider her answer as she took a sip of wine. Then, curling the glass against her chest like an evil villain plotting, Kit asked, "And what about David?"

She laughed at Kit as her friend waggled her eyebrows. Jesse shook her head. "Ugh. I don't even know what to say."

"Try telling me what happened."

"I need more wine for that."

"Easy enough to remedy." Kit rose and headed off to the kitchen, returning a moment later with the wine bottle. She topped them both off then plopped herself back down and gave Jesse an expectant look.

"I can't believe I'm going to tell you this," Jesse said. And then she proceeded to do just that. She told her friend everything, from what she'd said to what he'd said—she even told Kit about the kiss. When she was done, her friend was staring at her, wide eyed, her wineglass held loosely in her hands on her lap.

"Wow." Kit managed to say. "I'm proud of you. Surprised, but proud."

"Yeah, it felt great to lay it all out there, but I haven't heard from him since and I'm wondering if I ever will." Jesse was feeling a little snarky and didn't bother to keep it from her tone.

"You said he was working yesterday. Do you know if he is still working? You said he doesn't generally call when he works," Kit pointed out.

"I don't know if he's working or not. I imagine so. I think his last two shifts lasted three nights, but they both started on Fridays. I don't know if it's different when he starts on a Thursday."

They sat in silence for a long moment, each drinking their wine. Then, finally, Jesse asked the question that had been rolling around in her head ever since David had left her office.

"Do you think I'm being too demanding? I feel like kind of a bitch. If anyone knows relationships are about compromise, it's me, and I didn't leave much room for that."

"Do you want to get married again, Jesse?"

She drew her head back in surprise at the question then frowned. "I've always thought that no, I don't want to get married again. Don't get me wrong, Mark and I built a good life. We had fun together and raised two great kids together. But it's a lot of work. I'm not sure I want to do that again."

"But you aren't closed off from companionship?" Kit pressed.

Jesse gave a rueful laugh as she thought about that kiss. "Obviously not."

"Then I think you did the right thing. Hey, what do I know? I'm just your friend. I'm not a relationship expert and I've never even met David, but I'm glad you laid it all out there if only to make it clear to yourself."

"Meaning?"

"Meaning, even if you end up compromising on some of the things you want or don't want, he probably has a better idea of where you're coming from based on that conversation," Kit answered.

"But what if I don't want to compromise? Or what if maybe there are things I *might* compromise on, but based on that conversation, he doesn't think I will, so he's now walking away?" She paused for a moment then asked, "Also, is it just me or do I sound like I'm sixteen?"

Kit laughed, so did Jesse, even though she was feeling a bit melodramatic about it all.

"If you aren't willing to compromise, then it was even more important that you laid it all out like you did. And if he needs you to compromise on a few things and doesn't have the guts to at least ask, do you really want to be in a relationship with him anyway—a relationship of any kind? Finally, I know it sounds cliché, but if he turns out to be the type who walks away easily, he's the type you should let go."

Jesse hadn't quite thought it through like that. And when she did, in a way, it made her feel better. Because she knew enough about David to know he wasn't afraid of a little challenge or of speaking his mind. If she said something that didn't agree with him, he'd let her know. But then why hadn't he called yet?

"And he's probably not calling because he's trying to pick and choose what he really wants and what he cares about. That and I'd bet he's probably working." Her friend spoke, as if she'd read Jesse's mind.

"Thanks. I know I'm being pathetic, so thanks for humoring me."

Kit shrugged her off. "You're fine. Keep in mind, though, if you were like this all the time, it would be annoying," her friend smiled. "But I know you. You'll wake up tomorrow and everything will be fine again—not that all your problems will be solved, but you'll be tackling them instead of being momentarily overwhelmed by them."

"Momentarily overwhelmed?" Jesse grinned. She liked the phrase. "Speaking of being overwhelmed, where's your brother? Still with you?"

"He is. But he comes and goes at odd hours. I'm not really sure just what he's doing and I'd like to think it's legal since he does most of his work with the government, but then, you know, maybe it's not."

And just like that, Kit was right. Everything wasn't fixed, everything wasn't fine, but she was feeling a hell of a lot better than she had before her friend showed up.

• • •

The morning dawned clear and bright and Jesse snuggled into her bed and listened to the birds chirping and singing the morning away. She and Kit had finished the bottle of wine between the two of them, and then, to make sure Kit was sober when she drove home, they'd stayed up late, cooking a light meal, playing some card games, and watching a movie. As a result, for the first time since before the kids, Jesse had slept in past ten.

She contemplated this fact and then smiled. Her life was changing with the boys growing up and moving on. It was a tough adjustment, but there were going to be good things about it, too. Like learning how to sleep in again.

She spent the day running a few errands, working in the garden, and paying bills. She thought about going back into Mark's office but decided to take the day off from that. At three in the afternoon, she actually took a nap—like sleeping in, it was something she hadn't done in a long, long time—and was awakened by her phone ringing two hours later. James was due back in Windsor but was calling to ask if he could stay a couple of days to work with Vivi's twin cousins, Naomi and Brian. If it had been anyone else she would have said no, but she knew the cousins well and trusted them implicitly. They ran a security company that focused almost exclusively on digital security—just about the coolest business ever, according to James.

She called the twins to confirm and they enthusiastically repeated their offer, so she called James back and gave him permission to stay. Naomi would bring him home Thursday night when she came out to visit Vivi for the weekend. With Matt still down at the shore for a few more days, she found that the thought of having her house to herself, of being a parent to two adult children—not that she was quite there yet—might not be such a daunting thought after all.

With a charity event on her calendar for that night, she showered and changed. Blow-drying her hair into big, loose waves, she pinned it back on one side with an antique comb Mark had given her years ago. She slipped on a green, silk dress that draped and hugged her body in all the right places and a pair of black sandals with a four-inch heel. She wasn't interested in anyone other than David, but she wasn't too proud to admit that it would be nice to catch an appreciative look or two that night.

She applied her makeup, touched up her hair, and decided to drive Wanda to the event instead of Matt's car. She didn't usually drive her on the highway. Not because Wanda couldn't handle it, but because Jesse had seen the victims of too many accidents from older cars. They were big and heavy but just didn't have the same safety features as more modern cars. But still, a girl could use a little fun every now and then, and Wanda was definitely fun.

And the old car definitely caught people's attention when she came rumbling onto the scene. Jesse was still laughing to herself when she walked into the elegant hotel along the Hudson River in Albany. She wasn't sure what the valet stared at more, her or Wanda, and damn if she didn't feel just a tad bit competitive with her own car.

She headed straight into the ballroom and was greeted at the door by several friends. This event—one of many she attended throughout the year as head of Riverside Hospital—was one of her favorites. And as a board member, she was more invested than usual in the success of the evening. The event, an auction and dinner, raised several hundred thousand dollars for Children's Health Alliance, an organization that provided healthcare to children who would otherwise go without. They weren't going to solve the problem of children's healthcare in one night, but the gala went far to helping.

So she spent the next hour or so chatting with friends, driving up the bids on the silent auction items, and dealing with all the little last minutes details and problems that came up. By the time dinner was served, she was more than ready to take her seat. All the board members were seated at tables with major donors and, not having done the seating arrangement herself, Jesse was pleased to see Anna and Joseph Klinkenburg, and their guests, at her table. Anna and Joseph were as old as the hills but were still kicking it like people half their age. And they were, hands down, her favorite major donors because they did it from the goodness of their hearts. And though they loved coming to the gala to visit and catch up with friends, the hoopla around their generosity usually seemed to embarrass them more than anything else.

Jesse chatted with the guests at her table and caught up with Anna and Joseph over the salad. When the main course was served, Gerald, the president of the board, went up to the podium to give his talk and introduce the speakers for the night—a physician who volunteered with the Alliance to provide free care to children in need and a young family whose two small children had benefitted from that care. The doctor talked about how the Alliance connected with local physicians and healthcare suppliers to ensure that quality care and equipment were made available at no cost to the families. And the parents elaborated on how their doctor had worked with them for over a year to make sure that not only their children's basic medical needs—such as checkups and asthma medication—were met, but that they also received benefits such as eyeglasses and a new wheelchair for the youngest of the two.

When the physician and the family sat back down, Jesse doubted there was a dry eye in the house. Although the silent auction had concluded for the evening, she was pleased to see people pulling out their checkbooks to make donations.

Even as she glanced around the room to enjoy the moment, a small prickling sensation washed over her skin. She paused for a moment to let the moment of fear subside. She was fairly certain she was being watched, but that didn't always mean something ominous. She had hoped to catch an appreciative look or two tonight, maybe it was just that. When her heart rate dropped back down to normal, she casually scanned the room.

And two tables over, her eyes landed on David.

• • •

Holding a glass of sparkling water, David's hand stilled halfway up. He hadn't known Jesse was going to be here tonight and when he'd caught sight of her two tables away, well, warm and fuzzy didn't quite cover what he'd felt. No, it was something much more primal than that.

She had her hair mostly down but pulled up on one side, like a film star from the fifties. Her dress, what he could see of it, draped between her breasts and met at her shoulders in thin straps. He couldn't see the back, but he'd bet it draped, too. The fabric was soft, maybe silk, if he had to guess, and it moved with and clung to her as she shifted in her seat. And it was the same green as the color in her hazel eyes. He couldn't see her eyes clearly from where he sat, but he knew their color well.

And then those eyes landed on him and the world didn't exactly stand still, but it did narrow in. For a moment, the rustle of everyone around him, the jostling of chairs as people reached for their wallets, faded into the background, and all his attention focused on her. She held his gaze, though he could feel her giving him the same assessment he'd given her—taking in his tux, what she could see of it, and in general, his presence at this event.

Then someone bumped his arm and the moment was gone. They were still looking at each other, but he saw the questions creep into her eyes. They hadn't had a chance to talk since that day he'd visited her office. She didn't know what he was thinking, about her or about what she had—and hadn't—offered him. Still holding her gaze, he raised his glass in a small gesture. Tonight, they'd talk, he promised without saying a word. She nodded, then her attention was drawn to her neighbor and she turned away.

An hour later, David was never so glad for the opportunity to dance in his life. Not really much of a dancer under normal circumstances—he'd only gone to the requisite high school events and missed out on the club scene in his twenties—he was making an exception tonight. When he was sure the band was striking up a slow song, he crossed the room and asked Jesse to join him. The older couple standing with her looked a bit surprised, and maybe a touch delighted, and urged her to agree. Within seconds, he had one hand resting on her lower back, the other wrapped around one of hers and tucked against his chest.

They swayed to the music for moment and he was content just to feel her so close.

And then she spoke. "You didn't call."

He took another moment to absorb the feel of her pressed against him and then answered. "I did, when I got off work tonight, before I came here. If you look, you'll have a message."

He spread his hand wider across the small of her back and curved his fingers around her waist. He could feel her going soft under his hands—his body, of course, had the exact opposite reaction.

"Do I need to listen to it or are you going to tell me what you said?" she asked.

He didn't miss the hesitancy in her voice. He found it hard to believe she could wonder about his intentions, but obviously she was. He drew back just enough to look down into her face and spoke.

"Here's where I stand, Jesse. The last nine months have been the first in my adult life that I haven't been responsible for someone else. That I haven't had to worry about someone else's schedule or make sure homework or laundry was done or that food, good food, was on the table. The first time in my adult life that it doesn't matter to anyone but me if I don't do the dishes or if I eat takeout every night or sleep until noon when I'm not working."

He turned her around the dance floor, moving them away from the other couples. "And while all my friends spent their twenties bar hopping, dating, and growing up, I was changing diapers, coaching T-ball, and going to parent-teacher conferences."

He stopped talking for a moment and pulled her closer. She rested her head on his chest and as he turned them on the dance floor, he brushed a kiss across her hair when he knew no one could see.

"For the first time, I finally get to do what I want, maybe not all the time, but most of the time. Including dating whoever or however I want."

That got her attention and she pulled her head away from him and looked up.

"Look, Jesse, even if doing all the things my friends did in their twenties appealed to me—bar hopping, casual sex, and all that—it would be kind of creepy for someone my age. And just for the record, it *doesn't* appeal to me. But what does appeal to me is sex—like you said, 'hopefully good sex,'" he added with a smile. "And companionship—uncomplicated companionship. I get it," he said as his hand stroked her back out of view of the others on the dance floor. "I get what you want and why. But I need to make a few things clear." He waited until she nodded before continuing. "If we do this, it *is* a relationship. It's not just no-strings sex. It's friendship and all that, on *our* terms. I want to know I can call you if I've had a bad day, or that you'll call me if you've had a bad day, or if something funny happened and you just want to share it."

She nodded again.

"And it's also monogamous." That was non-negotiable for him. If he wasn't so interested in her, maybe, maybe he wouldn't care as much. But he was. And while he wasn't creepy possessive, he didn't want the complications that would come with an open relationship.

Thankfully, she nodded in agreement.

"I'm not going to sugarcoat it. What we'd be doing is unusual and it will probably have a few kinks to work out. Keeping things private and as uncomplicated as they can be between the two of us isn't always going to be easy. But I think, if we agree, it could work for us for as long as we both want it to."

Her big hazel eyes were staring at him. She swayed in his arms in silence for several long moments, and for a brief second, he wondered if maybe she'd changed her mind.

Then she spoke. "So, just to be clear, you're in?"

He smiled at her choice of words. Ducking his head to place his lips next her ear, he whispered, "Metaphorically and, I hope soon, literally too."

"Jesse!" The voice startled them apart and she drew back from his embrace.

"Gerald. Is everything all right? Oh, Gerald, this is David Hathaway from the Albany Fire Department. David this is Gerald Black, the president of our board." David shook hands with the short, older man who switched his gaze back to Jesse.

"I hate to interrupt your fun, but the hotel staff has some questions about the silent auction items, and since you coordinated that piece, I was hoping you might be able to help?" The man sounded sincere in his apology and David stepped away. She looked at him.

"Go. We'll catch up later," he said.

Gerald turned back to him and smiled. "Thank you, Mr. Hathaway, and please thank the department for their donation of the child's birthday party. It's always one of biggest sellers. Half the time, I'm fairly certain the parents are buying it so they can have an excuse to ride in the fire truck."

David smiled and nodded, thinking Gerald was probably right. Every year, the fire department offered to host a child's birthday party for the highest bidder, and every year, from what he'd heard, it was the adults who showed up with gleaming eyes.

Watching them leave, Gerald leaning in close to talk to Jesse, David wondered when she might be done for the night. And when they might be able to meet up again. Not soon enough, his body insisted, even as he turned away and went in search of his teammates.

• • •

He had seen neither hide nor hair of Jesse since she'd left the room to talk with the hotel staff over an hour earlier and his mind was starting to agree with what his body had been telling him all along. He was standing with his chief and a few folks from other fire stations having the one drink—a glass of whiskey—that he was allowing himself that night, but the only thing on his mind was when he'd see Jesse again. As he glanced idly around trying to catch a glimpse of her, a man bumped into him.

"Excuse me," David said, automatically.

"No, my fault," the man replied, glancing at David. Then, after a moment's hesitation, he cocked his head to the side and asked, "Don't I know you?"

David glanced back at the man. He was a few inches shorter than David and probably a few years older. His receding hairline and air of confidence made him seem even older. David frowned.

The man looked vaguely familiar, but he couldn't place him or the woman with him—a young brunette who wasn't quite managing to mask her bored expression.

"Wait, I know," the man said, with a vague gesture of his hand. "You were with Jesse that day in the hospital," he said.

David nodded when recognition dawned. "Oh, yeah. Dr. Bennet, right? You brought Jesse her phone?"

Dr. Bennet gave a distracted nod as he scanned the room, and David wondered how a man could manage to be both engaged and so seemingly disengaged in a conversation at the same time.

"Are you here with her tonight? I haven't seen her," Dr. Bennet asked, still eyeing the room. And now David knew why. He was looking for her.

He shook his head. "No, I'm not. A few of us came from the fire department," he responded with a nod in the direction of his teammates behind him.

Dr. Bennet's eyes cut back to his and, after a brief calculating look, he gave a sharp nod. "Then I'll let you get on with your night," he said.

David watched as Dr. Bennet pulled the young woman behind him. For a brief moment, he wondered if the physician was interested in Jesse or if maybe the two of them had been an item at some point. But that unpleasant train of thought was cut off when his eye caught on a waitress who looked to be making her way toward him.

"Sir?" she said. He turned his back to his colleagues to see what she wanted. "Are you Mr. Hathaway?" she asked

He frowned, wondering what was going on, but nodded. "Yes, I'm David Hathaway."

"Then this is for you." She handed him an envelope with his name on it. Not having any idea what it was all about, he watched her leave before breaking the seal. And when he did, he was glad his back was still to his teammates.

Inside was a slip of paper with "990 in 45 minutes" written on it. And a magnetic key card.

Tension and anticipation coiled in his body and his head jerked up. Scanning the room, he saw her, forty feet away, standing with a group of older women. Her gaze landed on him and held, even as she laughed at something someone said. Raising her glass of champagne to him in a mock toast, much as he had toasted her with his sparkling water earlier in the night, she gave him a ghost of a smile before returning her attention to the other guests.

"Hathaway? Everything all right?"

He turned back to his chief, tucking the envelope, and its contents into his breast pocket. "Yeah, fine. Just something I thought I won at the auction."

"And did you?"

David shook his head. "No, turns out I was wrong. But if you'll excuse me, I need to get going."

His departure was abrupt but there was no way he was going to be able to stand around and shoot the shit with a group of people who, with the exception of his chief, knew him too well. Not when he had a room key burning a hole in his pocket and a few things he wanted to pick up before he saw Jesse again.

He exited the hotel and walked a couple of blocks to a mini-mart. The cool night air seemed to help him get his anticipation in check. Picking up a pack of condoms had just about the opposite effect. Ever practical, he also picked up some toothpaste and a couple of toothbrushes, hoping they'd have a chance to use them. In the morning.

He didn't know what her schedule was—if the boys were back home, or if they would be expecting her home—but he hoped there might be a chance that they could stay all night. It had been a while since he'd had sex and an even longer time since he'd actually been able to sleep next to someone. Having a young child, then a teenage daughter, had put the kibosh on most of that. But he wanted both, tonight, with Jesse. Hopefully, lots of the former and little bit of the latter.

Heading back into the hotel, he took the stairs to the third floor then caught the elevator. He hadn't wanted to risk seeing anyone he knew while waiting in the lobby for an elevator to take him to the ninth floor. He was pretty sure no one would say anything to him, but was equally sure it would get back to his own station, and he'd be subject to the endless questions he, like Jesse, was trying to avoid.

Letting himself into the room, he glanced at the clock. He had ten minutes before she was due to arrive. He stripped off his jacket and bow tie. Laying them on the chair by the window, he looked out at the night view. The city lay vibrant and bright below him, the Hudson River cutting an empty, black swath through its urban surroundings.

Needing something to do while he waited, he tugged off his cufflinks and placed them on the table, then removed his shirt. Pulling his undershirt out from his pants, he sat down to remove his shoes and socks. When he was done, he debated whether or not to look in the mini-fridge for a bottle of champagne, then decided it would be too cliché. Turning back to the view of the city before him, he forced himself to still his own body.

And that was where she found him five minutes later—barefoot in tuxedo pants and a white cotton t-shirt, watching the Albany night, waiting for her.

He turned to look at her over his shoulder as she came in. She paused in the room's entryway as the door clicked shut behind her. It had been a long time since he'd wanted something or someone as much as he wanted this night and this woman. She took a few steps into the room, never taking her eyes off of him, and stopped again, dropping her wrap and purse on the desk. He turned to face her.

"I've never done anything like this before, David. I'm thirty-six years old and you're only the third man I've ever been with," she said.

He could hear a hint of nerves in her voice and he gave a fleeting thought to saying something soothing. But then she took a step toward him and her dress moved against her body.

"Good," was all he managed.

A hint of a smile played on her lips at his response. He realized then that all the tension he'd felt since first receiving her envelope had coalesced into a restrained calm—the kind of calm he felt before walking into a burning building.

He held out a hand and she walked toward him, closing the space between them. He slid his fingers into her hair and pulled her to him. Angling her face up toward his, he paused for a moment and just took her in. Then he dipped his head and met her mouth with his.

The kiss was as tempered as their first and he knew this was like the first few steps into the building. He knew what he was doing and where he was going, but the heat—the explosion— would come in its own time, at its own pace.

He felt her fingertips, then her hands, against his stomach. They lingered there for a moment, tentative. Then she slid them up his chest, over his shoulders, and sank her nails into his hair.

Suddenly, the explosion was there.

He wrapped his other arm around her, grabbing a handful of her dress, and tugged her against him. Her arms came down around his shoulders, pressing her flush against him, and he felt one of her legs come up toward his hip.

He dropped his hand and wrapped it around her thigh, pulling it higher, pulling her tighter against him. Her head fell back and he lowered his mouth to her exposed neck.

"David," she murmured.

Feeling the smoothness of her skin under his calloused fingers, he ran his hand up her thigh, taking the hem of her dress with it. When he reached her backside, she lowered her leg and moved back just enough to let him know she wanted the dress gone.

More than happy to comply, without a word and without taking his eyes off her, he pulled the silky, green gown over her head and dropped it onto the chair beside his jacket. She wore a cream lace strapless bra and matching underwear he was pretty sure were called boyshorts, though there was nothing boyish about them, especially not on her curves.

Looking at her, he clenched his jaw and forced himself to take a step back. It was either that or push her up against the wall and finish them both off in less than five minutes—it was a hard call, but he had enough presence of mind to recognize that this was their first time and he ought to try to make it more memorable than that.

She reached for his belt buckle and his stomach jumped. Without taking her eyes off his, she unbuckled it, released the button on his pants, and lowered his zipper. Stepping closer to him, she slid her hands down over his hips and to his thighs, taking his pants and boxers down with them.

Stepping out of his clothes, he then pulled off his shirt. For a moment, they simply stared at each other. It was possible she was taking him in as much as he was taking her in, but as far as he was concerned, his view of her standing there in her fancy underwear and heels, was much, much better than her view of him.

Unable to wait any longer, he reached his arms around her, unclasped her bra, and let it fall to the floor. She made an instinctive move to cover herself, but he caught her wrist in his hand and forced it back to her side. With his other hand he reached up and touched her, cupped her breast in his hand. When his thumb brushed over her nipple, she made a small sound that went straight to his groin.

Keeping hold of her wrist with his other hand, he wrapped his arm around her, taking her arm with his, and placed it against the small of her back, pulling her toward him, arching her up. He dipped his knees, lowered his head, and, still holding her breast, took her nipple in his mouth. She uttered a quiet curse as the fingers of her free hand tangled in his hair, holding him in place, then pulling him to her.

"David." It was a plea, nothing less than that. He let go of her wrist and soon she had both hands in his hair, holding him, guiding him, showing him exactly what she wanted. He hoped to god she did the same when he finally had the opportunity to taste her.

Her legs gave a slight tremble and her grip slackened. He

wanted to spend all night doing this, but knew neither of them was going to hold out much longer, at least not this first time. He looked up at her and that was all it took.

In a flash they were on the bed, her heels and underwear discarded on the floor. She lay on her back while he kneeled between her legs. Running a hand up her thigh, he slid a single finger inside her, testing her, even as he reached for a condom.

She made a small, needy sound as he pulled his finger out, then slid it back in. Her legs fell open as he tore the condom wrapper using his teeth and his free hand, then rolled it on. He thought about asking her to do it, knowing he'd enjoy the sight of her small hands on him, but seeing her spread out, waiting for him, he decided that could wait for another time.

Still teasing her with his fingers, he leaned down over her.

Her hands came up and cupped his face. "Now, David. Please."

He positioned himself, and with one last look before her eyes shut and his rolled into the back of his head, he slid inside.

• • •

Jesse awoke in the morning, naked and just a little bit sore. David was curled behind her, an arm draped over her waist. Her eyes found the clock and she wasn't at all surprised to see it was past ten in the morning. They'd been up most of the night, exploring each other, enjoying each other. She hadn't had a night like that in, well, forever, if she was honest. Of course, she and Mark had had their fair share of good times, but she had a different kind of confidence now than she did in her younger years with Mark, and those younger years had seemed to set the tone of their sex life. With David, it was all new, for good and for bad, and there was none of the baggage or expectations.

He stirred behind her and she craned her head to see if he was awake.

"I'm only half awake. In fact, how long did you book this room 'cause I might not move for another day or so." His voice was slurred with sleep, but as if to prove his statement wrong, a certain part of his anatomy stirred against her backside.

"Okay, maybe I'm a little more awake than I led you to believe."

She laughed softly and turned on her back.

His eyes popped open. "How are you feeling?" His hand came up and stroked her cheek.

In retrospect, it may not have been such a good idea to tell him he was her third lover ever, but it was sweet that he was concerned about her.

She smiled. "I'm sore, in a good way, and feeling more relaxed than I have in a long time."

A grin spread across his face. "You and me both." He lifted his head to look at the clock. "How much longer do we have here?"

"Checkout is at eleven, unfortunately."

"Hmm," his head hit the pillow and his eyes drifted closed again as his fingers made their way into her hair. "When do the boys get back?"

"Matt gets home Wednesday. James isn't home until Thursday."

His eyes opened again. "I don't have to work again until Thursday."

"Come to my place today." She hadn't thought twice before she'd asked. Maybe she should have been more subtle, but the thought of spending the day with him—lounging around her house, cooking a leisurely meal, maybe watching a movie—appealed to her and she didn't want to second-guess it.

"Are you sure?" he asked.

"Yes." She didn't hesitate. It was what she wanted. If he didn't want the same thing, he would need to say so.

One side of his mouth quirked into a smile. "Then that sounds good to me."

CHAPTER 13

IT TOOK EXACTLY TWENTY MINUTES from when she walked into her office for the glow of her weekend to wear off. She and David had spent Sunday doing exactly what they wanted—watching movies, strolling around her property, cooking, and of course, spending a good deal of time in bed.

But by nine thirty Monday morning, the sense of satisfaction and relaxation was gone, completely.

"Are you *sure* the lawyers signed off on all this?" Ed Greely, one of the hospital board members asked. For the third time.

"Of course they did, Ed," interjected Lucy Cantor, another board member. "What we should be worried about isn't the legal issues, but Jesse's safety, and that of our entire staff."

Jesse had set up this series of meetings to keep her board informed about Ian's investigation and this was the third conference call of its kind. The primary issue of the investigation was her safety, but because the hospital was involved, she had wanted to keep the board informed.

"Do the authorities think there might be a risk to anyone other than Jesse?" Ed asked.

Jesse sighed and took her phone off mute so she could talk. "At this point, they are fairly certain it is just me." Which felt just about as good as it sounded. "But we have taken extra precautions around the hospital and the regional clinics, just in case."

"And how much is that costing us?" Ed's question sparked another round of comments from the other board members on the call and she hit her mute button again. She knew this was par for the course. Some of them actually had constructive things to say. Others simply needed to talk. Half listening to the conversation on the phone, her head shot up when she heard Kayla's voice, much louder than usual, just outside her closed office door.

She frowned. She couldn't make out what her assistant was saying, but it wasn't like Kayla to raise her voice. Then Jesse heard Kayla's voice, loud and firm once again, followed by something bumping against the door, making her jump.

She took her phone off mute again. "I'm sorry everyone," she interrupted. "I have another meeting I need to get to. If you have any additional concerns, please let Kayla know and she'll schedule the time on my calendar. But between now and our next call, I'll send you regular updates every few days."

There was a bit of grumbling, but everyone hung up and in a flash she was up and opening her door.

"I don't care *who* you are, Mr. Forrester, you will sit down until I have the opportunity to ask Ms. Baker if she has the time to see you."

From her position in the doorway, Jesse could see that her assistant was doing a good job of holding her ground. She could also see Caleb towering over Kayla, attempting to intimidate her. When Kayla didn't back down, he muttered a not-so-silent curse, backed up a few steps, and sat down. A movement to Jesse's right caught her attention. She turned to find Ian, already seated, clearly enjoying the show.

She cleared her throat. Kayla spun around, and both Ian and Caleb stood.

"I'm sorry, Jesse. I tried to keep him out until you were done," Kayla said, glaring at Caleb.

"And it looks like you did a good job. I'm not sure Caleb is a man who's ever been put in his place before." She grinned at him as he glared back at her assistant.

"Ian." She turned in greeting. "Have you met Caleb Forrester, Kit's brother?"

Ian nodded a greeting to Caleb but neither man offered to shake hands.

"So, who was here first?" Jesse asked, looking to Kayla for direction.

"Sheriff MacAllister."

"Caleb, will you give us a few moments, please?" He was going to protest, she knew he would, so before he had the chance, she ushered Ian into her office and closed the door.

"Interesting guy," Ian said with a nod toward the door.

"Like Kit, in some ways."

"And not at all in others," he smiled. "So, I have some updates, not much, but I thought I would stop in and run them by you."

And for the next ten minutes he did. They'd eliminated two of the people they were looking into, which in some ways made her feel better, but since they were no closer to finding out who they were actually looking for, it also didn't go far. When Ian finished, she thanked him and walked him to the door.

Caleb was sitting in the same spot, still eyeing Kayla, who was doing a fine job of ignoring him. Jesse said good-bye to Ian and motioned Caleb inside. He gave a huff, which Kayla also ignored, and walked toward Jesse.

"Oh, Jesse," Kayla spoke as if Caleb didn't exist. "Ed Greely wants to have lunch on Wednesday and do you still want to go to that dinner on Thursday?"

"Go ahead and book the lunch with Ed and cancel the dinner. James is coming home Thursday. And while I'm sure he'll want to hang out with his friends, on the off chance he wants to have dinner at home, I'd like to be there."

Kayla nodded and Jesse followed Caleb into her office.

"I don't think I impressed her," he said, taking an uninvited seat.

"I don't know why. I'm sure you were polite and civilized and everything." She arched a brow at him when his eyes narrowed at her. She held his gaze as she sat.

"Your boyfriend was investigated for starting a fire back in California," he said.

She blinked. "Excuse me."

"Your boyfriend, David Hathaway. There was a complaint filed against him and he was investigated for starting a fire at a private home."

"It wasn't him." Of that she was certain. What she wasn't certain of was just how Caleb knew her relationship with David was more than what she had intimated when she'd spoken about him at brunch that day.

"Might I suggest you're biased?" Sarcasm laced Caleb's voice.

"Of course you can and you'd be right. But it still wasn't him."

He seemed a little startled by her certainty. But then again, if he did live in the shadow world, he probably never ran into anyone who could say anything with certainty.

"What was the outcome of the investigation?" she prompted.

"No charges were filed. The fire was arson, but they never caught who did it."

"And David's involvement?" she pressed.

"He was cleared." Caleb all but bit the words out.

"So I'm not the only one who knows he wasn't involved."

"Or he was just very careful."

She drummed her fingers on her desk and rested her chin in her hand. She appreciated his concern, she really did. But he was barking up the wrong tree. "When was this?"

"Three years ago."

"And was anyone hurt?"

His gaze slid to the side. "A young woman. She lived but suffered third-degree burns on about 20 percent of her body."

Jesse's heart lurched. "Why are you telling me this?"

"Because I think you should know about the man you're spending time with."

She studied his eyes, and for a moment, he looked uncomfortable but he didn't look away. She thought about asking how he knew she and David were spending time together, but decided that would sound too defensive. If he was guessing and she asked, it would confirm his belief.

"Thank you for telling me, but I know he wasn't involved. If you have information that is relevant to the case, though, you should be telling Ian, or even Vivi, his wife."

She saw his jaw tick and his mouth tighten, but he stood. She did the same.

"Be careful, Jesse. You have a lot of good things in your life, don't do anything stupid to put them in jeopardy."

She moved from behind her desk and stood in front of him, wondering again, what kind of man he was, or rather, what kind of life he led.

"I'm not a stupid woman, Caleb. I drive carefully, I use my alarm, I even carry pepper spray. But I work in a hospital. No one knows better than I do that sometimes shit just happens to good people and there isn't anything in the world we can do to stop or change it. I appreciate your concern, I really do. And I will be careful, because you're right; there are too many good things in my life to take dumb chances. But maybe, maybe while you're out there looking for answers, to my situation or any other, you should remember that—that sometimes it's just not anyone's fault." She believed in what she was saying, but even as the words were leaving her mouth, she wasn't sure why she felt the need to say them. There *was* someone after her—a very real person out there who *was* to blame.

But Caleb had demons, of that she was also certain, and having seen the same look in many a doctor's eyes, she knew he was blaming himself for something—something he thought he could have done better, something he thought he could have prevented, something he thought he could have changed but didn't. Maybe it was true.

But in her experience, more often than people wanted to admit—especially people like Caleb or the doctors in her hospital—even doing everything right wasn't a guarantee. The fact of that uncertainty was a burden to bear and everyone who worked with her had to shoulder it. She suspected Caleb did, too. And he was fighting it every step of the way.

"I'll be going then." He stepped away.

"Next time, stop by with some good news, or even no news, and we can just go grab a drink somewhere." She extended the offer as he reached the door. He looked at her over his shoulder, then gave a nod and left. She didn't worry that he'd taken her invitation the wrong way, but she did worry that he hadn't taken her seriously. If anyone looked like they needed a friend to just sit with, it was Caleb.

• • •

Time seemed to move at warp speed after that first weekend with David, with the exception of the investigation.

With no new leads, the investigations—the police's, Ian's, and hers—had slowed to almost nothing. David had concluded his findings about the explosive in Julie's shop and then turned everything over to the Windsor Police. Marcus and Carly hadn't been able to do anything with his report yet, since they had no leads. The patients and letters Ian had been looking into had come up blank, although there was still one more to look into—a man who would be out of town for the remainder of the summer. As for her own investigation into what exactly Mark had been looking into before he died—when she'd closed up the last box without finding anything, she'd *almost* convinced herself that he must have just simply forgotten to tell her.

On the one hand, it was frustrating not finding anything, not knowing anything more about any of the investigations. But the good news was, there had been no more "accidents," no more destruction of people, namely herself, or property, so she couldn't complain too much.

But while the investigations had slowed, the rest of the summer had flown by and it was with some surprise that Jesse found herself standing at the open trunk of her new Subaru—her little black one had turned out to be unsalvageable after the accident—looking at boxes packed full of Matt's things. With dismay.

"Come on, Mom. It's not like you didn't know this day was coming." Her son gave her an indulgent smile. She really couldn't believe he was headed off to college today. Classes didn't start for two weeks, but athletes had to check in early. Both her car and his were packed with his things; the plan was to drive into Boston and get him set up. Both she and James were going—she was going to drop her younger son off with Naomi and Brian for a two-week visit and spend a few days shopping in Boston on her own, before heading back home.

With James gone, it would leave her almost two weeks to spend time with David. They'd been seeing each privately whenever they could since that weekend in June and she was still enjoying their time together. Maybe it was because they were both older or both knew what it meant to have responsibility, but things seemed easier with him in some ways than they had with Mark. David cooked, did his own laundry, made his own schedule, and cleaned up without having to be asked—he took care of himself while still making an effort to be with her. He was considerate of her time, as she was with his, and so far, they'd made it work well. She would miss her kids over the next few weeks, but it would be nice to have more time with him.

"I know," she said, answering Matt's comment. "But just because I knew it was coming doesn't mean I have to be happy about it."

He grinned and wrapped an arm around her neck, pulling her close. He was so much taller than her; it always made her laugh. "You want me to go college, admit it."

"You know I insist you go to college, but again, it doesn't mean I have to like it," she said, jabbing a playful elbow in his side.

"Come on, let's go," James insisted, joining them and tossing his one duffel bag into the trunk of her car. She wasn't sure it was going to close, but between the boys, they got it shut.

"I don't suppose you plan to ride with me, James?" she asked.

The boys gave each other a look that she was pretty sure most parents were familiar with—the one that said something along the lines of "Mom's talking crazy but how do we tell her without hurting her feelings?" They had their moments, but she was glad they were close enough to have such conversations, even if they were silent.

"Never mind." She shook her head. It would be James's last chance to spend some time with his brother before college and she didn't want to take that away from him.

"I'll come with you, Mom, if you want." Both her boys were sweet, but James, the baby, was definitely the more affectionate of the two.

"Thanks," she managed a smile. "But your music will drive me crazy anyway. Go with your brother."

They hit no traffic as they headed into the city, making the trip an easy one, but it was still late afternoon by the time all Matt's things were unloaded and set up in his room. She dropped James off at Naomi and Brian's Back Bay townhouse, a building they'd divided into two large apartments, one for each twin. Then, after that, Jesse headed to Vivi's North End apartment. As a professor at the university, her friend often stayed over in Boston, so she'd kept her old apartment there to use as needed. It frequently sat empty, so Vivi was happy to give her use of it for the weekend.

She and the boys had agreed to meet up at one of the small Italian restaurants in the North End that Vivi had recommended. The area wasn't that far from the nearest T station, but the neighborhood, with its myriad of narrow, crisscrossing streets, also wasn't as easy to navigate as she would have liked. However, she figured it would be a good test of the boys' directional skills to not only get to the North End but then find the little hole-in-the-wall restaurant, as well.

She was pleased when they had both arrived, and on time, too. Together, they enjoyed a decadent meal before James headed back to the Back Bay and Matt set off to meet up with his new roommates.

Alone and back at Vivi's apartment, Jesse called David to check in. He still had two more nights on shift so he couldn't drive to Boston to meet her. She was seriously contemplating going home a night early but decided to see how she felt the next day. She had just hung up with him when the apartment buzzer rang, telling her someone was downstairs. She frowned. She wasn't expecting anyone.

She searched for the right button on the wall by the door and called down. "Yes?" she said.

"It's us."

Jesse couldn't help but smile. She wasn't altogether certain who constituted "us," but she definitely recognized Kit's voice. She hit the buzzer and in less than a minute Kit, Vivi, and Matty were bursting through the door.

"Kind of a last minute thing," Matty said, dumping an overnight bag on the ground.

"Thought you might not want to be alone tonight," Vivi said, stepping forward and giving Jesse a hug as best she could with her burgeoning belly.

"And we're going dancing!" Kit grinned and did a little jig.

"Dancing? I haven't been dancing in ages. Like, to a club?" Jesse asked.

"Yep, we're going clubbing." Kit started digging through her bag, found something, and tossed it to her. "Here, put this on."

Jesse looked at the piece of black fabric she now held in her hands. "This" didn't look like much.

"Everyone here is several years older than you, Kit." Jesse said. "And Vivi is almost seven-months pregnant. Exactly what kind of club are we going to?" she asked, eying the small piece of material. But secretly, the idea was starting to appeal to her. She hadn't had a real girls' night out in forever.

"The slutty kind. Probably Lansdowne Street, although the Alley is closer. Young men will buy you drinks and you can treat them like kids and they'll spend half the night trying to prove to you otherwise. It's very entertaining. You should try it more often,"

Kit said as her head all but disappeared into her bag as she dug around for something else.

Jesse glanced at Vivi and Matty to ask what they thought of this plan. She was surprised to find that they were both pulling out their own outfits for the night.

She grinned. "Then I guess the only question I have is, should I wear my hair up or down?"

• • •

David chuckled into the phone.

"Don't laugh, it hurts my head," Jesse said, which only made him laugh louder. She grumbled something unkind. She'd texted him the night before to let him know that her friends had shown up on her doorstep and they were going out dancing. He'd been glad to read that she was getting out but had felt a tug of regret at not being able to see her all dressed up for a club. As the night progressed, it was obvious she was having a good time, and maybe having a drink or two—or twelve. She'd sent a couple more text messages—some spelled correctly, some barely comprehensible, and most suggestive enough that, by the time the fourth one came in, he'd needed to excuse himself from the communal room at the station to read them.

"I wish I could be there to take care of you," he said now. And he did. He'd bet she looked cute all grumpy and hungover.

"Me, too," she mumbled. "I think it's safe to say that I'm going to miss any shopping I had planned, though. The thought of walking around and talking to people, let alone listening to the sounds of traffic on Newbury Street, so does *not* sound good right now."

He smiled to himself. She sounded so put out by the whole thing. "So, what *are* you going to do?" he asked.

"Take a bottle of ibuprofen and sleep, that is, *after* I drink a gallon of orange juice. God, in some ways I'm glad I missed this in my twenties."

"Yeah, me, too. But the younger you are the faster you recover. So they say."

"No kidding. Kit is up making breakfast. I think I hate her."

He laughed, and then wondered where Jesse was just then. Though he'd become less strict about not talking to her while he was at work, they still didn't usually talk when other people were around, since neither of them was inclined to want to answer any questions that might come up from anyone who happened to be listening in. It was one of the reasons why their relationship was the way it was.

She sighed. "I think I'm going to sleep it off and just come home. I'm not going to do any shopping, so I would rather just curl up in my own bed. Since you're on shift, Mike will have to do for company."

"I wish I could be there." And he did, a lot.

"Me, too. But you're off tomorrow, and the boys are gone for two weeks, so we'll have more time."

Thank god, he thought. It wasn't that they didn't spend time together; he just always felt greedy for more. He made a sound of agreement that must have let her know where his mind was going because she laughed.

"Maybe it's a good thing you're not off until tomorrow, since I'm not sure how much fun I'd be tonight anyway."

"You're always fun. And after some of those text messages you sent me last night, you have some payback coming."

"I texted you?" she asked, obviously trying to recall the action.

"Oh, yeah." He let his tone hint at just what kind of texts she had sent.

She paused. "Oh god, did I sext you?" She sounded horrified.

"And how." He laughed. "I know you'll have them on your phone, but I think it'll be more fun for me to read them to you when I see you tomorrow."

"No! You saved them?"

Her indignation made him laugh again. "Yep."

She groaned. "Am I going to be embarrassed?"

"I'm hoping you'll be inspired."

She laughed at that. "I guess I'll deserve what I get."

"You'll enjoy it, believe me."

"Promises, promises."

"Definitely." The bell rang in the station and he looked up at the board to see the location even as he started moving. "I'll call you later," he said.

She mumbled her assent and he gave a momentary thought to saying something more, but then she hung up. And while he might have spent some time thinking about just what that *more* might have been, he pushed it aside and pulled on his gear.

• • •

David smiled to himself as he drove up Jesse's driveway that evening. She'd left a message for him letting him know when she'd left Boston and he'd decided to surprise her. And after his long day, which had been one thing after another, his chief had told him to go home early and get some rest. Luckily, there hadn't been any fatalities, just two fires, a car accident, and the start of another arson investigation. He was looking forward to a leisurely night with Jesse. And maybe showing her those text messages.

The lights were on in her house when he pulled up, always a good sign. But as he got out of the car, he was struck by how quiet it was. He could usually hear Jesse moving around, or the radio on, but the only thing he heard was the distant sound of an animal as it moved through the forest on the back side of her property. He frowned. Maybe he was just overly aware of the silence after his long day. Or maybe she was already asleep; after all, he was supposed to be on shift and she wasn't expecting him. But still, judging by the time she left the message for him, she couldn't have been home for more than thirty minutes.

His curiosity ratcheted up into anxiety when he saw that the kitchen door was ajar. He called out her name. She didn't call back.

He pulled out his cell phone as he pushed the door open with his foot, careful not to touch the doorknob. Quickly, he thumbed in 9-1-1 on his phone, ready to hit send if needed.

"Jesse?"

Still she didn't answer.

He looked around the kitchen. He'd been over enough times when the boys were away that he knew everything looked normal. Jesse's bag was on the floor where she would have dropped it when she walked in.

But something wasn't right. At all. He wished he had Ian's number rather than the generic 9-1-1. But more importantly, he wished she would answer him.

"Jesse?" he called again walking into the family room. Nothing.

He walked toward the front of the house, then turned to the right, toward her bedroom, calling her name again. A sound to his left made him jump. Mike slinked out from underneath one of the throw blankets on the couch, looked at him, then curled back up on top of the blanket.

The light in her room was off, but he needed to look. He needed to know if she was in there before he checked the rest of the house. Stepping through the doorway, he flicked the switch on.

And saw Jesse, crumpled on the floor, blood oozing from her head.

CHAPTER 14

DAVID SANK TO HER SIDE, even as he hit the call button on his phone and switched it to speaker. Dropping it beside her, he felt for a pulse, a wave of dizzy relief washing over him when he found it.

"9-1-1 dispatcher what's the nature of your emergency?"

In a quick dispassionate voice, he gave the details of the situation, then added a request to have Ian MacAllister called personally. He checked her over and was, at this point, pretty certain that her only injury was to the head. But head injuries could be tricky.

"Come on, Jesse," he coaxed. Without more equipment or a doctor, there was little he could do beyond holding a compress to the wound. "Jesse, please, you're giving me a heart attack here." He murmured, needing to do something, say something.

He heard the dispatcher say that an ambulance was on the way, as was Ian.

Then her eyelashes began to flutter and her eyes slowly opened, causing him to let out a whoosh of breath. She blinked a few times, then focused her eyes on him.

"David?" She looked confused and made to move, but he held her still.

"Are you all right? Can you feel your arms and legs?" he asked. She looked even more confused, but she dutifully tested each limb, then nodded. And then cringed.

"My head. I didn't think I was this hungover."

For the first time in what felt like a lifetime, he gave a small smile. "Something happened and you hit your head. It's not your hangover. Or not entirely, anyway. Just relax and lie still," he directed.

She stopped trying to raise her head and lay back. One of her hands came up to wrap around his forearm. He couldn't help it; he leaned down and rested his face beside hers, cheek to cheek.

"God, you scared me, Jesse." His voice was rough, and raging through him was more than just adrenaline.

"I'll be fine," she managed to say, but he could sense the fear creeping into her as her confusion dissipated and the reality of the situation fell into place. He reached up and pulled the quilt off her bed. Keeping one hand on the compress, he wrapped it around her.

"I hit my head? What happened?" she asked.

He shook his head. "I don't know. Other than the fact that you were lying here unconscious with a gash on your head, I don't know." And there were so many things wrong with that statement that he couldn't even think about it just then. Not when she was still lying dazed on the floor.

He tensed as he heard a car drive up to the house, but then he saw the reflection of red flashing lights. He took her hand in his free one and kissed her palm.

"Ian's coming. As is an ambulance," he said.

"I don't need an ambulance."

"Maybe not," he answered as he heard Ian calling his name. "In here," he shouted toward the door before turning back to her. "But you do need to be checked out. I don't know how long you were out but I'm sure you have a concussion, at the very least."

"Jesse!" Ian cried as he pounded into the room. David saw Ian's eyes settle on him before jumping back to Jesse.

"How are you?" Ian asked, coming down to her side.

"I'll be fine. My head hurts, but I can still feel everything."

"An ambulance is on the way. Do you know what happened?" The sheriff pressed, though judging by his tone, David would wager the question was more out of concern than the beginnings of any future investigation.

She tried to shake her head, then winced and stilled. "I came in, set my bag down, and walked into my bedroom. That's all I remember."

Ian looked at him. "When did you get here?"

David looked at the clock. "Twelve minutes ago. The door was open when I got here, and I found her in here on the floor."

"Did you touch anything?"

He shook his head, then stopped himself. "The bottom of the kitchen door with my foot and the light switch in this room. It was dark when I got here," he added, looking to Jesse to confirm whether she'd turn the light on or not.

She tried to shrug, then just closed her eyes. "I didn't turn it on when I walked in. I was going to head straight into the bathroom."

Ian gave a curt nod. "You good in here?" he asked. "I want to make sure the EMTs don't disturb anything more than they need to."

He nodded, then called Ian back. "When I got here, it was quiet, unusually so. I heard what I thought was an animal crashing through the woods in the back part of the property. I didn't see any other cars on the road."

Ian seemed to take this in, including the fact that he had obviously been to her house enough times to have an idea of what was "unusual." Without a word, he turned and headed back toward the kitchen, just as a second set of red flashing lights appeared through the windows.

"I think our cover is broken," David said, looking back at Jesse. He couldn't have cared less at this point, but after almost two months of successfully keeping things on the down-low, they seemed to be coming out with a bang.

"Ian can be discreet." Her voice was quiet and tired, but she offered him a smile. "What are you doing here, by the way?"

He picked her hand back up and rubbed her palm, needing to touch her. "Long day, the chief gave me the night off since I have to pick up an investigation tomorrow. I thought I would surprise you."

"I'm glad you did."

He was, too. Her injury wasn't life threatening, but he hated the idea that she might have been alone, trying to deal with something like this when she came to.

The paramedics walked in a few minutes later and took over, though David refused to leave the room. He watched as they helped her get up, sat her on the bed, and went through the process of checking the wound, her eyes, and all her vital signs. He watched in an angry silence as they cleaned up the blood. Jesse seemed relieved when they declared that she wouldn't need stiches. Using some skin adhesive, they bound the edges of the cut together.

She had a concussion; of that there was no doubt. But she refused to be transported to the hospital for an MRI, at least not tonight. He was able to extract a promise from her that she would go in the morning, and he had every intention of making her keep it.

After giving David instructions about watching her while she slept, and only letting her sleep for short periods of time, the EMTs cleaned up and left. Leaving Jesse sitting on the edge of her bed, her hair a mess, looking a bit lost.

He sat down, leaned against the headboard, and pulled her into his arms. She went willingly and just lay there—her arms wrapped around his waist, her head resting against his chest.

Several minutes later, Ian found them in that same position. A look of disapproval crossed his face, but David didn't know if it was because they were so obviously together or because the information had been kept from him.

"Jesse?" Ian said.

She lifted her head from his chest and looked at her friend.

"Do you remember anything more?" Ian asked, his voice soft.

She dropped her head back down and shook it against David's chest.

"Was the door open when you got here? Or the alarm on?"

She seemed to mull this over before answering. "I think I unlocked the door, but I know the alarm wasn't on. I think I gave it some thought, but to be honest, I wasn't altogether sure I'd set it when we left. I think James was the last one out of the house and, well, things have quieted down so I just wasn't as vigilant about it when we left yesterday. And when I got home last night and the alarm wasn't on, I figured we'd just forgotten to set it."

"You said you think you unlocked the door. Do you not remember?"

"No, I remember putting my key in and turning it. But I don't remember testing the door before I did. So it's possible it was unlocked before I turned my key, but it might have been locked, too."

Ian frowned. "We need to look around the house and your room to see if we can find what you might have been hit with. Why don't you have David take you to our place and you can stay with Vivienne tonight?"

"Because I'm going to take her home to my place. She can stay with me tonight," David said. Her head came up at his proclamation. It wasn't negotiable as far as he was concerned.

Ian's eyes fixed on David's before switching to Jesse in question.

"We've been seeing each other for almost two months and haven't told anyone because, as much as I love your wife and Matty, they meddle and want to marry me off. My life is complex enough that I didn't want to deal with all the questions," she summed up.

Ian quirked a brow, then let out a chuckle. "She can be nosy."

"She's a shrink and a detective, she doesn't know any other way. And now that you've made her a happily married woman, she wants everyone else to be the same. Even though what works for her may not work for everyone else."

"So, no marriage in the works for you two?" Ian asked.

"And *that* would be exactly why we haven't told anyone," Jesse shot back. "It's none of your business until we decide it's your business."

Ian's gaze, now softened by good humor, came back to David. "And this works for you?"

"It works for both of us."

Ian seemed to weigh the situation, then gave a shrug.

"Whatever works for you is fine with me, but don't discount the hell Vivienne will likely put you through when she does find out. In a loving way, of course."

"So you're not going to tell her?" she confirmed.

"Not my place to tell her, is it?"

Jesse actually laughed. "The hell she's going to put me through is nothing compared to what's going to happen to you when she finds out you knew and didn't tell her."

"If you ever decide to tell her, that's probably true," Ian said, rising from his seat. "But the good news is, I know what I can do with all that energy." He grinned and winked at Jesse, who just laughed. "Now gather up a few things and get out of here. Hathaway, take good care of her and we'll talk tomorrow." He handed David a card containing his office, cell, and home numbers and left the room.

"Ready?" David asked, looking down at her.

She looked tired, and sounded it, too, when she answered. "More than you know."

• • •

Morning didn't even feel like morning when David rolled over and woke Jesse up for the umpteenth time. Since she wasn't hooked up to any machines to monitor her brain function, he wasn't about to let her sleep through her concussion. Thankfully, he could take her to the hospital for the MRI today, and then if they got the green light, they could nap as long as they wanted in the afternoon. Not that he'd be able to nap too long, he still had to head out to the scene of a suspected arson north of Albany, but he could have a short rest.

"Do I look as bad as I feel?" Her voice was gravelly as she pushed her hair out of her face. All things considered, she looked pretty good, and he told her so.

"You're biased." She cuddled up against him and he wrapped his arms around her.

200

"Yep."

He felt her laugh softly into his chest. Then she said, "And I'm glad."

She started tracing her fingers along the lines of his chest. Her gentle touch wasn't trying to arouse him, which was probably why it always did, because there was nothing coy in it, just her enjoying him.

"We need to get you to the hospital for the MRI." He picked up her hand and kissed her palm.

She mumbled an assent, but neither of them moved. He was just about to drift off to sleep again when his phone buzzed beside him. Picking it up, he read the number, frowned, then answered.

"Chief," he said.

"We need you up at the site, stat," came the abrupt reply.

At the tone of his boss's voice, David paused before answering. "I was planning to head up there this afternoon."

"Too bad, we need you up there now. Turns out the guy who owns the building is a key witness in a mafia racketeering case and the feds want to know everything there is to know about what caused that fire."

"Because they want to link it to their case?" he asked. It wasn't unheard of, but these kinds of connections, or potential connections, had come along very rarely in his career.

"Yeah, they want to know if one the mafia goons did it. Turns out the defendant in the case has some firebugs on his payroll and they would sure like to know if our fire shares any of the same signatures."

David sighed and looked at the clock. "I can be there in ninety minutes." That would give him enough time to get Jesse back home and then him back up to the site.

"Good, the feds are coming in and will be there about the same time." His chief rattled off the names of the people David would meet and then hung up.

He looked down at her. She was watching him.

"You have to go in?"

He nodded.

"Everything okay?"

He told her what the chief had told him and then they both reluctantly left the bed.

"You still need to get your MRI," he pointed out as he pulled on his clothes. They'd showered the night before when they'd arrived at his house. No doubt, he had crazy bedhead, but at least he didn't have to waste time in the shower this morning when he needed to make sure Jesse took care of herself. "You should call Ian and Vivi and have one of them take you."

She shook her head as she pulled her hair back into a pony-tail—no bedhead for her. "No, Vivi was a good sport going out to the clubs and all the other night, but she's almost seven-months pregnant and is tired as hell. I'll call Kit."

He was glad she wasn't fighting him on this, but he still needed to be sure it would be taken care of. "Call her now and make sure she can take you. I don't want to leave you until I know you have someone to drive you to the hospital."

She paused and gave him the kind of smile that did funny things to a guy's heart. "If I call her now, she'll be at my house before we are. I'll call her as soon as I get home."

"Promise?" He closed the space between them and wrapped his arms around her.

"Promise." She repeated.

He stared down at her for a long moment. He didn't think he would ever forget the sight of her crumpled body on the floor.

"God, Jesse." He pulled her close and took a moment to hold her. Her arms came around him in comfort and he brushed a kiss across the top of her head.

"We need to go, David."

"I know. I don't want to." He wasn't ready to let her go quite yet.

"I know. But you have to. Everything will be fine. I promise you. Kit will take good care of me."

He took in a deep breath and let it go, letting her go at the same time.

"I know. You have good friends. I think you should keep them close until we figure out what's going on."

She squeezed his hand as they left his house and walked to his truck. "Believe me, David, I plan on it."

• • •

Jesse sat in the passenger seat of Kit's little green convertible. Her friend was not at all happy about the fact that she hadn't been called the night before and was feeling suspicious about not just the break-in, but about all the events of the previous night.

She had called Ian and Vivi, dodged Vivi's questions, and made sure Ian knew she was going to head to Kit's after the MRI, just to have a rest. She had planned to go home, but the evidence collection team had left a bit of a mess that she didn't want to deal with quite yet, plus Kit wouldn't have it anyway.

"So, tell me again what happened last night," Kit said.

Jesse sighed and told her. For the third time.

"Who called the police? And where did you go last night?"

"Kit, can we just drop this? My head still hurts and if I'd known you were going to give me the third degree I would have called Matty."

That shut Kit up. For about thirty seconds.

"Oh my god! You're seeing that guy, aren't you? What was his name? David! That's what it was—or is. You've been seeing him all along and *he's* the one who found you last night. And you went to *his* house, didn't you? I knew Ian wouldn't just let you wander around all night."

Kit sounded so smug; Jesse didn't even bother answering. She closed her eyes and laid her head back on the seat.

"It is him, isn't it?" Kit pressed, but more gently now.

Jesse nodded, not opening her eyes.

"How long have you been seeing him? Why haven't I met him? I was wondering who you were texting all night at the club."

Jesse opened her eyes and rolled her head to the side in order to stare at her friend. When she didn't answer, Kit spared a glance in her direction a time or two. Then pursed her lips.

"This is why you didn't tell anyone, right? What we were talking about at lunch that day, all the endless questions from nosy friends."

"Something like that, yes."

Kit downshifted as they climbed a hill. "Sorry, I'll let it go."

"Thank you."

"After you answer one question."

Jesse let out another sigh.

"Is it as good as you hoped it would be?" Kit asked with an unholy grin.

Try as she might, she couldn't stop the twitch of her lips and the satisfied smile that crept across her face. "It's amazing."

"Hallelujah, amen," Kit said, making Jesse laugh.

"But, Kit. All joking aside, you and Ian are the only ones who know, and I would like to keep it that way for now," she said.

Kit's expression sobered. "Of course. But did you just tell me Ian knows and Vivi doesn't?"

"He said it's not his story to tell."

Kit let out a whistle, then laughed again. "I'd love to be a fly on the wall when she finds out Ian knew before her."

"I think Ian is kind of looking forward to it." Jesse smiled again, enjoying the sun on her face and wind on her skin.

"Yeah, I just bet he is."

• • •

Jesse rolled over and looked at the clock. She was in one of Kit's guest rooms and had finally had a good night's, or afternoon's, rest. Grabbing her phone she read through a couple of texts from

David. She'd sent him one earlier, letting him know the MRI had been clean and that she'd be staying at Kit's for the night.

Swinging her legs out of bed, she became aware of voices downstairs. Not just Kit's but a man's voice as well. Having slept in just her t-shirt, she slipped back into her clothes, then padded down to the main level.

Unlike most of the houses in the area, Kit's house was extremely modern, all glass and steel and split into three levels that descended, sideways, down the hill on which it was built. The middle level was the main living area, most of the bedrooms were on the upper level, and a gym, as well as the laundry, guest, and TV rooms, were on the lowest level.

Stepping into the kitchen, it was obvious she was stepping into an argument as well. Two sets of golden eyes turned to her as she stood in the doorway. Her own hazel eyes went to Kit and then to the man standing opposite her.

"Caleb," she nodded to him.

"Jesse."

"What are you doing here?" she asked.

"Good question," Kit interjected. Caleb shot his sister a glare.

"And what's bothering *you* so much?" Jesse asked Kit.

"Good question," Caleb mimicked Kit.

"Not helping," Jesse shot back. He put his hands up in mock surrender.

"Kit?" Jesse asked.

Kit shook her head and turned away to make some coffee. "I don't know why he's here. He just showed up while you were sleeping and he wants to know what's going on."

Jesse looked questioningly to Caleb, who met her gaze with an even, expressionless face.

"How did you know something was going on?" she asked.

He wagged his head, clearly not willing to answer her question.

"Ian's here," Kit announced with a glance at the security monitor. As a single, wealthy woman tucked away in rural Hudson

Valley, Kit had a decent security system. Nothing extreme, but a camera at the entrance to her driveway was a part of it.

"Caleb?" Kit drawled. *Are you going to stay* was left unsaid. He didn't bother answering. Jesse didn't understand the tension between the siblings, but for now, she didn't care. She'd ask Kit about it later. *After* she had heard from Ian about what he'd found.

Kit let Ian in and, not surprisingly, he picked up on the tension right away. His eyes went to Caleb, then to Kit, then back to Caleb. Jesse noted with interest that Ian didn't look surprised to see Kit's brother there.

"Jesse, how are you feeling?" Ian asked.

"Much better, thank you." She took over the serving of the coffee and soon all four of them were seated at Kit's sleek dining table.

"Vivienne wants you to call her," Ian started.

"After we talk, I'll do that. So did you find anything?" she prompted.

"We found some footprints in the field headed toward the woods, the trophy that was used to hit you, and some car tracks on the dirt road on the other side of the woods."

"A trophy?" Jesse frowned at the memory.

"One of Matt's," Ian supplied.

"He was in Matt's room?" The thought made her sick. "What about James's room?"

"It looks like whoever was there was searching for something. He or she must have started upstairs but was on the main floor when you came in and interrupted them. Was anything missing?" Ian asked.

"I haven't had a chance to look. Kit was going take me back tomorrow and help me clean up a bit. It sounds like we'll have more to clean than I originally thought?"

Ian nodded. "We fingerprinted a lot of surfaces. The rooms aren't too messed up, but they will need some picking up. Can you think of anything you might have that someone would want to take?"

"Just the usual things, computers, some jewelry, electronics, but nothing too valuable or unique. Maybe it was just a fluke thing, then?" A girl could hope.

Caleb snorted; Ian sent him a repressive look before answering. "It's always possible, but given that you lead a normal life and haven't really pissed off any one that we know of, I find it hard to believe that what happened yesterday and the events from earlier this summer are unrelated."

"But it's been almost two months since the car accident," Kit interjected. "Doesn't that seem weird to you?"

Ian shrugged. "Since we don't know who is targeting Jesse, or why, it's hard to say what's weird and what's not."

"What about the footprints?" Caleb asked.

"Small."

"Women's?" Caleb speculated.

"It's possible," Ian answered.

"What aren't you saying, Ian?" Jesse knew her friend well enough to know he was keeping something.

He sighed. "We don't have any proof, but we think it might be a woman."

A woman. For some reason, the thought sat heavy on her shoulders.

"Why?" Kit asked Ian.

"Given the size of the person you saw in the truck that tried to run you off the road, the footprint, and, well, the injury to your head, it leads us to believe it might be a woman."

"My injury?" Jesse repeated, confused.

"I talked to Vivienne about it last night, explained where you were hit, and showed her the photos of the injury. Judging by the angle and location, she thinks whoever hit you was no more than five foot six or seven."

"That could still be a small man or young person," Jesse pointed out.

"It could be, which is why we're not ruling anything out but rather expanding the investigation to include women."

Jesse frowned. "Okay. Any chance there were fingerprints anywhere?"

He let out a rueful laugh. "Yeah, lots of them. But I'm betting most of them are yours and the boys'. And maybe—" He cut himself off.

"Definitely David's," she supplied. Ian raised an eyebrow at her. "Kit figured it out. Caleb hardly matters, plus I know he won't say anything anyway."

Caleb put his hand over his heart. "You wound me."

Ian rolled his eyes. "We'll need his fingerprints to rule him out."

"I'm sure he'd be happy to provide them, but shouldn't they be in some system somewhere?" Jesse asked.

"Yes, but it's easier if we can get them from him."

She nodded, making a mental note to tell David.

"Wait, David was there when you were found?" Caleb asked, his coffee cup hitting the table.

"Caleb, don't," Jesse warned.

"Don't what?" Ian pressed.

"David was questioned in a suspicious fire in California. A young woman was seriously injured," Caleb said, ignoring Jesse.

"He wasn't involved," Jesse said with quiet certainty.

"I can't believe you dug into his life," Kit interjected with barely concealed disgust.

"How did you find out?" Ian asked, cutting them both off.

"I have my ways."

"So enigmatic," Kit said.

"Kit, your sarcasm isn't helping," Jesse said. Her friend looked like she was going to argue, then thought better of it and swallowed whatever she was going to say with a sip of coffee.

"I don't buy it anyway," Ian said.

"Oh yeah? Why's that?" Caleb sat back in challenge.

"Because I saw him last night. No one is that good of an actor," Ian responded.

"Meaning?" Caleb pressed.

"Meaning the guy looked like half of him wanted to go out and beat the shit out of someone while the other half was scared shitless to let Jesse go. Afraid something might happen to her if he did."

Jesse found herself staring at Ian. Was that really how David had seemed? To her right, Kit let out a little sigh.

"Seems like you know the feeling?" Caleb's voice was condescending and intended to provoke Ian. Why Caleb would want to do that, Jesse didn't know, but it worked. Just not in the way he'd probably hoped.

"Yes. I do," Ian said. "Last year a serial killer came after Vivienne. Not only was he a sadistic bastard, but he was also someone she'd known her entire life. So yes, I know what it's like to have someone you love threatened and believe me it wasn't something he was faking."

Someone you love? She glanced at Kit who was looking at her with curiosity, her head cocked to the side. She looked back to Ian who was still leveling his gaze at Caleb, not backing down from his assessment. Finally, Caleb shrugged off Ian's matter-of-fact pronouncement of his feelings and looked away.

"So what now?" Jesse asked.

"You go back to your house tomorrow, have a look, and let me know if anything is missing. Have you called the boys?" Ian asked.

She nodded. "Yes, I didn't tell them everything. I just said there was a break-in."

Ian gave no indication of what he thought of her decision. Kit and Caleb shared an indecipherable look—the first thing they'd shared since she'd come downstairs.

"We're going to keep following up on what evidence we have, like running the tire treads, and we're still combing the woods. In the meantime, you should spend some time thinking about who might be doing this. And even if you think there isn't any reason for someone to hurt you, try thinking of it another way."

"Such as?" Kit prompted.

"Maybe think of someone who would want something from you."

"Still a long shot," Jesse answered.

"I know, but you're going to have to give it a try. All these things started happening when you met David, maybe it's about him," Ian suggested.

She didn't think so, but then again, she'd had a hard time believing anyone would really want to hurt her and she'd clearly been wrong about that. So she nodded her agreement. As a group, they rose and walked to the door. Halfway there, Jesse's phone rang. With a glance at Caleb, because she couldn't help it, she said a quick good-bye then ducked away to take the call.

• • •

When Jesse walked back into the kitchen twenty minutes later, Caleb was the only one there. He handed her a glass of wine, then gestured for her to sit. She leaned against the kitchen counter instead. He shrugged, then did the same.

"Where's Kit?" she asked.

"She's in her office. Someone called, her agent or something. Said she'd be tied up for a while. So, you're still seeing him." His abrupt change of topic wasn't a question so she didn't bother answering. "That's too bad. I kind of like you," he said with another shrug.

She let out a huff of laughter. "I know you do. But not like that. What are you doing here, anyway?"

"You're a beautiful woman," he commented.

"And you're full of shit. Sit your ass down and tell me what you're doing here."

She moved to the table, sat down herself, and fixed him with a stern look. He sighed and followed her to the table.

"You *are* kind of pushy," he said, sitting across from her.

"I have two teenage sons, you haven't begun to see pushy. So let's try this again, what are you doing here?"

She didn't miss the glint of humor in his eyes, though his face didn't move a muscle. "I heard from a little bird about what happened last night. I was stateside so decided to fly up and see for myself."

"Why?"

"Because I can."

"Not good enough." She took a sip of the buttery chardonnay, not taking her eyes off him.

He tried to stare her down, but obviously it had been a long time since he'd teed off with a mother, if he ever had. Come to think of it, Kit had never mentioned her parents, maybe their mother was never in the picture. The errant thought made her frown.

No doubt taking advantage of her moment of distraction, Caleb changed the subject. "You're going to have to get used to the fact that there is someone out there who wants to hurt you, and until you accept that, you're never going to be open enough to start considering why."

"You and Ian have worked together, haven't you?" she countered. Two could play that game.

For a long moment they simply stared at each other, waiting to see who would give first. Her question had come to her out of the blue, but now that she'd asked it, she found she didn't really need him to answer. It was the only thing that made sense; it was the only way Caleb could have known about last night. Not to mention Ian's complete lack of surprise at finding Caleb in Kit's kitchen.

"Why do you care, Caleb?" She didn't have to stretch herself much to sound more curious than challenging. She wasn't upset about him being involved, but it just didn't make sense to her. She knew he liked her, as a friend and as a friend of his sister's, but none of it warranted the level of involvement she was sensing from him.

"What happened?" she pressed. His eyes slid away to the expansive view beyond the massive windows. Green hills covered

211

in maple trees and fields of hay dotted the landscape, but Jesse sensed that Caleb wasn't really taking in the scenery

"A lot of things have happened," he said. "A lot of people have been hurt by decisions I've made or haven't made. If I can help Ian figure this thing out before you get seriously hurt, I will."

There were so many layers to that statement that for several minutes she just sat there, sipping her wine, watching him watch the hills.

Then she spoke. "I see."

His eyes swiveled to hers. "What exactly do you see?"

"I'm curious, Caleb, what's the value of a human life these days?"

He flinched at her question then looked away again.

"I'm curious, really," she continued. "I mean do you have to save one person to make up for another person dying? Or is it two people you have to save? Or more?"

His jaw ticked and his hand tightened into a fist. "You have no idea what you're talking about."

"You're right, I don't. Tell me," she conceded simply.

"There's nothing to tell."

"If I'm some part of your redemption, if only in your eyes, I think I should know about it. Whose life will I make up for, Caleb?"

"Some things can't be made up for."

She was surprised he even managed to speak; his jaw was so rigid.

"You're right, some things can't. And yet you're trying, aren't you?" She'd cornered him. They both knew it. She no more believed he'd intentionally killed an innocent person than she believed David was involved in the fire all those years ago. But for some reason, he believed he had been responsible. And though she didn't doubt that, rationally, he knew one life saved did not make up for one life lost, emotionally, things weren't that clear. And emotions, for a guy like Caleb, were a messy thing.

"Look Caleb." She reached out and placed her hand over his fist. "I'm not going to pretend I know what you've done or what you've lived through. But I do know a thing or two about death and dying. Almost every doctor I know who has lost a patient wonders if there was something they could have done differently. A decision that might have changed the outcome. And the truth is, maybe there was. Maybe that person didn't have to die on that day. But the other truth is that we can only do what we can do. We can only make the best decisions we can with the information we have. And sometimes we just have to hope we're right."

"And sometimes we're wrong and someone dies," he said.

"And sometimes we're wrong and someone dies," she agreed.

The sound of Kit's office door opening down the hall brought the moment and the conversation to an end. Caleb withdrew his hand from under hers and stood up.

"I don't want to deal with Kit right now. I'm going out. I'll be back. Do not, I repeat, *do not* leave this house until I get back."

She thought his directive was a bit of overkill, but she also thought it best to pick her battles, so she just nodded her agreement. The front door was slamming behind him when Kit walked in.

"Where's he off to?" Kit asked, pouring herself a glass of wine and sitting in the seat her brother had just vacated.

Thinking of the weird tension between the siblings, Jesse leaned forward, "I don't know, but I think we have a few things to talk about, don't you?"

CHAPTER 15

Dᴀᴠɪᴅ ᴛᴀᴘᴘᴇᴅ ʜɪs ᴘʜᴏɴᴇ ᴏɴ the desk in front of him and pondered his last conversation with Jesse. This was her second night back in her house but the first night he wasn't with her. Being on shift had never sucked so much in his life. He hated leaving her, hated the thought of her being there alone. But she'd promised to set the alarm, including the motion sensors, and Ian had promised she would be well looked after.

All that aside, the conversation he'd just had with her had left him feeling more unsettled than it should have. Of all the things in her home to be taken, the only thing missing was a framed picture of Jesse's house and the surrounding landscape. He knew that fact was important, but for the life of him, he couldn't figure out why. Nor could he figure out why the perpetrator had taken one of Matt's trophies from his room—the one that had ultimately been used on Jesse. She had said that both items had more sentimental value than anything else—the trophy happened to include a small framed picture of Matt and his dad taken the week before Mark had died—and she could no more explain why those items had been picked than he could. And judging by the conversation he'd had with Ian earlier that day, the apparent randomness of those two items was pissing Ian off, too.

"Don't you look preoccupied? What's up, Hathaway? Contemplating how to grow your perennials next season?" Dominic leaned on the doorframe, crossing his arms. David's life was much quieter than most of the other guys, or so they thought, and was, by default, the subject of much ridicule. Usually, he played along, but he wasn't in the mood tonight.

Dominic must have sensed it because he moved in and sat down across from him.

"Everything okay?" The teasing was gone from Dominic's voice.

David flicked a look at his friend. He didn't want to open the can of worms that would be Jesse with his teammates, but he could use a little insight, another brain on the subject.

"A friend of mine has had a couple of weird things happen to him lately," he started, intentionally changing the gender of his "friend." "He's had his tires slashed, someone tried to run him off the road, and then someone broke in and stole a few things. It just doesn't make a lot of sense." He had also intentionally left out the bombing of Spin-A-Yarn since any mention of that would make it patently obvious just how much he was altering the story.

"Jealous girlfriend?" Dominic suggested.

David shook his head. That was about the only fact he knew for certain—it was not a jealous boyfriend. But maybe there was someone stalking her? Maybe there was a man out there who thought *he* should be her boyfriend, instead of David, and was upset about having David in the picture? But why the photo and the trophy?

"Angry husband?" Dominic offered.

"Meaning?"

"If he's running around with a woman who happens to be married, maybe it's the husband doing all those things," Dominic explained.

David almost said the spouse is dead, but then the ghost of a thought settled in his head. He sat forward, frowning.

"Jealous husbands suck," Dominic added. "Of course, that's not to say I didn't deserve what I got," he added. His "relationship" with the hot little redhead with the rings had ended much like David had thought it would. But since he'd never said "I told you so," he'd felt a growing sense of loyalty from the younger man.

"I don't think it was a jealous husband, but you did give me an idea." David stood and looked around for a moment, sorting out his next move. "Excuse me, I need to go check on some files."

Dominic watched him, then stood, too. "Sure, just let me know if I can help."

David nodded as he walked out of the room and headed down to the archives. Everything was online, now, all fire reports, suspicious or otherwise, but the main computer was down in the basement.

Flicking on the light as he walked into the rarely used room, he sat down and turned on the computer. A few minutes later, he was culling through the reports of the fire that had killed Mark Baker. If the threats to Jesse weren't about her, maybe they were about her husband. It still didn't make a ton of sense, but at this point, he felt they were all grasping at straws and this was just one more.

When he was through researching, he leaned back in the chair and thought about what he'd just read. It seemed like an accidental fire, but all he had was the report. Some of the pictures were online, but not all. Neither was the schematic of the building. He picked up the phone and dialed the extension of the central office that provided administrative help. After being told the schematics would be available to him in a few days, he printed out the report and placed it in a folder.

"Hathaway?" Kurt, one of his teammates, called from the top of the stairs.

"Yeah, down here," he answered.

"There's someone here to see you. In reception."

Not expecting anyone and figuring they could wait two minutes, he shut down the computer, made sure the workspace was tidy, and after turning off the light, made his way back to the main part of the station. Walking into reception, he saw the form of a man, dressed in jeans, a t-shirt, and boots, standing with his back toward him. He was tall—taller than David—and stood with a military rigidity that gave David pause. And when the man turned around, his gold eyes flashed with something not altogether nice.

"I'm Caleb Forrester."

David knew the name, of course he did. Jesse had told him about the few times she and Caleb had talked earlier in the summer and he also knew from his earlier call with her that Kit's brother had just arrived back in town.

"Is everything…" His voice trailed off. He was unsure why Caleb would be there unless something had happened to Jesse.

"She's fine." His reply was curt and David was beginning to get the sense that whatever conversation Caleb had in mind, it would be best not to have it in the fire station.

"Let's go outside." Not bothering to see if Caleb followed, he headed through the front doors. Looking around the parking lot, he spotted a black Range Rover backed into a spot. Knowing it didn't belong to anyone from the station, he headed toward it.

"Jesse and I have chatted quite a bit over the last few months," Caleb said, coming to David's side. They reached the car and David leaned his hip against it, crossing his arms over his chest. He didn't doubt Jesse's fidelity for a second. But she had said she and Caleb were friends, and there was nothing friendly about the man in front of him.

"I know, she told me," he replied.

"She's a beautiful woman, Hathaway."

David knew when he was being provoked and didn't want to give this guy any satisfaction by responding. But still, it was hard not to tell the guy to go fuck himself. The only thing that stopped him was knowing that Jesse *did* consider him a friend.

"What do you want, Forrester?"

"I want to know if you have anything to do with the shit that's been happening to Jesse."

A moment of rage crashed through him at the thought and he wasn't quite as successful biting his tongue this time around.

Caleb continued, not the least bit fazed by David's language.

"It all started when she met you. *The day* she met you, I believe," he pointed out.

David's eyes narrowed. "It's not me." His voice was quiet, like the calm before the storm, and it seemed to catch Caleb's attention.

"Prove it."

David considered this. He didn't have to have this conversation, but in some strange way, he sensed that if he could get Caleb's focus off of him, he might actually be an asset on this case. The guy seemed to care about Jesse. He wasn't really sure how he felt about that, but if the man could help keep her safe, that was what was most important.

"I was here filling out reports when her tires were slashed, I was on shift when the bomb went off at the shop, I was at the restaurant waiting for her when she was run off the road, and the men's size-seven shoe prints they found in the field? I don't think so." Both men looked down at his size-ten-and-a-half feet.

Caleb grunted. "How did you know about the shoe size?"

"Ian's taken a liking to me." Sort of. Well, at least Ian believed that David cared enough about Jesse to keep him informed.

"Ian never thought you were good for it when I suggested it to him," Caleb conceded with a shrug.

"Ian's a smart man."

The two men stared at each for a long moment. Caleb opened his mouth to say something, but the ringing of the firehouse bell cut him off.

David straightened. "I don't know what your story is, Forrester, but I can't be there with her all the time. If you can help keep her safe, have at it."

Caleb actually cracked a smile. "That's very brave of you. Like I said, she's a beautiful woman."

He inclined his head as he began backing away toward to the station. "She is, but you're not her type."

"How do you know?"

David cracked a grin, one that was probably cockier than nice. "Because I am."

He left Caleb staring after him as he went to gear up. But the call was just a small fender bender so after sending one truck out to respond, David removed his gear and made his way to the station's communal room. As much as he trusted Jesse, he still wanted to check in. They only called each other every so often while either was at work, but they texted quite a bit. They laughed about feeling like teenagers whenever they did, but it let them have conversations—as stilted as they were—without being overheard.

"Met your friend Caleb." He typed in. He wasn't sure if she had her phone or was in a position to answer so was pleased when her response came less than a minute later.

"???"

"He stopped by. Wanted to know if I was involved." In what, David didn't need to say.

"I don't think I like him as much anymore." Her reply made him smile.

"He's worried about you. I get that."

"I know. It's his only redeeming quality right now."

"Are you home?" He thought she was, but he wanted to make sure.

"Yes, with the alarm on."

"Good girl."

"I'm calling Dash about a dog tomorrow."

"I'll be there tomorrow."

"I know." Who knew two little words could be so suggestive?

"You never read me the texts from my night out." She added.

"I'll be there as soon as I can."

"I know."

"Be safe."

"You too."

And that was that. He would much rather have heard her voice, but with all the people around, it was easier to keep thing private this way.

"You look smug," Kurt said, walking into the room.

219

"Any news on the fender bender?" He wasn't about to discuss anything but work.

Kurt rolled his eyes at David's refusal to respond but answered. "They're already on their way back. Ralene from the admin office called and said the plans you requested were ready."

"Wow, that was fast. She said it would take two days—it's been less than two hours," David replied.

"She has a thing for you," Kurt grinned.

"She's the same age as my mother, I think she just feels sorry for me. All of you have family around here. I don't."

"You have Miranda. Speaking of which, when are you going to bring her around?" Kurt asked.

David chuckled and shook his head. "Not going to happen. Not for a while anyway." Miranda had spent her summer doing an internship down near DC. He'd seen her a few times over the summer and they talked a lot, but on the few occasions she'd been to Albany, they'd spent their time hiking, checking out the historic sites, and generally hanging out. Not meeting his colleagues.

"I hear she's pretty cute." Kurt egged him on.

David's brows went up. "That's my daughter. Do you really want to go there? I may have a few years on you, but in my book that also means a few more years of experience."

Kurt let out a bark of laughter. "Okay, old man, I'll let it go. You're not that old, anyway. You just got started young."

"Yeah, tell me about it."

"You ever regret it? Feel like you missed out?"

David glanced at his teammate, surprised by the sudden seriousness in Kurt's voice. "Regret it? No." He shook his head. "Would I recommend it? No to that too. As for missing out, sometimes, yeah, it crosses my mind. But then I see all my friends just settling down with young kids and I kind like knowing I'm done with all that. Besides, you know what they say, that youth is wasted on the young. Now I have all that freedom *and* know how to appreciate it."

"But *do* you appreciate it?" Kurt asked. "You never go out with us after shift, we never see you at the bars. As far as we know, you live like a monk. And do you really think you'll never get married? You're young enough to have another family. Do it all again."

He shook his head. "Not doing it again. I love my daughter and in many ways she is the best thing that ever happened to me, but I'm not about to do it again."

"What if you meet someone who wants kids?"

He thought of Jesse. She knew exactly where he stood on the issue and why. And more importantly, she agreed with him. "Not going to happen."

"You sound awfully certain."

"And you're asking a lot of questions. Something on your mind, Kurt?"

His friend shook his head. "No, you're still just a little bit of an enigma to us, that's all. We work together, live together a few days out of the week, we generally know more about each other than is probably healthy, but we have no idea what goes on in your life outside of here." He gestured around the station.

David shrugged. "It's not that exciting. There's nothing to know." But he was living the life he wanted and that was good. Well, except for someone being after Jesse. His face must have darkened at the thought because Kurt sat back and gave him a questioning look.

"Did Ralene say when I could pick up the schematics?" David asked.

"I told her you were on shift until tomorrow so she's going to drop them tonight. Are they for a case?"

David shook his head. "No, just an old fire I'm looking into for a friend."

"Which one, maybe I was on it?"

He gave Kurt the date and the specs.

Kurt leaned back, mulled it over a minute, then nodded. "Yeah, I remember that fire. A guy died. A professor at the university. It was gnarly. One of those old university houses. It went up in minutes. The guy never had a chance."

"What guy?" Dominic asked entering the room.

"That fire a couple of years ago at the university. The one where the professor died," Kurt supplied.

Dominic let out a whistle. "Yeah, that was bad. The building was nearly consumed by the time we got there."

David winced internally at the description. It was hard to believe they were talking about Jesse's husband.

"Was there anything suspicious about the fire?" he asked. He didn't miss the how-much-should-we-say look the two men shared.

"Your predecessor investigated it. He'd been on the job for over twenty years," Dominic answered.

Which could mean any number of things in David's mind, so he tried a different tack. "Did you guys notice anything unusual when you were in there?"

"We didn't even make it in." Kurt shook his head. "Like Dom said, the place was engulfed by the time we got there. We had to do everything externally."

"And did anyone ever think an accelerant might have been used, for something to go up that quickly? Or something had helped the fire along?" he pressed.

"Of course," Dominic responded. "But the walls were insulated with hay. The building was a hundred and fifty years old. It was a tinderbox waiting to happen."

David didn't like the sound of this. "It was a public building. Wasn't it retrofitted with a sprinkler system?"

Kurt wagged his head. "It was, but the temperatures were below freezing and had been for a while. The sprinkler never went on."

"The pipes froze?" He supposed it was possible, but it didn't sound right. In all his years working in the Truckee and Lake Tahoe area, an area that regularly saw subzero temperatures in the dead of winter, he'd never seen sprinkler pipes freeze.

"That was the finding," Kurt supplied.

David thought about asking more questions, but decided he needed to do a little research first. When he was better armed with the facts and circumstances, he might come back to his team and dig a little deeper. Dominic and Kurt seemed to sense that the conversation was over; Dominic got up to pour himself a glass of water.

"So, was he in here texting again, Kurt?"

Kurt grinned. "Yep."

David rolled his eyes.

"Someday we'll find out what that's all about." Dominic gave David a mock salute with his glass.

"You'll be disappointed, I'm sure," David retorted.

Dominic's eyes slid to Kurt's before he answered. "Somehow, I doubt that."

David thought of some of the messages on his phone. Especially the ones he was saving to show Jesse from her girls' night out. Yeah, he kind of doubted it, too.

CHAPTER 16

OVER A WEEK HAD PASSED since someone had rifled through her home, and though she had moments when panic slammed into her, all in all she was beginning to feel back to normal. She had the week off, ostensibly to get ready for the coming school year, but Matt was already at school and James was still in Boston. She and David had already spent a few days together, but she was still looking forward to having more time with him once he got off his shift later that night.

But as Jesse looked at the text he'd sent moments earlier, she frowned. It was a far cry from his previous, flirty messages.

The message simply read, "On a call. It's bad. Will talk later."

She flipped on the news and was somewhat mollified not to see any reports of dangerous fires. There was a report of a single-house fire but it was already out. There had been fatalities but the victims had not yet been identified. The reporter mentioned it was being investigated and they would have more news later. Given that the death or serious injury of a firefighter would have been included in the news clip, at least she knew David wasn't hurt.

Not knowing when he would be done for the night, Jesse poured a glass of wine, drew a bath, and slipped into the bubbles for a good long soak. After turning her skin nice and pink, she got out, dried her hair, and slid between her sheets without bothering to dress. If David was able to come tonight, she wanted him to know she'd been thinking of him. In the meantime, she turned on the television, curled under her blankets, and watched an old Audrey Hepburn movie.

She was just drifting off when her phone buzzed beside her.

"Hello?" She assumed it was David, given the hour, and hadn't bothered to look at the number.

"Are you awake?" His voice sounded grim and angry.

She hesitated. "Yes."

"Good. I'm pulling up your drive now."

She sat up and saw the reflection of his headlights wash through her bedroom as he drove up the long drive. She got up, pulled on a robe, and went to meet him in the kitchen. He was already toeing his boots off and resetting the alarm when she came in. She paused in front of the island. Something was off. Something was very off.

Wearing an expression she'd never seen on his face before, but one she recognized all too well, he paused and looked at her. His text message flashed through her mind. "It's bad." And she *knew* how bad it could be.

She opened her arms to him and he came forward, burying his hand in her hair. Tilting her head up, he drew back, then covered her mouth with his in a punishing kiss even as his other hand yanked the tie of her robe. It fell off her shoulders and gathered beneath her on the island.

He pressed into her, crowding her, pushing her against the counter. She didn't know what had happened at that fire, but he was exorcising it with her and she was going to let him.

The counter dug into her back and he lifted her up just enough so that she perched on the edge. Stepping between her legs, he continued kissing her, nipping at her lips, her neck, and her breasts, not saying a word.

Leaning back, she braced herself with her hands and offered her body up to him. There was no doubt in her mind that he knew who he was with, but at that moment, he was lost and angry and blindly taking it out on her. She knew he wasn't going to hurt her, but he wasn't going to spare a thought for her pleasure either; he was only hoping to kill his own pain.

His mouth closed over a nipple and he sucked hard enough for her to feel it throughout her entire body. Pulling her closer to the counter's edge, roughly, he slid two fingers all the way inside her without any warning. She sucked in a breath at the sudden intrusion but forced her body to take him, for his sake.

One hand still tangled in her hair, pulling her head back and keeping her body arched for him, he nipped and bit and sucked her breasts as his fingers moved in and out at an angry tempo.

But still, it was David, and she trusted him completely. His rough treatment didn't scare her and she soon found herself pressing her pelvis into his hand. She felt a small tremor begin in her thighs, and she opened them more, encouraging him to continue. For both their sakes.

With a curse, he yanked his hand away. Confused and dazed, Jesse tried to see why, but with his other hand still holding her hair, her head stayed back. Suddenly, she felt him, thrusting himself into her, without much more than the sound of a foil packet being torn open as a warning to her. Her body froze at the new sensation but David didn't seem to notice. He gripped her hair with one hand and her hip with the other as he thrust himself in and out, pushing her farther back onto the counter with each movement.

There was nothing she could do but hold on and let him ride his demons out. But the heat and the friction, coupled with the knowledge that he'd come to her, that he needed her for this, refused to let her stay passive.

She wrapped her legs around him and the sudden movement on her part made him pause. He drew back enough to look at her, then looked down at the two of them, joined. A long moment passed, and then, with deliberate intent, he took each of her feet, one at a time, and placed them on the barstools on either side of him. Moving the stools out inch-by-inch, he spread her wide open.

With a gesture for her to stay still, he slid his pants and boxers all the way down, then somehow managed to kick them off along with his socks, without withdrawing himself from her. After pulling his shirt off and tossing it on the floor, he was finally as naked as she. Pausing for a moment to look at her, he traced a line from her neck, down between her breasts, and across her belly with a fingertip. Then, leaving his hand there, he gently pushed her upper body down onto the counter.

From her position lying on the island, her legs spread and David between them, she raised her head and watched his face as he lost himself in her. Her hands curled into the robe that still lay beneath her as he touched, stroked, and tasted as much of her as he could. And then, finally, he started to move within her again.

She laid her head back down, closed her eyes, and focused on the feel of him. This time, he kept one hand on her breast and the other on her hip as he moved slowly, intently, in and out, as if he were studying her, memorizing her.

She squirmed against him as much as she could and tried to encourage him with her own small movements, but he refused to let her set the pace or call the shots. And he didn't vary his rhythm by so much as a beat.

And then she understood. This was all about control. Whatever had happened that night, at that fire, had left him feeling so out of control that he needed to gain it back. In whatever way he could. He needed to know that there were some things he still had a say in. Some things he could dictate.

So she acquiesced. Completely.

She quieted her movements, and while she normally let her body tell him what felt right and what didn't, tonight she did nothing. Intentionally, she let him do what he wanted, what he needed, to her body. Handing over all control wasn't easy for her, but to her own surprise, she heard sounds coming out of her mouth and words leaving her lips that she'd never made or said before.

And when she heard herself tell him how good he felt inside her, how he could do anything he wanted to her because he made her feel so good, his pace changed.

"Tell me," he demanded.

She almost couldn't speak anymore, the sensations in her body were so strong, but she managed a few breathy words here and there. And when his finger very gently brushed over her, everything burst. She arched up off the counter, but his hand on her hip held her in place. The restraint seemed to make everything that much more intense, seemed to concentrate the energy, and for a moment, her eyes rolled into the back of her head and she stopped breathing as her entire body jerked in spasms.

When she was finally able to open her eyes again, she found David braced above her—head fallen forward, face and chest beaded with sweat. They were both breathing hard and she felt her own body damp with perspiration.

She managed to raise a hand and draw a finger down his forearm. He looked up at her and she saw that the anger was gone from his eyes. But the pain, the sadness, was still there. Without a word, she sat up. He withdrew from her and she swung her legs down. With a tentative step to make sure she could bear her own weight, she stood before him and, taking his hand, she led him to her room.

In silence, they showered, dried off, then climbed beneath the sheets where she curled up against him. His arm came around her, pulling her close, and against her bare skin she felt his heart beat beating strong and steady.

"Do you want to tell me what happened?" she asked in the quiet of the darkness.

He took a few breaths before speaking. "Did I hurt you?"

She shook her head against his chest and waited, letting him decide when he was ready. After several minutes, he spoke.

"It was just supposed to be a single-house fire. Of course, we always worry about people inside, so we were sweeping the structure as best we could. Then we found the first body. We got the fire out pretty quickly and were hopeful that we'd only lost the one. One is bad enough. And the fire hadn't done as much damage to the rest of the house as it had to the room where we found her."

He paused in his story as he rubbed his eyes with his free hand. "But it was a smoky fire. Some fires are just like that, depending on the materials that are burning. When we got in to search the rest of the house, we noticed a chair up against a closet door. The door had some fire damage, but was still intact. When we opened it—" His voice cracked and he took another break. After a few deep breaths, he seemed to get his voice back under control and continued.

"When we opened the door, there were two kids inside. A brother and a sister, holding each other. The little boy was eighteen months old and his sister was three. They died of smoke inhalation."

Jesse felt her own tears fall for the two young victims. Babies. Locked in a closet and left to die.

"Who… ?" She managed to ask.

"We think their father. We don't know for certain, but the police are looking for him. His wife, the first body we found, was stabbed to death. We think she might have hidden the kids there when he arrived. And that he knew they were in the closet when he set the place on fire. We think he's probably the one that locked them in."

What could she say to something like that? Jesse was speechless at such a horror and words would never make it better or easier to understand. She had no doubt that everyone at the station would feel this loss, this anger. But those who were parents, like David, would feel it more. And while she would never understand the actions of a person who could do what that father had allegedly done, she now understood him better. She wished there was more she could do for him, more she could do to ease his pain. All she could do was be there for him.

"I'm so sorry, David."

His arm tightened its hold on her and he leaned down and brushed a kiss across the top of her head. "I know, Jesse."

• • •

David wrung out the wet rag and wiped it over the controls of the big red truck. He'd left Jesse that morning, sleeping sated in bed, and come in to work to start his report. He wasn't technically on duty, but he wanted to make sure that everything that could possibly be done to bring justice to whoever was responsible for the deaths of those two little kids was being done. Everything. Including his small piece of the puzzle.

He was still furious about what had happened, but after his night with Jesse, he felt more focused and certain of his role in bringing justice. He no longer felt the blind rage and fury he'd felt when he'd arrived at her place. Being with her had soothed him. Which was ironic because very little of what they had done had been soothing. Thinking back on the night before, it was possible there were things he should feel bad about, but try as he might, he couldn't regret the way he'd needed her, the way he'd taken what he'd needed. And the way she'd given it to him.

And she had given—her trust, her control, her body, and her soul. As if just being with her wasn't enough to take the edge off, her complete submission to him—if only for a few hours—was enough to humble him, to bring him back to some sort of balance that allowed him to face what he had to face.

"Yo, Hathaway. You gonna shine that chrome right off or you just wishing you were rubbing something else?" Dominic shouted.

David had only come by to write the report, but the guys were taking advantage of the sunshine and lack of calls to wash one of the trucks and he'd felt compelled to join in. Classic rock was playing loudly in the background, and the sun was doing its best to take away some of the darkness they'd all experienced the night before.

"Go fuck yourself, Dominic," David shouted back, tossing the rag in the bucket.

"It would be more action than you're getting, I bet," Dominic responded with a laugh.

"Not hard," Kurt joined in, emerging from the cab. "Didn't you just tell me you thought he was a monk?"

David laughed, thinking of what he'd been up to just twelve hours ago.

"Nah," Dominic said, tossing his rag in the bucket. "I said he wants us to *think* he's a monk."

"One of those 'still waters run deep' kind of things?" Kurt

asked. David was just about to cut them off when the rumbling of an engine caught the attention of all three of them. They watched in appreciative silence as a classic Shelby convertible, with its top up, pulled into the guest lot. The sun glistened on the shiny black paint and chrome trim. The car rumbled to a stop, and even though the music was still playing, when the driver killed the engine it seemed suddenly so quiet.

Dominic whistled. "Nice."

"The woman or the car?" Kurt asked, clearly thinking both deserved the compliment. David said nothing as he watched the driver's door swing open and a single, bare leg, ending in a four-inch heeled stiletto, hit the pavement. With one leg out of the car and one leg in, the woman's dress rode high up her thigh, and when she turned to pick something up from the passenger seat all three men got a good long look at her backside. Sitting upright again, with her long blonde hair swinging in a ponytail behind her, the woman held a phone to her ear. She paused in that position for a moment, and minus the cell phone, she looked like a pinup girl from the fifties.

"Holy shit," Dominic breathed.

Holy shit indeed. David grinned and jogged over to the car.

Jesse was just finishing her call when he stopped beside her open door. Without a word, he pulled her up from her seat, slid a hand under her ponytail, tilted her head back, and claimed a deep, intimate kiss. He thought he should probably stop—at least it crossed his mind that he might want to consider it—but when he noticed that she'd risen up on her toes to meet him and then felt her nails dig into his biceps, he slanted his head and deepened the kiss even more.

Just on the brink of backing her up against the car, David forced himself to pull back. With deliberate care, he ended the kiss. He opened his eyes and looked down at her; she met his gaze from beneath her lashes and a small smile played on her lips. A breeze lifted her hair, tickling his hand, and he smiled back.

A moment went by before he spoke. "Uh, not that I'm not happy to see you—"

"Hmm, I noticed," she cut him off, pressing herself against his obvious arousal.

"But, what are you doing here?" For the first time, he realized she held something in her hand. His phone.

"I found it this morning," she said, handing it to him. "It kept buzzing and Miranda's name was on the screen. I thought it might be important so I wanted to get it to you ASAP."

He looked at the phone, two messages from his daughter. He was pretty sure he knew what it was about—his signatures on her loan documents—and it wasn't an emergency, but it was nice of Jesse to worry.

"Where did I leave it?" he asked.

Jesse tilted a brow. "You didn't leave it anywhere. I found it under the fridge. It must have fallen out when, well, you know."

He traced her bottom lip with his thumb. "Yes, I know." He smiled.

"That's a very self-satisfied smile if I ever saw one." She nipped his thumb and he felt it *everywhere*.

He reached for her hand and brought her palm to his lips then kissed each of her fingers. "Believe me, there was nothing *self*-satisfying about last night, at all."

Her head tilted back as she laughed. He caught a glimpse of his two teammates, neither of whom was being discreet in their attention.

"Has our cover been blown? Again?" she asked with a small gesture in their direction.

He wagged his head. It was bound to happen sooner or later. He found he really didn't care all that much and told her so. He offered to introduce her to them, but she declined for the moment. She looked worried by her decision, like he might be offended that she didn't want to meet his teammates, but he knew she had some errands to run and that she might want a little more notice before taking that step. At this point in time, it didn't matter to him—if she wanted to meet them, great. If not, he was more than happy to continue to keep the relationship private—well, as private as they could, anyway.

He kissed her again—this time gently but quickly—and helped her into her car, promising to head back to her place as soon as he finished at the station. Shutting the door, he stood by as she revved the engine, gave him a saucy smile, and waved good-bye. He watched her drive off, then turned and jogged back toward the station. Only to be hit square in the face with a blast of cold water.

"What the hell?" He sputtered to a stop—his face dripping with water, his shirt plastered to his chest. Kurt and Dominic stood there staring at him, Kurt holding a hose. Both men were wearing flat, pissed-off expressions.

"We thought you might need a little cooling off after all that," Kurt said.

Uh-oh, they were pissed.

"Look guys, it's nothing."

"Oh, sure, it's 'nothing,'" Dominic threw up his hands, mocking David. "Did that look like 'nothing' to you, Kurt?"

"Definitely didn't look like 'nothing' to me." His teammates crossed their arms over their chests. David was starting to dislike their attitudes. Or, maybe he was feeling a little guilty for having kept Jesse a secret. But really it wasn't any of their business and he told them so.

"Oh, it's none of our business. I see." Kurt said, then turned to Dominic. "Does that work for you?"

Dominic shook his head. "Hell no."

"Me neither. What the fuck, Hathaway?"

"Hathaway!" Saved by the chief calling from inside the station. With a last look at his teammates, David turned and walked away. In silence, he followed his boss upstairs to his office.

"What the fuck was that?" the chief demanded with a gesture toward his window once he'd shut his office door. His window that looked out onto the guest parking lot. Nice, everyone and their mother knew now. Served him right for losing his head for a moment. And Chief Perotti wasn't one to let things go. He was a small man, not more than five foot six, with a slim frame and thinning dark hair. But he was tenacious as a bulldog. Something David tended to appreciate since usually the chief was fighting for his men. This was the first time that Chief Perotti had turned the full force of his personality on *him*.

"*That* was a woman I've been seeing for several months," David answered.

"Thank god." The chief's voice was heavy with sarcasm. "I'd hate to think she was someone you met last night with a display like that and all. Your teammates are going to be pissed you didn't tell them."

"It's not their concern."

In response, Chief Perotti simply stared at him, his tiny, dark eyes unwavering in their disapproval. David let out a sigh. It wasn't their business, but in the same way, it wasn't his mother's business either. He knew that in some ways they had a right to be pissed. They all but lived together three or four days a week. They knew each others' strengths and weaknesses, likes and dislikes, and they knew when their teammates were having problems, in their relationships or otherwise. Partly, it was the fact of this closeness, their being together so much, but it was also a safety issue. If someone had something going on that was taking their mind from the game, their teammates needed to know.

"I'll fill them in," he acquiesced.

The chief gave a sharp nod. "Now, since that didn't look like a fly-by-night kind of thing—"

"I've already added her to my paperwork, sir," David cut him off. His paperwork, the names and contact information of those who would be notified if anything happened to him. Miranda and his parents were always on the list. Two months ago, he'd added Jesse.

"Good. Now tell me about the investigation," Chief Perotti switched topics.

"My report's been filed. The lab is still looking at the evidence."

Again, his boss nodded. "I just got a call from the lead detective. The husband was caught early this morning and confessed to everything. His confession aligns with your findings."

"Which should be corroborated by the evidence." David finished and let out a breath he didn't know he'd been holding. Whatever justice befell the father of those two kids wouldn't ever be enough to pay for what he'd done, but knowing he would pay in some way had to be enough for now.

"You did good work last night," the chief said grudgingly.

"I wish I hadn't had to."

The chief inclined his head in agreement. "Me, too. But since we do have to do that kind of work sometimes, I'm glad you're around."

Chief Perotti wasn't a mean guy, but he also wasn't free with his compliments, especially to relative newcomers to the force. David muttered a thank you.

"Now, go explain her to the guys," the chief said with a vague gesture toward the parking lot, "before they go and do some dumbass shit to get back at you."

David grinned at the dismissal and jogged back downstairs. Dominic and Kurt were picking up the cleaning materials when he stepped outside. They both stopped and eyed him. He closed the space between them and stood before them.

"Look, I'm sorry. Her name is Jesse Baker. She's the hospital administrator at Riverside Hospital. I met her when I was investigating that single-house fire in Windsor a few months ago."

"Three months ago," Kurt clarified.

"Yes," he conceded. "Three months ago. We've had our reasons for keeping things just between the two of us, and up until a few days ago, no one knew at all."

"And what happened a few days ago?" Dominic asked, not masking the fact he still wasn't happy.

David pursed his lips. He thought about not telling them everything, but the looks on their faces convinced him otherwise and he went ahead and spilled it all. His friends took a moment to absorb what he'd told them.

"So your 'friend' that was almost run off the road?" Dominic pressed.

"Jesse."

"And the slashed tires?" Kurt interjected.

"Also Jesse."

"Hey." Kurt was snapping his fingers, the way someone does when they're recalling something. "Wasn't that the last name of the professor who was killed in that fire? The one you requested the schematics for?"

He nodded. He didn't want to drag his friends into this, but it didn't look like they were going to give him any choice. "It was Jesse's husband. We can't think of any reason why someone would be after her, so it made me wonder if it has something to do with him."

"Does she know you're looking into that fire?" Dominic asked.

David shook his head. "And she won't, unless I find something."

He fixed each man with a pointed look. No way did he want Jesse to know he was beginning to wonder if there was more to Mark's death than an accidental fire. She and the boys should go on thinking it was an accident until he had absolute proof otherwise—*if* he had proof otherwise. At this point, he had nothing but curiosity and intuition.

Dominic threw up his hands. "Hey, don't look at us. It's not like we've ever talked to her. Not like we'd ever have a chance to slip up and tell her or anything like that." His rebuke was tempered and David knew then that he and his teammates were okay. It probably helped that he'd let them in on a secret.

"Why don't we go look at those schematics Ralene dropped by yesterday?" Kurt suggested.

David looked at his watch. "Nice as that sounds, Jesse and I only have two more days together before life, work, and the like gets back in the way. I think I'd rather spend the afternoon with her."

"Yeah?" Kurt laughed. "No shit. I never would have guessed by the way you shoved your tongue down her throat. We should all be glad the back seat of that sweet car isn't big enough for the two of you or we would have seen a lot more than us young 'uns should. I think I'd have to bleach my eyes after that."

David rolled his eyes and offered an alternative suggestion to the two of them that made them laugh as he headed out the door.

"Hathaway?" Dominic called as he walked across the lot toward his truck. David turned back to see both men watching him from the doorway. "Name the time and place and we'll be there."

He didn't need to ask what Dominic meant. They'd meet Jesse when and where he decided. He gave them a salute and turned to head to Windsor.

CHAPTER 17

DAVID HADN'T REALLY GIVEN MUCH thought to Jesse's growing desire to have a dog. In general, he thought it was a good idea. But as he shut off the water in her outdoor shower, where he was rinsing off after a quick, early afternoon run along her property's perimeter, he heard voices and realized just how handy a dog might be. The shower had drowned out the sounds of the car coming up the drive. It never would have drowned out the noise a dog would have made barking at the car. And now he had to face whoever had arrived in that car. Wearing only a towel.

"Whose car do you think that is?" he heard a woman ask. The voice sounded vaguely familiar but he couldn't place it.

He heard a man chuckle and say, "This ought to be interesting." *That* voice he knew.

"Do you know something I don't know, Ian?"

"Hello, Dr. DeMarco," David said, stepping out from the shower. Her hand flew to her chest and he felt a little guilty for startling her, but really, there was no other way around it.

"Oh, Mr. Hathaway." She blinked at him and he watched as her eyes grew wide. "Oh."

She was staring at him, having already put two and two together. He crossed his arms and waited. For what, he didn't know.

"Vivienne, you're a married woman. Stop staring." Ian's voice held more dry humor than anything else. She waved him off.

"I'm a doctor, Ian. It's hard not to appreciate the human form."

David felt his lips quirk into a grin as he looked at Ian.

Ian shook his head. "Go put some clothes on, Hathaway."

He smiled. "I'll do that. And I'll wake Jesse, let her know you're here."

"Jesse's napping?" Vivi frowned, causing David to pause in his path. "It's two in the afternoon."

David glanced at Ian, who waved him on. "I've got this. Go get dressed."

"Oh, for god's sake, I get it," he heard Vivi say as Ian chuckled.

Ten minutes later, he and Jesse emerged from her bedroom. He'd pulled on some shorts and a t-shirt, she'd thrown on a dress and pulled her hair halfway into a ponytail. She still looked sleepy and rumpled and he wished he'd had a chance to wake her properly.

"Vivi, Ian. Is everything okay?" she asked, checking the coffee pot one or the other of them must have started.

"I'm fine, how are you?" Vivi looked at Jesse and no one was fooled by her innocent expression.

Ian hid his laugh behind a cough; David leaned against the counter and avoided the other man's gaze, fighting his own smile.

"Uh, I guess you met David. Again."

"I did. He was just getting out of the shower. Practically naked. It was quite a surprise. Visually, not a bad one, I'll admit, but a surprise, nonetheless."

David was pretty sure that, until this moment, he hadn't blushed since he was fourteen. Jesse shot him a startled look before turning her attention back to her friend.

"The, uh, the coffee is done. Maybe we can go out on the porch and chat?"

Vivi arched an eyebrow. "Yes, I think we have quite a bit to catch up on. But before we do, I just want to make sure I understand something. You," she said, turning to her husband. "*You* knew all about this, correct?" Her finger wagged between David and Jesse.

"I asked him not to say anything," Jesse offered Ian her protection.

Vivi's eyes narrowed on her husband, not in anger, but in calculation. "Hmm, somehow I doubt that. Let's go have that chat,

Jesse. And, you," she said, with another look at Ian. "*You*, I will deal with later."

David watched in silence as the good doctor and Jesse poured coffee into their mugs then headed out to the porch. When the door shut behind them, he turned to the sheriff.

"You at all worried about that?" David asked with a gesture in the direction of Vivi.

Ian grinned and grabbed a muffin from a basket on the counter—a remnant of the decadent breakfast David had just tried to run off.

"Nah," he said, taking a bite. "I'm kind of looking forward to it."

David had to laugh at the man's easy-going nature when it came to his wife.

"So, anything new in the investigation?" He raised the topic Ian and Vivi had no doubt come to discuss. Pouring the remaining coffee into two more mugs, he took a seat at the breakfast bar. Ian sat across from him.

"The shoes were Converse sneakers, which makes the footprint useless. They're unisex, so it could still be either a man's or woman's shoe. Other than that, nothing. Have you had any luck getting Jesse to think about who this could be, or if not who, why?" Ian asked.

David shook his head slowly, thinking of the building schematics at the station.

"There something you want to say, Hathaway?"

"Did you know Mark Baker?" he asked. He wasn't sure what kind of ground he was treading here, so he was trying to tread lightly.

Ian shook his head. "No. He and Jesse met around the time I left for the service, and I came back right after he died. I always thought it was kind of weird, their age difference and all, but I never heard anything bad about him and by all accounts he seemed like a good husband and father. Why?"

David was gratified to hear that someone else thought the

fourteen-year age difference between Jesse and Mark was odd. It wouldn't have been all that strange if she'd been in her thirties. But she had barely been an adult, eighteen, when she'd married a thirty-two-year-old man. It might have turned out fine, but when David thought of his daughter dating a man fourteen years her senior, it had big creep factor to it.

"David?" Ian prompted.

"I was just thinking about something someone said to me about why these things might be happening to her. I hadn't told him all the details, like the fact that Mark is dead, but when I told him about what was happening to Jesse, his first theory was a jealous lover followed by his second suggestion of a jealous spouse. Since I'm the boyfriend, I ruled myself out, but it made me think about the spouse. Obviously, it's not Mark doing all this, but what if it's *about* him?"

"Meaning?" Ian leaned forward and rested his elbows on the counter.

"I'm not sure. But I figure there are only three options that possibly make any sense whatsoever."

"Lay it on me. At this point in the game, I'm open to anything."

"Well, since someone else, namely Kit's charming brother Caleb, pointed out that the things didn't start happening until after Jesse and I met, I wonder about a stalker."

"Someone stalking her?"

"Or me. Either option would work. Someone is stalking her and gets mad when she meets me."

"Or someone is stalking you and gets mad when you meet her."

"Seems weird to say it, but it's a possibility."

"Have you been keeping your eyes open, then?"

David took a sip of coffee and picked at a muffin. "I have, sort of. I don't actually go out that much and when I'm on the job, I'm pretty focused and it's hard to be aware of anything other than the job."

"Not to mention not very safe."

He inclined his head. "That, too."

"So, what's the third option?"

"Maybe all this has something to do with Mark."

"Like?"

David shook his head. "I don't know. I really don't. And I can't explain why it would be happening now, when he's been dead more than two years."

"But?"

David looked toward the porch, making sure the women weren't headed back in before he spoke. When he heard nothing but the murmur of their voices outside, he answered. "I may not find anything, but I pulled all the files on the fire that killed Mark. I know nothing about him, but if what is going on now had something to do with something that was going on then, maybe the fire will tell us something."

Ian sat back. "You're seriously looking into his death? What do you think you're going to find?"

Again, David shook his head. "I don't know. Maybe nothing. Probably nothing. But like you said, at this point we've drawn so many blanks I can't think it will hurt."

"It might if Jesse finds out."

David set his mug down. "Which is why I'm telling you and not her. And neither of us will mention a word of this unless, or until, I find something worth mentioning."

Ian regarded him for a long moment before finally giving him a nod of agreement. His face was expressionless so David had no idea if the sheriff thought he was crazy or on to something. Either way, it didn't matter, he needed to do something and this was something he could do.

"Don't you all look so serious," Vivi said, entering the kitchen with Jesse right behind her. David had been so focused on making his intentions clear he hadn't heard them coming back in.

"I was just telling David what I can expect from you when we get home. You know, for keeping *this* from you and all." Ian wagged a finger between David and Jesse, mimicking what his wife had done a short time ago. David was pretty sure the man was goading her on purpose.

"Dr. DeMarco," David started.

"Call me Vivi."

"Vivi, thanks for coming by. I'm sure I don't need to tell you why Jesse and I made the decision we did. It was our decision to make. But all things considered, MacAllister might deserve whatever you plan to dish out. After all, she is one of your closest friends."

He draped an arm around Jesse as he watched Vivi's eyes go from him to her husband. Ian winked at Jesse.

Vivi rolled her eyes. "Come on, you big lug," she said, hooking an arm through her husband's. "I think it's time to leave these two alone. Not to mention, you and I need to have a little chat."

"A chat, eh. So that's what we're going to call it—ow!" He cried out as she stomped on his foot.

"Bye Jesse. Bye David. Do stay in touch," Vivi said.

And they were gone.

David and Jesse listened to sound of the car making its way down her drive. When they could no longer hear it, they both started to laugh. Turning toward her, he wrapped his other arm around her, encircling her.

"So, was she mad?" he asked.

Jesse wagged her head from side to side. "More curious than anything."

"About?" He wasn't sure he liked the sound of that.

"About us—how long we've been together, why we've kept it secret. Those sorts of things."

"But not mad?"

She shook her head. "Maybe I underestimated my friends. Maybe she won't try to steamroll me into having the same kind of relationship she has."

"Maybe she just wants you to be happy."

"She definitely wants that. But it's also possible that at this very moment her shrink mind is dissecting everything I've just told her and I'm becoming a case study."

David chuckled. "I doubt it. My guess is Ian will keep her too distracted to do that. Or at least do too much of that."

"He did look a bit gleeful about all this, didn't he?" she agreed with a smile.

He moved his hands to the back of her head and began to massage her scalp. Her head fell back and she closed her eyes. It was all well and good that their friends were taking things in stride, but there was one topic he and Jesse hadn't covered in all this.

"What about the kids?" he asked. One of her eyes popped open for a moment, then closed again.

"Meaning?"

"Meaning, my teammates know, a few of your friends know. Do we need to tell our kids so they don't hear it from anyone else?"

Both her eyes opened now and began to search his. He was ready to tell Miranda, had been for a while. But his relationship with his daughter was very different than Jesse's relationships were with her sons. Miranda had never had a mother and was off at college starting her own life. That wasn't the case with Jesse's boys.

"Do you think we should?" she asked, her voice tentative.

"I think Miranda would want to know, but your situation is different than mine. Do I want Matt and James to know? Yes, but only if you feel it's the right thing to do and only when you feel it's the right time."

Her eyes never left his as his fingers continued to massage her. "It would change things," she said.

He nodded. But things were already changing.

"I don't know how they would react," she added.

He didn't either. Putting himself in their shoes, he wasn't sure how he would feel. But the man in him wanted her to be sure enough *of him* to take on whatever reaction her boys might have. Of course the parent in him understood her hesitancy.

"But then again, I'm not all together certain they'd be surprised. And even if they are, while they will always be my kids, at some point, my life is my own. Just as their lives will be their own."

David said nothing, not wanting to interfere with her reasoning process. It had to be her decision and her decision alone. She knew where he stood; the rest was up to her.

"I think I should tell them."

His hands stilled. "Are you sure?"

She nodded. "But I want to tell them in person. Matt will be home at the end of September for homecoming. I'll do it then."

It was about a month away. Part of him wanted her to tell them now. Right this minute. But another part of him, a much bigger part, was just as ready to take this next step at whatever pace she set. They'd done the right thing starting out as they had. And he trusted that as they moved forward, as long as they continued to do what felt right for each of them, they would figure out what worked for them, what was the best for them, what would make them the strongest. Because there was one thing they both knew all too well and that was that life didn't always make things easy. But, if you had someone in your corner, sometimes it was easier.

CHAPTER 18

JESSE REACHED FOR HER RINGING phone and checked herself moments before she growled a sleepy, grumpy greeting. She didn't want to sound like she'd just woken up on the off chance it was one of the boys calling; they would find it weird that she was still asleep at close to ten o'clock in the morning.

"Hello?" she said, trying to sound more chipper than she felt. David slung an arm around her waist and tugged her close. They'd stayed up late watching BBC's *Inspector Lewis* and because she had a bit of a crush on the series' character Sergeant Hathaway, her own personal Hathaway had felt the need to prove just how much more crush worthy he was, which had kept them up even later.

"Jesse?" Kayla's voice came across the line. Instantly, Jesse was more awake.

"Yes, it's me, Kayla. Is everything okay?" There was very little her assistant couldn't handle so that fact that she was calling wasn't a good sign.

"Everything is fine, it's just that, well, I wanted to let you know we've had an abandoned child brought in," Kayla said.

Jesse pulled herself into a sitting position as she tried to process what she'd just heard. "An abandoned child? Who? Where?"

"A toddler really, we think she's about a year and a half. She was found in the park a few blocks from here, the one at the top of Philips Street. Someone called the police and as a matter of procedure, the police brought her here."

Jesse knew the park; it wasn't far from the hospital. "Is she okay?"

"She appears to be fine, but we're waiting for a child advocate to get here before we do an exam."

"And where is she now?" Jesse asked.

"She's with Gabby Sanchez, the pediatric ER nurse, and Roxanne Bly, the social worker."

Everything sounded under control. But an abandoned child? Occasionally, they had women abandon their babies in the nursery, but this was the first time in her career an abandoned child had come to the hospital.

"And the police?" she prompted, knowing Kayla would have any necessary details.

"They are working on it. Checking missing persons reports and AMBER Alerts and talking to anyone who might have seen the person who left her."

Jesse's mind was working a mile a minute. The poor little girl must be terrified, but it was also potentially a media issue—which was no doubt one of the reasons Kayla had called. If word got out about the child, the local media would most definitely show up, since, in their area, most news consisted of reporting community events and high school athletics. They didn't have a lot of stories like this, not even in Riverside, and it would be a big news day for the few media outlets in the region.

"I'm going to call Colin at the Riverside Police Department. He's their head PR guy. I'll make sure that we're on the same page with who handles the media and what they say. I'm sure you've already told everyone to keep this quiet?" Jesse asked.

Kayla gave her confirmation.

"Good, not only do I not want any media crawling around the hospital, I don't want anyone at the hospital to do anything that might hinder the police investigation or get in the way of helping the child," Jesse added.

Kayla rattled off a few of the precautions she'd already put in place. Together they came up with a few more ideas to ensure that the little girl stayed safe and any media stayed away and then hung up.

Jesse slid out of bed, pulled on a robe, and padded out to the kitchen, leaving David to sleep. Turning her computer on, she found Colin in her contacts and placed the call.

The department was as baffled as anyone but was following procedures, just as Kayla had told her. She learned that the little girl had been found sleeping in some blankets under the swing set at eight o'clock that morning and, with the exception of having been left there, seemed relatively happy and healthy. They agreed that the police would handle all inquiries and that she would instruct her staff not to give any comments. She also learned that the child would be placed in protective custody until they had more information, and while the police would release general information about her, like her approximate age and gender and where she was left, they wouldn't release her picture or any details.

It all made perfect sense to her, even though the situation in general made no sense. Who would abandon a child in a park? She didn't have an answer for that but called Kayla to give her the update.

She was still pondering this question over a cup of coffee when David walked in. He'd pulled on a pair of shorts but still looked sleepy—yawning, rubbing a hand over his bare chest, and sporting a serious case of bedhead.

"Everything okay?" he asked, dropping a kiss on her head before pouring himself a cup of coffee and sitting down beside her. Still contemplating the plight of the little girl, she filled him in.

He reached out and rubbed her arm in support. "Are you going to go in?"

She shrugged. "I thought about it, but Kayla has things under control. She's worked with Colin from the police department before, so I think they'll cover all the bases. I'll stay on call today, but I think that once the child's exam is done, as long as it doesn't show anything, they'll take her into custody and move her from the hospital."

He picked up her hand. "I'm sorry. I can't imagine what would cause a parent to abandon his or her child."

She frowned. "I know, me neither. But then, maybe it wasn't a parent. Or maybe the parent isn't fit and knows the little girl will be better off without him or her. Any way you look at it, it's going to be a sad story."

• • •

And it got even sadder as the days passed and no one claimed the little girl. Jesse looked at the calendar on her desk; it had been five days since Jane, as they called her, had been found. And still not a word from anyone. It was hard to believe no one would miss such a sweet child. The temporary foster parent and the social worker assigned to the case had brought her into the hospital a few times for additional checkups. So far she was healthy, which was good, but made the fact of her having been abandoned seem even more bizarre. Developmentally, she was a little behind in her speech, but other than that there was no malnutrition or special needs to indicate hardship of any sort. And Jesse wasn't the only one confused by the whole thing; the police department, though proceeding through the motions, was as befuddled as she was.

An instant message pinged on her computer and she glanced at the screen. Then frowned.

"Hi Mom," the message from James started. "In my computer programming class. It's so basic I may have to hack into his lesson plan to make it more interesting. Just thought I would let you know."

"Don't even think about it," she typed back instantly. He was home from Boston and back in school. If the way things had been going so far were any indication, this year was going to be interesting.

"Ha! Nice to know you think so highly of me. Actually, in the library for morning break right now. Going to Chelsea's house after school. Be home by dinner."

She sighed. "Just be glad I think so highly of your skills, if not always your judgment. Have fun and tell Chelsea I said hi."

"Nice save, Mom." And he ended the conversation.

She smiled thinking of her younger son. He and Chelsea had grown closer over the summer and Jesse was happy to see a true friendship developing between them. She'd been convinced early on that James had actually been interested in Heather, Chelsea's best friend who was calmer and seemingly more James's type. But after all the problems her mom had been going through, Chelsea seemed to have settled down a bit. She seemed to be figuring out what was important and what wasn't. And her friendship with James was currently ranking pretty high on her list.

"Jesse?" The intercom on her phone buzzed. "Sorry to interrupt you, but Dr. Martinez is down in the emergency department and was hoping to speak with you today. You have back-to-back meetings starting in about twenty minutes," Kayla said.

"So if I don't go now, I'm out of luck."

"If you don't go now, *she'll* be out of luck," Kayla corrected.

"I'm on my way."

Jesse left her office and headed down to the ER with orders from Kayla to be in the conference room on the second floor in twenty minutes for one of the departmental budget meetings.

The ER had always been her least favorite place to visit in the hospital. It was a hive of activity, not just with patients coming in, but also with doctors and nurses moving quickly about triaging those patients. And then there was the near constant presence of the support staff—pushing carts, opening cabinets, and moving in and out of rooms in an effort to keep all the supplies stocked. It ran like a well-oiled machine, even on the worst of days, and Jesse was proud of how successful it was—of their patient-satisfaction rates and patient-care scores—but it was also the one place in the hospital she felt well and truly out of place.

And this day was no different. She skirted an empty gurney being pushed by an orderly, then dodged a food cart, no doubt on its way to another part of the hospital, as well as a supply cart, before stopping in front of the nurses' station. She hated to disturb the nurses, who all seemed to be doing four things at once, but managed to ask one where she might find Abigail and was directed toward the back of the department.

"Abigail, Kayla said you wanted to talk to me?" Jesse asked, approaching her friend, who was scrubbing out in one of the back rooms.

Abigail turned and smiled as she finished rinsing her hands. "Miss Matt yet?"

"Not yet, but I'm sure it will come if I allow myself to acknowledge the fact that he's in college. But for now, denial and I are like this." Jesse held up her crossed fingers. "And Danielle?"

"I do miss her, but I'm glad she and Matt are at the same school. I think it will be good for her to have a familiar face in the sea of humanity that is college. But," she paused to drop the paper towels she'd used to dry her hands into the bin, "that's not why I asked to see you, and thanks for coming down. I wanted to talk to you—"

Abigail drew up short when they both heard a crash and someone not quite yelling, but speaking very loudly in the hall. Jesse glanced at her friend, who frowned and shrugged, then they both stepped out to see what was going on.

"Where is she?" a man demanded. Jesse took in his slipshod appearance and shot a glance at a nurse standing behind a nearby counter. *Call security*, she tried to communicate with her eyes. The nurse seemed to get it and gave her a sharp nod before sitting down and picking up the phone as discreetly as she could behind the counter. The man, who appeared to be in his midtwenties, was wearing a faded red sweatshirt covered in holes and brown cotton pants with frayed hems that fell just above his ankles. Based on his build, which was slightly pudgy but not overweight, he looked like someone who led a mostly sedentary life. And though he looked unkempt, Jesse didn't think he seemed all that dangerous, more agitated and confused. Still, no one was about to take any chances, especially with so many people around.

"Can I help you?" Jesse stepped forward and asked in her most soothing voice. The man's dark-brown eyes shot to her and for a moment she had the strangest sensation that he recognized her. His eyes narrowed and his mouth moved, but he didn't say a thing. He raised a hand as if to beckon her to him and she saw it was shaking. She glanced quickly at the nurse, who gave her a slight nod, then turned her attention back to the man.

There was something seriously wrong. And she wasn't the only one to sense it. Quietly, and without making a production of it, nurses and doctors had begun herding patients and their families into rooms, and staff, such as stocking clerks, out of the area.

Tuning out the activity going on around her, Jesse kept her gaze locked on to the man, trying to figure out if he was a junkie, either coming down or high as a kite, or just someone who was mentally unbalanced and off his medications. She didn't know what was off about him, but something was definitely off. He fumbled in his jacket pocket and when his hand emerged, her heart slammed into her chest.

Wavering in front of her was the barrel of a gun.

CHAPTER 19

JESSE FELT A TREMBLING BEGINNING within her and a cold sweat gathering on her skin. But she forced herself to swallow, placing her faith in the knowledge that security would be there soon.

"Tell me your name," she coaxed.

To her right she sensed Abigail moving. From where she stood, Abigail wouldn't be able to see the gun, but if she was listening at all to the panicked sounds coming from the few nurses and doctors remaining in the area, she would know something was very, very wrong. And she knew that Abigail was not one to abandon another person in danger.

Knowing Abigail's inclinations, Jesse made a desperate attempt to motion her friend back. As it was, the man was only focused on her and she was hoping to keep him talking to her, and only her, until security arrived.

At least they weren't in the ER lobby or any of the more public parts of the hospital, she thought to herself. Standing in that hall, it was now just Jesse, three nurses, and one doctor other than Abigail. As if that wasn't enough.

Staring down the barrel, Jesse wondered how many bullets it had, how many people he could kill if he decided to shoot. For a fleeting moment, she wished she'd learned more about guns. Then she quickly acknowledged that it wasn't guns she wished she knew more about, but how to get them away from people.

"You asked where *she* is when you first came back here. Who are you looking for?" Jesse asked, taking a step to the side toward the room she'd come out of. She wasn't going to duck and hide but she wanted to get closer to Abigail so that her friend could see that she was, relatively, okay at the moment.

"My, my sister," he stuttered.

"And who is your sister?"

"G-G-Gabby."

"I know Gabby. She's one of our pediatric nurses, right?"

He gave a jerky nod. "Why are you looking for her, is there something I can help you with?" Jesse asked, trying to keep her voice soothing.

"I want to g-g-get m-married and she won't let me."

Jesse tilted her head to the side. "Are you sure about that? That doesn't sound like the Gabby I know."

"Ye-s-s, she said I c-c-can't get m-married be-because I can't hold a j-job, but she wo-won't let me get a job!"

The only thing that made any sense to her was that the man was getting more and more agitated. And when security picked that exact moment to show up, Jesse, with a growing sense of dread, watched as the man's eyes went wild. She didn't dare look at Abigail—if she showed any sign of needing help, her friend would be there in a heartbeat and she didn't want that. At all.

Jesse stood, frozen in place, as four security guards yelled repeatedly at the man to put the gun down. She had hoped their presence would help, but judging by the look of anguish that washed over the young man's face as he howled and clutched at his ear with his one free hand, "help" wasn't what was happening. It was getting more and more chaotic by the second and she knew she needed to get the guards to back down for just a second before things got even more out of control.

And then, suddenly, Abigail was at her side.

"Stop it!" Abigail shouted at the guards. Too caught up in what they were doing and not noticing they were making it worse, they ignored her.

But the man did not.

It felt like the world slowed to a crawl as she watched the man's gaze focus on Abigail. His expression changed from tormented to calm and with a deliberateness that belied his earlier state, he raised his gun and fired twice.

Jesse was on the ground before she knew it, dimly aware of people screaming, shouting, and running past her. The noises became louder as she realized that she hadn't been hit. Then her eyes flew to Abigail.

A bright red stain was blossoming on the front of her friend's green scrubs. Abigail's eyes watched her in silent confusion. Jesse heard herself shouting "No!" repeatedly as she scrambled toward her friend, clawing at Abigail's clothes, desperate to find the wound, to prove that it wasn't as bad as it looked. Frantic to stop the bleeding, to stop the pain, Jesse screamed for help. And for a moment, no one heard her. Then, suddenly, finally, a nurse was beside her.

"Is it safe?" Jesse demanded, compressing the wound with her hand. Blood seeped between her fingers as she fought back tears.

"Yes," the nurse answered, handing her a thick towel.

"Get Dr. Bennet. Where is Dr. Bennet?" Jesse demanded, shouting at anyone who would listen in the hall. The towel gave the illusion that her friend wasn't bleeding underneath it, but she knew better.

"I'm right here." The doctor kneeled on the other side of Abigail. He looked lost and in shock as he stared at his colleague. And utterly useless.

"Dr. Bennet," Jesse barked, bringing his attention back to her. "We need a board. We need to get her onto a gurney, and into surgery. Do you understand?" He stared back blankly. "Do. You. Understand. Dr. Bennet?"

He blinked then started shouting orders. A nurse took over Jesse's compression and then two more pushed her out of the way. Jesse backed up against the wall and, barely holding back her tears, watched as one of her closest friends was wheeled away. Within seconds, Abigail was gone.

"Jesse!" one of the other nurses came running up to her. "Are you okay?"

Jesse just looked at the older woman. "Where is he?" Her voice was flat and devoid.

"He, um, he shot himself."

Jesse turned and saw that whoever it was had indeed shot himself. She took in the blood splatter on the walls then let her eyes fall to the blood on the floor at her feet. She raised her hands and looked at her red-soaked skin.

"Jesse?" the nurse said.

"We need to secure the hospital. We've run this scenario a hundred times during our emergency trainings, everyone should know what to do," she said through a tunnel of emotions. "And someone needs to call her husband. I need to call Joe," she added, her voice breaking.

"Ma'am?" One of the security guards approached with a police officer who must have arrived within minutes of the shooting. She knew she would need to talk to them eventually, but now she needed to make sure the hospital was indeed safe. And then she needed to call Abigail's husband.

"Jesse," Mike Mitchel, her head of security, said as he rushed toward her.

"Mike, where are we? What's the situation and what's being done?" How she managed to ask these questions, she didn't know. They *had* run this scenario during their emergency planning. But training for it and living it were two different things. Especially when one of the victims was one of her best friends. *That* was something no one could ever train for.

In a succinct manner that Jesse, and the policeman standing with them, appreciated, Mike filled her in. All of the processes and procedures they'd put in place were being implemented. The hospital was being searched, the public areas were in lockdown, and security and the police were coordinating to contain the situation.

Feeling dazed, Jesse nodded and issued the orders and directions the training had instilled in her. When she finished, Mike left to implement his part of the response. She turned to the policeman standing beside her and felt a complete loss for words.

Maybe sensing her impending shock, a nurse beckoned her over.

"Jesse, in here," she said.

Jesse looked up just as the nurse reached out to take her hand. After guiding her into a hospital room, the nurse turned on the tap in one of the sinks and scrubbed Jesse's hands with soap, washing most of the blood away as Jesse stood and watched the pink-tinged water circle the drain and disappear.

"Jesse!" Kayla came running into the room. The police officer had stationed himself at the door, but Kayla had completely ignored his attempt to keep her back. Her eyes were red rimmed as she watched the nurse help Jesse dry her hands. All three sets of eyes lingered on the pink tinged cloth for a moment, then Kayla cleared her throat.

"Come in here," she said, taking Jesse by the arm and leading her into a sitting room. Kayla pushed her into a seat and when her damp shirt touched the skin of her stomach she realized just how much of Abigail's blood she had on her. She may have gotten most of it off her hands, but still, she felt like it was everywhere. There was too much of it.

"I'll call Joe," Kayla said, taking a seat beside her, wiping at her eyes and nose as she tried to dial.

Jesse held out her hand. "I need to tell him, Kayla."

Her assistant studied her face for a long moment, then handed her the phone.

The conversation was short, but no one knew better she did just how much a few words could change your life forever. At the end, she offered to call Danielle, too. She wasn't sure she'd be able to have that conversation, that she'd be able to tell the young woman her mother had been shot and they didn't know whether she would live or die, but knowing that Joe wasn't in a position to make *any* calls gave her the strength to try.

She dialed Danielle's number and it went straight to voice mail. She tried again with the same results. Finally, she tried Matt. He answered on the second ring.

"Mom?"

"Matt."

"What's wrong?" he asked instantly.

"Have you seen Danielle?" she asked.

He hesitated. "No, but I'm on my way to meet her at the gym right now."

She tried not to cry, but the tears started to fall silently. Closing her eyes and drawing on all her strength, she told Matt what had happened. That he needed to get to Danielle before she heard it anywhere else went without saying.

"Are *you* all right?" he asked. She could hear the shakiness in his voice. And though she wasn't all right, and wouldn't be for a while, she told him she was fine.

"Okay." He took a deep breath. "I'm going to get Danielle and bring her home. We'll be there as soon as we can."

"I'm not sure you should be driving now, honey," she managed to say.

She could hear him take another breath. "I know you're okay. But Danielle isn't going to be. I'll get her there just fine. We'll be there as soon as we can."

She agreed, against her better judgment, and hung up. Blindly, she handed the phone to Kayla. She felt like a lead weight sat heavily in her stomach.

"Jesse?"

She looked up.

"Why don't we get you cleaned up?" Kayla's voice was gentle but persuasive, and Jesse was once again grateful for her young assistant as she let herself be led her to the staff room and into the shower.

CHAPTER 20

"HATHAWAY!"

David started and looked up to see Dominic jogging down the stairs, jangling a key chain in his hand.

"Yeah?"

"Get up, we need to go."

David frowned. The bell hadn't rung and he had no idea what Dominic was talking about. Even so, he felt sweat begin to bead on his brow.

"What's wrong," he demanded.

Dominic swallowed. "There's been a shooting at Riverside Hospital."

David felt like the floor was falling out from under him as the denial started to form on his lips.

"Let's go. We'll talk on the way," Dominic ordered.

Dazed for a moment, David watched his teammate head toward the door, then leapt up to follow him out to his car. Without a word he climbed into the passenger seat. Dominic revved the engine and backed out.

"What do you know?" he asked, his voice shaky. He fumbled with the radio dial, hoping to find some news.

"Not much. SWAT was deployed, the police, and first responders," Dominic replied, turning onto the road that would take them to the highway, the fastest route down to Riverside.

"Why would they need first responders at a hospital?" He asked the question and then felt sick because he knew the answer.

Depending on how many people were shot and who they were, they'd need all the help they could get. "Oh, god," he choked out.

He kept his face turned to the passenger window, away from Dominic's concerned glances, for most of the drive, praying the entire time that when they got there he'd see her. Fifteen minutes away from the hospital, his chief called with an update. Two people had been shot, one bystander and the shooter himself. That increased the odds that Jesse wasn't a victim, but there was no way he was going to relax until he actually knew she was okay.

They pulled into the parking lot of the hospital and it was a zoo. Cops and media were everywhere. He scanned the police line and wondered whether or not they'd let him through. He wasn't a responder and he wasn't law enforcement, they'd have every right to keep him out. But that wasn't going to happen.

"David!" Dominic tugged his sleeve. "That's her, isn't it?" he asked, pointing to a hospital entrance.

At that moment, the moment he saw Jesse standing by the doors talking to a police officer, he felt something he had never in his life felt before: the overwhelming urge to drop to his knees and thank god, or whoever it was who had been listening to his prayers.

"Jesse!" he shouted. He was smart enough not to break through the police line and go running across the parking lot when they'd just had a shooting, but it was hard to hold himself back. She didn't seem to hear him so he called again. And then, slowly, she turned.

Her eyes met his and he saw her hand come to her mouth, as if she was fighting off the urge to cry. She started walking toward him and he ducked under the tape. An officer made a move toward him, but she called to the officer and waved him off.

He was incapable of words when she walked straight into his arms. He pulled her against him, holding her tight. His cheek came down on her head and he closed his eyes and breathed her in, feeling her heartbeat, absorbing her vitality. He didn't ever want to let her go.

"I'm okay, David," she finally managed to say. Then her

arms tightened around him and she let out a small, choked sob. "But Abigail, Dr. Martinez, she's been shot. She's in surgery." She paused, unable to go on for a minute. "We don't know if she's going to make it. I was standing right next to her."

If he hadn't been holding her when he'd heard that, he wasn't sure he would have remained standing. He felt himself start to shake at the thought of her so close to death, and with a sense of desperation he'd never felt so strongly before, he needed to get her out there, away from it all.

"Dominic is here. He can drive us home." His hand slipped down to hers and he started to pull her with him toward his friend's car. It took him a second to realize she wasn't moving. He turned back and looked into her eyes.

"I can't, David." Her voice was small, but certain. "It's my hospital. I can't leave my people."

He blinked, unsure he was hearing her correctly. "You were almost shot, your friend is lying in surgery, no one expects you to do your job right now."

She gave him a small smile. "But they do. I'm the head of the hospital, we're in the middle of a crisis; I'm not abandoning my staff."

Intellectually, he understood what she was saying, but everything in him rebelled against it.

"Joe is here, Abigail's husband. Matt is bringing Danielle, her daughter, back from Boston and they should be here in less than hour—I want to be here for them. I also have staff I need to settle, a hospital I need to get back in functioning order, police to work with, and a nurse, the sister of the shooter, we need to find. Not to mention handling the media. Of all the times to leave, this isn't it. And I know you know that." She added the last bit so softly that any anger or frustration he felt dissolved and all that was left was his need to protect her.

"Jesse, don't ask me to walk away."

"I'm not," she shook her head. "But I have a job to do. I don't know how long it will take or when I'll be done, but I need to do it."

He took a deep breath. "Okay, I hate it. I hate leaving you." She smiled at his petulance. "But I get it." He ran a finger down her cheek. "Promise me you'll stay close to the police and with groups of people. Promise me you'll be as safe as you can be?"

She nodded against his hand then kissed his palm. "I'll call you as soon as I'm able to take a break," she said.

He cupped her face and stared into her eyes, memorizing every detail. Then he leaned down and brushed his lips against hers.

"If I don't hear from you by the end of my shift tonight, I'm coming back and dragging you away."

She gave him another soft smile, then nodded. He didn't want to let her go, but she took a step back. His fingers still held hers, but no other part of them touched.

"Thank you for coming."

He managed a nod and then she turned and slipped away. He stood, watching her back, as she walked toward the hospital. A police officer joined her just outside the door and the two disappeared from sight.

• • •

At six thirty that evening, David stood at the door to Jesse's house. She'd called him when she'd left the hospital so he knew she was inside. He also knew Abigail hadn't pulled through surgery, and that despite the loss of one of her closest friends, Jesse had forged her way through the day. He had no doubt, judging from her actions and the tone of her voice when they'd spoken on the phone, that she had stuffed her emotions way down deep in order to get through the day. She'd even snapped at him when he'd asked, for the second time, how she was holding up. He didn't take it personally, people had to do what they had to do to get through times like this. Not only had she lost a friend, but she'd had to run the hospital and stay strong for Abigail's family, and her own two sons, too.

But enough was enough and he was going to make sure that she had what she really needed, not just what she thought she wanted, to deal with the events of that day.

"Can I help you?" Matt stepped through the door, holding it close behind him. "Aren't you that arson investigator?"

He nodded. "I'm here to see your mother."

Matt's eyes were red rimmed and his expression blank.

"Matt, who is it?" James's head popped around the door behind his brother.

"Mr. Hathaway, right?" Matt asked, still obviously confused as to why he was there. David nodded and looked at both the boys. They weren't about to let him in, let him invade their space. Or their mother's space. He didn't think it was because they didn't like him, but more because they were protecting their mother, trying to give her some of the peace she hadn't had all day.

"I'm sorry about Dr. Martinez," he said.

Both boys nodded and James looked away, blinking.

"Is your mother here?"

"Matt? James? What are you doing? Oh, David." And there she stood. Shielded by her sons, wearing a robe and holding a glass of wine. It looked like she'd just finished a bath and he was glad to see she was doing something for herself. He felt himself relax for the first time all day.

"Jesse."

The boys moved aside as she stepped forward. He could feel the change in their expressions, curiosity creeping into their minds.

"I didn't know you were going to stop by," she said.

He looked at her in disbelief. She'd almost been shot less than ten hours ago and she thought he was just going to let it go. His eyes flickered to the boys standing behind her. Maybe she was still trying to keep her relationship with him a secret, but as far as he was concerned, there were bigger things to worry about right now.

"Matt, James," he spoke, addressing the boys. Both sets of eyes met his. "Your mother and I have been seeing each other for over three months. I have a tremendous amount of respect for her, and if you are wondering, yes, I do love her. But we can talk about that later, because right now, your mom and I need to have a chat."

Jesse looked stunned and he seized the opportunity. Taking hold of her hand, he moved past the boys and pulled her into the house.

"Mom?" Matt called.

"It's fine," she managed to say as he dragged her behind him, not stopping until they got to her bedroom and he'd shut the door behind him.

For a moment, she just stood there, glass in hand, looking at him. Then she burst.

"What the hell was that about?"

"Have you cried today?" he asked.

"What? Of course I have," she brushed him off. "I thought we agreed that *I* was going to tell the boys? I can't believe you just said that to them! Without talking to me first or even giving me any warning. What were you thinking?" she demanded.

"I'm sorry about Abigail." Her voice had risen, but he kept his quiet.

"What?" she demanded.

He'd seen this before, too. It was hard for her to hear anyone through her own pain.

"I said, I'm sorry about Abigail," he repeated.

"You have a funny way of showing it. Things are already getting complicated between us and now you've complicated them even more. David, I care about you, you know I do. I even love you, too, although I'm not really feeling it right now. But you've just made my life monumentally—hey, stop! What are you doing?"

He cut her off by gathering her in his arms and sitting them on the bed, with her in his lap. He took the glass of wine and placed it on the bedside table and then just held her.

"What are you doing?" She demanded again, sitting rigid in his arms.

"Holding you."

"I'm fine. I think you should go." She was wooden in his arms, staring straight ahead.

He ignored her and just held on. She was a strong woman but she'd break eventually. Not because he wanted her too, but because she needed to. But he also knew it was a place she wouldn't let herself go without a fight. There were a hundred and one reasons for her to stay strong and stoic and only one to let go. He wanted her to take that reason, to value herself as much as she did everyone around her. So he just sat, his arms looped around her, his cheek resting against her shoulder.

He watched ten minutes click by on the clock before he felt her start to relax. Ten minutes after that, she was crying silently against his chest. Crying for her friend, for herself, for Abigail's family, and for the tragedy of the day. Easing them back onto her bed, he lay beside her, never letting her go as she clung to him and finally let herself go.

• • •

It was dark when David slid from her side and made his way to the kitchen. Matt was sitting at the breakfast bar when he walked in. They nodded to each other silently and David watched the young man's eyes search his before they dropped down to his shirt, still wet with Jesse's tears.

"She cried," Matt stated, sounding a bit surprised. David nodded, making his way to the coffee maker.

"She never cries."

He raised the carafe, silently asking Matt if he wanted coffee. When Matt nodded, David filled it with water and started the pot.

"Everyone cries sometimes," David said.

"Even you?" Matt challenged.

David thought of the night he'd come to Jesse desperately trying to escape the reality of the little brother and sister. "Even me," he conceded. "But only when I know I don't have to be strong anymore."

"Meaning?"

"Meaning, sometimes it's hard to let yourself cry when you know you need to be strong for other people. When you have other people relying on you."

Matt got up, walked around the counter, then leaned up against it. "Who does she need to be strong for?"

"You, your brother, Abigail's family, the hospital. A whole shitload of people."

It crossed his mind that maybe he should be watching his language. But he'd spoken the truth and the situation wasn't exactly normal anyway.

"She doesn't need to be strong for us," James said, joining them.

"You're her kids, of course she needs to be strong for you."

"You sound like you speak from experience?" Matt asked, crossing his arms over his chest.

"I have a daughter. She's a year older than you, a sophomore in college in Rhode Island."

Both the boys seemed to take this in.

"And you're dating our mother?" Matt asked.

He nodded. He wasn't fooled by the mock-easy way Matt spoke. This was the moment—the moment when they could reject him, get angry with him, or worse, get angry with their mother. He didn't know which way it was going to go.

"And you love her?" James asked.

Again, he nodded, feeling tension creep into his body.

And then Matt gave a small smile. "So, she's been sneaking around for what, three months? Really? *Our* mom?"

"Ooh, I think I'm going to be able to get away with *a lot* from now on," James added with a laugh.

For the first time all day, David smiled. "I wouldn't count on it, James."

● ● ●

For a moment, when Jesse woke up, she wondered if she was alone. The house was silent—no voices, no one moving about. And then she remembered.

David.

She buried herself under the covers for a little longer, thinking about what had happened. She'd told him she was fine, he hadn't believed her. She'd been rude to him, yelled at him, he'd ignored it. She'd told him to leave and he'd gathered her in his arms and held on. And let her fall apart.

Thinking about it again brought another set of tears to her eyes. For Abigail yes, but also tears of loss and of hope. When she'd had two miscarriages between giving birth to Matt and getting pregnant with James, Mark had left her to mourn on her own. Not that he hadn't loved her or checked in on her or taken care of her, he had. He had doted and tried to fix things that couldn't be fixed. But when Mark had asked how she was and she had answered "fine," he had left it at that. When she'd been anything but fine.

She always worked through things and sorted them out. But she always did it on her own, in her own time. She thought Mark was being respectful by leaving her to her own process. But after what David had done earlier, she was starting to wonder if maybe she and Mark had had it wrong all those years.

David hadn't pushed or tried to fix things, he just hadn't let her run away from them. And he hadn't freaked out or offered her platitudes when she'd cried. The memory of his physical body holding her, keeping her still, was a new sort of comfort. And the way he'd just held on while she cried, letting her break into a million pieces, even knowing he couldn't put her back together, wasn't embarrassing or frustrating at all. Unlike how she had always felt with Mark.

She had hated crying in front of Mark because he would immediately try to make it right. She knew he responded that way out of love for her, but sometimes things just can't be made right, or sometimes she knew she had it in her to make them right herself but needed a moment before she did so. And when Mark tried to fix things or point out how she could fix them—as if she didn't know—it would make her angry. And then he would get hurt and she would have to deal with his pain as well as hers. So, over the years, she'd just stopped showing him that side of her.

But David had just let her be herself. Or, more precisely, he'd let her be more than who she had become over the last several years. He hadn't let her get away with ignoring herself, and because he had stayed rock steady with her the whole time, she felt a new solidity and strength about their relationship. Oh, it was always good, and she'd told the truth when she'd said she loved him. But this was different. This was more. This was feeling like their relationship had taken root and no matter what way the wind blew, it wasn't going anywhere.

She knew she had a long few days and months ahead of her as she mourned the loss of her friend, but she felt a renewed sense of energy knowing she wouldn't be alone as she pushed through the coming weeks. And when she heard a muted chuckle coming from down the hall, she knew she wasn't alone now, not by a long shot.

As she walked into the kitchen, three sets of eyes turned toward her. David was sitting at the breakfast bar playing penny poker with her sons. Matt and David each had cups of coffee in front them and James had a glass of juice.

"Mom," Matt said, rising from his chair. He enveloped her in a huge hug. She held on to him for a moment, burying her face against him.

"How are you?" she asked, stepping back. "Have you talked to Danielle?"

He shrugged in answer to the first question. "I told her I'd come over after you woke up." He glanced at the clock. "Do you mind?"

She shook her head. "No, I'd say take something with you, but from experience I know they aren't going to want to eat tonight. So just go and be with her." Matt gave her a long, steady look then squeezed her hand and let go.

"I'm not sure how late I'll be," he said, gathering his keys.

She waved him off. "Go, stay as long as you want or as long as she needs you. We'll be here."

When he was gone, she turned her eyes to David and James. Both were watching her. She offered a small smile and brushed a hand over David's hair as she walked past to get herself her own cup of coffee. He reached out and gave her hand a quick squeeze.

"Can I get you anything, Mom?" James asked.

She stopped short, sat down beside David, slid her empty mug over, and let her son help her. "A cup of coffee?"

David reached for her hand and held it in his against his thigh as James took the mug, filled it, and brought her the coffee.

"How's the game?" she asked, taking a sip.

"Your son is a card counter. I just thought you should know." David said with a nod toward her younger son.

James tried for a look of innocence but couldn't quite pull it off when a grin spread across his face. "How did you know?"

"We play a lot of poker in the firehouse."

"Are you going to tell Matt?" James asked.

"Matt doesn't know?" Jesse asked. It didn't come as a shock to her that she didn't know, but the fact that he'd been able to keep it from his brother was surprising.

"Nah," James answered. "I lose enough on purpose that he hasn't figured it out yet."

"And his brain is wired a little more straightforward than yours would be my guess," David interjected.

She thought about being offended at his insinuation of James's deviousness, but since he was right, and because it was, in general, good-hearted deviousness, she just let out a small laugh.

"Ian and Vivi are on their way over," David said, changing the subject. She glanced at James, knowing what Ian would want to talk about and thinking it might be better to have her younger son upstairs.

"Mom, I'm fifteen. I think I can handle it considering everything we've already been through."

His tone was lighthearted, but she didn't miss the undercurrent of weariness and wisdom in it.

"You're right," she said, clearly surprising him. "If you want to stay when Ian updates us, you're welcome to. But I'm not sure what he'll have to say, and if it's not public knowledge it will be up to him whether you stay or not."

James considered her for a moment then nodded.

"Good, then how about another game while we wait. A *fair* game, James," she added with a wink.

James smiled, shuffled, and dealt the cards.

Two games later, they heard Ian's truck pulling up the drive, and within minutes Jesse and Vivi were hugging each other, each shedding tears for their friend. Even Ian looked like he had shed a few.

"So, do we know anything more than what I knew when I left the hospital a few hours ago?" Jesse asked as they all took a seat in the family room. Ian wasn't officially on the investigation but knew the chief of the Riverside police well.

Ian cast a glance at James, then looked back at Jesse. David reached for Jesse's hand and tugged her against him as she answered Ian's unspoken question. "He's old enough, Ian, and unless you're going to tell us things that aren't public, I've told him he can stay."

Ian took another look at James, whose earnest expression made him look much more like Mark than usual, then started filling them in.

"You know they found Gabby, who wasn't able to tell the police much more than what you knew when you left. Her brother was mentally impaired but always harmless. He took medication and had someone who came by and helped him during the day when his sister was at work. He didn't need twenty-four-hour care, which was why he was living with her, but he did need some help every now and then.

"She doesn't know what did or could have set him off. She doesn't even know where he would have picked up a gun. She didn't have one in the house, and as far as she knew, they didn't even know anyone who would have that type of gun. Rifles, sure, but not a handgun."

"I assume the police are tracing it?" David asked.

Ian nodded. "They are. Sameer, at the state lab, is running the ballistics tonight; he might know something tomorrow. We do know it wasn't registered, which sets the detectives back a little, but we'll see what the ballistics say."

"I know where Gabby lives. If her brother needed assistance, how did he even get to the hospital? She doesn't live close enough to walk," Jesse asked.

Ian shot a glance at Vivi before answering. "We aren't sure, but we're checking local traffic and security cameras to see if we can find anything."

"What aren't you telling us, MacAllister," David asked, his protective tone earning him a curious look from James.

Again Ian looked at Vivi, but this time Vivi answered. "Two of the tapes show a large blue SUV around the time we think the shooter was dropped off."

Jesse blinked. David straightened beside her.

"What the hell?" David said.

"Mom?"

"What did it show? Did you get a license?" David demanded.

"Mom?" James asked again, sensing the change in dynamic. For a moment she felt frozen. It couldn't be possible that the person who ran her off the road all those months ago could have been involved in the shooting at her hospital. It was too much of a stretch. But looking at Ian and Vivi's faces, it looked like maybe she should consider it.

And then the guilt crashed down on her. If her friend was killed because of something to do with her, how would she ever face Joe or Danielle?

"It's not your fault," David said, rubbing her hand in his, obviously sensing her train of thought.

"No, it's not," both Vivi and Ian said.

"Will someone please tell me what the hell the blue SUV

means and why it's freaked you all out!" James's outburst brought all their attention back to the here and now.

Jesse frowned. "James, your language."

Her son shot her the kind of you-must-be-kidding-me look that only a teenager can.

Beside her, David spoke in a measured tone and told James just what he wanted to know, including why the blue SUV was important.

"But that doesn't make any sense. How could it possibly all be connected?" James said when David was done speaking.

The three other adults looked at each other, then settled their gazes on Jesse; David gave her hand a squeeze. They meant to convey to her that what she told her son about what had happened over the summer was up to her. She looked into James' face, a face full of worry, and accepted that he wasn't a baby anymore. The more she held back from him, the more he would worry, the more his imagination would take hold. She didn't like the idea of telling him everything that had happened and their suspicions that someone wanted to hurt her, and he would worry once he knew, but it would be better to have the truth out there than not. So she told him.

When she was finished his face was pale and his fists were clenched in his lap. "Why didn't you say anything earlier?" he demanded, trying to sound angry, but the fear came through.

"Because it's still conjecture," Ian answered. "We don't have anything solid, and we certainly don't have any motive for why someone would want to hurt your mother."

"Maybe it doesn't have anything to do with her. You said everything started when you met David, maybe it has something to do with him!" James said, with an angry glare at the man.

Jesse glanced David's way, but Ian answered, his tone soothing but confident. "It's possible. We're looking into that option, too. We're also looking into the possibility that maybe it has something to do with your father."

That was as much of a surprise to Jesse as it was to James and both gawked at Ian.

"Again, we don't have any proof of anything, but we have to look. If we can't find a reason for someone to be after your mom or David, the only other adult in the equation is your father, so we're looking into him, too."

Remembering her talk with her lawyer and her subsequent search of Mark's office, she avoided Ian and David's gaze. She didn't think what was happening now had anything to do with Mark, but he *had* been acting differently before his death, and the fact that she was looking into him, too, and hadn't told anyone made her feel just a tad guilty.

When no one spoke for a while, she looked up. Worried about how James was taking this, she stole a look at his face and then stared. He seemed to actually be considering what Ian had said. He didn't look convinced either way, but he didn't seem angry that his father was being brought into a situation in which he couldn't defend or explain himself.

"I don't see how he could have anything to do with it, but since he's not here to answer for himself the way my mom and David are, have you looked through his things?" James asked.

Ian gave her a look, silently asking permission to continue this discussion with her son. She nodded.

"We haven't gotten that far. Do you have any suggestions?"

"His papers are in the office and I have his old computer."

Jesse frowned. She'd forgotten about that. James had taken Mark's laptop after he died. "There isn't much on it and I haven't looked at it in a while, but I have it upstairs if you want it."

Ian looked at her again, then nodded. "That would be good, thank you, James."

James got up and went upstairs. When he was out of earshot she spoke.

"It's a longer story that I don't want to get into right now," she said, gesturing with her head toward the stairs. "But I went through Mark's papers this summer. My reasons were not related to what happened to me, which is why I haven't said anything, and I can explain them later, but there was nothing unusual in them."

All three sets of eyes stared at her. Ian and Vivi stared in curiosity. David's expression was somewhat different. Not jealous, but maybe confused or a little bit hurt that she hadn't told him about this before.

James came bounding back down the stairs again and she hoped everyone would let it drop now that her son was back.

"Here," he said, handing the computer to Ian. "I had it under my bed and had mostly forgotten about it. It's a little dusty, but it should work."

Ian thanked him, and he and Vivi rose to leave.

As Jesse and David walked the couple to the door, Jesse spoke. "James leaves for school at seven thirty. I can be a little late to work tomorrow, so come by then if you can and I can tell you the rest. Matt will likely still be asleep or back at the Martinezes'," she added.

Her friends nodded, gave Jesse a hug, then left.

When the sound of Ian's truck had faded away, they all returned to the living room.

"Are you staying tonight?" James asked.

Jesse swallowed and fought the urge to jump in. David took a strong grip on her hand.

"I'd like to."

James studied the man. "But you won't if I don't want you to?"

She couldn't help it, her hand tightened on David's. She didn't want to be alone tonight, but she didn't want her son to feel alienated either.

"Maybe, maybe not. Jesse and I would need to discuss it."

James didn't look belligerent or even particularly upset. He did look a little confused and unsure about how to handle the situation. So she was grateful when David continued.

"Look, James. I don't want to cause any more problems for this family than you've already had, and now you're all dealing with yet another crisis. But the thing is, I love your mom and I want to be here for her in a way that, as her child, you can't—or she won't let you because she feels the need to be strong and protect you. So I need you to be honest with yourself and with us. If you don't mind me staying, I'll stay. But if you do mind, I expect you to tell us, so that we can deal with it. Because what I don't want to happen is for you to lie to me and your mother and tell us you don't mind when you really do."

She watched as James' eyes searched David's face for a long, long moment. Her heart was thudding in her chest and even as she recognized the truth in David's words, that James needed to be honest, she wanted her son to say it was fine. She wanted James to be okay with her and David.

Finally, James gave a little nod. "I'm not going to lie and say it's not going to be weird to have a guy other than my father in our house with us. But after everything that's gone on, more than anything, my mom deserves something or someone that makes her happy and makes her feel safe."

Her eyes welled with tears. "So you're okay with it?" she clarified.

His eyes came to hers and she saw a hint of a smile. "Yeah, I'm okay with it. But you know, since you've been sneaking around all this time, I think that maybe next time I, uh, push the boundaries," he said euphemistically, "maybe you should be a little more lenient?"

She arched a brow at him in the way only a mother can.

He laughed. "Yeah, that was what David said, too."

• • •

She crawled into bed a short time later, exhausted but knowing from experience that sleep would be hard to come by. David slid in and lay on his side, facing her.

"I'm sorry about your friend," he said again, tracing a line down her cheek.

His sincerity touched her. He was a good man in so many ways and she realized she'd never told him that.

"Thank you, David."

He tucked his hand under his head and looked at her. "For what?"

"For being you, for being there for me, for handling my boys with respect and honesty."

"I wouldn't have it any other way."

"I know. That's kind of my point. You're a good man and I do love you."

He took the palm of her hand and pressed it to his lips. Then he smiled.

"What?"

"I just realized that I'm thirty-seven years old and I've never been in love with anyone before. Except for my daughter, of course, but that's different."

She smiled back. "Does it freak you out? Worry you or scare you?"

"No, not at all." His answer was immediate. "Now isn't the time for me to show you how it makes you feel, but I promise I will soon."

She pressed up against him and knew exactly how it made him feel. Taking the initiative, she pushed him onto his back and slid her legs on either side of him. Lowering her head she feathered kisses along his cheek, then down his neck and back up to his ear. Nipping at his earlobe, she whispered, "Show me how much you love me, David."

She felt his body tense in reaction and then she was on her back.

"That's about the best thing I've been asked to do in a long time."

She grinned up at him, wrapping her legs around his thighs. "We'll have to be quiet," she said gesturing her eyes toward the floor above them where James slept.

"Not a problem. I love a good challenge."

CHAPTER 21

DAVID COULD SEE THAT JESSE was jumpy. No two ways about it. After a late-night phone call home, Matt had decided to spend the night in the Martinezes' guest room, and just ten minutes ago, James had headed off to school with a friend. Now, he and Jesse were just waiting for Ian and Vivi to arrive. And if her face was anything to go by, she looked to be waiting for the grim reaper rather than her friends.

"Here," he said as he walked out onto the porch. Stopping beside her, he handed her a cup of coffee, then wrapped a blanket around her. The day was bright and sunny, but fall was definitely moving in and there was a distinct Northeast chill to it. It even smelled crisper than the lazy, humid days of summer.

He was about to offer her a platitude when Ian's truck pulled up the drive. Followed by a black Land Rover. He groaned internally.

"Caleb's here, too." She sounded as confused as he was annoyed.

Not that he thought the guy was bad news, but his intensity wasn't going to do anything to calm Jesse down. Regardless, there was nothing he could do and within a few minutes they were all seated in her living room, Caleb and his sister Kit, who David met for the first time, and Ian and Vivi. Judging by the introductions, it was the first time Vivi and Caleb had met, too.

"DeMarco," Caleb said. "Any relation to Jeff DeMarco?"

Vivi drew back and Ian put a hand on her shoulder. "He was my brother," she managed to say.

Caleb gave her a sad look. "He was a good man. I'm sorry for your loss."

Vivi threw a glance at Ian before answering. "Thank you."

Caleb gave a curt nod then sat down next to his sister, who seemed to be studying him like he was some sort of rare species.

"Let's get started." Ian called everyone to attention. "I just want to mention why Caleb is here. He and I did some work together when I was a Ranger. I trust him—his brain and his skill—and I think he can be an asset to us even if he never lifts a finger. Vivienne is here, well, because she's Vivienne, but she's also officially a consultant on this case."

"And Kit?" Jesse asked.

Her friend stuck her tongue out at her and grinned. "I'm here because I threatened to castrate both of them if I wasn't invited," Kit said, pointing her finger at her brother and then Ian. "Vivi took exception, of course, and lobbied to include me."

Ian rolled his eyes.

Vivi gave a soft laugh and said, "So let's get started."

"Okay, what about the computer?" David asked. "Have you had a chance to go over it?"

Ian bobbed his head. "We took a look last night. Couldn't find many files and what we did find was fairly benign."

"Fairly?" Jesse asked.

"Some e-mails and some paperwork that, without any context, could be interesting. But it could also be nothing if we knew the context around it," he explained.

"So, what now?" she pressed. David reached for her hand and wrapped it in both of his.

"Well, it actually looks like some files were either deleted or hidden, but Vivienne and I aren't computer savvy enough to tell. Do you know if James would have done something like that?" Ian asked.

She shook her head, then, seeming to change her mind, shrugged. "I don't think so, but I can't say for certain."

"Okay, fair enough. Naomi and Brian are coming tonight and

we thought we might have them take a look. With their skills, we should be able to get a better idea if there is anything on the laptop worth looking at. Do we have your permission to let them have a look?" Ian inquired.

She looked at David before turning back to Ian and nodding.

"Good, thanks. Now, last night you said you had gone through some of his papers. Do you want to tell us what that was about?"

Beside him, he could feel Jesse tense up. He gave her hand a reassuring squeeze, but she didn't seem to notice.

"Jesse?" Kit said, sitting forward.

Jesse shot David a quick look, one that looked awfully apologetic, then her eyes fell to the floor as she answered the question.

"I went to see my lawyer after I was almost run off the road. I wanted to make sure the will was in place for the boys if anything happened to me. He mentioned to me that Mark had been in a few months before he died asking about setting up a trust for the kids. He'd never mentioned anything to me so I was curious. I went through his papers in his office to see if I could find the information our lawyer had given him or any reason why Mark was looking into it."

The corners of David's mouth turned down. She hadn't mentioned any of this. He wasn't too worried about it, but if had been bothering her, it would have been nice to know.

"And did you find anything?" Vivi asked.

She shook her head and a cascade of blonde hair hid her face.

"Jesse?" Vivi spoke softly. "Is there something you think you need to tell us?"

His gaze locked onto Jesse's profile. She bit her lip and closed her eyes. He brought her hand to his lips and held it there for a few moments, hoping to give her some strength or encouragement or whatever it was she needed to continue.

Finally, she looked up, straight into Vivi's eyes. "Mark was a good father and, for most of our marriage, a good husband. We were talking about separating, though, when he died."

David's chest constricted at her announcement. He felt a flash of anger but was smart enough to know it was really hurt disguising itself as anger. Why hadn't she told him? In the grand scheme of things, it wasn't a huge deal, but still, it wasn't nothing.

"Why, Jesse?" Vivi prodded in a soft but encouraging voice.

He saw Jesse's throat work. "Because he'd had an affair. Two actually. I knew about one, and we tried to make it work after I found out. It was when James was about ten. It wasn't a lot of fun, but I thought we were working it out." She paused and her hand went limp in his. "But then I found out about a second. And well, one might be a mistake, but two?"

She let the question hang in the air and refused to meet David's eyes. Like she thought he might blame her for something or, worse, think less of her. He took a tighter hold of her hand and pulled her closer to him.

"Why didn't you ever say anything?" Vivi asked, trying to mask her own surprise.

"Because it hardly mattered. I didn't even know you when it was happening, Ian was in the service and it was unlikely I would have told him anyway. Kit was the only person around when all this was happening."

"But you never said anything to me either," Kit pointed out.

Jesse looked down again. "Because I was embarrassed. And then he died and it just didn't seem to matter. There was no reason anyone needed to know."

Only there was, and, judging by the look she gave David, she knew it. He had needed to know, not because he would judge her or blame her or take pity on her, but because it was a part of who she was. Not all of who she was, but certainly a part of her.

"What the hell do you have to be embarrassed about?" Caleb interjected, breaking the moment. "As far as I can see, the only thing you did was try to save your marriage. Excuse my French, but *he* was the dickwad that fucked up."

Kit smacked her brother on his arm but he didn't even flinch. His gaze was focused on Jesse, and for the first time, David thought he could actually grow to like the guy. Maybe.

"I have to admit, I agree with Caleb," he said.

Jesse's eyes flew to his, searching for any hint of anger or betrayal in his face. The only thing he was capable of thinking when she looked at him like that was how lucky he was to have walked into the hospital that day. She offered him a tentative smile and squeezed his hand.

"Okay," Caleb once again interrupted. "Now that we've established that your husband, though he might have been a good father, was an unethical scumbag, what does that mean for the investigation?"

Jesse was about to mouth her objection, but David silenced her by directing her attention to Vivi and Ian, who were looking at each other, clearly having a silent conversation.

"Well, it doesn't give us anything concrete," Ian started, shifting his gaze back to Jesse. "But it does align with some of the theories Vivienne came up with last night."

"Theories?" Jesse asked.

"Yes," Vivi answered. "Theories as to why you are being targeted. And, knowing about Mark's past actually makes me more certain I was on the right track."

"Meaning?" David prompted, pretty sure he wasn't going to like where this was going. He knew Vivi was an FBI profiler and profilers usually only worked the worst of the worst kinds of cases. If she was putting her mind to this case, it wasn't going to be pretty.

"Well," she started. "The kind of violence we're seeing against you is unusual. When a woman like you—a single, working mother with no real ties to anything shady—becomes the subject of systematic criminal violence, it's usually either a stalker, who may or may not also be a serial killer." At her use of the phrase, Ian reached out and stroked a hand down her back. She turned and gave him a soft smile before continuing. "Or it's related to someone she knows, usually a parent or spouse.

"We know your parents live on the West coast, closer to your sister, so it's unlikely they would be the origin of what's happen.

And because Mark has been dead for two years, I've been struggling to figure out how he might be the cause of this."

"But now," Caleb interjected, "because you know his past and know it wasn't as apple pie as it seemed, you think it fits your profile?"

Vivi wagged her head. "Yes and no. Yes because the things that have happened to you, Jesse, are classic manifestations of jealousy. If Mark were still alive, I would be much more certain that one, or both, of the women he had an affair with was jealous and acting out on that emotion. I still think it's likely, and it does fit the pattern, but the fact that he's been dead two years isn't something we can discount. Why now? What would a woman like that have to gain two years—or more—after the fact?"

Jesse stood and walked to the window. Everyone watched her but no one moved. David ached to go to her but knew instinctively that she needed some space to think. She wasn't sold on Vivi's theory and he didn't blame her. Beside the time gap, for all intents and purposes, Mark had been a good father and he knew she was struggling to comprehend or even contemplate that his actions all those years ago might be the cause of what was happening to her today.

Finally, she turned and asked, "What do you mean 'a woman like me?' I know you said a single working mom, but is there something else to that comment?"

Vivi frowned. "I'm not sure I follow your question."

Jesse paused, her eyes darted to David, then went back to Vivi, then she spoke again. "I mean, what if I were some other kind of woman. More specifically, what if I weren't single?"

Vivi tilted her head. "Well, we all know you're not, but not many other people do. Is there something you're trying to tell us?"

David felt his stomach sinking; this was a morning for revelations that was for sure. And though he hated hearing Jesse air her secrets in this kind of forum, selfishly, he hated that *he* had to hear them in this kind of forum, too.

"Jesse?" he pressed.

"I just, I mean," Jesse paused, took a deep breath, and continued. "I do think whatever was going on with Mark before he died was, well, maybe something to look into. But would it be worth looking into any exes, of mine or David's?"

David heard the words, but the meaning refused to sink in for a moment. And then *he* frowned. She had told him he was only her third lover and not that he cared about numbers, but he had assumed her first had been *before* she'd married. And that would be a long time to go back.

"Do you *have* any exes?" Kit asked. Now that he and Jesse had successfully kept their relationship a secret for so many months, David could hear the speculation in Kit's voice—had there been *another* secret relationship?

Again, Jesse's eyes flitted to his before they landed on the floor in front of him.

"Not an ex, not really, anyway."

"Jesse?" Vivi prodded gently. Both Caleb and Ian had gone preternaturally still.

Jesse let out a big sigh. "Look, I'm not saying I think it's him, but since we're looking at Mark and *that* seems like a stretch, it seems like maybe we should just lay everything out there."

"I agree," Vivi said, keeping her voice soft and encouraging.

Jesse hesitated, fiddling with the hem of her sweater, then she looked up and met his gaze. "About nine months after Mark died, I was at a holiday party for an organization supported by a few of my board members. It was the first holiday season I was on my own, and even though Mark and I had been having problems before he died, I think, well, I think I was just feeling lonely. And probably a little bit sorry for myself."

She paused and took another deep breath. "Ken Bennet, a doctor in the hospital, was there. He's kind of a pompous jerk, you know. Almost a caricature of himself as a surgeon," she said as an afterthought. "Anyway, he was always flirting and he has a reputation for not wanting much from the women he's with."

"And," Vivi pressed when Jesse paused.

283

"And I went home with him that night," she said in a rush. "I'm not, believe me, I'm not proud of it, but I did. And again, while I don't think he has anything to do with what is going on, if we're stretching for things to look into enough to include Mark, I just, well, I just thought it might be worth knowing about."

"And did it last more than that one night?" Ian asked.

David already knew the answer to that. If Jesse had found someone she wanted to spend time with, she wouldn't have been so embarrassed to say something.

She shook her head. "No," she said, confirming his assumption. "But he wanted more," she added and David noted a sad hint in her voice.

"Meaning?" Ian asked, obviously taking more notice.

Jesse dipped her head. "I went home with him because I was feeling lonely and sorry for myself on that night. He had a reputation for going through women so I figured there wouldn't be any messy aftermath."

She paused and pursed her lips together. Obviously, she'd been wrong, but how wrong was something he didn't know. He remembered meeting Dr. Bennet, twice, and it was hard to imagine him with Jesse. Not that he was biased.

"But there was a messy aftermath," Jesse continued. "Not too messy, he has too big of an ego to let anything get too messy around him. But it turned out that he had been interested in me for a very long time before that. He wanted more than just one night. And when I didn't, I think I hurt him. Badly."

Everyone in the room was silent for a long moment. And then her gaze came back to David's and he could see the regret for the pain she'd caused—even to someone as arrogant as Ken Bennet—reflected in her hazel eyes. He held out a hand and she came back to sit beside him. Wrapping an arm around her, he pulled her close.

"Is Dr. Bennet the good-looking, dark-haired guy, on the short side?" Vivi asked.

"He has a receding hairline, but what hair he has is dark, and he's about five foot six or so," David said.

Ian frowned, "You know him?"

David gave a quick nod. "I met him at the hospital once. I was with Jesse and had come down to visit Aaron Greene. I also met him at a fundraiser this past spring," he paused, remembering that meeting. "Actually," he said, his brow shooting down, "he asked if I'd come with her."

Jesse turned in his arms and looked up at him, "He did?"

"Yeah, he did. I thought it was a little strange that he would think that, but then again, his only context for knowing me was because he'd seen me with you at the hospital, so I figured it wasn't *that* strange." But now with this new twist, Ken Bennet's curiosity about Jesse seemed to take a sinister bent. It could have been a harmless inquiry, but then again, maybe not.

Vivi sat back in her chair and stretched out her pregnant belly as she took a deep breath, then refocused on Jesse. "Okay. Thank you for telling us, we will definitely look into it, especially given that statistically, exes do show up quite a bit in cases like this. But before we move on, I have to ask, has there been anyone else?"

Jesse shook her head.

"Ever?" Caleb almost goaded.

David looked down in time to see Jesse roll her eyes at Caleb. He wasn't sure what she would say in response, but she surprised even him when she answered.

"I didn't date in high school, I married when I was eighteen, and unlike my husband, I was faithful for all the years we were together. I had that one regrettable night with Ken and many more memorable ones with David since. So, as prim and proper as you might think it sounds, no, other than the three you know about, there has never been anyone else."

That seemed to shut Caleb up and David almost, almost, hid the smirk he wore as he cast the other man a smug look. It wasn't very forward thinking of him, but he couldn't help throwing it in Caleb's face that clearly Jesse was a discerning woman and still, she'd chosen David. And again, it wasn't about the number of men she had or hadn't been with, it was her take on, and belief in, what relationships meant to her. Different people had different views, for sure, but what he admired about Jesse was that she knew what she wanted and valued it enough to live it.

"Okay," Vivi said, "Then that takes care of Jesse, what about you, David? We haven't asked you if you have any exes."

He felt Jesse raise her head to look at him. Then Caleb chuckled and David shot him a glare and cleared his throat. "There hasn't been anyone between the time I moved here and when I met Jesse."

"No dates, no dinners, nothing?" Vivi clarified.

He shook his head. "No, I was pretty focused on my new job for the first several months, then between Miranda, my daughter," he clarified, "and then meeting Jesse…" He let his voice trail off.

"And before you moved?" Ian asked.

He frowned. "I lived in California, and, yes, I dated. But given that you aren't looking at any connection to Jesse's family who live in Washington, wouldn't it be just as unlikely to be connected to someone from my past in California?"

Vivi lifted a shoulder. "It's not exactly the same thing. We're not looking at Jesse's family as a reason because when family *is* used against each other, whoever is conducting the violent behavior typically wants their true target to see and suffer with the actual target. So in Jesse's case, if someone wanted to go after her parents for something, they would be way more likely to go after her sister, who lives near them.

"But in a romantic relationship, it's a little different," she continued. "We have seen men and women follow an object of romantic interest around the country, and sometimes even the world. But I'm inclined to agree with you that anyone you might have dated in California probably isn't going to be relevant here for the simple reason that you were here nine months before you met Jesse, right?" Vivi asked.

He nodded.

"If someone followed you from California, it would be more likely than not that she would have tried to make some sort of contact in those first nine months. It's very hard for people with that kind of personality to go unnoticed for so long, so she probably would have done something to make you notice her."

David's eye narrowed. "That is really creepy."

"Yes, welcome to my world," Ian said, earning a small laugh from all three women in the room, which was, no doubt, his intention.

"Okay, so we add Dr. Bennet to the list to look into and, Jesse, I hope you know how much I hate to do this, but I really do think we need to take a deeper look at Mark's life," Vivi said. The question that was left unsaid: *Who's to say what other secrets he might have had?*

For a moment, Jesse rested, unmoving, against David's side. Then she looked at each person in the room before her gaze landed on Vivi and she spoke.

"Look, Vivi, I'm not arguing with your logic and I'm not dismissing your theory, but it's hard for me to even think it through, let alone accept it. And I wouldn't have the first idea where to start looking into whether or not you're right."

"But you don't mind if we do?" Jesse's head swiveled to see Ian better, his question made it clear that this was something he and Vivi had already discussed.

Slowly, she shook her head. "But not a word to anyone outside this room. If Mark has nothing to do with this, I don't want the trash dragged out in front of the boys for no reason." She held up a hand cutting off something Caleb was about to say. "And it's my decision and mine alone. I'm not saying bury things or hide things from me. But until we know, if we ever know, if Mark's—" she paused, searching for the right word but then settled on calling a spade a spade. "Until we know if any of Mark's affairs had anything to do with this, we keep it quiet."

When everyone nodded in agreement, Caleb reluctantly so, she leaned back into David. And though he wasn't happy with this turn of events and with having had a big part of the last few years of her life kept from him, he knew it would be all right. Because despite everything she'd been through, the lies and the betrayals, she was still beside him.

CHAPTER 22

"JESSE, YOUR ASSISTANT IS IGNORING me."

Jesse looked up to find Caleb walking into her office without knocking. She sighed; she should be annoyed, but the truth was, she was having a hard time trying to concentrate on anything at the moment. She really wanted to be with Abigail's family. Unfortunately, she had some work that just couldn't be put off, so after the meeting that morning with Vivi, Ian, Kit, and Caleb, she'd come in for a few hours.

"You're a hard man to ignore, Caleb. Then again, I always say Kayla is an overachiever."

He shot her a bemused look and then perched on the side of her desk. She drummed her fingers and stared at her computer screen. Finally, she gave up.

"Why are you here again?" Maybe blaming him for distracting her would work.

"Because your boyfriend told me I needed to stick with you."

She made a face at him. "My *boyfriend*? I'm thirty-six, David is thirty-seven, Caleb. We're not sixteen."

"What else am I supposed to call him?"

"Maybe his name?" she suggested, not without sarcasm.

"Nah."

She sighed again and rested her chin in her hand. "Do you think Mark's involved—or *was* involved in something before he died that led to all this?"

He shrugged. "I just met Vivi, but I knew her brother and he was always bragging about how smart she is and how good she is at her job. I'm not sure it's the tack I would take, but when she laid it all out there this morning, I have to say it made sense. I'm not sure I'm ready to give up my other theories just yet though, not until we find something more solid on Mark."

"You don't still think David is involved?" She didn't bother to hide her disbelief. His gaze slid away.

"As much as I would like to say otherwise, no, I don't think he's involved."

She gave him a smug smile. "Then what are your other theories?"

"Either you have a stalker or David does. Dr. Ken Bennet might be a good candidate for that," he added.

She thought about this for a long moment. She didn't want to reject it, but it seemed so unlikely. Ken Bennet was a jerk, but she didn't think he'd get involved in anything as messy as what was going on. And she just didn't believe that she was the kind of woman who would attract a stalker. But David? Maybe, especially after hearing some of the stories about the firehouse groupies.

"Makes sense," she said. "More for David than for me."

Caleb raised an eyebrow. "Last time I checked, which was barely seconds ago, you're pretty smoking hot."

She gaped at him; he reached forward and tapped her chin from below, closing her mouth. She knew she was relatively good looking, but she'd been married for so long, and with two teenage kids, "hot" was not a word she would ever have used to describe herself. He must be bluffing.

She narrowed her eyes. "Isn't it true that stalkers aren't always about looks anyway?"

He gave her a feral smile. "Yes, it's true. But I would wager in your case, if you do have a stalker, it probably has something to do with your looks, and the fact that you work in a place that saves people, and that you're a mother. You have a lot of things to work with in the fantasy department, whether a person's crazy or not."

"Are you trying to make me uncomfortable?"

He shrugged again. "No, just trying to point out the obvious.

Mark might have walked all over you, but surely there must have been other men interested between the time he died and when you finally hooked up with Hathaway. Why is it so unreasonable to think you could have a stalker? It's not any more of a stretch than to consider Mark being involved in something that is causing all these things to happen to you."

She thought about this. Mark hadn't really walked all over her, but Caleb did have a point. The stalker scenario was just as likely as the Mark scenario.

"Mark didn't really walk all over me, Caleb."

She didn't really care all that much about what he thought, but oddly enough, talking about Mark's infidelities seemed easier than talking about stalkers. It felt like so long ago.

"He cheated on you, twice."

"Relationships are more complicated than that, Caleb."

"They aren't that complicated, Jesse. If you make a vow of fidelity to someone, you keep it. Or end the relationship before you break it. It's the only honorable thing."

She wanted to point out that he wasn't married, and likely never had been, so what did he know about it? But she didn't. Couldn't, because, truth be told, she kind of agreed with him.

She lifted a shoulder, then rose to turn on the electric kettle set up on the meeting table.

"I suppose you're right. I think people cheat for two primary reasons. Because they are too cowardly to face what's wrong in a relationship or because there is something much deeper, psychologically."

"Meaning?" He joined her by the table and they both sat. Dropping tea bags into cups, they waited for the kettle to boil.

She tilted her head. "I don't know, really. But it seems like when all these stories of infidelity come out, more often than not, it's because there was something fundamentally wrong in the relationship that one or the other party didn't want to face. But then there also seems to be the situation where there's some kind of power thing going on. And," she paused, not certain she wanted to continue.

"And?" Caleb prompted, pouring hot water into her cup before doing the same with his.

In for a penny, in for a pound. "And I wouldn't be surprised if that's what it was with Mark."

"How so?" He sat back and studied her.

She couldn't believe she was going to say this. And to Caleb, of all people. Then again, it might be easier with him than with any of her friends or David.

"Mark was fourteen years older than me when we married. And I know both of his affairs were with much younger women."

"Students?"

She nodded. God she hated feeling sullied by her late husband. The women had been above consent, but barely. And Mark had been close to fifty at that time.

"Do you think there were more than just the two?"

Her eyes shot to his. She searched his expression, finding no judgment, no hint that he had just spoken her biggest fear, the thing she had never let herself consider. Suddenly, she knew, deep down, that it wasn't that she'd never let herself consider the option, but rather that she'd never let herself acknowledge the reality.

She nodded. She didn't have any proof. But once she found out about Mark's second affair, she just seemed to know, even as she blocked it out. Denial wasn't just a river in Egypt.

Caleb's mouth went flat.

"Earlier, when I said I was embarrassed, Caleb, I know you, and probably everyone else, thought it was because Mark cheated on me. But really, what I think I'm most embarrassed about is that I didn't catch it sooner. And don't say some people are good at hiding things," she cut off whatever he was about to say. "I know that. But this was someone I was married to for *sixteen years*, Caleb. Someone I shared my life with, someone I raised children with. How could I not have known?"

She blinked away the water welling in her eyes. Caleb said

nothing, there was nothing to say. He reached out and placed a hand on top of hers. They sat there for several minutes before she stirred.

"Karen Ross."

"What?" he said.

"Karen Ross. That was the name of one of the women. And the other was," she paused, trying to recall the name she had intentionally tried to forget. "And Susan Parmenter. I didn't remember the names until now. I should text that information to Ian."

Someone knocked on the door as she reached for her phone.

"I've got it," Caleb said, pulling out his own device and motioning her toward the door.

"Come in," she called.

Colin Gray, one of the detectives and the main PR guy for the Riverside police, walked in. Jesse stood and walked into a big hug. He was also an old friend.

"I'm so sorry about Abigail," he said, dropping his arms and giving her a look of concern.

She inclined her head. "Thank you. Do you have any more ideas yet as to why that man turned violent? How is Gabby?"

"She spent a long day with us yesterday and is probably more shocked than anyone else. I'm sure Ian filled you in on the blue SUV, and we're looking into that, too. But no, nothing new since last night. That's not why I'm here today, though. I'm here about baby Doe."

The toddler. She'd almost forgotten about the little girl in the upheaval of the previous day.

"What about her? Is she okay?"

"She's fine. Healthy and happy in her temporary foster care. But we think it's time to release a photo of her. As you know, we didn't at first because we were hoping a parent or guardian would step forward once they realized she was gone. But it's been almost a week now and no one is coming forward. We've decided to put her picture out there in the hope that someone might recognize her and have information about her."

"It sounds like you're not hopeful about a parent or guardian coming forward now," she said sadly.

He shook his head. "Not now, not after so much time has passed. There are any number of reasons why that might happen, not the least of which is some kind of foul play, so we're hoping if someone knows the little girl, they might also know about her family, so then we can locate them and make sure they are okay."

"The poor little girl. I hope you find someone who can help."

He reached out and squeezed her shoulder. "I do, too. I just wanted to give you the heads up that we're releasing the photo today. We will say she was brought here for a routine checkup as part of the press release, so you may want to remind your staff that if anyone calls, all inquiries and information should be directed to us. I already mentioned this to Kayla on my way in, and she offered to send an e-mail to the staff if you need her to."

She nodded. "Yes, of course."

Colin's eyes skittered to Caleb, but since Colin was obviously on his way out, she didn't bother to introduce them. Instead she gave the detective another hug and walked him to the door. After saying her good-byes, she looked out at Kayla who was watching her.

"Everything okay, Boss?" she asked, gesturing her head toward Jesse's office and the man still inside.

"Everything is fine. Was he bugging you?" Jesse asked, also gesturing her head toward Caleb.

Kayla let out a laugh. "Not hardly. I think he *thought* he was bugging me, but it's not like we aren't busy around here."

Jesse felt a wave of guilt sweep over her. She'd been staring off into space all morning, then spilling her guts to Caleb, while her staff was slogging away.

As if sensing her thoughts, Kayla stood and gave her a quick hug. "Hey, I didn't mean it like that. You're scheduled to take the afternoon off. We're fine here, really. The things I have to do are paperwork, forms, that sort of thing. Nothing that needs your attention today. Why don't you go deliver Detective Gray's message to the various departments and then head out for the day. Do they know when they'll be holding Dr. Martinez's funeral?"

At the mention of Abigail's funeral, Jesse's eyes misted. "Thanks, Kayla. I might do that if you don't mind?"

Kayla shook her head.

"And the funeral is on Saturday."

"I'll be there."

"Thank you, Kayla. Someday you'll leave me and I won't know what to do."

Her assistant smiled. "Nonsense. I have no plans to leave, and even if I do, you'll know exactly what to do. You always do. But thanks for the vote of confidence. Now, why don't you grab your jacket and that man and head out."

"*That man* is listening to everything you're saying and *that man* thinks that's a good idea." Caleb stepped into the doorway and slid Kayla a look of faux indignation before handing Jesse her coat.

"I should send the e-mail about the little girl," Jesse protested her rapid removal.

"I'll send the e-mail, you can just make some rounds and make sure people will read it. How's that?" Kayla suggested.

Jesse smiled at her. "Once again, thank you. I promise I'll be better tomorrow."

"You're already the best, but I know what you mean. You," she said with a pointed look at Caleb, "take care of her."

In response, he gave Kayla a mock salute and herded Jesse away.

• • •

The rest of the week passed in a blur of activity. The hospital received a few calls about the little girl, which they dutifully directed to the police, and the investigation into the shooting was wrapped up as far as the hospital was concerned. The case wasn't closed, but the police were done interviewing everyone, watching the videos, and doing everything else they needed to do with respect to the hospital and its staff. And Abigail's funeral was on Saturday.

Jesse, David, and James attended together; Matt was one of the pallbearers. And while her heart bled for the family, the whole day brought back so many memories, she had to shove them into a little box to make it through.

Most of the reception she spent sitting with Joe, helping in any way she could. His daughter stayed close to him, too, and then, toward the end of the reception, Jesse noticed that Danielle and Matt had taken off. She gave a fleeting thought to the two young people and wondered if maybe their relationship had developed into something more than just friendship. For any number of reasons, she didn't think that would be a good idea—not right now, at least—and she hoped Matt felt the same, hoped her son was smart enough to know better than to start a relationship in the midst of so much pain.

By unspoken mutual consent, Saturday night was a quiet night. She, James, and David watched a late-night movie. Matt wandered in around midnight, looking spent, and the four of them ended up in the kitchen, drinking hot chocolate and telling stories about Abigail and the Martinez family. It was cathartic; it felt good to laugh and remember the fun things about her friend. But when she finally crawled into bed, David simply gathered her in his arms and held on tight as she worked through everything she was feeling, everything she was thinking.

Come Sunday, things were different. At eleven a.m., she and David found themselves sitting at Ian and Vivi's kitchen table. Ostensibly, it was brunch, but the real reason they were there was to discuss *the case*. Jesse was taking a sip of her coffee and admiring the view of the fall colors just starting to turn the tops of the trees when Rooster, Vivi and Ian's dog, started barking—announcing the arrival of another party.

"Caleb," Vivi answered Jesse's question before she even asked. Jesse looked at David to see if knew anything about this, but he gave her a quick shake of his head.

They found themselves seated at the kitchen table shortly

thereafter, a spread of bagels and fruit in front of them. It wasn't quite the feast Matty and Dash had prepared, but it did the job.

"We're waiting for one more person," Vivi stated as they sipped their coffees and skirted around the issue at hand.

Within five minutes, Kit joined them. Shooting her brother a dirty look, she sat down and grabbed a bagel.

"Not that I don't appreciate having my friends around," Jesse started, "But I'm not sure why Kit is here, again. I mean, you two are both law enforcement," she said, pointing to Vivi and Ian. "David is an investigator, and you," she said, looking at Caleb. "Well, I'm not altogether sure what you are, but you're probably more like Ian and Vivi than like me. But Kit..." She let her voice trail off.

"I thought you might want a friend with you, a friend who knew Mark," Vivi answered. "The rest of us weren't around before he died."

Jesse looked for some meaning in her friend's words, and the only thing she could derive was that it wasn't going to be good. And so she asked.

Vivi's gaze skittered away, met Ian's, then came back to hers. "No," she said. "It's not going to be pretty."

David took her hand. "Lay it out, Vivi. Let's just hear it."

Vivi's gaze dropped for a moment, then she took a deep breath, looked up at Jesse, and spoke. "Naomi scoured the laptop hard drive last night and we found at least four other women we think Mark had affairs with."

Jesse went very still for a long moment, as the world seemed to slow down around her.

"Jesse?" David said, his voice quiet beside her.

"Oh, god," she rocked back in her seat. "I think I might be sick." And it was true. Two she knew about, but another four? If there were four more, was it possible that there were six or ten more? How could she have been that naïve?

Kit came to sit on the other side of her, wrapping her arm around her. Between Kit and David, she was anchored firmly in the here and now, but the information had shaken her foundation, her sense of self.

For several long minutes, everyone let her process what she needed to. They didn't press her, nor did they make excuses or offer platitudes. When her mind shifted enough to recognize the people around her, when it came back to the present, she took a deep breath and asked the sixty-four-thousand-dollar question.

"Okay, what does it mean?"

"Nothing, on its own," Ian offered.

"But?" she pressed, sensing there was more bad news.

"But," David spoke. "I've been looking into the fire that killed him, and I'm not as certain as my predecessor was that it was an accident."

She physically jerked at that piece of information and he hurried to continue.

"I didn't like what was happening to you and it just didn't make sense for all the reasons we've talked about. There just isn't a reason for someone to target you, so I started to wonder if maybe it had something to do with Mark."

"And so you decided to just go ahead and investigate his death?" *Without telling me*, was unspoken.

David looked like he would rather say anything than what he was about to say, but he plunged on. "I didn't want to tell you because I didn't know if I would find anything, and if I didn't, I didn't want to upset you."

"But why would you even think to do something like that?"

He took a deep breath and looked her in the eye. "Because, like I said, it just doesn't make sense to me that someone would want to come after you. I started to wonder if it had something to do with Mark, and if, on the off chance it did, his death might tell us more. I know it was ruled an accident, but I needed to do *something* to make this," he made a vague gesture to all the people in the room, reminding her why they were all there, "all go away. And looking into the fire record to determine if the accident ruling was legit was something I could do. And on the off chance it wasn't legit, I hoped that maybe his death might tell us something about his life before he died."

Jesse frowned. "But you did find something?" The question was barely out of her mouth before she knew the answer. "What did you find?"

She watched his eyes move from her to Ian, then to Caleb before landing back on her. He was talking to her and her alone, but he wanted to be sure everyone else was listening.

"I didn't find anything conclusive. But what I did see, I didn't like."

"Meaning?"

The look in his eyes told her just how much he wished he didn't have to have this conversation; it was an apology and empathy rolled into one. But he continued. "His body was found fairly close to the door. It was damaged enough that the autopsy would only have been able to pick up something if that 'something' were really off. Meaning that unless he'd had a bullet in him, it would have been hard for the ME to find anything other than the fire as the cause of death."

"But you don't think it was the fire?" Ian pressed.

"No, I do think the fire is probably what killed him, but what I also think but can't prove, is that he might have been incapacitated when it happened."

"I don't understand," she said, feeling like she was swimming in a sea of Jell-O.

"His office was on the first floor. Granted, it's a raised first floor, but it's only about five feet off the ground. He had four sets of double windows in his office. The report stated that the fire started in the back of the building, in the kitchen. But even with the hay insulation, I have a hard time believing he couldn't have made it out one of the windows or the door."

"Leading you to believe he was incapacitated," Caleb interjected and David nodded.

"How?" Vivi asked.

David shrugged. "That's the question. Like I said, the ME

didn't have enough of the remains to run a comprehensive toxicology screen, but even if he had, I'm not sure if it would have shown anything. If you asked me to guess, honestly, I would say he was probably electrocuted somehow before the fire. The jolt would have knocked him out and the subsequent fire would have killed him."

"And the fire would have then erased all evidence of the electrocution," Ian supplied.

"Electrocuted?" Jesse found herself repeating the word. When it had just been about her, everything that was happening had seemed unlikely but something she could deal with. But now that it was possible that Mark was murdered, everything just seemed surreal.

David held her hand between both of his. "It's just a hypothesis, but it's one I think we should consider."

She held his gaze for a long moment. What she was trying to read in his expression she didn't know, so she asked the most relevant question. "Okay, so if we think Mark might have been murdered and we think he had multiple affairs, where does that get us in terms of trying to figure out who is doing all these things now?"

"Maybe nowhere," Caleb supplied, not surprisingly.

"But maybe somewhere," Vivi countered. "If he was having an affair with someone who took exception to him ending it, that would be a motive."

"For his murder, maybe, but what about me and what about the time lag between Mark's death and the events that have happened to me?" Jesse pointed out.

"There are a hundred and one reasons why a jealous lover would come after the wife. As for the time lag, we don't see it all that often, but we do see it."

"And what is it attributed to?" David asked.

"The two most common things are a change of location and incarceration," Vivi supplied.

"Meaning maybe after she killed Mark she left the area for a while to avoid detection?" Kit asked.

Vivi nodded. "Or she, assuming it's a she, which we are at this moment, was incarcerated on an unrelated charge. We tend to see equal numbers of both in situations like this."

"But I still don't get why she would come after me once Mark died. It's not like she's going to woo him away from me."

"Anger, hatred, feeling wronged—she might even blame you for his death in some way. All those things might affect her perception when she thinks of you. And might drive her to want to hurt you, to want to punish you," Vivi explained.

It was all still so unbelievable, but she had to give it some credit. She wasn't in a position to think clearly about it, and her friends, with the exception of Kit, were all trained in this kind of stuff. If nothing else, she felt she needed to trust them and go with it just to see where it went.

"So, where does this get us? I mean, what do we do next?" Jesse asked.

Vivi turned to David. "How certain are you?"

He seemed to consider the question for several moments. "If it had been my case from the beginning, I would have looked into it a lot more than my predecessor did. But going off of the old files, it's hard to say. Even so, my gut tells me something is off."

She saw Ian look at Caleb, who gave a nearly imperceptible nod. Then Ian turned back to the group and spoke. "Then this is what we do. We look into the women we know he was involved with as well as take a look at his student list from the semester he was teaching when he died."

"No," Jesse interjected. "I know Mark, or thought I did, but even so, he wouldn't go for his current students. He was killed in the early spring. I would look for students he'd had the previous fall semester. And I would look for students who weren't economics majors."

She couldn't believe what she was saying, what she was ready to accept, but the truth was, she didn't have much of a choice.

"I was a public policy major and had to take an economics course as part of my degree. I took it as a summer course before my first fall semester, that's how we met. I know the first woman he had an affair with was a political science major and had to take economics for the same reason. I don't know about Susan Parmenter or any of the others, but I would look into that. If they were in a similar situation, I would probably focus my attention on other students with the similar setup."

Everyone was silent for a long moment. She wasn't sure if it was because what she'd said was way off base—after all, she was in hospital administration, not law enforcement—or because it was right on target. But either way, an awkward few moments passed before Vivi jumped in.

"Thank you, Jesse. I know this can't be easy for you, but believe me, what you've just told us, the insight you've shared, is tremendously helpful." Vivi turned to her husband. "Ian, I think Jesse is probably right. Let's start with looking into those female students who took Mark's classes in the semester before he was killed who were not economics majors. Those parameters should narrow down the search considerably. Once we have that list, we can go from there."

Ian nodded and shared a look with Caleb who also nodded, then stood. Taking Caleb's cue and needing to be out of there, Jesse stood as well. Kit rose and gave her a silent hug before collecting her things.

"I want to have a quick talk with Ian before we leave," David said before brushing a kiss against Jesse's hair and stepping away. She watched him go, feeling disconnected from everything around her. On automatic, she grabbed her coat and made her way toward the front door. Toward fresh air.

Caleb stepped in front of her and bracketed her face in his hands, forcing her to look at him. "Do not blame yourself for any of this."

"I don't know what you're talking about," she shot back.

"Don't play dumb. It's beneath you."

She glared into his gold eyes. And then her shoulders slumped. "It's hard not to, Caleb. I was married to him for sixteen years."

"You work in a hospital. You know how convincing sociopaths can be, and from what I've heard, Mark was a sociopath."

"And that's supposed to make me feel better? He's the father of my children, Caleb."

"Yeah, he is, but they have you for their mother. Look," he said, moving his hands down underneath her hair. "You have a lot of good people in your life. A lot of solid, honest people who care for you. Don't let what Mark did ruin or taint that. Don't let his life and his choices echo through yours."

She'd been so wrapped up in trying to process what she'd learned today, what Caleb had just said to her wasn't anything she thought she was ready to hear. But once the words were out, she knew it was exactly what she needed to hear. She needed to be reminded that Mark was only one person.

She offered him a smile. "You like David, don't you?" she asked, changing the subject.

He grunted.

"So, what was the story with that fire in California you were so hung up about?"

His lips thinned. "Turns out the woman was a firefighter groupie. She and David had gone out a time or two but he called it off. She took exception to that and set her own house on fire and blamed him."

"And she injured herself?" Jesse asked with a frown.

"Last ditch effort. She thought her chances with him might be better if he felt sorry for her."

The thought turned her stomach. "Or if she wasn't crazy," she added, sad sarcasm in her voice. He inclined his head.

"So then, you're okay with him?" She teased him.

"He's sleeping with you. On principle that means he's going to bug me." She knew he wasn't being serious. She reached up and slipped a hand behind his neck, brought his face down and placed a kiss on his cheek. When she drew back she looked at him again. He was stooped, his knees bent and his back hunched. She laughed.

"See it's the mechanics of it all, Caleb. It never would have worked."

"That and the fact that you love me," David said, coming up beside her and slipping an arm around her waist.

"And the fact that I love him," she repeated. Caleb rolled his eyes and walked away.

• • •

They watched Caleb walk back into the house, then David led Jesse to his truck and held the door as she climbed in. She'd taken a blow today and he wasn't sure how she would handle it. Learning that the person you shared your life with for over a decade had been lying to you for years was enough to shake anyone. And adding that piece of information on top of everything else, like the possibility of Mark having been murdered, well, he could hardly blame her if she retreated into a protective shell.

"How are you?" he asked once he was behind the wheel. He turned and traced a finger down her cheek.

"Honestly? I don't know." Her big hazel eyes looked straight into him.

"You know I would never do that, right?" He didn't need to elaborate on what he was talking about. She gave him a soft smile and cupped his cheek with her palm.

"Yes, I know." Her complete lack of hesitation almost took his breath away. He leaned forward and kissed her, lingering over her lips. When he finished, he rested his forehead against hers. She smiled at him.

"Caleb was right," she said. He raised an eyebrow at her. "He said I shouldn't let Mark's decisions, Mark's life and his betrayals, echo through my own. That I shouldn't give him that power."

"Caleb said all that?" David asked with a smile tugging one side of his mouth.

Jesse smiled. "Well, maybe not all of that, but he did imply it and he did say that I shouldn't let what I learned today ruin the good things in my life." She gave him a pointed look.

"I really, really don't want to like that guy, but it's getting hard to keep it up," he responded.

"He likes you. Doesn't want to admit it, but he does."

David pulled back and laughed. "I'm not sure I'd go that far, but I get the sense he's reluctantly accepting me."

She picked up his hand and kissed it. "He doesn't have a choice if he wants to help me. Now, let's go home. I need to get the kids ready for the next week and I want to talk to Matt about heading back to school."

"He's not going to want to do that," he said, starting the truck.

"I know, and I want to be sensitive to that. But he does need to go back."

"Well, then, let's go see what we can do."

In the end, they compromised. Matt wanted to stay another week, Jesse wanted him to go back Monday, as it was, they agreed he would get up early Thursday morning and head back in time to get to his classes. They had a quiet night at home, and David was awed by Jesse's ability to stay focused on the boys, on the here and now, given what she had learned earlier in the day. The only time he saw her falter was as she was saying goodnight to Matt that night. David had been waiting for her at the bottom of the stairs and had watched as she'd poked her head into Matt's room.

"Good night, honey," she'd said. David had expected her to come right down after a perfunctory response from Matt but something had held her back. "How are you?" she'd asked her oldest son.

"I'm okay," he'd heard Matt say. They'd filled him in on everything they'd told James about what had been going on. The boys both now knew about the potential of their father being involved, but both were more focused on the fact that their mother might be in danger. Jesse had seemed to think the reason for Matt wanting to stay was because of Danielle, but David suspected it had something to do with looking out for his mother, too.

"Mom, do you miss Dad?" Matt had asked. David had watched Jesse lean against the doorframe, giving the illusion of being relaxed when he knew she was anything but.

"Why do you ask?"

"Just with Danielle and everything, you know."

She inclined her head. "Yes, I do know. How is she?"

"As good as can be expected, I guess. Mom," Matt had paused, hesitating. "How old were you when you met Dad?"

"I had just turned eighteen. A few months older than you."

"And do you regret anything? Getting married so young, having us so young?" David's heart had climbed into his throat as he'd watched her struggle with the question.

"How could I regret anything when I have you and James?" she'd said.

Matt had laughed at that. "I figured you would say something like that. But if James and I weren't in the equation and it was just you and Dad, would you have done things the same?"

David had wanted to interrupt, had wanted to save her from having to answer the question, especially on this day of all days. But he had known she needed to do this on her own so he had just stood there and waited.

Finally, she'd shaken her head. "Knowing what I know now, I don't think I would have. Maybe I still would have ended up with your father, but I probably would have taken more time to grow up, to have a life of my own."

"To figure out who you are?" David had heard the smile in the boy's comment.

"We're always figuring out who we are, but yes, to get to know myself better. But Mark was a good father, Matt. He was smart and funny and kind." And that's when David had heard her hesitate for the first time since starting this conversation, but she straightened and continued. "And I did love him, Matt."

"I know you did. And he loved us."

Jesse hadn't answered but did acknowledge the comment with a small gesture of her head.

"Thanks, Mom."

"For?"

"Just because."

David had seen her smile at that.

"Good night, Matt. I love you."

"Love you, too, Mom."

She had shut the door quietly and then turned toward the stairs. When he'd held out a hand to her, she'd walked down and straight into his arms.

Now, standing at the bottom of the stairs, he held her loosely in his arms. "Have I told you how amazing you are?" he asked. She didn't say anything but just nuzzled into him.

Knowing sleep would come easier for her tonight after her long day, he led her into her room and they slid into bed together. Tomorrow, James would be back at school. Tomorrow, Jesse had to go to work. And Tuesday, he was back on shift. Life would begin to get back to normal, at least the normal routine of things. Unfortunately, there was still the little matter of someone out there who wanted to hurt Jesse.

As she slipped off into sleep, he lay awake thinking about everything they'd talked about at Ian and Vivi's home earlier that day. He was glad he had never known Mark and couldn't imagine doing what that man had done to Jesse and his family. Six affairs. At least.

In the dark, he frowned, as a thought came to him. Susan Parmenter was the woman Mark was having an affair with right before he died—the second woman Jesse found out about and the one that initiated the talks about divorce. If Susan was his most recent, did that mean he'd met her the semester before the affair? The fall semester Jesse had suggested they look into?

He wondered if Ian had looked into Susan. Since the sheriff was given her name a few days ago, David guessed that he had. So, assuming Susan was in the clear, since Ian hadn't mentioned her today, maybe the person they were looking for was from a prior semester. Of course, it was possible Mark had more than one affair at a time, but what if he just picked one a semester or so? That would mean that whoever they were looking for was probably a student *before* Susan.

Checking on Jesse, he reached for his phone. Hitting a few numbers he texted Ian to look back another two semesters with a short explanation as to why. It wasn't too late at night, but with Vivi more than seven months pregnant, David didn't want to take a chance on waking her with a call.

But less than a minute later he received a text back from Ian. "Done" was all it said.

Setting his phone back down, he turned to curl up behind Jesse. At his touch, she shot bolt upright. In a flash he was beside her. She looked wildly at him for a moment then gripped his arm so tight he could feel her nails biting into his skin.

"Jesse?"

"He wasn't supposed to be there that day," she said, her voice flat. He brushed a piece of hair away from her face, wishing he could take all this pain away.

"I know Jesse, no one should have been there that day," he answered, speaking of the fire that had killed Mark.

"No," she said firmly, her eyes boring into his. "You don't understand. *He* wasn't supposed to be there that day," she repeated. "*I* was."

CHAPTER 23

DAVID'S MIND FROZE FOR A moment then sputtered to life.

"What?"

"I was supposed to be there. I was supposed to pick up his files," she said, her eyes searching his.

"Whoa. Wait a minute. Ian needs to hear this." He reached for his phone.

"David, it's late."

Her voice was returning to normal he noticed, but he didn't stop dialing. "He's awake. Trust me."

"Hathaway," Ian said when he answered.

"Jesse just remembered something you need to know," David said, putting the phone on speaker.

"Ian, I'm sorry to bother you so late," she started.

"Not a problem. Tell me what you remembered," Ian coaxed.

She took a deep breath. Holding David's gaze, she spoke. "Mark was at a conference in Boston that week. He wasn't going to be back until late Friday night. I was headed into Albany for a board meeting on Friday afternoon, so he asked me to swing by his office to pick up some of the papers he wanted to grade over the weekend."

She paused, swallowed, and then continued. "We had a crisis at the hospital that day and I had to skip the board meeting. I called Mark and he said it wasn't a problem. He'd decided to leave a little early so he would just swing by and pick up the papers himself. So it wasn't supposed to be him in his office at all. If his death was intentional, I think it might have been meant for me."

David could see the reality of what she was saying come crashing down on her. He was pretty sure that, up until now, up until she put herself in Mark's place and maybe saw herself burned and dead, the idea of someone wanting to hurt her had been more theoretical than anything else. He would wager that she knew it intellectually and believed what she was being told by him and Ian and the others, but she hadn't really accepted the reality of it. Until now.

"When did you talk to Mark?" Ian asked.

"That Friday afternoon, when he was on his way home."

"No, I mean the first time, when you made the plans for you to stop by his office?" Ian clarified.

She seemed to think about this for a second before answering. "Thursday, sometime. I think it was in the afternoon, but it might have been in the evening."

"This, well, this doesn't really change a lot for us in terms of how we were thinking about things, but it does give us a new lead. And does remind us of how serious this can be. Whoever is doing this, might have already killed one person. I know this isn't what you want to hear—"

"I can hardly deny it now, can I?" she interjected.

"True. And to be fair, we still don't know for certain if Mark was murdered. But please take this seriously. If for no other reason than that it would upset my wife greatly if something happened to you."

Jesse's eyes softened at Ian's teasing plea. "Believe me, I'm taking this very seriously now, Ian. Aside from wanting to know the truth about what happened to Mark, I'm not at all interested in leaving my kids without either of their parents."

"Then you'll be safe?"

After she agreed, Ian requested to speak to David.

He took the phone off speaker. "Yeah?"

"You're going to work on the fire reports right?" Ian said without preamble.

"All day tomorrow. I'll probably bring in a few friends as well, to weigh in."

Ian grunted. "When do you go back on shift?"

"Tuesday night."

"I want someone watching her," Ian stated.

"You won't get any arguments from me," he countered.

"Not even if it's Caleb?"

David could hear the humor in the other man's voice. "Do you trust him?" he asked.

"With my life," Ian answered without hesitation.

"But would you trust him with Vivi's?" David asked, more to the point.

Ian hesitated at this point, but David was fairly sure it didn't have anything to do with Caleb. A thought that was confirmed by Ian's next statement.

"Yes, if I had to."

"Then yes, even if it's him. Can you arrange it?"

Ian said he'd take care of everything and they hung up.

Jesse looked at David with curiosity and he filled her in.

"God, this is just getting worse and worse, isn't it?" she said, lying back down beside him and tucking herself in close.

"It's not any better, that's for sure. But you have a lot of good people in your corner. Ian and Vivi are a solid team."

"And Caleb?" she added, her voice teasing. He chuckled.

"Like I said, I don't want to like the guy, but if he can help keep you safe, I will definitely revise my opinion."

· · ·

David stood by as the man in question came to pick Jesse up for work the next morning. Matt had gone off to visit Danielle, James was at school, and he had plans to hit the station, review the reports from the fire that killed Mark, and maybe ask a few more questions. He was just closing the door after setting the alarm when Matt pulled up.

"Everything all right?" he asked as Matt climbed from his car.

Matt nodded. "Yeah, I was just, well, I was hoping to catch you alone."

David leaned against his truck and waited. He had an idea where this conversation was going, but he wasn't looking forward to it.

"How is my mom? And I don't mean just with what happened with Dr. Martinez and everything."

"She's hanging in there," David said. "She has good moments and bad ones, but she's a smart woman and is listening to what people like Vivi and Ian are telling her with respect to her safety."

"Is there more going on than you guys are telling us? I know you're looking into my dad's old computer, and my mom seemed a little out of it yesterday. Is there something more going on?"

David knew he had to tread carefully here. Matt was almost a grown man, but he was also Jesse's son and what he was entitled to know wasn't David's decision.

"You and your brother both know what you need to know."

"That's a nonanswer if I ever heard one," Matt responded, showing his teenage years.

Again, David shrugged. It was a nonanswer, but it was the only one he was going to give.

"You seem pretty laid-back about the whole thing. My mom is off at work by herself, you're here headed off somewhere else, I'd bet."

David knew when he was being egged on, and he also knew that fear quickly turned to anger, especially in teenage boys. In grown men too, for that matter. Still, he forced himself to take a deep breath before he answered.

"Look, Matt. I saw what your mom's car looked like, I saw Spin-A-Yarn, and I was the one who found her after the break-in. I can't even begin to put words to how I feel about it all. But believe me, no one is laid-back about this. Your mother has someone with her now. Vivi and Ian are doing their part, and I'm looking into a few things myself. We all have our parts to play in finding out who is doing this and in protecting your mother. And right now, she has someone far more qualified than me to play bodyguard."

He saw Matt swallow. "But she does have a guard, someone looking out for her?"

David nodded, thinking this was probably the crux of Matt's concern, his mother's safety. He'd already lost one parent, the thought of losing another was more than any kid should have to bear.

"What can I do?" Matt asked.

David considered the boy in front of him. He couldn't say "nothing," but he knew Jesse wouldn't want Matt involved, not just because she would worry about his safety but because of what he might find out about his father.

"Don't give her any cause to worry," he said. "Be where you say you are going to be, be home when you say you will be. Call her and let her know if your plans change. This is hard for her, none of us need to do anything that might make it harder."

Matt's eyes searched his and David knew he had been looking for more and was disappointed in not getting it. But he wasn't about to budge on this, plus, he believed every word he said. Matt must have sensed his honesty, because, finally, he nodded.

David looked at his watch. "If I recall, you're supposed to be at Danielle's house right now."

Matt opened his mouth to say something, then closed it. But as he reached for the door handle on his car, he turned back. "I'm sorry I insinuated you didn't care, but where *are* you off to today?"

"I need to go over some reports at the station. Your mom should be home by six. I was thinking of coming back a little earlier and getting dinner ready. Thoughts?"

Matt gave him a small smile. "She really likes lasagna. I mean *really* likes lasagna."

David was still smiling when he pulled out of Jesse's drive and headed to Albany.

• • •

But he wasn't smiling several hours later as he stared at the fire report and the photos spread out on the table before him. There wasn't any proof to be had, but he'd bet a year's salary the fire that killed Mark Baker was no accident. He picked up a photo of the remains of the man himself—what very little of him was left—and his stomach lurched at the thought of Jesse being the possible intended target.

"Having fun?" Dominic and Kurt joined him, pulling out a couple of chairs across from him.

"This is crap," David said, gesturing to the report. "What do you see here?" he asked, handing them a photo of what had been a hallway before the fire consumed it.

"A burn pattern. It's hard to see with all the damage, but you can definitely see it," Dominic said, taking the photo and studying it.

"Right. And this?" David handed them a report claiming the cause of the fire was old wiring and a small gas leak emanating from the faculty kitchen at the rear of the building.

"That the fire started with the gas leak in the kitchen," Kurt said.

"Exactly." David said, reaching for the photo Dominic still held. Placing it next to the schematics of the building he slid the two images across the table. "And what do you see now?"

Both men leaned forward and studied the two documents for a long moment. Then Kurt let out a low whistle.

"You see what I see, don't you?" David insisted.

All three men sat back. "Why do we have a burn pattern indicating that flames were moving from the front of the building toward the back if the fire started in the back?" Dominic stated.

David shot them a frustrated look. "Exactly my point."

"So you think that the fire actually started in the front of the building? Maybe in Professor Baker's office itself?" Dominic asked, taking another look at the photo of the hallway.

"If the fire—or a fire—started in his office, I think it would explain the position of his body and why it doesn't look like he tried to make it out at all," David posited as Dominic picked up a few more photos.

"But look at these patterns here." Dominic pointed to another picture. "This charring is consistent with a fire emanating from the kitchen. Not to mention the fact that the ceiling burned out in that room, too." David knew what Dominic was talking about and it was something else he found disturbing about the fire and the findings of his predecessor.

"What?" Kurt prompted.

David took a deep breath and let it out before he spoke. "I think there might have been an explosion of some sort, maybe even gas, in the office. I think, well, in my opinion, I think we should consider the possibility that when Baker went into his office to find his files and he turned on the lights, there *was* a wiring issue and it sparked a small but forceful explosion. In his office."

"And the flames from that explosion then travelled back toward the kitchen and ignited a much bigger, hotter, and more destructive fire when it came in contact with the gas leak from the old stove," Dominic finished.

"And the first explosion is what did him in," Kurt added. "Maybe it didn't kill him, but it incapacitated him enough that he was already down when the second, larger fire came through. The whole series of events could have happened in less than a minute," he mused.

All three of them studied the images and the report for several more minutes before David finally asked the question that had been on his mind since he'd started looking into the fire.

"Am I crazy? Am I finding things because I want to blame Jesse's husband?"

Both men looked up, then at each other before Kurt spoke. "Look, we didn't want to say anything, but Rodgers, the guy before you, was done about three years before he finally left. There were a couple of instances where he called things that the chief caught before the final reports were filed—things he had to go back and change. Rodgers was a good guy, but at that point he just wanted to be done.

"And this fire was one I remember. None of us were convinced it was accidental. We weren't convinced it was arson, either, but it just seemed that Rogers reached his conclusion too easily. Especially considering the location and state of the body. We all thought it deserved a little more attention. A couple of us said something to him about it but he blew us off. We mentioned it to the chief, even, especially when we learned the victim had a wife and two kids. We wanted to make sure they had justice, you know, if it was called for. He promised to look into it, but then we had a rash of serious arsons and a couple of big summer brushfires, and it got a little lost in the shuffle, I think."

"Anyway," Dominic picked up where Kurt had ended. "By the end of that summer, we were all done for. It was a brutal year with the drought and the heat and, not that it's an excuse by any means, but I honestly think it fell through the cracks."

David heard what they were saying and even understood it. But that didn't mean he had to like it. Even so, what was done was done, and while he believed that if Mark was murdered, the murderer should be brought to justice, he was more concerned with knowing whether Mark's death had anything to do with Jesse, and if learning more about it would help him protect her.

He sighed. "So if the fire started in his office, how did it happen?"

The three of them thumbed through the photos for a few minutes. He hated investigating this way because he was limited to whatever the photographer had decided to take pictures of and he didn't know what he was missing. But the pictures had already shown him one discrepancy, maybe they would reveal more.

"Here," Dominic said, pushing a photo across to David. "Is that what I think it is?"

David studied the picture and though he thought he saw what had caught Dominic's attention, he spread the rest of the pictures out, found the one he wanted, and compared it to the one Dominic had handed him.

"Jesus, how could he have missed this?" David muttered to himself about his predecessor.

"What?" Kurt demanded, reaching for the two photos. After a minute, he let out a low whistle. "Well, hot damn, does it look to you like the light switch was tampered with?" The question was rhetorical. By this point, all three of them had seen the scratch marks on the plate that covered the switch.

And the distinctive "V" shape that indicated the origin of a fire.

The shape was faint and hard to see with all the other fire and smoke damage on the wall, but it was most definitely there. Which meant that even if a much bigger fire had come from the kitchen, another fire, a smaller one, had ignited in Mark Baker's office.

David felt his jaw tense as he laid the two pictures aside and continued to thumb through the rest. If a fire had sparked in the office, it would explain the burn patterns he'd seen in the first photo he'd shown to Dominic and Kurt. But faulty wiring on its own wasn't enough to cause the kind of fire that produced the charring he'd seen. There had to have been more.

Studying the photos for several more minutes, David finally saw something. "What's this?" he asked, handing a photo across the table and pointing to the lower right hand corner. His teammates looked at the object.

"A fire extinguisher?" Dominic answered, clearly not convinced himself.

David opened his computer, pulled up a screen and found another picture.

"Have a look at this," he said, sliding his computer across the table.

"It looks like the same kind of canister," Kurt commented.

"What are you showing us here?" Dominic asked, gesturing to the picture on the screen.

"That is a picture of the canister for the explosive used in the Spin-A-Yarn fire."

"Shit," both men said in unison.

"They're the same," Kurt added to no one in particular.

"Yes they are, and I think I better call the sheriff."

• • •

Jesse set the phone back in its cradle just as a knock sounded at her office door. Calling to whomever it was to come in, she watched as Colin Gray popped his head through the doorway.

"You have a few minutes?" he asked.

She smiled at the detective. "Definitely. Anything to avoid having to write the next newsletter. For all sorts of reasons, this month's edition is going to be hard to get out."

He gave her a sympathetic look then paused halfway to his seat. "Any chance you're up for some coffee? We could talk as we walk to the hospital café?"

Jesse glanced at the clock. With Caleb keeping guard, she hadn't left her office all day except to attend a lunch in one of the conference rooms down the hall. It was now heading on four p.m., and coffee, and a walk, sounded heavenly.

Caleb tried to stop her as they walked through the outer office, but she'd been a mother for almost eighteen years and knew just what kind of a look to throw at him to convey exactly what she wouldn't say out loud. With a grunt of exasperation, Caleb threw up his hands and followed them out.

"That anything I should know about?" Colin asked, nodding his head in Caleb's direction. "Ian filled me in some, but he didn't mention you having protection."

She shrugged it off, not wanting to make a big deal. "Ian is just cautious. So are David and Vivi, for that matter. I'd say I'm just humoring them, but truth be told, it does make me feel better, coward that I am."

Colin chuckled. "Smart, I'd say. Not a coward. Everyone can

use someone at their back every now and then, and now seems like as good a time as any."

Jesse smiled, grateful he wasn't making a bigger deal out of it all.

"So, did you have something to talk to me about?" she asked as they passed through the hospital's main lobby. Jesse glanced at the visitors in the waiting room and noticed that it was unusually crowded: a single woman, a couple with a fussing baby, an older couple, and a man dressed in construction gear—along with all the requisite staff. She knew Caleb was taking everyone in, assessing them as potential threats, but to her they just looked like people waiting in the lobby usually looked—equal parts anxious, worried, and annoyed.

"We got a lead on the abandoned toddler and I wanted to fill you in," Colin started speaking as they hit the stairs and headed down to the lower-floor café. "A woman by the name of Evelyn Jackson called. She lives in Albany and has been out of town visiting her daughter in Vermont for the past month. She didn't get back until yesterday. She says the little girl and her grandmother, a woman named Virginia Carson, used to live across the street from her."

"I'd be excited about that, but I get the sense it would be premature to start thinking happy endings," she commented.

"You'd be right. We did learn the little girl's name is Emma Carson and she's about twenty months old. Virginia Carson, however, died a week before Emma was abandoned."

They paused the conversation as they ordered their coffee and took a seat. All the while, she was aware of Caleb standing guard, trying to look as inconspicuous as he could—which wasn't very.

"Then how did Emma get down here?" Jesse asked when they were settled.

"Evelyn didn't know. Emma was Virginia's daughter's baby, but other than knowing that, she said Virginia never talked about her daughter."

"But is it possible her daughter came back for the baby? And then changed her mind?" she posited. It seemed incomprehensible to her, but she was learning a lot lately about what people were capable of.

"It's possible. The court records on Emma Carson are sealed. We're working to get them unsealed and should have some more information tomorrow or the next day. In the meantime, we're looking for the daughter, too."

Jesse let out a deep breath. "What about Emma, what happens now and what can we do to help?" she asked instead.

"For now, she stays in foster care until we can figure out what is going on with her mother. I also got the name of Virginia's attorney from her priest and have an appointment with him tomorrow. According to the priest, Virginia left nearly everything to Emma in a trust."

"How would he know that? And I thought you said no one knew about Emma other than Evelyn."

"Virginia left the church a little something as well, so he had dealings with her attorney. Apparently the attorney let it slip about Emma, but the priest didn't think anything of it since he figured it wasn't too uncommon to have a grandparent leave things to a grandchild. Of course, he didn't know that Virginia had been raising Emma."

She took a sip of her coffee and felt it burn its way down her throat. "Did she have much of an estate?"

Colin shrugged. "Hard to say. The house was nice enough but not fancy."

"I hate to ask, but is there any chance that Virginia's death might have been something other than old age and the daughter had something to do with it?" As the words left her mouth, Jesse realized what a dark perspective she seemed to be taking on life these days.

"At this point, anything is possible, but I should know more tomorrow."

She nodded absently, then asked again if there was anything the hospital could do.

"Actually," Colin said. "We do want to bring Emma by for one more test. We collected some samples from Virginia's house and ran her DNA. We want to do a blood draw on Emma so that we can run her DNA against Virginia's and establish some familial markings. Given that it looks like we might not find Emma's mom, we'd like to have the two sets of DNA on record as something to compare to if anyone does come forward claiming to be family."

Jesse frowned. "Of course we'll do the blood draw as long as it's properly ordered and agreed to by Emma's advocate. But you knew that, so what is it that we can really do to help you, Colin?"

Colin had the grace to look a little sheepish. "Well, I know you and Dr. DeMarco are friends and I was kind of hoping that you might be able to ask her if she could run the test. Like in the next day or two."

Her brows went down. In the grand scheme of things, this wasn't a big favor.

"Of course," she agreed. "But can I ask why you just didn't ask Ian? After all, your office and his share the same building."

Colin cleared his throat and his eyes darted away for a moment. "We, uh, we actually did."

"And?" she prompted.

"And, uh, he reminded us that his wife was nearly eight months pregnant and then walked away."

Jesse's lips twitched. That was so like Ian.

"Of course I'll ask her," she reiterated as a look of relief passed over Colin's face.

"Thanks," Colin said, standing. "I was hoping you'd say that. I also just wanted to let you know that we at least have a name for her now. And we know that she was taken good care of. Evelyn said that Virginia was a very doting grandmother and the two always seemed to be very close. Everyone here at the hospital was so good to Emma, I figured they would want to know how she's doing."

"Thank you, yes, she endeared herself to quite a few of the nurses," Jesse said, rising as well. "And while I'm not sure what

Emma's life will be like from this point onward, I am glad her first couple of years were good."

"Yeah," Colin answered with a cop's weariness. "You and me both."

When she got back to her office, Jesse picked up a message from Ian. They'd received the warrant for the information on Mark's students that afternoon and would be executing it in the morning with Naomi's help. Vivi's cousin wasn't technically law enforcement but she worked extensively with the government and Ian tended to bring her on as a consultant when he needed someone with her scary computer skills—and of course, if it meant she got to spend time with Vivi, Naomi always jumped at the opportunity. Ian also asked Jesse if she would be available the following afternoon to meet with him and review the list. He wasn't sure she would see any names she recognized, but he wanted her to look anyway.

The task was one she knew she needed to do but wasn't looking forward to. Still, she pulled up her calendar for the next afternoon. She had a few meetings Kayla would need to either handle or juggle for her—she wasn't going to look at the list while at work so she'd need to leave the office. Like Ian, she didn't think she'd see any names she recognized, other than the two she already knew, but on the off chance she did, she didn't want to be at work when it happened.

Once she'd cleared her schedule, she called Ian to let him know what time she would be home the next day and that he could just stop by when he had the list. She then popped out of her office to let Kayla know about her calendar and invited Caleb back into her office to fill him in on the plan she and Ian had agreed to.

He looked at her as if he wanted to apologize for his entire gender when she told him what she was going to have to do, but thankfully he didn't say a thing, just nodded and said he would be wherever he was needed.

A few e-mails had come in while she was out with Colin so she sat to read them, but after a few minutes she realized she'd been sitting there reading the same one over and over. As sure as she was that looking at the list wouldn't reveal anything, clearly, her subconscious was not looking forward to it.

Letting out a big sigh, she looked at Caleb, sprawled deceptively casually in one of the chairs across from her. "I'm losing focus," she said.

His lips twitched into a grin. "I heard a rumor your boyfriend was cooking for you tonight. Why don't I get you home, I'm sure he'd be glad to take your mind off things."

"You know," she said, rising from her seat and grabbing her coat, "one day that snarkiness is going to bite you on the ass."

He chuckled. "If only my life was that exciting."

• • •

The next day didn't go as planned, for her or apparently for Ian, judging by the time she finally got a hold of him. A complaint filed against the hospital took up her morning so she wasn't able to leave as early as she would have liked. When she placed a call to Ian, she found that he was still at his office, too. Since the sheriff's department was housed in the same building as the Riverside police department, not a mile from the hospital, she agreed to meet him there at three o'clock.

She wasn't crazy about the idea of David being with her, but he'd convinced her the night before that he should be. So, after calling David to fill him in on the new plan, she popped her head out to let Caleb know as well. She thought he probably liked this plan better as it would mean she was in an area surrounded by law enforcement, but all he did was nod and say he'd drive. Which was an unnecessary statement, since he'd been driving her everywhere for the past two days anyway.

Somehow she managed to focus and finish her work. She spent the last hour running through the afternoon's meetings with Kayla, who would sit in for her. It was a big step for the young woman, and Jesse was a bit nervous about it, but she wanted to give Kayla this opportunity so they plunged ahead. By the time they were done briefing, she felt more confident. Until she saw the look on Caleb's face when he finished a call on his cell at the same time. She felt the blood drain from her face.

"What?" she asked.

Sensing something, Kayla came to stand beside her.

"Caleb?" Kayla said. Distantly, Jesse noted this was the first time she'd heard her assistant call Caleb by his name.

Caleb's eyes went between the two women before finally settling on Jesse.

"We need to talk," he said. Without waiting for an answer, he ushered her into her office.

"Caleb?" Jesse asked, echoing Kayla's question.

Before answering, he went around her desk and sat down in her chair.

"Do you have access to everyone's schedules?" he asked.

She frowned. "Yes, I have access to department schedules through a single program, but the other schedules, schedules of the support staff, are in several other programs depending on whether they are hospital employees or contractors," she answered. "Why?" she pressed. "Does this have to do with Dr. Bennet?" she asked.

Caleb glanced up, then motioned her over. Rising from her chair, he all but pushed her into the spot he'd just vacated.

"Ian is still looking into Dr. Bennet. Did you know he was married before coming to Riverside?"

She glanced up at him and shook her head.

"Turns out his wife's death was ruled suspect, but there was never enough proof to build a case."

She blinked and took in the information. She wasn't even sure she knew what he meant, but it *was* clear that Caleb thought Ken had a past worth looking into. She turned back to the keyboard and started to pull up the program that held the doctors' schedules. But Caleb's hand came down on hers, stopping her progress.

She looked at his large hand, resting on hers then slowly, confused, she raised her gaze to his.

"I need you to look up the schedule of the food service people."

"The food service people?" she repeated, then frowned. "They're contractors. Why would we need to see that?"

Caleb took a deep breath. "Because Rosy McIntire now works for the company that manages the service here at Riverside."

"And Rosy McIntire is?" she pressed, not altogether sure she really wanted to know the answer.

"Rosy McIntire is the woman who was obsessed with David back in California. The one who started the fire. The one who nearly killed herself to get his attention."

Jesse stared at Caleb for a good, long moment. She might have even opened and closed her mouth a few times in an effort to say something, only she never managed to figure out what that something might be.

Finally, she seemed to pull it together. "The woman who was obsessed with *David* now works *here*?" she repeated, almost unable to comprehend the coincidence.

Caleb nodded.

"For how long?" she demanded. Though why the information was relevant wasn't very clear in her mind, it was just something she needed to ask.

"About a year," Caleb answered.

"A year," Jesse repeated, mostly to herself. After a pause, she closed down the program with the doctors' schedules and started to open the one that would show her what Caleb was obviously looking for. As that program began to boot up, her mind seemed to do the same.

"So if it *is* a coincidence that she's here, since obviously she came here before David did, what does it mean?" she asked.

Caleb lifted a shoulder. "It could mean a lot of things. Maybe she heard him talking about Miranda coming east and his plan to join her and she came first. Maybe it's actually a coincidence that she ended up here, and then, when she saw you with him, it triggered something. At this point, I don't know what it means, only that it's a coincidence I don't like."

Jesse bit her lip in thought as the program came to life. Keying in her password, she brought up the main home page, then looked at Caleb for guidance. She could pull up schedules by employee or she could look by date.

"Pull up Rosy McIntire's file," he directed with a nod to the screen.

Dutifully, she typed in the name. A few seconds passed, then Rosy McIntire's hospital badge photo popped up. Below it was her schedule for the week. To search for past weeks, she would need to key in a few more dates, but for a moment, her eyes rested on the photo.

"Do you recognize her?" Caleb asked. He must have seen something in her expression because his voice had gotten quiet.

Jesse tilted her head and studied the picture again. Rosy McIntire *did* look familiar.

And then it clicked.

"Yes," she said, dread thick in her voice. "I was walking with David one day and we ran into Dr. Bennet. As Ken turned to leave, he bumped into her. By the time I turned to make apologies for Ken's rude behavior, she was already halfway down the hall."

"And is that the only time you remember seeing her when you were with David?" Caleb asked, pulling his phone back out of his pocket.

Jesse wagged her head in indecision. "There are always food delivery carts being pushed around. I see them all the time, but I don't always remember the face of the person pushing them. And I may not know all of them since that service is provided by a contractor. So if you're asking if I specifically remember seeing her," she gestured to the picture on the computer screen, "any other time, then, no, I don't. But chances are high we've crossed paths many times between the time David first came to Riverside and now."

Caleb nodded, then turned and placed a call. She could hear him talking to Ian, giving the sheriff Rosy's name. She glanced at the computer again and noted that Rosy wasn't currently on duty. She gave Caleb this information and he repeated it to Ian.

After another minute or so of conversation, Caleb hung up and refocused on her.

"How did you find out about Rosy if not from Ian?" she asked. He gave her an enigmatic look, which had her shaking her head. "Never mind," she said. "So what now?"

Regret flashed through his eyes before he spoke, but then he answered. "Ian will look into Rosy McIntire, but in the meantime, I believe you have an appointment at the sheriff's office."

Jesse's stomach sank at the stark reminder of what lay ahead of her. For a moment, she'd been distracted by the thought, by the possibilities, of Rosy McIntire. She glanced at the clock and noted they'd be late for her three o'clock appointment. As she silently gathered her belongings, she recognized how out of sorts her world had become when thinking about David having a stalker constituted a reprieve.

As she walked toward the door, Caleb put a hand on her arm, halting her.

"I'm sorry," he said. And for the first time, he allowed real emotion to show on his face. She'd seen glimpses of it before, but this time, his open sincerity and sympathy nearly brought her to tears.

She managed to clear her throat before answering. "Thank you, Caleb. For that and for everything else you're doing."

He looked about to say something else, then his lips thinned and he gave a simple nod.

Fifteen silent minutes later, they were pulling up to Ian's office.

David was waiting for her outside, and without a word, he took her hand and walked beside her into the lion's den.

Vivi, Ian, and Naomi were in Ian's office when they entered. Naomi, whom Jesse hadn't seen in a few weeks, stood and gave her a hug. Jesse tried to tell herself that it was a nice-to-see-you hug but suspected it was more likely an I'm-sorry-you-have-to-do-this hug. She gave Naomi a smile, then sat.

She looked to Caleb to see if Caleb and Ian were ready to share the information they'd just learned yet, but he gave a sharp shake of his head. "After," he seemed to be saying. Her gaze lingered on his for a moment, then she nodded and turned back to Ian.

"Okay, lay it on me," Jesse said as she held out her hand for the list.

Ian looked to Vivi. When she nodded back to her husband, he handed Jesse a sheet of paper.

"These are the names of female students who took a class with Mark over the three semesters before his death. None of these women were Economics majors," Ian said.

Jesse scanned the list of about forty names. Not one looked familiar. She'd started to let out a little of the tension she hadn't realized she was holding when a name caught her eye. About two-thirds of the way down the list.

"Ian?" she said, frowning.

"Do you see a name you recognize?" he asked, sitting straighter in his seat.

Jesse shook her head. "Not from talking with Mark, but this woman, Stacey Carson," she said, pointing to the name.

"What about her?" Vivi urged softly.

Jesse looked up and met Ian's intense gaze. "The little girl who was abandoned a few weeks ago in Riverside, her grandmother's last name was Carson."

CHAPTER 24

JESSE SAW IAN LOOK AT Naomi, who immediately began keying something into her computer.

"Are you sure?" he asked.

She nodded. "Colin stopped by yesterday to fill me in. The grandmother died a few weeks ago," she said and then recounted the details Colin had given her. "I know he was supposed to go see the grandmother's lawyer today. And I know they were looking for the mom. He didn't give me her name, but he did say they were looking for her."

"And no one knew about the granddaughter?" Ian asked.

"Colin will have to fill you in, but it sounded like she and her grandmother stayed pretty secluded."

"And do you know if they found the mom?" Vivi asked with her hand resting on her own big belly.

Jesse shrugged. "I don't know. Again, you'll have to ask Colin, but is it possible Stacey Carson is Virginia Carson's daughter and Emma Carson's mother?"

"Not only possible, but probable," Naomi interjected. "Stacey has a criminal record and her mother, Virginia Carson is listed as next of kin."

"What is she in for?" Caleb asked.

"What *was* she in for is more the question. She *was* in for involuntary manslaughter. She was released earlier this year after serving two years of her four-year sentence," Naomi supplied.

"Involuntary manslaughter?" David repeated.

"And get this," Naomi continued. "The driving accident

in which she killed an old man happened the day *after* Mark was killed."

"Oh god." Jesse felt her stomach roil as it all sank in at once. "Emma is Mark's daughter, isn't she?"

"Jesse," David warned.

"No, it all makes sense now." She held up a hand to stop David's protest. "Or at least some of it. She didn't want Mark dead, she wanted me dead because she was pregnant and she wanted Mark. And *that* is why Mark was looking into creating a trust. It wasn't for me or the boys, it was for his daughter."

"Jesse, you don't know that," he tried to appease. But when Naomi cleared her throat, she knew the other shoe was going to drop.

"I have Emma's birth certificate here." Her eyes skittered between Ian and Vivi before settling on Jesse. "It does list Mark as the father. Emma was born in the jail where Stacey was incarcerated and then promptly turned over to Virginia Carson."

Jesse felt David's hand engulf hers. His felt hot and dry against hers. She felt so cold.

"What else do we know about Stacey Carson?" Vivi asked.

"I have her mug shot and driver's license picture." Naomi's offer was clearly halfhearted.

"Let me see," Jesse said. Her voice sounded a million miles away.

Naomi looked to David before she slid her computer across the table. Jesse studied the images. The woman was young, just like *she* had been when she and Mark had first met. Stacey Carson had blonde hair and looked petite. No doubt, Mark had a type.

She leaned closer to the screen and frowned.

"Jesse?" Ian said.

She cocked her head, trying to recall a memory. "I think I've seen her before."

No one spoke as she studied the picture.

"I know," she remembered suddenly. "I saw her in the hospital lobby yesterday. Colin and I were walking through on our way to the café. Normally, I wouldn't remember since there were so many people, but I've become more vigilant lately. Here," she said, handing the computer to Caleb. "You probably have a better memory than I do. What do you think?"

He picked up the computer, glanced at the image, and nodded without hesitation.

"Shit," Ian said.

"She's probably been at the hospital a lot. I bet if we go back before each of the incidents that Jesse was involved in, we'll probably see her face on the security videos," Caleb offered.

Ian took a deep breath. "Okay, we may want to go back and do that to build a case against her. But for now, we need to know where she is so we can bring her in. I'm calling Colin now, but Naomi, see what you can do, too, okay?"

Jesse only half listened to what was being said. The truth of everything was sinking in even as she was sure it would take weeks or even months to fully process. Mark had another child. A little girl. With a student. Stacey's name wasn't one she'd known before seeing the list, so if they added up the two women she knew about, the four Naomi thought were likely that Vivi had told her about last Sunday, and this one more, Mark was up to seven women in their sixteen-year marriage. The thought made her stomach roil, and though she knew anger would come at a full boil later—she could feel it simmering—all she wanted to do right at this moment was curl into a little ball and be alone.

"Jesse?" David spoke beside her. "Jesse?"

She stirred.

"Your phone is ringing," he said gently, with a gesture to her purse.

She stared at him for a long moment, before the words filtered through and she reached for her phone. Glancing at the number, she almost didn't answer. It was James and she wasn't sure she could face him right now. But the mother in her wouldn't let go and she hit the answer button.

"James?"

"Mrs. Baker?"

Jesse frowned and looked at the number again. It *was* James's number but a woman's voice. Or a girl's.

"Yes, who is this?"

"Um, sorry to bother you but it's, um, it's Chelsea."

"Chelsea? Is everything okay?" Jesse could feel herself start to hyperventilate. There was only one reason James's would have someone else call her and that was if he couldn't do it himself. As if sensing the change in her attention, the room had gone silent around her. She looked at David and he mirrored the concerned expressions of everyone else in the room.

"I, uh, I don't know," Chelsea started. "I'm here at the school and we were supposed to take a run together. I had to go home and get my stuff, but he said he'd meet me here. But I'm here and he's not. But, I, uh, I found his phone."

Vaguely, Jesse noted the concern in Chelsea's voice, but it was drowned out by the roaring in her own head.

"Jesse?" Vivi was speaking to her. "Tell me what's going on. Now," she added when Jesse didn't immediately answer.

The directive was what she needed and she quickly repeated what Chelsea had told her, her voice and her body shaky. When she was done, Vivi took the phone and hit speaker.

Ian was picking up his own phone as Vivi spoke to the young woman. Jesse listened, feeling more and more numb as the seconds ticked by. She heard Vivi tell Chelsea to stay put, in her car, with the doors locked and that Officer Marcus Brown or Carly Drummond would be there shortly. Being Windsor police, they were much closer to the school than Ian or the rest of them sitting there in Riverside. Still, Jesse rose, needing to be where James was supposed to be.

Vivi's hand wrapped around her arm, stopping her. She tried to shake it loose as Vivi finished her call, but her friend held fast.

"Vivi," she warned. David was at her side, solid and sure.

"I know you want to run off, but we need you here for just a minute."

"My son, Vivi!"

"I know."

The calm of Vivi's voice annoyed her even more and she made to move away.

"We need to know who else to check with," Vivi said, almost pleading. "We need to be certain he isn't just at home or with one of his friends. If we know where he isn't, it will help us find where he is."

The words sounded reasonable, but Jesse was feeling anything but at the moment. Then David slid his arm around her.

"It will just take a few minutes, honey. I'll call home while you make out a list of his friends. I'm sure Naomi can track them down and place the calls while we're on the road." She looked at him and tears welled in her eyes. He brushed a hand across her face. "Just a few minutes, honey. Then we can be on our way."

Finally, she nodded and sat back down. David pulled out his phone and, in a shaky hand, she took the pen and paper Ian handed her. She had three names on the list when her phone rang again. Not bothering to look at the number and hoping it was James, she answered before the first ring stopped.

"James?"

"Mom!" he answered.

"Hello, Mrs. Baker."

Jesse froze. She had never met Stacey Carson but she was dead certain she just had. "Stacey." Her voice was oddly calm, she knew. But she also knew, for the first time in her life, what it felt like to well and truly want to hunt someone down. She felt the phone being taken from her hand and Stacey's voice filled Ian's office as someone hit speaker, again.

"So, you figured it out? I knew you would when I saw you talking to that cop yesterday about Emma. It was only a matter of time."

"Where is my son?" Jesse said.

"With me, of course. You know, all this should have been

mine. Mark loved me. More than he loved you. You should have died that day, then Emma and I would have everything we deserve."

"But I didn't, and now you have my son."

Stacey laughed. "I do. He looks like Mark. A pity he has your eyes, though. Anyway, all good things must come to an end and I'm going to enjoy watching you watch it all slip away."

"In order to watch me, you'd have to be close by. Are you close by?" She saw Ian make some gesture, urging her to keep the conversation going. But right now, she didn't need any help from anyone. Stacey Carson had her son and she was going to get him back.

"Close enough for you to come to me. I can almost feel Mark here, where I am. Although it's different than it was when he brought me here. But like I said, everything changes, doesn't it?"

And just like that, the line went dead. Jesse shot out of her seat needing to get out, her entire body was shaking, and she was more scared than she had ever been in her life.

"Whoa, down." Caleb shoved her back into a chair and pushed her head between her legs.

She slapped him away and sat up. The world was spinning but that hardly mattered. "Don't tell me what to do, Caleb. She has my son! My son, damn it."

"I know. And as soon as you look like you're going to stick around and not pass out like a little girl, you can start ordering us around."

"Little girl, my ass, Caleb. I'm fine," she shot back.

He shrugged. "I know. Now what?"

She drew back, then glared. The bastard had tricked her. But then again, she didn't feel lightheaded anymore. And as he met her glare, she acknowledged it was a good question. She didn't know the first thing about what she should be doing next, only that she needed to be doing something. David took her hand as she looked to Ian.

"We need to figure out where she is. It sounds like a place she and Mark went to when he was seeing her." Ian cast an apologetic look at her.

"Please, Ian," she rolled her eyes. "The bastard can rot in hell for all I care at this point. It was his dick that got us here. What little affection I had left for him is gone." She saw Caleb's lips twitch and she shot him a glare.

"I'm pulling up his credit cards now," Naomi said.

Jesse shook her head. "I paid the bills, I would have noticed if there were charges on the card that didn't make sense."

"Not these bills, I'd bet." Naomi slid her computer over again and Jesse took a look.

"He had a secret credit card. Of course he did." Later, she knew she would need to sort all this out to process just how much, and how often, she'd been betrayed. But right now, that was a luxury she wasn't going to allow herself.

"Jesse, are there any other properties you know about where he might have taken someone? A cabin somewhere or a favorite hotel?" Vivi asked.

"Matt," Jesse said.

Ian looked confused. "Matt would know?" he asked.

"No," she shook her head and frantically grabbed for her phone. She should have been listening to Ian, but when the thought hit her, it hit like a ton of bricks.

"I need to make sure Matt is okay."

Ian snatched her phone away and handed her his. "We need to keep your line open. Use mine."

"Or better yet, let me call him," David said, already dialing the number on speaker.

"David?" Matt answered, after David had identified himself. "Is everything okay?"

Jesse let out a long breath.

"Where are you?" David asked.

"At the Martinez's, like I said I would be. Where is my mom?" Jesse could hear the tension rising in her son's voice.

"I'm right here, Matt. Are you sure you're okay?"

He paused. "I'm fine. What's going on?"

She looked at David. She couldn't say it, couldn't bring herself to vocalize what was going on.

"We're at Sheriff MacAllister's office and we just received a call from your brother," David started.

"James? And?"

"And, there's no easy way to say this, but we know who the person responsible for all the attacks on your mother is," he continued.

"That's a good thing, right?" Matt interrupted.

David took a deep breath and answered. "Yes, but she has James."

"What? No!" her older son exploded. "Mom, what the hell is going on? Where's James? Why aren't you out looking for him?" The pain and fear in his voice was almost too much to bear.

"Matt," Ian stepped in. "I need you to listen to what I'm saying." When it was clear Matt was going to stay quiet, if not necessarily attentive, Ian relayed the gist of the phone call from Stacey.

"Mom, I need to go look for him," Matt pleaded.

"No!" she shouted.

"Matt," David intercepted. "We need you to stay where you are. Your mother needs to know you are somewhere safe. If you go out looking for your brother it's going to be that much harder on her and everyone here. Do you understand?"

"But, David…"

"There's no buts, Matt," Ian spoke. "David is right. We need to focus on finding James, and if we have to worry about you being out there too, possibly being another target, it's going to make it harder for everyone involved to do what we need to do." Matt made a small sound, but Ian continued. "Is Joe Martinez there?"

"I'm here," came Joe's voice. It was obvious from the concern in his voice that they'd been put on speaker phone and Joe had heard everything.

"I'll send someone out to sit with you, but keep the kids in the house with the doors locked," Ian ordered.

"Please, Joe." Jesse choked back a sob.

"Mom," Matt's voice broke through. She gripped David's thigh, willing strength back into her body and mind.

"I'm here, Jesse." Joe's voice was calm and certain. "No one is going to hurt these kids. I promise you that."

"Thank you, Joe."

"Promise me you'll call as soon as you know something, or anything," Matt demanded.

"We will, I promise," she answered. "I love you, Matt."

"Love you, too, Mom."

And then he was gone. She closed her eyes, wanting so badly to hold her children. To feel them in her arms.

"Jesse?" Caleb said, bringing her back to the task at hand.

If she didn't pull it together, she might not ever have the chance to hold them again. "I'm ready." She took a deep breath and looked at Naomi.

Naomi didn't miss a beat. "I pulled the records for the semester after Stacey was Mark's student. There are six hotels or B&Bs that might be options. All the other charges are restaurants or other places it would be unlikely she would be able to hold someone captive. Ready?"

It was a loaded question, but she nodded.

"The M Hotel in Boston," Naomi read out the first location on her list.

The name didn't ring a bell with her and she glanced around the room.

"I don't know anything about it, but school gets out at what, two forty-five? No way would she have had time to make it to Boston," Caleb offered. Naomi nodded and moved on.

"The Cottage in Red Hook?"

"It's possible to have made it down to Red Hook, but it sounds small," Vivi said.

"A four-bed guest house," Naomi said, reading something from the screen. "Not exactly the kind of place you can take a hostage. How about the Craymore in Lenox?"

"We were just there for brunch last month," Jesse roused. "But that place hasn't changed in fifty years. She said that where they are is different than it was."

Naomi inclined her head. "Good point. What about the Silver Spring B&B down in Houstonic?"

"We looked at that place to get married," Ian said. "It underwent a major renovation about a year and a half ago."

"And it has small guest houses scattered around the property," Vivi added.

"Then let's go," David said. But Ian held up a hand.

"We need to go through all of them before we make a plan. I don't want to miss something because we jumped the gun."

"What about the last two, Naomi?" Jesse prompted urgently.

"The Westerbrook in Albany and the Saranac in New York. The Saranac has the same issue as The M, she couldn't have made it down to the city by now. The Westerbrook anyone?"

"It burned down about seven months ago," David said. "It was my first arson investigation here. Insurance fraud."

"Could be that's what she means by it looks different," Ian posited.

David shook his head. "It was razed to the ground this summer. There is nothing left. Not even the basements. They were filled and the land was donated to the city for a park when the owner was convicted of the fraud."

"So then it's the Silver Spring," Caleb said. "What do we know about it and how soon can we get there?"

Jesse listened to the voices around her but one was filling her head. The sound of Stacey taunting her, telling Jesse that it all should have been hers and that it was all going to slip away.

"Wait!" she blurted out. Caleb was moving toward the door but stopped. Ian looked up from holstering his gun.

"She said that she could almost feel Mark. Wouldn't that mean he would have some kind of history there? How many times was there a charge at the Silver Spring?" she asked, turning to Naomi. Naomi tapped in a few keys, then frowned.

"Five. But only one when he would have been seeing Stacey. The others were right before he died."

"When he was seeing Susan Parmenter," Jesse supplied.

"He could have been seeing two women at once," Ian suggested.

"Possible," Naomi spoke. "But judging by what we found on his laptop, I think it was only one at a time."

Jesse could feel everyone's eyes on her, but she held her gaze fixed on the floor. A germ of an idea was taking hold in her mind.

"She said 'all this should be mine,'" Jesse stated. She repeated the phrase again out loud. Then over and over in her head. And then she knew.

She looked at David.

"She's at my house."

CHAPTER 25

DAVID'S HEART STUTTERED AND HE knew she was right. Fury ripped through him. There was nothing Mark Baker hadn't fucked up in her life. He wished like hell the guy was around to witness all the destruction his appetites had caused. His hand tightened around Jesse's, she had lost so much already, so much was already at risk. And yes, a house was a house, but on top of everything else, it was one less sanctuary, one more thing of beauty in her life that was now tainted.

"It would make sense, Ian," Vivi said, confirming both Jesse's insight and David's own belief in Jesse's assessment.

"We need eyes on the place," Ian replied, reaching for his phone.

"I've got a guy. He came in two days ago. I had him watching her at night. He's at Kit's and can be there in five minutes," Caleb added, pulling out his own phone.

David turned to Caleb. Had the situation been less fraught, he would have been stunned to know that they'd had a night guard last night. As it was, he just absorbed the information and hoped the guy knew what he was doing.

"Does your guy know the property?" Ian asked. Caleb nodded. "Good, have him come in on the east side by the old barn. Tell him my guy, Deputy Chief Brown will be coming in from the north, the wooded side."

He half listened as the two men made plans even as everyone gathered their belongings.

When Ian hung up, he looked at Vivi. "Any chance you'll stay here?" he asked her.

Vivi shook her head.

David could see Ian didn't like it, but he wasn't going to waste time arguing. "I'm calling in some local help and I want the paramedics on standby at this address," he added, handing a slip of paper to one of the deputies they passed on the way out.

"Ian," David said. "She's a firebug."

Ian looked supremely unhappy about that reminder. "Roger that," he said. "We'll want the fire department on standby. And even though it will take them a while to get down here from Albany, I want the bomb squad, too," he added as they left the building.

The only saving grace, to David's way of thinking, was that at least the past few days had been a bit foggy and drizzly. If Stacey did decide to blow something up, the fire probably wouldn't spread.

"This way," Caleb said, taking hold of Jesse's arm and pulling her to his truck.

David reached for her other arm and stopped them. "My truck, Forrester. I have some gear in there if we need it." He didn't bother to see if Caleb had agreed or not, he just walked her to his truck, opened the door, and helped her into the back seat. Caleb appeared behind him carrying a duffel bag.

"Your truck, I drive," Caleb ordered. David thought about arguing but decided it wasn't worth it. If Caleb drove, he could focus on Jesse.

They weren't on the road two minutes, following behind Ian and his flashing lights, when David began telling her what he had planned.

"If she's there, you're not going in alone. I'm going with you," he said.

She gave an adamant shake of her head. "You can't, David. It's me she wants. You might make her nervous or she might just kill you. I can't, I don't…" Her voice faded.

"You're right, it isn't me she wants, but she wants you to suffer. She isn't going to do anything too quickly because that wouldn't be satisfying enough. Whether I'm there or not isn't going to make a difference in her plan. She may try to make you think it will, but I promise you it won't."

"And you know this because?" Her voice was part worried, part sarcastic, but he chalked it up to nerves. And fear.

"I've investigated a lot of arson and arsonists. I may not have studied people exactly like her, but crazy is crazy. And you don't spend your summer plotting against someone, making plans and executing them, only to throw those plans out the window at the last moment. It just wouldn't fit her personality."

"For what it's worth, I agree," Caleb weighed in.

"But what if she has a gun or something and shoots you or James?" Jesse persisted.

"Or you," David added.

"Don't speculate," Caleb ordered. "We'll know more in about—" his voice cut off as he answered his phone. Since David hadn't heard it ring, he assumed Caleb had set it to vibrate.

"Tell me," Caleb said, then he listened for a moment. "Got it... shit. Hold on," he ordered as he turned to David.

"Hathaway, there any chance you have something that will register if there is gas present? Assuming we can't smell it."

"Yeah, of course. It's in my kit. Why?"

"Good man," he said and then went back to his call. All David heard him say after that was, "Ten minutes, east side."

"Well?" Jesse demanded when Caleb got off the phone.

Holding up a finger, Caleb pressed a couple of buttons and put Ian and Vivi on speaker.

"I just talked to my guy," Caleb informed them all, "and he's spotted James and the woman in the barn that used to be Mark's office. James is okay. He's alive. According to Cantona, my guy, it looks like he might have been slapped around a bit, but he's holding up."

David heard Jesse suck in a breath and he reached back and took her hand in his. Whether to reassure her or himself, he didn't know.

"He doesn't see any firearms, which is good news. But David was right; she's a firebug. He spotted a canister he thinks has an explosive device on it. He can't be sure from his angle, but it's all she seems to be carrying," Caleb finished his report.

David tuned out at that point and focused completely on Jesse. Ian and Caleb would make the plans they needed to make. In his mind, the only thing he was going to think about was walking into that building with Jesse and out of it with her and James.

"You can't, David," she pleaded in a whisper. "Think of Miranda."

But he already was thinking of Miranda. He wanted to walk out of that building as much he wanted anything in his life. But he also knew that if he didn't walk *into* that building with Jesse, he would never be able to live with himself. He wouldn't want to. And then he'd be no good to anyone, especially Miranda.

"It's not up for debate. I'll turn my phone on and slip it into my pocket so Ian and Caleb can hear what's going on inside. I'll be able to tell them about the device, Jesse. I'll be able to feed them information that can help them."

"But Caleb can do that, too," she insisted.

He glanced at Caleb, who shrugged, seeming to take her sacrifice of him in stride.

"But Caleb has other skills. Skills I don't have. If I'm not inside, I'm no good for anything. At least if I'm in there, I can help, which frees Caleb up for other things." "Other things" being a euphemism, he hoped, for taking this Stacey woman out of commission in whatever way posed the least risk to James and Jesse.

"Right," Caleb interrupted, pulling the truck to the side of the road about forty feet from Jesse's drive. Ian's lights and sirens had been turned off and he was now parked about fifty feet on the other side of the drive. Neither car would be visible from the barn.

"I'm out of here," Caleb said. "David, the sniffer would be good right about now." As Caleb climbed out, David and Jesse did the same. Jesse moved to the front seat while he rummaged through his kit and handed Caleb the device. With a nod and a quick admonishment to stay safe, Caleb started to jog up the hill. Within a few feet, he was joined by another man with some serious weaponry slung across his back.

"Any idea who that is?" David asked as he slid into the driver's seat.

Jesse shook her head. "None."

He went to put the truck in gear, then paused and turned toward her. Sliding a hand into her hair, he pulled her toward him and brushed a quick kiss across her mouth. "I love you, Jesse. Remember that. You're not alone."

She blinked away the moisture in her eyes. "I love you, too."

"Do you trust me?" The question was about the here and now. But it was about so much more and they both knew it.

She nodded.

He sat back and put the truck in gear. "Then let's go."

• • •

"He can't be here," were the first words Stacey Carson uttered to Jesse. The woman was standing behind the open door, using it as a shield. Jesse cast him a look and he silently begged her to trust him. She gave a tiny nod.

"Too bad, he's here and he's not going anywhere," Jesse said as she pushed her way inside, David at her side.

"James!" she said. David stopped just inside the door and watched Jesse rush to her son's side.

"Mom! She has a bomb! You need to get out of here," James cried. David had to admire the boy's spirit, but leaving wasn't an option. And though he was relieved to see the boy alert and looking defiant—relieved, but not surprised—he didn't like seeing James with his hands tied behind his back and his body tied to a chair. David could feel the anger coiling inside him, but he forced himself to take a deep breath and do what he was here to do.

Stacey had quickly stepped away when they'd entered and now had her back against the wall opposite the door, giving her a good vantage point to watch the entire room. She was framed by two large windows on either side of her, but the wall was otherwise empty. In her hands she held a small device, not much bigger than a can of soup, made of what looked like some kind of plastic.

He noted the device and glanced around the room looking to see if she'd tampered with any electrical plates—like those he'd seen in the pictures of the fire that had killed Mark—and for places she might have hidden a bomb other than the one she held in her hand. Based on what he knew about her from her other fires, she was a single-device kind of arsonist, so he had no reason to think there would be more than the one she held. But he also knew she was crazy.

The door they'd come through was in one of the corners of the room and from where he stood he could see everything he needed to. The space itself was about twenty feet by forty feet and though it had originally been a barn, it was hard to see any remnants of that past in the updated interior where they now stood. The floors were wood, but wide-planked and with a shine and evenness to them that was too modern to make them original. Two of the walls, the one to his right and the one that Stacey stood in front of, were finished and painted a pale gray with white trim. The other two, the two to his left, were lined with empty built-in shelves and cabinets of a deep ebony color.

A desk had been pushed into the far corner to his right and boxes, stacked two and three high, covered the top. The room had been cleared of everything else so he assumed those boxes contained Mark Baker's files, papers, books, and whatever else he'd kept in the office. A few looked to have been opened recently and only hastily shut—a reminder that Jesse had been in here looking for clues as to what her husband had been up to before he died. He cursed silently, thinking of just what they'd *all* found.

Noting to himself that with the desk, boxes, and cabinets there were more than enough hiding spots for a second device, he turned his attention to James. And the chair he sat in. Placed a little to the left of the center of the near empty room, it was definitely large enough to have a device attached to the bottom of the seat. David's jaw tightened.

"You." Stacey's voice drew his attention back to her. "Shut the door and empty your pockets."

She waved the device in front of him as a threat. He knew she wasn't likely to set it off now, but since he'd taped his phone to his stomach under his shirt he had no qualms about closing the door behind him and emptying his pockets, as Ian had expected she'd demand.

"And you," she said, turning to Jesse. "Step away from your son and empty your pockets."

Jesse took one step away but went no further. "I have no pockets." She raised her hands and gave Stacey a good look at her fitted dress and cardigan.

"Move over there," Stacey demanded, her eyes fixed on Jesse as she waved the canister in David's direction. While Stacey's position allowed her to see the whole room fairly easily, she still had to turn away from him to face Jesse. And when her back was to him, he gave Jesse a shake of his head.

"I don't think so, I think I'll stay by my son," Jesse said.

"Mom!" James protested. In response, Jesse laid a hand on his shoulder and moved to stand at his back.

"What do you have there, Stacey?" David asked, drawing her attention back to him. Gesturing with his head to her hand. "Is that another gas canister? It looks like it has a trigger device on it this time. No timers today?"

She sneered. "That damned timer was the stupidest idea I've ever had."

David could argue that but didn't.

"I should have just stuck around and triggered it when I knew she would be in the store," Stacey continued. "I took a chance because Mark was always complaining about just how damned predictable she was," she added with a gesture of disgust in Jesse's direction.

"And you failed," he pointed out. Her eyes narrowed on him.

"What about Emma?" he asked. He didn't dare look at Jesse but hoped like hell she was sliding the knife they'd taped to her thigh out from under her skirt.

"What about her?" Stacey demanded.

"You abandoned your own daughter," he pointed out.

She looked at him like he was a moron and it was in that moment that he realized just how deranged she was.

"Yeah, so," she shrugged. "She was supposed to bring Mark back to me but he was already seeing that bitch Susan when I told him I was pregnant."

"Then why didn't you end the pregnancy?" he asked, cringing inside. He wasn't necessarily adamantly pro-life, but it wasn't easy being so flip about a human life.

"Because I knew he wouldn't be able to turn away from her once she was born. Mark *always* talked about his sons. I knew when he met her he wouldn't be able to cut me out anymore."

There were so many things wrong with Stacey's reasoning that David didn't even begin to try to dissect it all. He just wanted her to keep talking. He just wanted her to stay distracted enough that Jesse could cut James loose.

"And when he didn't take you back, that's when you tried to kill Jesse, wasn't it?" he asked, taking a step farther into the room.

Stacey turned red at his comment and spun back to Jesse. His chest clenched and his heart rate leapt.

"You bitch," she raged, pacing toward Jesse. "You were supposed to pick up Mark's files. I was with him in Boston. I heard him make those plans with you. But noooo, you're too lazy to help your own husband, you stupid whore. And because of you, he's dead. I don't think you understand how much I hate you."

Stacey raised the device and both Jesse and James drew back in anticipation of the blast. His heart climbed into his throat.

"Was it a device like you have now, Stacey?" he asked hurriedly. He was starting to sweat and he knew if Stacey paid enough attention, she would see the panic on his face, hear it in his voice. But he *had* to get her attention away from Jesse.

She spun back around to him and he forced himself to take a small breath, willing his own anxiety under control.

"No, it released gas over time, so when the lights got turned on, the little extra electricity I arranged for would spark it. I turned on the gas in the kitchen when I left, just to be sure," she paused for a moment and frowned. He realized that her statement confirmed his assessment of what had really happened in Mark Baker's office that day, but that thought was fleeting.

He watched Stacey's eyes refocus on him from wherever her mind had gone, then she shrugged and added, "This is trigger based. So I get to control it."

"That's pretty clever," David said, thinking he might be going overboard, but doing what he could to keep her attention on him. From the corner of his eye, he saw Jesse give him a small sign. He knew James was free. Now they just had to figure out how to get out of there alive.

He glanced at the canister in her hand. He had no idea if gas was leaking into the room already or not. He couldn't smell anything, but as Caleb suggested, it was possible that she was using the odorless kind or something else altogether. He wished he had the sniffer he'd given to Caleb, but he knew, in reality, she never would have let him into the room with it. He just hoped Caleb was able to put it to good use.

"You're a fire girl, what about the shooting at the hospital?" he asked, trying to buy them some time to figure out how to escape. Or possibly get some sort of sign from someone outside about what they should do.

But his attention returned to Jesse when he saw the startled look on her face at the question. She'd known a blue SUV had been spotted, but she'd been so caught up in James's abduction that she probably hadn't put the two together yet.

"Oh, that," Stacey said and then made a face. "I hate guns. But I needed to get her out of the hospital if I was going to be able to arrange a little meeting." Stacey gestured to Jesse with her head as she spoke.

"I don't get it. Obviously, you had some sort of plan, but I'm not seeing it," he coaxed as he moved into the room a bit more. Stacey's body turned as she followed him and, from the window, he caught a glimpse of a flash of light. He didn't know for certain, but he hoped that meant Caleb or someone else was up in the hills he could see through the windows.

He hadn't talked to Caleb or Ian about it, but David would bet that between the three or four men out there, there was probably a sharpshooter or two between them. Hopefully, by now, Caleb knew if there was a gas leak or not and whether someone could take a shot or not. And the only way for him to find out was to try and maneuver Stacey toward a window. If no one took a shot, then he would know they had other problems, likely a gas leak. In which case, he would need to come up with another plan.

"I said I needed her out of the hospital. There were too many security cameras there, too many security guards." David brought his attention back to the room and, as Stacey spoke, he inched sideways. She followed him with her own movements.

"If there was a shooting in the hospital, maybe she'd be put on probation or maybe, as it turned out, it would be a friend and she would take a couple of days away from that place," Stacey continued. "God, I hate hospitals. How can anyone stand the smell?" she added, following a train of thought that was obvious only in her own mind.

David took a few more steps to his right and she followed. Her back was to Jesse, but she was standing between them.

"So how did you manage it?" he asked.

Her personality seemed to shift again, and she shrugged casually. "You hang out in hospitals enough, you hear things. I heard the nurse talking about her brother and how worried she was about him and his care. The daytime help she hired wasn't there all the time so I took the opportunity to meet him myself. Turns out she should have been worried. He was very malleable. I had him convinced after a week that his sister was screwing with him. That all the things he wanted—a house of his own, a girlfriend, a life—he could have. But that his sister stood in the way."

Again, he saw the flash up on the hill through the window. She followed his gaze this time and as she looked away from him, he spared a glance at Jesse. She had her hand firmly on James's shoulder, keeping her son silent, but she gave him another nod just as Stacey turned back.

"So you gave him a gun?" he asked, hoping to distract Stacey from whatever she might have seen through the window.

"I did. I hate guns, but I know how to use them. My dad was a cop and he taught us young. It didn't take much to convince that guy that if he took care of his sister, he could have it all," she paused and seemed to give something some thought. He didn't like the little smile that played on her lips. "You know, that's who he was supposed to find, his sister. But I think it actually worked out better for me the way it happened, you know, with that woman he shot being one of *her* friends and all," she said with an offhand gesture toward Jesse.

David heard Jesse suck in a quick breath and James shift in his chair. Forcing himself not to look at them, he kept talking.

"You must have known he wouldn't make it out," he said. If he'd let himself think about what she was saying, her callousness would have rendered him speechless, so he kept a tight rein and focused only on keeping her talking. And getting everyone out alive. Although, come to think of it, he wasn't sure how *she* planned to get out alive.

That thought raised a whole set of new questions. Had she planned to tie Jesse up, leave the bomb, then trigger it? That seemed too haphazard, even for someone as crazy as Stacey. She *had* to have known that Jesse wouldn't come alone. He glanced around again, looking at all the spots other devices could have been placed, a second bomb *could* give her leverage to get herself out of there alive. Assuming she intended to get out alive.

Stacey shrugged again and responded to his comment about Gabby's brother. "Sure, I knew he wouldn't make it out. But it didn't really matter to me. I just needed him to get to her," she said, using the device to gesture toward Jesse.

But her arm only made it halfway through the motion when he heard the sound of glass breaking and the report of a rifle. A look of shock crossed Stacey's face, then she pitched forward.

David saw Jesse pull James out of the chair in his peripheral vision as he lunged forward, hoping against hope that he could catch the canister. He knew it was on a trigger, but he had no idea what kind.

"Get out!" he yelled even as he dove for the floor.

He was vaguely aware of Jesse yelling for him, Stacey screaming in the background, and the sound of boots crashing against the wood floor. And then he hit the ground.

CHAPTER 26

"Do you have it?" Caleb demanded as he rushed the room. David lay panting on the floor, his arm outstretched, the device cradled in his hand.

"I do but it's got a trigger and I don't know what kind," was all he got out before Ian stepped in and slowly removed it from his hand. He wasn't hurt, not yet, but the air had been knocked out of him when he'd hit the floor.

"No one come in," Ian ordered. "You," he said to David. "Unless you know how to defuse a bomb, get out." David let the words sink in, and judging by Ian's tone, while they weren't out of the woods yet, death wasn't imminent.

He got up on his knees then, reaching for the wall, pulled himself up. Through the doorway, he could see Jesse outside, straining against someone who was holding her back.

"This is the last time I'll say it, Hathaway. You've done enough today, now get out. We've got this," Ian barked.

He didn't question how Ian and Caleb would handle it, how they knew whatever it was they needed to know to defuse the bomb, he just gave one last look at Stacey, writhing on the floor with blood oozing from her shoulder, and left. But before he reached the door, he turned back, something niggling on his mind.

"Ian?"

The sheriff looked up.

"She had to have an escape route. I think it might have been that," David said with a gesture to the bomb Caleb was studying. "At first I thought she meant to use it against Jesse, but now I think she might have planned to use it as her getaway." Which meant that she'd had another plan for getting to Jesse. And the more he thought about it, the more certain he was that there was another bomb somewhere in the office. But he was going to leave that part up to Ian. Right now, he just wanted to see Jesse. Once Ian nodded in recognition of what he was saying, David turned and left the two men to do what they needed to do.

When David cleared the police line, Jesse launched herself into his arms, sobbing, laughing, thanking him, and chastising him all at once. Ignoring everything she was saying, he gathered her in his arms, buried his face in her hair, closed his eyes, and just held on. Eventually she quieted, but still he held her, unwilling to ever let her go.

"David?" His head came up and his eyes met James's. For a long moment, they just looked at each other, then David opened an arm and James stepped into the embrace. Her arm came around her son and the three of them breathed in life.

"Mom!"

David didn't know how long they'd been standing there when Matt's voice interrupted them. He looked up and both Caleb and Ian were outside, holding pieces of the canister. The bomb squad was starting a search of the office and property and an EMT was inside with Marcus Brown, working on Stacey. He wanted to tell them not to bother, but when Matt came running up, David decided he had better things to focus on.

Jesse's older son threw his arms around his mom and brother as David stood and watched. When Matt finally stepped away, everyone's eyes were red.

"Mom?" James's voice was quiet as they stood and watched the activity. "Was what she said about Dad true?"

"What who said about Dad?" Matt asked.

David watched Jesse look at both her sons. She had wanted to protect them from this but knew it wasn't an option now.

She nodded. "Yes, James it was true. Matt, I promise you, we'll talk about this later."

He could see Matt wanting to protest, but Joe and Danielle were striding up to them. Without a word, Joe gathered Jesse in an embrace. Then Danielle came forward to do the same.

"You okay?" Joe asked, looking both Jesse and David over.

David nodded.

"Joe, there's something you should know. Something you and Danielle should both know," Jesse said. And she proceeded to tell them an abbreviated version of what they learned about the shooting of Abigail. When she was done, Joe turned and looked toward the open door of the barn.

"She still alive?" he asked.

Jesse nodded.

"And she'll stand trial?"

Again, Jesse nodded. "We have the whole thing recorded," she said quietly.

For a long moment the man just stood there, watching the barn. Finally, he turned and nodded. "Ian will see to it she gets justice then."

David thought Joe was more generous than he would have been, but he said nothing, turning instead to catch a glimpse of the EMT loading Stacey onto a stretcher. She was quiet and he wondered if they had sedated her. Out of curiosity he walked back toward the barn. The EMT was pulling the stretcher and Marcus was pushing it from behind. Stacey was wearing an oxygen mask and her hands were cuffed to the sides of the gurney.

David wasn't the kind of guy who'd ever considered himself bloodthirsty, but looking at Stacey and thinking of all the pain and destruction she had caused, he realized he wouldn't have cared one way or another if she had died by that bullet.

He glanced at the deputy to see how Marcus was handling the situation, then frowned. Something was wrong. Of its own accord, his head drew back and cocked to the side. Then his gaze landed back on Stacey and his blood ran cold.

She smiled at him.

"Out!" he yelled, his heart in his throat. "Everyone out.

Get back, get back," he shouted chasing everyone away. The EMT looked startled then bolted away from the building. David watched, blood pounding in his ears, as Marcus tried to make it around the gurney and out the door.

"Marcus," Ian yelled as the officer finally rounded the stretcher and hit the doorway.

Then everything exploded around them.

• • •

"Jesse!" David yelled, panic clawing at his chest.

"David? Are you okay?" she said, sounding just about how he felt as she came running to his side.

Slowly he rose, dusting the dirt off his hands. He'd hit the ground as soon as he knew what was happening and was now a bit scratched, a bit scraped, and a bit stunned, but otherwise unhurt. Flames were growing greedily, consuming what had once been Mark Baker's office, and smoke, thick smoke, bellowed out the shattered doors and windows, enveloping the area.

"I'm okay. The boys? Ian? Caleb?" he shouted, frantically look-ing around. He saw Joe with his arms around all three kids, his body sheltering theirs from the blast. David let out a deep breath when he watched Joe straighten and saw that James, Matt, and Danielle were unharmed.

Turning toward where he'd last seen Caleb and Ian standing, he called to them again.

"We're good." He heard Ian call back as he saw them both emerge, coughing, through the smoke.

"The deputy. He was right there. Have you seen him? What about everyone else?" David asked going into work mode. The smoke was still thick on the ground but it was also starting to form a column as it rose into the sky.

"Everyone out here is accounted for," Ian said, still surveying the scene. "But we need to get in and find Marcus. I think he was out when it hit, but I can't see anything through the smoke."

"That's my job," David said racing to his truck, ignoring Jesse's pleas to wait for the fire department just coming down her drive. But he knew how important minutes—no seconds—could be to life or death. Grabbing his work coat, a mask, and gloves, he approached the building.

Judging by the blast, he estimated the trajectory of where Marcus would have been thrown and started searching for him in a grid pattern. Without his full gear, the smoke stung his eyes and his throat burned even through the mask. But still he searched.

In less than a minute, he came across a body. Dropping to the ground for a better look, for a moment he lost hope. Marcus lay on his side, his left leg burned and shredded by debris almost to the bone. The gurney that held Stacey Carson was tipped on its side and was lying across the deputy's knees. Her body lay across his lower legs, one hand still handcuffed to the rail.

Not one to give up, David ripped off his gloves and felt for a pulse. By some grace of god, or whoever was listening, he felt a slow, weak, rhythmic beat under his fingers.

"I've got him," he shouted, and triggered the light that others would use to locate him, even in the smoke. "He's down and we need backup." Already he could hear the sound of the fire truck sirens and the crunch of their tires on the driveway.

From experience, he knew less than a minute had passed before someone else reached him, but holding his finger on that pulse, and feeling it weaken with every beat, made time slow down to a surreal pace. There was no saving Stacey, and two of the firefighters unceremoniously shifted the gurney and body off Marcus.

Together the three of them lifted Marcus onto a board and David shouted that they were heading out. Even before they hit the clear air, the EMT was back, beside a different stretcher now, barking orders and helping to load Marcus into the ambulance.

"We need an airlift," David demanded, taking off the rest of his gear.

"There's no time. We'll get him to Riverside and they can airlift to Boston or New York from there," Jesse said, already calling the hospital to prepare them for Marcus's arrival and ordering the helicopter.

David wasn't sure Marcus would make it to Riverside, but Jesse was right. They could have him in care before a chopper was even ready to lift off. Riverside wasn't equipped to handle the kind of injuries he suspected Marcus had incurred, but he figured that some care was better than no care as he watched them load and pull away, sirens blaring.

He turned to see James, Matt, and Jesse standing there watching the fire with shock on their faces. He didn't think their shock was for the destroyed property, but rather for Marcus, a man who been a part of helping them.

"David." Jesse looked to him for some kind of reassurance. He couldn't give her exactly what she needed, but he could give her something.

"Come here." He opened his arms and she stepped right back to where she should be.

• • •

Darkness had descended hours earlier and yet no one seemed able to go to bed. Jesse looked at the three men sitting around her table and gave thanks, yet again, that they were where they were. Everyone was cradling coffee or hot chocolate and the conversation had dimmed.

She had told Matt and James everything she knew about Stacey, and though it was a conversation no parent wanted to have, she answered their questions about their father honestly.

"Did Dad really have an affair with that woman?" James had asked. "And who was Susan?"

Jesse had answered the best she could, telling her boys about their father's infidelity with Stacey, Susan, and Karen Ross. She told them they had been talking about a divorce once she found out about the second affair. But she assured them she'd had no idea about Stacey until earlier that day.

When asked if there were others, she wasn't sure what to say to that. Thankfully, David had jumped in and said that it was possible, based on what Naomi had found in Mark's old laptop, but they had no proof.

The conversation moved on when Ian called with an update on Marcus. They'd airlifted him to New York and he would pull through but it was going to be a long road. One of Marcus's knees needed to be replaced, the other was shattered but repairable, his hip was crushed, and he'd suffered severe burns on his right leg and lower torso. Ian, Vivi, and Carly were at the hospital with him.

A few hours later, they got another call from Ian. One that made everyone smile. It was a few weeks early but it seemed that Vivi's body had decided to take advantage of the convenience of already being at the hospital and she was in labor. Everyone was doing fine and the families were already starting to descend. Ian promised to call as soon as the baby arrived.

And now the four of them were sitting quietly, lost in their own thoughts. The house had been swept four times over to check for any surprises Stacey might have left, but after David insisted on bringing the dogs through a second time, Jesse felt comfortable that at least her home hadn't been invaded again, and with the help of a little whiskey in her coffee, she was finally starting to relax enough to consider going to sleep.

When David's phone rang, she glanced at the clock. It was late, very late. But it had only been an hour since Ian had called to tell them about Vivi. She watched as David answered.

"Yeah?" A look of surprise crossed his face and he got up and looked out the window. Ian had placed a sheriff's deputy at the end of her drive, mostly to make sure folks left them alone.

"Yes, of course." He hung up and she saw headlights sweep the room as a car came up the drive. "Miranda is here," he said.

He sounded as confused as she felt. And then his words sunk in. Of course his daughter would want to be here, would want to see him. But Jesse was a wreck and, for a moment, a little bit of panic set in at meeting David's daughter. Then James's hand came down over hers as he reminded her of the important things in life. Miranda wouldn't care that they were exhausted and ratty looking, she would just want to know her dad was okay, and that was something Jesse understood.

"Miranda," David said, as he stepped into the little mudroom and opened the door for her. Jesse and the boys stayed at the table, giving the father and daughter a few minutes together.

"Dad," she answered. Jesse could hear the rustle of clothing and she assumed the two were hugging. "How are you? I mean, really, how are you?"

He chuckled. "I'm fine. Better than I was twelve hours ago. We're tired and James is a little banged up, but other than that, we're all fine."

"James is the younger son, right?" Miranda asked. Obviously, David had told her about them.

"Yes, come in and meet everyone," David said.

Jesse watched as he rounded the corner with the young woman in tow. She was tall, not as tall as her dad, but close to five foot eight, and athletically built. She had David's dark brown eyes and curly brown hair streaked with gold highlights. Her coloring looked more Mediterranean than David's, but she was definitely his daughter.

Jesse and the boys stood.

Miranda's eyes swept over each of them before landing back on her.

"Jesse, this is my daughter, Miranda. Miranda, Jesse," David said.

Jesse stepped forward to offer her hand but Miranda offered her a big hug instead.

"I know you don't know me," Miranda said, stepping back. "But for my dad's sake, and the sake of your boys, I'm really glad you're okay. All of you," she added, looking directly at each boy in turn.

They all sat back down again, and once a cup of coffee was

placed in front of Miranda, she peppered them with questions about the day, discreetly avoiding asking too much about Mark.

Jesse watched Miranda talk with the boys and felt a sense of calm wash over her at their easy interactions. That's not to say they were instant best friends, but it was clear that they were all being as grown-up as they knew how to be in this sudden blended-family situation. And she was pleased to see that the kids were more interested in getting to know each other as people than as children who were protective or possessive of their parents. She didn't know what the future held for her and David, but for now, this was good.

Matt was telling Miranda about the running trail around their property when David leaned over to Jesse and asked in a whisper, "Are you ready for bed?"

She'd been enjoying the sounds of the kids' voices and hadn't yet thought about calling it a night, but the moment he asked, she yawned and her eyes dipped.

"Come on," he said rising. "Let's get you to bed."

"The kids," she mumbled.

"The kids will be fine," Matt interjected. "We'll set Miranda up in the downstairs room. You go on to bed. You deserve it."

She looked at the boys, then stepped forward and gave each one a kiss on the top of his head. "Good night, love you. And Miranda, thank you for coming, it's so nice to meet you."

"Love you, too, Mom," James and Matt answered.

Miranda smiled. "It's nice to finally meet you, too. I'm sorry it took what happened today, but I'm glad to be here."

"We're glad you're here, too," Jesse answered.

After David gave his daughter another hug, Jesse took his hand as they made their way toward her room. And just before she shut the door, she heard something that let her know it would truly be okay.

Miranda's voice drifted down the hallway. "You guys like playing poker?"

CHAPTER 27

So much had changed in the last four days that Jesse couldn't quell the jitters in her stomach. Intellectually, she knew Matt and James were safe picking up bagels for breakfast in town. But memories and images of James tied to that chair still echoed through her at times and she thought they probably would for some time to come.

Vivi, Ian, and their new baby were already home. Jeffery MacAllister, named after Vivi's brother, had weighed in at seven pounds three ounces and was, naturally, the center of attention in the MacAllister and extended DeMarco families. He had his father's eyes and his mother's hair and, so far, neither of their personalities, but time would tell on that one.

Marcus Brown was out of intensive care but had a long road ahead of him. His surgery had gone well and he would walk again, but there was likely some sustained nerve damage that they hadn't been able to fully assess yet. Still, he was alive and would recover enough to live a productive life. He would probably never win a marathon, but they no longer worried about his survival.

And then there was the change she and the boys had talked about over the last three days. They had come to a decision that would affect all their lives, and though it was scary in more ways than one, all three of them knew it was the right decision. That it might end her relationship with David weighed heavily on her, but in her heart of hearts, she knew even that wouldn't change her mind.

"Jesse?" the man himself said as he walked into the kitchen

carrying a bundle of firewood with Miranda trailing behind him carrying a load of her own.

"Oh, thanks, go ahead and put that in the bin by the fireplace. You didn't have to do that." Jesse followed them into the living room and watched as he stacked the wood. By unspoken agreement, after that first night, David and Miranda had stayed at his house—all of them had been through a lot over the previous week and blending the families was an additional stress neither had wanted at that point.

"I noticed you were almost out when we left last night so we decided to grab some from your woodpile on our way in," he said with an easy smile.

Because that was the kind of guy he was.

"Thanks," she said, moving back to the kitchen. "The boys are in town but should be here any minute with the bagels. Coffee?"

Her stomach was too tied up in knots to drink any herself, but she poured some for Miranda and David. They made small talk about the weather, which had gotten colder, and college, which both Matt and Miranda were headed back to tomorrow. She was worried about the fact that Matt had missed his first two weeks of classes, but Miranda did her best to reassure her everything would be fine.

However, when Matt and James pulled up, she was feeling anything but fine. After dropping the bagels and cream cheese on the kitchen island, Matt took one look at her and suggested that he, James, and Miranda go for a walk around the property before they ate. Miranda gave him a curious look but agreed, and soon Jesse and David were alone.

"You want to tell me what's going on?" David asked, taking their moment alone to wrap his arms around her.

She looked into his eyes and knew this was going to be one of the hardest conversations she would ever have.

"Jesse?" His voice was starting to sound worried.

She pulled away, needing her own space, and walked around the kitchen island away from him.

"What's going on? Is everything okay?" he pressed.

She took a deep breath. "Everything is fine. It's just that," she paused and his eyes searched hers. "It's just that the boys and I have made a decision that I think you aren't going to like."

He drew back and frowned. "Why don't you let me be the judge of that?"

She could tell from his voice that he wasn't defensive quite yet, but he was ready to go there fast.

"This isn't about us, David. I want to say that first. I love you, you know I do, so this isn't me ending things or anything like that."

"Then what is it?"

Her attempts to appease had obviously had the opposite effect as his eyes narrowed on her.

"I've decided to file to adopt Emma Carson," she blurted out.

"What?" He sounded more confused than angry.

"The boys and I have talked about it. She has no family left and, well, she's James and Matt's half sister. None of us feel it's right for her to be punished for the sins of her parents. I can afford it and I'm still relatively young. It's just," her voice wavered as she saw David's expression close down. "It's just something we need to do," she finished, her voice quiet, pleading with him to understand.

"But you've already raised two kids. *I've* already raised a daughter. You said you were done." She could tell he was fighting to stay reasonable, but was losing that fight.

She looked down, knowing now where this conversation was going to go. "I know. But you of all people know how quickly life can change. And this isn't something I would ever have asked for. But it's happening. And all we can do is deal with it the best way we know how."

"And so you're going to adopt her? Have you even met her?" His voice was incredulous.

"Yes and yes. I have met her. She's a lovely little almost two-year-old who is living with strangers because the woman who raised her died. And yes, I am going to adopt her as long as the courts don't have any objections. But I also know how you feel about having more kids. I know because I felt that way, too. Until this happened. So I'm not asking you to do this with me. I am going to do it. I *need* to do it. And I'm going to leave it to you to decide if you want to be a part of it. Don't get me wrong, David, I want you to be a part of it, I really do. But—" her voice cracked on what she was about to say, but she pushed on. "But you've always been clear about what you did and didn't want when it came to having more kids, so I will understand if you choose not to do this with me." She was blinking back tears at this point and hated that doing the right thing wasn't always the easy thing.

"This is what you want?" Judging by his tone, he was still struggling to understand her decision, was still trying to give her the benefit of the doubt, but was not at all happy with what she was saying. Raising another child wouldn't have been something she would have chosen if the world were perfect, but the world wasn't perfect, and most importantly, it wasn't perfect for the inno-cent little girl who was caught up in all this. If she and her boys had it in them to make a family with her, to be her family, then yes, she wanted that.

But to lose David because of that? She'd known it was a possi-bility when she and the boys had first started talking about it, but now, standing in front him, watching him slip away, well, it was harder than she'd ever thought it would be.

"It's the right thing to do."

"So I have no say in this? I have to accept having another child if I want to be with you?"

It wasn't fair, none of this was fair, but they both knew life wasn't ever fair. Sometimes it was good or great and sometimes it sucked. Sometimes bad things happened to good people and sometimes it was the other way around. Fairness had nothing to do with it. But even so, she couldn't bring herself to answer.

David let out a low curse, ran his hand over his face and turned away.

"I don't know what you want from me, Jesse," he said, turning back. "You and the boys have been talking about this enough to have reached a decision and then you just dump it on me? Didn't it occur to you that maybe I should have been a part of those conversations?"

She blinked at him, taken aback. In all honesty, no, she hadn't thought he should have been a part of those conversations. Not because she didn't know it would affect him—affect them—but because she knew how he felt about raising another child. Not to mention that their relationship, as good as it was, was still fairly new. They had kept things to themselves for so long, but even after they'd been "outed," they hadn't had any conversations about their future. They'd never talked about living together or doing anything other than carrying on as they had. That he'd have wanted to have been a part of a conversation about adopting Emma hadn't crossed her mind.

"Mom?"

"Dad?"

Matt and Miranda entered with James following.

"Everything okay?" Miranda asked, her eyes going between the two of them. Jesse remained silent, letting David take the question.

Jesse saw his jaw tick, then he forcibly took a deep breath. "Yeah, everything is fine. Are you guys ready to eat?"

None of the three kids looked like they believed him and Miranda slid Jesse a sympathetic look. And by the way Matt and James were avoiding her, she'd bet they'd told Miranda exactly what was going on.

The only easy thing about their breakfast together was the fact that it was fast. They ate mostly in silence—what little conversation that came up was between the kids, with Miranda and Matt comparing class schedules and talking to James about colleges. For her part, she tried to swallow a bite or two of bagel, but it felt so dry in her throat she gave up and drank water instead.

David said next to nothing and when he and Miranda put on their coats to leave, the perfunctory kiss he dropped on Jesse's head felt like a guillotine. But as hard as this was, as awful as she felt, she still knew, bone deep, that adopting Emma was the right thing. And that David would have to make his own decision.

• • •

"You are being a complete boob, Dad," Miranda said, snatching the keys from his hand as he went to insert them into the ignition.

"I don't know what you're talking about." He held out his hand and glared at his daughter. Then forced himself to relax. It wasn't Miranda's fault this was happening.

"I know exactly what I'm talking about. Jesse is going to adopt Emma, Mark's baby by that crazy woman, and you just totally freaked out on her."

He stared at Miranda for a long moment then held out his hand again for the keys. "We are not going to have this conversation."

"Why not? Because you think if you express reservations about raising another kid, you're going to hurt my feelings? Because you're afraid it might make me feel like an unwanted burden?"

"You were never unwanted. You might have been a burden for a few of those teenage years, but you were never unwanted." He really didn't want to be having this conversation, mostly because Miranda was right.

"Nice, Dad. Using humor to deflect. It's a good thing I took that psych class last semester 'cause I never would have caught on."

He shot her an irritated look.

"Well?" she prompted, unrelenting.

"Well, what?"

"Well, what are you going to do?"

He rubbed his hand over his face again. Raising another child? He couldn't imagine it. He'd just created a life of his own for the first time.

"I don't know," he answered honestly.

"It's not like you would be on your own this time around," Miranda said. He looked at her questioningly. "I mean, it would be different if you decided to do this with Jesse, instead of walking away and letting her do it on her own," she continued. "You're older now, you have a career, a house, a life, and you'd have a partner this time around. And based me, you know you're a great parent." She gave him a cheeky grin. She made it sound so easy, but he it knew it wasn't.

"You don't understand and I hope you don't have to for many years," he said with a pointed look.

She rolled her eyes.

"Raising kids is amazing, Miranda, it really is. But it's hard work. It's a lot of responsibility but it's also a lot of logistics and planning and lot of—" He stopped himself, not wanting to risk hurting his daughter's feelings.

"A lot of giving up your own life to make things work for your kids?" She finished his thought.

She didn't sound hurt or like she was judging him, but when she said it, he judged himself. And that was why he was so hesitant to even contemplate the decision with Jesse. If he was already feeling anxiety about having to change his schedule and his life, didn't that make him too selfish to be a parent again?

"God, Miranda, it's amazing you've turned out as good as you have. I may love you a lot, but I probably wasn't the best parent."

She smiled at him, like she had all her life. "You're a great dad, Dad. Sure we had some ups and downs, like most families do. But the thing is, I always know you love me, I always did. Even when you wouldn't let me go to Mexico for spring break my senior year or when I got in that fender bender. Or when we couldn't afford to go on any vacations other than camping because you were in school.

"To be honest, Dad, I don't know how you did it. But the thing is, this time around, you won't be on your own. Not only would you have Jesse, but Matt, James, and me, not to mention friends who actually have kids the same age, unlike when I was a kid and all your friends were out bar hopping."

"It's not that easy, Miranda." He laid his head against the

headrest. Something was shifting in him, and he was, for the first time in the last two hours, starting to feel a little calmer.

"You're right, it's not. But what you feel for her isn't a whim, Dad. You run into burning buildings all the time for people you don't know, but you walked into a building with a crazy woman and a bomb for Jesse and her family. Whatever that was, whatever that feeling was that day isn't going to go away."

He closed his eyes and thought back to that day and the days before it. To the photo of Mark's body and what he'd felt when he realized how easily it could have been Jesse. To the certainty he felt when he knew he was not going to let her walk into that building on her own. And then to happier times—to their first meeting and then their first night together. And how much he had needed her that night he'd found that little girl and her brother.

And when he thought about losing Jesse, really losing her, pain seared a hole through his heart so deep that, for a moment, he found it hard to breathe.

David looked at his daughter who was patiently watching him. She was one of the best things in his life and every day he was grateful for all the work, all the hours, all the worry he had, and would, live through for her. Looking at her sitting there— smart, capable, confident, and compassionate—he knew what he needed to do.

Miranda gave a little squeal when he opened his door and slid from his seat. He heard her car door shut behind him as he opened the kitchen door and reentered Jesse's house. Three sets of eyes landed on him as he stood in the doorway. James and Matt were at the breakfast bar, Jesse had been wiping the counter and now stood frozen with a sponge in her hand.

Striding toward her, he slipped the sponge out of her grip then sank his hands into her hair on either side of her face.

"If we're going to do this, we're going to do it my way, Jesse," he said.

Her eyes went wide. "Do what, David." She might have been confused, but he could hear hope in her voice.

"If we're going to raise a child together, we're going to do it the way I didn't get to do it the first time around."

"Meaning?" She bit her lip and he could see moisture welling in her eyes.

"I know we never talked about it, but you're it for me, Jesse. If things had never changed, I would have been happy to stay your partner for the rest of our lives, marriage or no. But things do change and now there is a little girl who needs parents and a family. If you want me to raise Emma with you, we do it as a family that is tied together in every possible way. If you want me to do this with you, then I want us to get married and start the process together."

She blinked back tears. "We don't have to get married to raise her together, David. I don't want to get married just because of Emma."

In that moment, he wanted nothing more than to hold her, to pull her to him and never let her go. But he needed to make something very clear first.

"We may be doing the paperwork because of Emma, but did you hear what I said? You're *it* for me. I'm pretty sure I knew it that first time I saw you. But I know I've known it for a while. Whether we're married or not isn't going to affect how I feel about you or my commitment to you in any way. But I think it will make it easier to process the adoption, and besides, it might give *me* some assurance that *you* won't be going anywhere. I raised a child once on my own, and while I don't regret it," he flashed a smile at his daughter, "I think I'd like to experience it with a partner this time. So, what do you say? Do you want to do this together?"

She looked at him for a several beats then slid her gaze to the boys. He didn't think she was looking for permission, but he knew she'd like their support. Both boys gave small nods. She turned back to him and he knew his life was about to change. And he couldn't have been more ready.

EPILOGUE

SITTING AT THE TAVERN, DAVID took a sip of beer and contemplated Dominic's question. Would they or wouldn't they?

"You know you won't," Kurt taunted.

David smiled. "Probably not," he agreed, easily. "Miranda offered to take Emma for the night so we could get away for the New Year but we kind of want to spend it all together. Matt and Miranda are going to stay in town, so we'll probably make it a family thing. And no, we probably won't make it to midnight."

He grinned, not caring too much. Especially since "not making it to midnight" usually meant he and Jesse had some time to themselves, alone, in their room. As far as he was concerned, there were worse ways to spend New Year's Eve.

"Any second thoughts? Do you regret it at all?" Dominic pressed.

David's memory floated back to that time. It turned out that Rosy McIntire had sought mental treatment after the fire in California. Mortified to find herself in the same area as David, she'd tried to keep a low profile at the hospital and in town. She had been cleared of any involvement, as had Dr. Bennet. The investigation into Stacey Carson had taken over a month. But within days, it had become clear that neither David nor Jesse could provide any additional insight, so they'd left everything in the hands the police and sheriff.

And taken off and gotten married.

The weekend after he'd asked her, they'd married in a tiny ceremony in the San Juan Islands in Washington State. They'd flown out, with the kids, brought his parents up from California and married at an inn Jesse's parents had found on Lopez Island. The short ceremony was part of a long weekend that both families spent together. It was fast, simple, and just what they'd wanted. It took another month to get custody of Emma and now, just over three months after the wedding, they had four months before the six-month probation period would be over and they could officially adopt her. But no one doubted it would happen. Emma had settled into her new family, and they into her, faster than either he or Jesse could have anticipated. They'd even acquired a puppy that Dash had found for them. Emma had named him Bob after her favorite member of "Aunt" Matty and "Uncle" Dash's dog pack.

Thinking of his family, David smiled to himself. His life, and Jesse's, could have turned out so differently. They could have let the echoes of their pasts catch up to them. Between the two of them, they could have let the pain, the sorrow, the betrayals, and the fear guide them. But, together, they hadn't. Together, they were building a new life. One built on a solid foundation of love, trust, and family. Oh, he knew they would have ups and downs, but he also knew, beyond a doubt, that he hadn't been lying that day in Jesse's kitchen when he'd told her she was it for him. They were strong together; they were better together.

So, were there any second thoughts?

He was about to answer when the door flew open and a gust of freezing wind blew into the restaurant. Jesse walked in holding Emma by the hand, followed by Miranda, Matt, and James. With a little squeal, Emma broke free and ran to him.

"Daddy!" she exclaimed as she jumped into his lap and threw her little arms over his shoulders, her tiny fingers catching the hair at the nape of his neck. Her language skills had rapidly caught up with her age group once she'd come to live with them and she'd started calling them mommy and daddy just a few weeks before. And every time he heard it, it felt better and better.

Jesse followed Emma over, said hi to Dominic and Kurt, and placed a kiss on David's head. Moving his beer out of toddler reach, she took off her hat and coat and dropped into the seat beside him. Emma snuggled her body against his as the older kids waved and headed off to play a game of pool before sitting down and ordering.

"Did you order me a beer?' Jesse asked. He slid one in front of her, making her smile. She leaned over and gave him another kiss, on his cheek this time.

Second thoughts? Regret it?

Not a chance.

ACKNOWLEDGEMENTS

IT'S HARD FOR ME TO believe that this is my fourth book. What's not hard for me to believe is that I still have a lot of the same people to thank, including my family and my mountain-mover friends, Sarah and Angeli, as well as former-neighbors-but-always-friends, Lisa and Jere. A new addition to my list is Division Chief Ron Karlen, Dixon Fire Department. I'm particularly grateful that he took the time to not only read some of the scenes from this book but also walk me through arson investigation 101. Ron, you'll see your fingerprints on this version of the manuscript and it's the better for your input. As always, any mistakes are mine, or, as I prefer to think of them, "literary license." And last, but definitely not least, Julie, my editor. I recently found the following quote: "I don't make the same mistake twice, I make it three or four times, just to be sure." I'm sure it applies to me when it comes to edits. When I read her redlines, I have visions of her strangling back swear words, pulling out her hair, and muttering to herself, "I've already told you a million times that's not how we do things!" Thankfully, she has kids so is probably used to the feeling.

Keep reading for a preview of Tamsen Schultz's

THE FRAILTY OF THINGS
WINDSOR SERIES BOOK 4

Independence. Kit Forrester is a woman who wears her independence like armor. Despite keeping secrets and hiding her past, she's built a life she loves and is accountable to no one. Until, that is, one of the world's most wanted war criminals sets his sights on her and she must weigh the risk to one against the chance of justice and closure for many—a decision Kit couldn't make on her own even if she wanted to.

Certainty. As a man who makes his living in the shadows of governments and wars, certainty isn't a part of Garret Cantona's vocabulary, and he's just fine with that. But when Kit walks into his life, he realizes he's never before been so sure about anything or anyone. Suddenly, he finds that he's looking at the world, *his* world, in a different light. And now that he is, he's determined to protect it, and her, in whatever way he can.

Frailty. No one knows better than Kit and Garret that an appreciation for what is, or what was, or what might be, can be born from the uncertainty and fragility of life. But when a hunt for a killer leaves Garret no choice but to throw Kit back into her broken and damaged past, even his unshakable faith in what they have together might not be enough to keep it from shattering into a million pieces.

CHAPTER 1

KIT FORRESTER TOOK A SIP of her beer and eyed the man sitting across from her. Drew Carmichael looked every inch the business tycoon he was. At over six feet of lean muscle, his blond hair, blue eyes, and strong chin gave him a hint of New England aristocracy. And she knew that, truth be told, Drew *could* trace his family back to the Mayflower. But it was his presence more than his appearance that conveyed an inherent sense of authority.

And authority was good, considering what Kit knew his *other* job to be.

She set her glass down and leaned forward. "Drew, in all the years I've known you, you've never, and I repeat *never*, asked me for a personal favor."

Her eyes stayed on his face even as he flicked a look out the window. Under normal circumstances, she might think he was just taking in the view of the beautiful winter night through the front picture window of the small restaurant in which they sat. But as charming as the Hudson Valley of New York, and particularly Old Windsor, was this time of year, she suspected Drew was being vigilant rather than appreciative.

His eyes came back to hers. "I know, Kit. Believe me, I know. And you can say 'no.'"

"But you'd rather I say 'yes,'" she said, finishing his thought if not his statement. Drew gave very little away but she'd known him long enough, nearly twelve years now, that she could see in the shadows of his expression the unease she heard in his voice. "Tell me what you need," she said.

She watched some of the tension leave his eyes, but he paused before answering as a couple came through the door, with a gust of cold wind following them, and headed toward the bar. Once the new patrons were well away, Drew set his elbows on the table and moved closer to her.

"Jonathon Parker is an agent with MI6, which, as you know, is the British version of the CIA."

Kit nodded. She traveled a lot for her job, met a lot of interesting people, knew a lot of interesting things—especially considering the fact that for the past eight years she'd been one of Drew's assets.

His position as one of the board members for his family's multi-national conglomerate was a perfect foil for his real job with the CIA. And Kit, well, she was the high-flying daughter of a very wealthy, and very deceased, businessman. That, coupled with her own international success as an award-winning writer of modern literature, gave her easy access to people and places. She didn't work for the CIA, but she did help them out on occasion.

"Jonathon was placed on probationary leave three days ago," Drew continued. "They're investigating his potential involvement in the release of information that compromised several key MI6 assets in the Middle East."

"Uh, that's not good," Kit said, leaning even closer to Drew. She knew what she did for him, for the agency, was potentially dangerous, but she never really gave it much thought. She knew Drew well and trusted him, and trusted that if he asked her for help, it was for a good reason. Still, she didn't like the idea of anyone else knowing what she did on the side.

Drew let out a little huff of air that could almost, but not quite, be called a sardonic laugh. "No kidding. It's not good for anyone involved. Not Parker, not the assets."

"So what do you want me to do?" she asked. "This sounds professional, but you said you needed a personal favor."

Drew took a sip of his own beer, set it down, and took a deep breath. "You're already going to Rome later this week. I was hoping you could stop by London on your way through and hand off some information for me."

"Drop it to Parker?" she asked.

Drew gave a single, sharp nod.

Kit stared at her dinner companion even as her mind went through the logic. She didn't know all the ins and outs of the CIA, but she was pretty sure that passing information from an active agent to an agent being investigated wouldn't be looked upon kindly. Especially considering that the agent being investigated was foreign. She also didn't know what would happen to Drew if he were caught, but she was certain it wouldn't be good.

"Drew," she said, concern lacing her tone.

"You don't have to do it, Kit. And if you choose not to, I won't hold it against you."

"But?" she prompted. Drew wasn't the most straight and narrow guy she knew—she figured, in his job, he couldn't be—but he *was* one of the most principled. If he wanted to involve himself with an agent under suspicion, he had to have a reason.

Again, his gaze traveled out the window before returning to her. She could see he was debating whether or not to answer. Finally, his eyes slid closed, and for a moment, he looked older than his forty years.

"Drew?" She leaned forward and laid her hand on his arm. He opened his eyes.

"I'm not going to lie, Kit. It got bad. Three of the four assets were killed within days of the information leak. Whoever did this deserves whatever justice the British decide to mete out. But it wasn't Parker. He's being framed."

"Framed?" she couldn't help the single eyebrow that shot up. When spooks started framing each other, it was bound to get messy.

One side of Drew's mouth ticked up into a smile. "I know, it's like a bad version of *Who's On First* when spies start playing these games. If it ever gets unraveled, it will be a miracle."

"But you know Parker wasn't involved?" she pressed, tucking a strand of her auburn hair behind her ear.

"He wasn't," Drew answered with certainty.

"And why can't this go through official channels?"

Drew let out a sigh. "Because the information I have isn't information that we, the Agency, want to share with MI6. And before you ask," he said, raising a hand to stave off her question, "the official Agency answer is still "no," even when we know that it will likely ruin the life a great agent."

Kit sat back in her chair and, for a moment, regretted getting into this conversation in the first place. There wasn't any doubt in her mind that she would help Drew, she'd just been so stunned when he'd asked for a personal favor that she'd started asking questions. And, not surprisingly, she didn't like what she'd ended up hearing. She didn't like that her own government seemed to value life so little. She wasn't naïve and knew that there might be a very good reason why the CIA didn't want to share whatever information Drew was referring to, but still, the thought that they might have information that could help someone and choose to not use it didn't sit well on her shoulders.

"If you don't want to—"

"Of course I'll do it, Drew. I was just thinking that I'm glad I'm not the one who has to make these decisions. I'm glad I'm not the one who has to weigh the value of sharing information against the lives it might help or harm." She took another sip of her drink and set it down with a small smile. "I'd totally suck at it," she added.

Drew smiled back—a real smile. "That's because you have a heart and you're human."

Kit rolled her eyes. She was a softy; she'd freely admit to that. But Drew wasn't giving himself any credit. He had a tough job, and she knew how much he cared about just about everything. Maybe too much.

"So, then," she continued. "Now that we've settled that, what are the particulars?"

Drew slid two business cards across the table to her. Both were printed with her name and generic contact information, one had a small, Celtic design in the upper right corner, a design taken from her first book, *Celtic Shelter*, and the other had a similar design, only it was in the upper left hand corner. The cards looked normal and bore nothing unusual that would draw attention to them.

"This one," Drew said, his finger tapping the card with the mark on the right side, "is for Ambrose."

Fabio Ambrose was a diplomatic liaison located in Rome. She'd met him on numerous occasions and had already been planning to see him, at Drew's request, on her upcoming trip to Europe. Ambrose was her official assignment.

"And this one," Drew said, sliding the other card over, the card with the design on the left, "is for Parker."

"And how will I meet Parker?" she asked, taking the cards and tucking them into her purse. She wasn't sure what information was on the cards or how the intended recipients would retrieve it, but she assumed it was some sort of old-school dot technology where information was encoded in tiny pixels that made up the print.

"That's easy," Drew said, leaning back in his chair, looking a little bit more relaxed than he had just a few moments before. "His sister is a journalist who covers financial news."

Kit laughed. "And, let me guess, financial crimes as well?"

"The two do tend to go together," Drew said with an answering grin.

"How fortuitous then that the book I'm currently working on revolves around the impact such a crime has on a small community."

Drew's grin widened into a smile. "I thought so, too. Isabelle Parker would make an excellent interview subject. She's older than Parker by several years and has been on the beat forever. A request from you to meet wouldn't be unusual."

Kit shook her head and smiled. "I'll do some research on her and have my publicist contact her tomorrow. Provided she'll be in town, I can fly through London and spend a few days there before heading to Rome for Marco Baresi's party."

Marco was a fellow writer and her mentor. He was also, at one point, years ago, something more. Marco had recently received a very prestigious European book award and his publisher was throwing him a huge party to celebrate. Of course, she would be there. When Drew had found out, he'd asked her to contact Ambrose while in town. And now, it would seem she was adding Isabelle Parker to her list, as well.

She looked down at her purse and contemplated the two business cards inside. One was Drew doing his job. But the other, well, thinking of it gave her pause. She wasn't about to back out, but that didn't mean she wasn't concerned.

"Drew? Are you sure?" she asked, bringing her gaze up to his.

She knew he saw the seriousness of her question and her concern for him. His expression softened even as a world-weary look stole across his face.

He nodded. "Yes, I'm certain. He's a good agent and I've known him for years. When I heard what was happening, I knew it wasn't him. And when I found the information that could prove it, well, that just made it all that much more clear in my mind. But," he said, taking a deep breath and then letting it out, "as much as I hate to admit it, I can see why we don't want to share what we have with our counterparts in England. I even agree with the decision."

"But?"

"But Parker will know what to do with it. I trust him not to share it, but to use it to clear his name."

"That's a lot of trust to put in someone, Drew," she pointed out.

He gave her a wry smile. "Ironic, isn't it? Since spooks aren't supposed to trust anyone with anything, yet I'm entrusting him with information that could not only pose a threat to the US but also get me fired and likely imprisoned, too."

Kit studied him for a moment and saw the resolve in his eyes. "Well, if it makes you feel any better, I'm not sure of the wisdom of your decision either, but I *do* trust you." She took the last sip of her beer and looked around the room. It was sometimes surreal meeting with Drew, knowing the shady world he operated in, then looking around and seeing couples laughing, families dining together, and the world going on.

"Is there anything else I should know?" she asked, bringing her attention back to her companion.

Drew finished his drink and set the glass back down on the table. He didn't look up as he answered, but kept his focus on his fingers as they caught the moisture gathered on his glass. "I'm not going to lie and say this meeting with Parker is like all the others, because it isn't. I haven't heard anything that would indicate that there could be problems, but just be safe, Kit. Be aware of what's going on around you. You have good instincts; use them. If something doesn't feel right, trust that feeling."

Kit frowned. Drew had given her this same speech any number of times when she'd first started shuttling information for him. But he hadn't given it in years. That he felt the need to now shouldn't have come as a surprise, but for some reason, it did.

It made her want to ask, yet again, if he was sure he wanted to go forward with his plan. But remembering the look of certainty in his eyes the first time she'd asked, she knew she already had her answer. And so she nodded in response to his warning.

"Always," she said.

His eyes watched hers for a moment then traveled down to her empty beer glass. "Shall we?" he asked, nodding toward the door, ending the meeting.

"You go on ahead," she said, suddenly feeling like she wanted a little time alone with a glass of whiskey. Drew frowned. She smiled. "Really, Drew, please. I know you have to drive back to New York City tonight, so go on ahead. I'm just going to have another drink, enjoy this view," she said with a gesture toward the picture window, "and then head home."

"You sure?" he said, concern still lacing his tone.

"Yes, I'm sure. Go. Drive safe. The roads are cleared from the snow last night, but they get icy."

"Yeah, yeah, yeah," Drew said, rising with a smile of his own and donning his black cashmere scarf and coat. "I know, the Taconic Parkway winds a lot and ice builds up and people don't drive safe." He mimicked what she told him nearly every time he visited in the winter months.

"Just call me 'mom,'" she said with a laugh as he pulled on his leather gloves.

Drew rolled his eyes, then bent down and kissed her cheek. "You're almost decade younger than me, but you do give my mom a run for her money in the worry department."

"Just be safe," Kit said, grabbing his scarf and stopping him from straightening away. He might joke, but she meant every word and wanted to make sure he knew it. His face was a few inches away from hers and it occurred to her that the position was an intimate one. Though it had never been like that between the two of them, she knew that if anyone she knew saw them, gossip would ensue—the joys of a small town.

"Be safe," Kit repeated, quietly.

Drew's eyes held hers for a moment, then he gave a tiny nod. "You, too," he said then dipped his head and gave her one more kiss on the cheek. Reluctantly, she released him and watched him walk out the door.

Through the window, she saw him climb into his silver Mercedes SUV and back out of the plowed parking lot. She glanced down at her purse again, hoped like hell Drew knew what he was doing, then ordered a shot of whiskey.

• • •

It was just after ten when Kit finally made her way to her car. Consisting of a post office, a general store, and Anderson's, the restaurant she'd just come out of, Old Windsor was never a very happening spot. It was even quieter on this cold, Sunday evening.

Her boots crunched the snow as she crossed the street toward her car. Kit loved the winter, but in temperatures hovering around zero this time of night, she was glad for her gloves, hat, and scarf, not to mention her long down coat that nearly reached the top of her boots. A small gust of wind blew and the frigid air snaked under her scarf and down her neck. She hunched her shoulders in protection as she reached into her pocket for her keys.

Concentrating on where she was putting her feet. Kit was startled to hear the sound of a car door opening. Her head shot up and her step faltered. Parked next to her own vehicle was a black Range Rover. She knew a lot of people who drove Range Rovers, especially this time of year, but only one who would show up like this. Despite the cold, she paused about ten feet from her destination and watched as a jacketed figure unfolded itself from the ominous-looking car.

"Kit," her brother said.

"Caleb," she responded. She hadn't seen or spoken to her brother in five months. Almost enough time to believe he wasn't a part of her life. Almost enough time to accept that she was fine on her own, that she was fine with having no family.

"We need to talk," he said. Kit didn't respond for a moment. She and her brother didn't *talk*. They never *talked*. Not anymore. There had been time in their lives when that hadn't been the case. There had been a time when she'd idolized her older brother, when he'd looked out for her, when they'd gone fishing together, and when she had believed that he had the answers for everything.

But that time had long ago passed and they hadn't been in each other's presence for more than a few days a year for over a decade. Kit started to speak but stopped short when a second figure emerged from the passenger side of Caleb's car.

She was glad her face was hidden in the shadows of her hat and scarf as Garret Cantona, her brother's right-hand man, straightened to his full height. Kit was tall, easily five foot ten, but Garret's six-foot-three form dwarfed hers. Like Caleb, he wore jeans and work boots, but rather than a jacket, Garret sported a black sweater and a gray beanie hat. She knew the hat covered light-brown hair that, if it got too long, curled in ways that bothered him. And she felt, more than saw, his light-blue eyes—eyes rimmed with thick, black lashes—studying her.

"And I see you brought your Mini Me," she added, forcing

her gaze from Garret back to her brother in time to see a look of irritation flicker across his face.

"Kit," Caleb warned.

She let out a little breath of annoyance. It was too cold to be having this conversation now. "I'm going home. If you'd like to follow me, feel free. You know I have enough room for you. If you don't want to stay with me, there are dozens of bed and breakfasts around. I don't care either way, but I'm too cold to be standing out here right now." She almost added that they could feel free to camp on her property, too, since that was exactly what Garret had been doing when she'd first met him. Her brother had been in town helping a friend of hers and had brought Garret along. Why her brother hadn't had him stay in the house with them was a mystery to her. She'd discovered Garret camping on the back edge of her eighty acres—close enough to a road to be easily accessible, but far enough away from everything to be seen.

"Cantona will go with you," Caleb all but ordered. Kit laughed.

"I don't think so, Caleb. You can meet me there." Both cars had been backed into their spots and Kit had to pass Garret as she made her way to her driver's side door. Keeping an eye mostly on the icy path, she glanced up at her brother's companion as she drew alongside him. His eyes were trained on hers but she could read nothing in his expression. She wished it were the same for him—that he would find her expression as neutral as she found his—but she wasn't as good at this game as either of the two men who stood with her. Still, he stepped back and let her pass.

Unlocking her door, she slid onto the leather seat and shivered as her cold jeans pressed against the backs of her legs. She reached for the door but Garret was already there, closing it. And for a moment, for a very brief second, she thought she saw a question in his eyes. But then the door shut.

"Go with her," Kit heard Caleb say as she fumbled with her key in her gloved hands.

"No," she heard Garret respond. "It's not as though she's going to run, Forrester. You just dropped in on her after five months of no contact. Give her space," he added.

Kit heard Caleb start to respond but whatever he was saying was lost as her engine roared to life. She pulled out onto the road and turned west toward home. Through her rearview mirror, she saw both men climb back into Caleb's Range Rover. She wasn't sure what to feel when their headlights appeared through her back window.

Not wanting to think about the sudden appearance of both Caleb and Garret, Kit turned her mind to her meeting with Drew. She wasn't going to back out, but the more she thought about it, the more anxious she became—for Drew, not herself. She didn't know the half of what he did in his job, but she knew he was committed to it, almost too much so. She also knew he wasn't married, and from what she could tell—from her conversations with him and with their mutual friend Dani Williamson, now Dani Fuller—he'd never even had a relationship that lasted more than a month or so.

If the MI6 agent, Parker, was playing him, Drew could lose everything—everything he loved, everything he had worked so hard for, would disappear. The thought made her stomach turn. Drew was one of the good guys and he deserved some happiness in his life—in whatever form that came.

Kit made a promise to herself to do what she could to help Drew and was already mentally planning the adjustments she would need to make to her schedule in order to accommodate his request as she pulled onto her long driveway. In the distance, she could see the top of her home. That sight, and the drive from the road to her abode, always brought her a sense of calm.

That sense of peace was why she lived in the Hudson Valley. She was young, not yet thirty-two, and had a career that kept her in the public eye to a certain extent, and over the years more than one person had asked her why she chose to live alone in such a small, rural town. Ironically, since she was a writer, it was a question she couldn't adequately answer with words—it was just this *thing* she felt each time she came home that drew and kept her here.

Her house came into view as she rounded a gentle curve. Unlike most houses in the area, hers was modern in design. From the driveway, it resembled the side of a staircase, with three levels climbing the hill. The lower level held a guest room, laundry room, and all those rooms that only occasionally got used, like her TV room and gym. The middle level was the main living area and kitchen, and the upper level had two more guest rooms and her massive master bedroom suite with an attached office. Every side of the house that wasn't tucked against the hill was lined with floor-to-ceiling windows.

It was bigger than she needed just for herself. But when working with the architect, she'd been adamant that the home be designed in such a way that it would be easy to sell if she ever wanted to—which meant standard things like more bedrooms, a big, easy living area, and nothing too crazily custom. At least that's what she'd told the architect. Although it was something she thought about less and less with each passing year, in rare moments she wondered if she'd really been hoping to fill the house with her own family. It wasn't that she thought she was getting too old; age had nothing to do with it, she knew she was still young. But, after having lived on her own since she was seventeen, she often wondered if she might be too set in her ways to ever be able to live with someone else, let alone raise a family.

Taking a deep breath and forcing those thoughts from her head, Kit pulled around to the parking area carved into the hill at the back of the house. After parking in her garage, she didn't bother to wait for her brother and was in her kitchen pulling off her hat and gloves when Caleb and Garret came in, each carrying a duffel bag.

Her eyebrow went up. "So, I guess you're staying."

"We need to talk," Caleb repeated what he's said earlier as he dropped his bag and stepped into the kitchen.

"I wasn't planning on seeing you tonight, and believe it or not, I don't actually have time to talk with you right now," she said as she hung her coat up.

Garret had placed his bag on the floor and was leaning against the wall, arms crossed, watching her.

"Kit." Again, Caleb's voice held a hint of warning.

"Look, Caleb, as Garret pointed out, you just dropped in on me. I do have a life and, in fact, I'm not even going to be here very long. I'm heading to Europe the day after tomorrow to attend a party for a dear friend of mine. Between now and then, I have a number of things I have to do, some of which I need to do tonight." Like reschedule her flight through Heathrow so she could meet up with Isabelle Parker.

Her brother opened his mouth to say something, but she cut him off. "The downstairs guest room you use whenever you show up is made up. You," she said, turning to Garret, "can either sleep on the sofa down where Caleb sleeps or there are two more guest rooms upstairs. Both are made up and both have attached baths."

"You can sleep on the sofa," Caleb interjected. Kit let out a sardonic laugh at the order issued from her brother. At one point in their lives, hearing the protective tone in Caleb's voice would have felt normal, would have made her feel cared for. Now it was just ridiculous. Not only were they all adults, but Caleb had long ago given up the right to be protective of her in any way.

Garret chuckled. "I don't think so, Forrester. Between a bed and a couch," he shook his head, "it's a bed for me." And to prevent any further discussion, Garret grabbed his bag and headed up the stairs. Neither she nor Caleb said anything as he left. And when they heard the door to one of the guest rooms click shut, the silence between she and her brother suddenly felt heavy.

"He won't bother you," Caleb finally said. "We've worked together for years," he added. *He wouldn't dare* was left unsaid.

"I know," Kit said. "Ian told me about Garret when he was here with you last fall helping Jesse with that mess." She didn't mention that she had actually met Garret. It seemed easier not to. Saying she'd heard of him from Ian MacAllister, the county sheriff and friend of hers and her brother's, seemed reasonable.

Caleb and Garret, had come to offer their help, and considerable expertise, to Ian when Jesse, another one of Kit's good friends, had gotten caught in the crosshairs of a woman who had stalked Jesse and nearly killed her on more than one occasion.

While Kit was grateful for the help Caleb and Garret had provided, the fact that both had upped and disappeared from Windsor before she'd even had the chance to thank them served to remind her of just why Caleb was no longer a significant part of her life. Not even when he was standing five feet in front of her in her own kitchen.

They stood for another silent moment, and with every passing second, the gulf between them seemed to open wider and wider.

"I have some things I need to do," she said abruptly, breaking the building tension.

"We do need to talk, Kit," Caleb said as she started to walk away.

She paused at the bottom of the stairs, tempted to just keep walking. But she didn't. He was watching her, still standing where he'd stopped when he walked in. She and her brother didn't have much of a relationship, but he was still her brother and he *had* come to help her friend Jesse when he'd been asked.

"I have some things I need to do tomorrow, but I should be free by the afternoon," she said. She saw another look of irritation flash across his face, but it was gone almost as fast as it had come. He gave a small, sharp nod. She waited for him to pick up his bag and head downstairs. But when he didn't, she said her good night and climbed the stairs to her own sanctuary.

• • •

Two hours later, Kit was still awake. She'd changed her ticket and added a layover in England rather than flying straight to Italy. She had also researched Isabelle Parker, the journalist, and e-mailed her own publicist to see about setting up a meeting with Ms. Parker while she was in London.

The change to her schedule had been easy, but given that she was expected at a party in Rome on Friday and had anticipated arriving Thursday, she needed to move her departure up a day to give herself enough time in England. That meant she'd be leaving tomorrow rather than the day after. Caleb wouldn't like that, but it's not like he'd given her any warning that he was coming, so what little guilt she felt at not sticking around, she shoved aside.

After finishing things up in her office, she'd taken a shower in an effort to quiet her mind and body. But it hadn't worked. And now, at just after midnight, she stood alone in her room, in her pajamas, staring out at the winter night through her floor-to-ceiling windows.

And it came as no surprise when, behind her, she heard her bedroom door click open and shut. Even without the soft sound, she would have known when Garret walked into the room. For good or for bad, it was just like that between them. Looking over her shoulder at him, she watched as he paused a few feet into the room and met her gaze.

"Mini Me?" he said, his lips quirking into a shadow of a grin.

"If the shoe fits," Kit responded in the quiet of the night. He had showered and his hair still looked damp. He was in jeans again, with a white t-shirt and bare feet.

"I'm three inches taller than your brother," he said, coming toward her.

She turned her attention back to the window. "Being a Mini Me is more a state of mind than a physical state."

He chuckled as he came to stand beside her but she didn't feel much like laughing. He ran a finger down the side of her face, brushing her hair away from her profile. "I've missed you," he said.

She couldn't deny the little hitch in her heart at hearing those words, but she didn't want to go there with him. It would be so easy to turn into his arms and finish what they'd started all those months ago. But all the months apart had made her realize something—while her body might want Garret, the life he could offer her, that he could offer *them*, wasn't one she wanted. So she changed the subject.

"It's for nights like this that I built all these windows," she said, placing her palm on the glass pane. It was cool to the touch and the heat and moisture from her hand created a small ring of fog. She paused and watched as it disappeared. "There are maybe four or five nights a year when we have both snow and a full moon, and even fewer that are clear nights with new fallen snow," she said.

Kit kept her gaze on her little valley, letting the raw beauty of it seep into her soul. A fox trotted across the driveway several yards away from her house, then disappeared into the woods. The full moon hung in the dark sky, its light reflecting off the snow and casting the night into an encompassing kind of blue. And trees created shadows that fell in muted patterns onto a ground that looked blanketed with diamonds.

"It is almost enough to make me believe in magic," she said quietly as she let her hand drop.

"Kit," Garret said. He made a move that would bring him closer to her but stopped when she shrank away. The peace that had flirted with her as she'd looked out at the night vanished.

"You're upset," he said.

The funny thing was, she *wasn't* upset. She had every right to be, but she wasn't. She was something much worse; she was disappointed. Sad.

She shook her head. "I'm not going to deny we have chemistry, Garret."

"Chemistry?" His voice was flat as he cut her off.

"Yes, chemistry," she repeated, then finally turned to look at him again. In the light of the full moon, she could see his blue eyes locked on hers. He didn't blink; he didn't so much as move a muscle. Then he seemed to take some internal deep breath and relax. His shoulders dropped an inch and a small smile played on his lips.

"I read an interesting article on my flight here," he said.

His non sequitur caught her by surprise and she frowned in question.

"It was about love at first sight. Do you know how many women believe in it?" he asked.

Too many, she thought to herself, but she said nothing and just shook her head.

"34 percent," he answered. "Do you know how many *men* believe in love at first sight?" he continued.

"A lot less," she guessed, feeling cynical.

"73 percent," he stated.

She simply stared at him for a long moment. He couldn't possibly be telling her he was in love with her. They did have some chemistry—chemistry like she had never experienced with anyone else, but they had only spent less than two days together.

She cleared her throat and looked away. "Well, it's not the love at first sight that's most important, it's the love at the one-hundredth or -thousandth or ten-thousandth sight that really matters."

For a moment, Garret said nothing. Then he sighed. "I'm sorry I didn't call. I could have," he admitted. "But I wasn't sure what I would say. Or if you would even have wanted me to."

That last sentence was said more as a question. Would she have wanted him to call? The girly girl in her said yes, of course he should have called, but the woman in her, the woman who had her life figured out and knew what she wanted out of it—including what she did and didn't want out of a partner, was a little bit glad he hadn't.

"I don't know." She answered what he hadn't really asked. She knew her honesty hadn't been what he had wanted to hear and it had hurt him. It was crazy to think that she could feel his energy change, but there was no other way to describe it. She wasn't looking at him, hadn't seen his expression, but still, she knew. She hadn't intended to hurt him, but she wasn't going to lie—not to him, not to herself.

Gathering her strength, she turned to face him. She could feel the heat coming off his body and was once again struck by how easy it would be to just slide her arms around him. But she wouldn't.

"There is *something* between us, Garret. I've already conceded that. But what I want for my life isn't what you can give and I'm not interested in asking you to change."

"Then don't," he said.

She shook her head. "I'm not, Garret. The man you are is someone I admire and like and, yes, am attracted to. But don't ask me to change, either. Sometimes love or lust or chemistry or whatever you want to call it isn't enough. A wise woman I know who has been married for over fifty years once told me that it's often not the big things that ruin a relationship but all the little things. And though I don't doubt your sincerity, I've had enough people in my life like you, people that can't or don't talk about their work and that come and go as the job dictates, to know that it's not what I want for *my* life."

She saw his jaw tick at that. But she needed for him to hear this. It wasn't him she was rejecting, it was the kind of life he led, and she wasn't about to try and change him. She'd been honest with him about that, too.

"It doesn't have to be that way," he said.

"It doesn't?" she challenged. She couldn't see any other way it *could* be. Garret led a life of secrets. A life that required him to be places within a moment's notice. A life that didn't allow him to share when he'd be going, where he'd be going, or why he was going, let alone when he might come back.

"It doesn't," he insisted.

"Fine, then," she said. "What are you doing here?" she asked.

Garret shrugged. "I don't actually know. Caleb said he needed to talk to you and I came along for the ride because I wanted to see you."

"Where did you fly from?" she pressed.

He gave her a hard look as he realized what she was doing.

"How long will you be here?" She hated throwing these questions at him, but he *had* to see her point.

"I don't know, Kit." He didn't like that she was pushing, but she needed him to understand.

"And where will you go when you leave?"

"I don't know," he bit out.

"And how long will you be gone?"

"I couldn't say," he managed to say, as his jaw ticked again from the tension.

Kit paused as exhaustion suddenly overwhelmed her. Letting out a small sigh, she spoke. "I know, Garret," she said, her voice quiet in the darkness. "I know you can't say or don't know. And I know you're okay with living like that, but I'm not. So, as easy as it would be to lead you to my bed right now, I'm trying to be a grown up about it and put some value on what I want, what I really want for the long term rather than just what I want right now."

She felt the tension radiating from his body and knew this was as hard for him as it was for her, because she did believe he was sincere in whatever feelings he had for her. Which made it all that much more important to be honest about where she stood, about what she was feeling.

"And I think you know as well as I do that if we end up finishing tonight what we started five months ago, it's going to be more than a one-night stand," she said. "We can't cross that bridge and expect to be anything other than completely involved."

Even as she said the words, a sense of sadness swept through her. She'd half expected it, but it still didn't feel good. And though she knew in her heart she was doing the right thing—she knew in her heart that now was not the time or place for her and Garret—she still felt the sting of loss.

Maybe Garret felt it too, but his expression shifted from one of frustration to something infinitely more kind and intimate. He didn't take a step toward her, but he did raise his hand and slip it under her hair at the nape of her neck. His thumb brushed across her jaw and she stood still under his touch. After what seemed like forever, he bent forward and softly, gently, brushed his lips against hers. For a heartbeat, she allowed herself to close her eyes and just feel him.

Her eyes opened when he pulled back a few inches. He held her gaze. "I understand what you're saying, Kit, I do. I even respect it. But this isn't the last conversation we're going to have on the issue."

She wasn't sure what to say to that, but even if she'd had a response, Garret wasn't going to wait around to hear it. He dropped his hand, turned, and walked away.

For a long time after the door closed behind him, Kit just stood and stared at the place he had been.